Songbird and the Spy

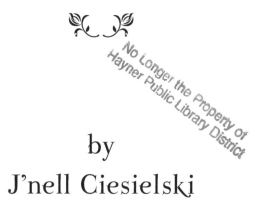

by
J'nell Ciesielski

SMITTEN
HISTORICAL ROMANCE
LIGHTHOUSE PUBLISHING OF THE CAROLINAS

SONGBIRD AND THE SPY BY J'NELL CIESIELSKI
Published by Smitten Historical Romance
an imprint of Lighthouse Publishing of the Carolinas
2333 Barton Oaks Dr., Raleigh, NC 27614

ISBN: 978-1-946016-79-9
Copyright © 2019 by J'nell Ciesielski
Cover design by Elaina Lee
Interior design by Karthick Srinivasan

Available in print from your local bookstore, online, or from the publisher at:
ShopLPC.com

For more information on this book and the author visit:
http://www.jnellciesielski.com/

Brought to you by the creative team at Lighthouse Publishing of the Carolinas (LPCBooks.com):
Eddie Jones, Karin Beery, Pegg Thomas, Shonda Savage, Steven Mathisen, Jennifer Leo, and Christy Callahan

Library of Congress Cataloging-in-Publication Data
Ciesielski, J'nell
Songbird and the Spy / J'nell Ciesielski 1st ed.

Printed in the United States of America

Previous Books by J'nell Ciesielski

Among the Poppies

PRAISE FOR *SONGBIRD AND THE SPY*

With lovely prose and her impeccable attention to history, author J'nell Ciesielski once again delivers a riveting, romantic adventure in *Songbird and the Spy*. In this gripping tale of espionage and romance, the perils of WWII come to life as forbidden attraction between a German captain and a mysterious French waitress threatens to expose their secrets, jeopardizing themselves and countless others trapped inside Nazi-occupied France. Intrigue, danger, and romance abound in Ciesielski's sophomore novel and will guarantee to keep you on the edge of your seat. *Songbird and the Spy* is a must-read for those who love WWII historical fiction!

~Kate Breslin
Best-selling author of *High As The Heavens*

Fans of historical romance (or any romance with an element of suspense) will enjoy *Songbird and the Spy*. In this story, Ciesielski takes an ordinary American woman named Claire and throws her into very extraordinary events swirling in France during World War II. Claire isn't looking for love, but love comes knocking for her in a most unexpected way. Read it!

~Rick Barry,
Author of *The Methuselah Project*

Acknowledgments

Stories start with the spark of an idea, a flash springing from the sea of possibilities, but it often takes a team of believers to bring it to life. Linda Glaz, agent extraordinaire, believes in dreams like no other. She's taken me further on my publication journey than I could ever hope to dare. Karin Beery and Pegg Thomas, my oh-so-patient editors who push me to find the diamond in my lumps of coal. They also have the privilege of pulling me off the ledge when I think I can't handle one more rewrite. To the entire team at Lighthouse Publishing of the Carolinas, who spend countless hours making my novel the best it can be. To all of you, thank you from the bottom of my heart.

I wouldn't be who I am today without my mom. Mom, I know you don't enjoy reading about Nazis … sorry. And my dad who I wish could be here to read this. My sister-in-law Carrie who took the chance on reading one of the early drafts, and who loved it so much she may have shed a tear. My brother, Steven, well, you'll just have to wait your turn for a thank you. The pirate book has your name all over it. My amazing magical unicorn of a muse and dear friend Kim. My stories wouldn't be half of what they are without you.

Oh, Miss S. You are one of a kind, kiddo. My days are filled with laughter, sunshine, and lots and lots of horses because of you.

Bryan, Viking on.

DEDICATION

Bryan, the other half of my blade

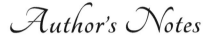

Author's Notes

On 22 July, 1940, Winston Churchill ordered his War Cabinet to form a single sabotage organization that would "set Europe ablaze." The Special Operations Executive, also known as "Churchill's Secret Army" and "Ministry of Ungentlemanly Warfare," was created for a deadly trifecta of purpose: espionage, sabotage, and reconnaissance during WWII by destroying the Axis powers and aiding local resistance movements.

Criminals, smugglers, bootleggers, and even an Indian princess filled the ranks of this new fighting force as each recruit was chosen for their deep knowledge of the country to be operated in, how to kill with their bare hands, disguise themselves, detonate trains, and escape from handcuffs using only thin wire and a diary pencil. If they managed to pass the test, they would be dropped into enemy lands. Many did not survive their first few months in country.

One of the most vital tools for the SOE was clandestine radio communications using a wireless set that weighed less than 40 lbs. These transceivers were instrumental in coordinating attacks, setting drop zones, and sending information back to Allied Headquarters. Transmitting procedures were not always secure when messages had to be sent on set frequencies at fixed times, too often allowing Germans to triangulate the operator's position. Caught operatives found themselves with a bullet to the head, or worse, an interrogation at 84 Avenue Foch—Gestapo Headquarters in Paris. Transmitting was a series of complicated and often time-consuming steps that I simplified down to the most basic steps for Michael to complete in the novel. The important note for readers to take away was how incredibly skilled and brave these men and women were, knowing death breathed down their necks every second of every day. Yet they kept fighting. Without them, the war may never have been won.

The organization was officially dissolved on 15 January, 1946. Only recently have their heroics become known to a grateful world.

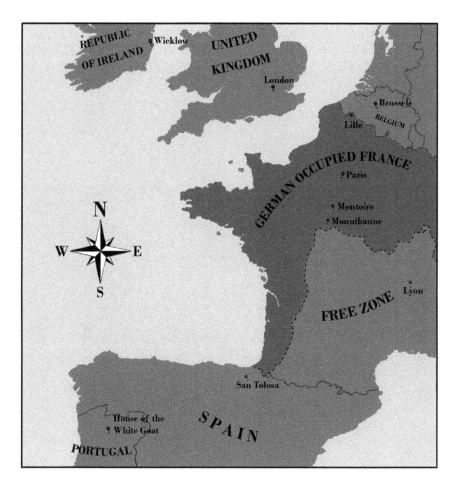

"And now go and set Europe ablaze."

– Winston Churchill, 1940
Upon founding the Special Operations Executive

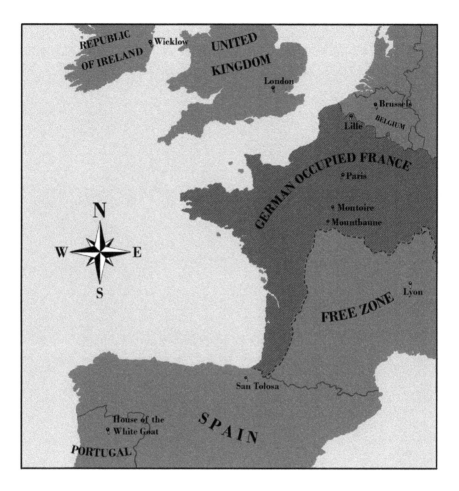

"And now go and set Europe ablaze."

— Winston Churchill, 1940
   Upon founding the Special Operations Executive

PROLOGUE

May 1940, France

Claire Baudin jittered with excitement as she checked her stocking seams. One final tweak to her new red straw hat and she slid out of the cramped ladies' water closet. Tottering her way along the swaying railcar's aisle, she bumped three elbows before falling into her seat.

"*Mesdames et Messieurs, dix minutes jusqu'à Montoire.*" The conductor walked the aisle with practiced ease, thumbs hooked behind his dark blue lapels. "Ten minutes until we arrive in Montoire."

Claire leaned out of her seat to catch his attention. "*Excusez-moi, m'sieur.* Could you please tell me what time it is?"

He pulled a large gold watch from his breast pocket and squinted at the numbers. "*Midi.* Are you switching trains in Montoire?"

"*Non.* My family is waiting for me there. I've never met them before."

He smiled under his bottlebrush mustache. "I'm sure you will make a very fine impression. There is a bench in front of the station if you have to wait."

"*Merci beaucoup.*"

As the conductor moved away, she caught sight of two of the brightest blue eyes imaginable watching her from the next seat back. With burnished hair and a clean-shaven face, the man sat straight without a wrinkle in his clothes, unlike the rumpled passengers surrounding him. Below his unwavering gaze, he neither smiled nor frowned.

"*Pardon?*"

Claire startled at the passenger at her elbow. The woman gestured to go around Claire where she blocked the aisle. "*Excusez-moi.*"

Embarrassed warmth filling her cheeks, she faced front again, and smoothed the folds of her red skirt, eager to be off the hot train once and for all. Her poor backside screamed for relief from the loose spring poking under her seat, and her nose had suffered for over three hours from the cloud of cigar smoke four rows ahead.

In less than fifteen minutes, she would finally meet the cousin her father and *Grandmère* had talked about from their life long ago in France. Or was he her second cousin, being her father's first cousin? It didn't matter. Momma had instructed her to call them Uncle Emile and Aunt Helene, and Claire was to make herself useful on their farm. Or else.

Turning her attention to the bountiful kingdom of slender grass blades and towering golden wheat outside the window, she imagined the smells of rich earth, sweet leaves, and mellow grain that grew at her Virginia home far across the Atlantic Ocean. It had been too long since the familiar notes had surrounded her.

Her days as a *conservatoire* student gave her little time to do anything but study and practice the violin. In the three years that she'd been in France, she'd yet to spend an afternoon in Paris.

Paris! Her heart skipped double time at the mere thought of visiting the vibrant city, especially after hearing so many thrilling stories from *Grandmère* and fellow students. Once Claire completed her classes at the *conservatoire,* she'd apply to play at every music hall in that wonderful city.

She pulled out a small, heavy suitcase from under her seat and placed it beside her. She flipped open the locks and ran a reverent finger over her most prized possessions: Bing Crosby, Glenn Miller, Billie Holiday, Louis Armstrong, Tommy Dorsey, Cole Porter, Wagner, Tchaikovsky, and Stravinsky. All arranged by genre, then alphabetically, shining at her with their promising black ridges peeking out of their cases. Would Uncle Emile have a record player to—

KABOOM!

The earsplitting noise ripped through the center of the train. Claire screamed as she slammed the case shut and threw her arms over her head. Metal screeched against metal. She slammed into the seat in front of her. Pain jarred down her arms.

Another explosion rent the air. The car pitched forward, throwing Claire to the floor. Terror galloped in her heart and blocked sound from her ears. Was she dying? Her body wouldn't be in so much pain if she were dead, would it? Tears flooded her eyes. She squeezed them shut to staunch the panic from overtaking her.

The train shuddered, shaking her teeth together. With a groan, it collapsed on the tracks. She clamped her teeth together and waited for another explosion to finish them off. *One Mississippi, two Mississippi, three …* nothing came.

Sucking in several deep breaths to calm the fear crackling through her, Claire forced her eyes to open. The train leaned heavily on its side with suitcases and tangled bodies spilling into the aisles and onto the floor. Numbness tingled Claire's arms and pain squeezed around her head like a rubber band. The acrid scent of charred metal assured her death had not taken her. Yet.

Hands shaking, Claire grabbed the armrest and hauled herself up, clawing at the seats on either side of her to keep her balance on the tilted floor. The deafening whirl in her ears faded, leaving behind howls of pain and confusion from the other passengers.

"Mademoiselle? Excusez-moi, mademoiselle."

Claire turned to the voice. It called to her from behind as if through a tunnel. Blue eyes stared anxiously at her. The impeccable, wrinkle-free man.

"Mademoiselle, are you all right?"

"Oui." She gingerly touched the knot forming on the side of her head. "Yes, thank you. Just a little bump."

"Would you mind taking your nails out of my hand?"

"What?" She followed his gaze. Her fingers were embedded into the back of his hand. "Oh, I'm so sorry. I didn't realize."

"Shellshock will do that to you." She let go, and he rubbed the red marks. While everyone around him scuttled like lost ants, he stood with confidence. A rock in the sea of pandemonium. "Are you sure you're all right?"

Who besides her grandfather and his old war buddies used the word *shellshock* anymore? "Yes, yes. I'm fine. Are we in a war zone?"

"Off the train! Everyone, now. Get off!" The conductor staggered down the aisle, jabbing people in front of him and snatching the dazed from their seats. Blood from a gash above his eye dribbled down his cheek. "Get a move on, people!"

"Sir, what's happened? Have we been bombed?" Claire grabbed for the conductor's arm, but her foot stuck between the case of records and the seat in front of her. She yanked at her leg. The foot refused to budge. People shoved one another like stampeding cattle as they raced to get off the train. Biting back a cry, she tugged desperately at her foot.

The impeccable stranger vaulted over the back of her seat and landed in front of her. Fishing one hand between the seats, he curved his fingers around her ankle and yanked. Her foot popped free. She pitched forward and smacked into his chest. The scent of washed cotton and soap wound around her pulse, pulling it from the frantic edge.

Grabbing Claire by the shoulders, he pushed her into the crush of people clawing their way to the rear door. Frightened passengers knocked her out of the way as they crawled from their seats and shouldered their way into the teeming mass. The man's firm grip on her shoulders kept her upright as her feet slid down the skewed aisle and outside. Only when she jumped from the platform did his hands leave her.

Claire staggered away from the warped metal. She searched for her blue-eyed guide, but the chaos had swallowed him whole as people wobbled into the field. Then she saw the train and gasped.

The first two railcars had split in half, the blackened metal sides jutting out as if sliced with a can opener. Bleeding and broken, people wriggled from the cars' bowels.

A crippling ache knotted in Claire's stomach. She pressed a fist to her mouth as tears spilled down her face. Dear God, what had she survived?

Claire pulled an embroidered hankie from her pocket and wiped the dirt from the toes of her shoes. Once a beautiful red that matched her new hat, they now looked like they had marched through the Dust Bowl and back. So much for arriving looking spotless. She shoved the handkerchief back into her pocket and looked around. Thank God she had arrived at all.

The unfortunate souls from the first two cars were laid out next to the tracks with tablecloths from the dining car covering them as the local police jotted their identifications on notepads. Survivors meandered in the field amongst the weeds, but it was difficult to keep them separated from the locals rushing to help with armloads of food, water, and torn sheets for bandages.

A long shadow pounced on her. *"Nom, s'il vous plaît."*

"I've already given my name and traveling papers to another officer." Claire shielded her eyes as she looked at the *gendarme* holding a stub pencil over his clipboard.

He frowned. "Who?"

How was she supposed to tell the difference between all the uniformed men scurrying about in the chaos? She pointed left. "He went that way."

"You people need to stop moving around so we can do our job." He shook his head and scratched his pencil on the paper. "How are we supposed to keep track of everyone?"

"No one is sure what to do," she said, hugging her knees to her chest. "Best of luck."

Claire's nerves were as precarious as an egg balanced on a clothesline. She'd tried to find a place far from the carnage to string her emotions back together, but the chaos crept toward her, picking at the fragile cord.

He made an annoyed noise and moved on to the family sitting next to her. The sweet scent of wheat and grass brushed her nose, coaxing her stomach into a gurgle. She'd last eaten a stale croissant that morning, back when the day was innocent and full of possibilities. Her only possibility now was finding a way to the nearest village in hopes they could point her to her family's farm. She held her hand up and counted the finger lengths between the sun and horizon. Four o'clock, well past her arrival time. Surely they wouldn't be waiting for her at the station after all these hours.

A bleating horn cut through the late-afternoon haze. She shielded her eyes against the sun as a black truck with wooden slats around the bed trundled between rows of wheat stalks. The horn beeped again, and a girl's head popped out of the open window.

"*Cousine* Claire!" The girl's frantic eyes roved over the sea of faces. "*Cousine* Claire!"

The driver had yet to pump the brakes as the girl threw open the door and vaulted out, a brown braid streaming behind her. She ran from person to person, gesturing wildly as they shook their heads or shooed her away.

Claire pushed to her feet and waved to catch the girl's attention. "My name is Claire. Are you M—"

The girl threw her arms around Claire's neck, kissing both of her cheeks. "*Oui, oui*. I am Maurelle. Oh, Cousin Claire, you cannot imagine our worry when we arrived at the train station, and they told us—oh, Papa. Look, I have found her."

Uncle Emile unfolded his long body from the truck and jogged around the front to stand beside his daughter. His blue eyes—identical to Claire's father's—examined her. "Are you hurt?"

She shook her head. "A little bump on the noggin, but my headache isn't throbbing anymore."

He pointed to the box at her feet. "Is that your bag?"

"My records." Once the threat of danger had passed, the porters had climbed back into the train to toss out what personal items they could find, her box among them.

Frown lines creased his tan face. "You survive a train wreck, and you don't think to get your suitcase?"

"It was in the baggage car." She pointed to the metal remains.

He snatched the record box and headed back to the truck. "Come."

Claire hesitated as she looked back at the policeman with his clipboard. "I don't think I'm allowed to leave yet. They told us to stay put."

Uncle Emile slid her box onto the back of his truck and climbed behind the steering wheel. "Their captain is on the German payroll. Get in. The goats need to be fed."

Dazed by her rollercoaster of circumstances, Claire hopped in next to Maurelle and slammed the door. Uncle Emile threw the truck into gear and sped away. Glancing out the back window, she realized not one person watched them leave.

CHAPTER 1

Michael Reiner smoothed the front of his jacket with his palm and adjusted the perfectly polished row of buttons. It had been nearly a year since he'd last slipped into the confining sleeves, but one made concessions when ordered to appear before the base commander. Raising a hand, he gave two precise raps on the heavy oak door.

"Enter." A voice boomed from the other side.

Michael opened the door and stepped in, snapping to attention with a salute.

"At ease." Colonel Walthers touched his hand to his forehead in a return salute. "Come in and have a seat."

Michael took the chair next to Major Gunston, his commanding officer, and pressed his feet to the floor. Beads of sweat popped out on his forehead.

"How are you, Mike?" Gunston drew on his cigar and blew out perfect gray rings. "Enjoy your time in France?"

"Yes, sir."

"Nothing to complain of?" Gunston propped a booted foot against his opposite knee and peered at him through the smoke haze.

Michael rubbed the tips of his sweating fingers against his knees. He'd lost all of his belongings during that train explosion on his way back to England, including an entire folder on the training exercises of the German troops along the French and Belgian borders. And that blonde girl. He'd looked for her after she jumped from the train. Staying behind to help others off, he had scanned the tear-streaked faces and haunted eyes, but she had disappeared into the throngs of crying people. "No, sir."

"Bit of a liar, aren't you?"

The air in Michael's lungs froze. "No, sir. I mean, I'm proud to do whatever job my country calls me to."

"What a conveniently diplomatic answer."

Michael dug his fingertips into his thighs. "Sir, I don't know where these accusations are coming from, but I assure you that—"

"Relax, son." Gunston chuckled. "Men of action don't like to be stuck in classrooms, but your linguistic skills are invaluable in teaching those Frenchies to intercept and decode the Jerries' mail. What better teacher could we offer than the chap who speaks three languages—fluently I might add—has a German birth certificate, and a German education?"

"Yes, sir. Of course."

"Good, but I didn't call you back to England for a pat on the back." Colonel Walthers walked to a table in the corner of his office and poured a healthy amount of brandy into a tumbler. "Care for a drink?"

"No, thank you, sir." It was barely two o'clock in the afternoon.

The Colonel sloshed back his glass and poured himself another. Swirling the amber liquid, he perched a hip on the corner of his desk and stared at Michael with falcon-like gray eyes. "Lucid, good. You will need to be, but you also need to learn to take a drink every now and then. Germans like their beer, like to smoke too, but I don't advocate you give that a whirl while you're there. Smells the uniform."

"I don't smoke, sir." It took a second, but Michael's brain finally registered the colonel's words. "What do you mean while I'm there? Am I being transferred?"

Walthers took a long swig of his drink. "In a manner of speaking. A new branch is being set up, commissioned by Churchill himself. The Special Operations Executive is to set Europe ablaze by espionage, reconnaissance, and sabotage behind enemy lines. All very under the table, you understand. We need people who speak the language and know the customs. In other words, people who blend in."

"And I know how to do those things."

"Better than anyone. You will be promoted to captain. Gunston tried to get you a major's badge, but I'm afraid you're a bit too young in the face to pull that off. Not enough gray hairs or circles under the eyes."

A mixture of excitement, fear, and apprehension tingled along Michael's spine. Espionage. They wanted him to be a spy, to be in the middle of the action again. And to use the bittersweet heritage of his boyhood to blend in with the enemy—his own people. He could help bring this war to a swift end. "When do I start?"

"Depends on how fast you complete the training. From your record, I suspect you'll breeze through. Then it's off to France, where you'll meet your contact. You leave tomorrow."

Michael stood and saluted, barely able to keep the grin from his face. "Thank you, sir."

"Oh, one more thing. *Captain.*" Walthers drained his glass and placed it on his gleaming desktop. "Stop off to the chaplain before you leave and beg forgiveness from the Almighty for every '*Heil Hitler*' you're about to spit out."

Michael's footsteps echoed off the black-and-white tiled floor like staccato pops from a rifle. The gleaming white hallway held an endless row of windows that cast sunlight onto gilded frames that once held pictures of French leaders but now displayed Hitler, Goebbels, Himmler, and Hess. The four men of the apocalypse eyed every person who dared call themselves pureblood and walk the halls of the converted Parisian military headquarters.

More than anything Michael wanted to kick the toe of his shiny black leather jackboot into every glassed face. Maybe another time, when the halls didn't slither with ranking German officials.

High heels clicked as secretaries swished about carrying files and notepads, their golden-blonde hair curled atop their heads with eager smiles always on their cherry-red lips.

He approached one of their desks. "*Heil* Hitler."

"*Heil* Hitler. May I help you, Captain?" An oil painting of Hitler with his German shepherd filled the wall behind her chair.

"My name is Captain Reichner. I'm here to see Major Heydrich."

She smiled and buzzed the intercom. "Sir, Captain Reichner is here."

"Let him in," came a voice through the box.

The secretary swayed to the double oak doors and pulled one open, flashing Michael a smile as he walked in. The door clicked behind him. Michael tapped his heels together and stuck his right arm straight out. "*Heil* Hitler."

The man sitting behind the wooden desk returned the salute before motioning Michael across the plush carpet. The major's chest barreled out, showing off the colorful medals tacked across his impeccable uniform. He didn't ask Michael to sit. "You come highly recommended. All your paperwork is in order, which stands in your favor since we have much on our plates right now trying to sequester France. They surrendered much easier than we thought."

Michael's spine strained from standing so erect. "A victory for the Fatherland, sir."

"Indeed. Today France, tomorrow England, and next week the world." The smirk disappeared from his face as his heavy brow turned down. "But where are we as conquerors if we do not have intelligent communications? That is where you will come in." He reached into a drawer and pulled out a thick folder, sliding it across his desk.

Michael took the folder and glanced at the contents. A more perfect assignment he could not imagine.

"You will be the Commanding Officer of Communications in Montbaune, a village some three hours southwest of here. Resistance is starting to rear its belligerent head. People are talking,

and spies are prowling. The Führer wants to know who and what is going on at all times in his vast empire, and it is our job to see it done."

"Are we to be listening to our own people, sir?"

"All communications from the region will go through your wires, friendly and enemy, civilian and military. Depending on the subject matter, you will then direct it to the appropriate office. They will take it from there. You're the middleman, with a very good ear I might add." The major's thin lips curved.

"Thank you, sir. I'm proud to use my ability for the Führer."

"*Wunderbar*. Now, the men under you are trained in French, three in English, and one in Spanish. Not the multilingualism one would hope for, but what can you expect of the enlisted?"

"If I may be so bold, sir. I intend to see their limits pushed far beyond what they are currently capable of. If we are to have these countries in our grasp, then it is imperative we learn their languages." Michael dropped his shoulders and allowed one corner of his lip to pull up. "At least until they all learn German."

"*Ja*, you have the idea, Captain. I never cared for the French, although their chocolate is delicious." Heydrich slapped the arm of his padded chair and boomed with laughter. "I know you're fresh in, maybe even wanting to take in the sights of Paris, but not today. Be ready to leave at 1400."

Michael's jaw clenched. The sights of Paris? Like rubble and ash, homes blown apart by tanks, soldiers goose-stepping through the Arc de Triomphe, and terrified citizens waving swastika flags? "Ready and eager, sir."

"Dismissed."

Leaving Heydrich's office, Michael shot to the men's room. He turned on the cold water and splashed it over his burning neck. He was surprised it didn't sizzle as soon as it touched his skin. His fingers gripped the porcelain basin, and he let the cool surface soothe the burning pulse throbbing through his fingertips. He lifted his head and gazed into the mirror. Amidst the somber gray of his tunic and ashy face, the only color staring back was his blue eyes. He gave a quick nod to make sure the stranger before him was not an imposter. He'd passed.

CHAPTER 2

April 1941

Claire trudged up the porch steps of her French family's farmhouse. Her Aunt Helene, eighteen-year-old cousin, Odette, and much younger cousin, Maurelle, sat in wicker chairs shelling peas.

Aunt Helene looked up, the welcoming smile sliding from her worn face. "What did they say?"

Claire shook her head. The folder holding her identification papers weighed like lead in her hands. "No."

Uncle Emile stomped up the steps behind her and slammed his hat on the peeling porch rail. "Those *imbéciles* do not care that she is a citizen of a neutral country. They will not allow her to return to Lyon to resume her studies. She lives in occupied France."

A deep V creased Aunt Helene's forehead. "But that is ridiculous. Did you explain everything?"

"*Oui*, but that man's brain is no better than a mashed potato. Worthless cowards rolling beneath the Nazis' thumbs to save their own necks." He rubbed his hands over his face. His nails were clean, scrubbed free of dirt for the important visit, not that it ever mattered.

What had started as a few weeks with her family had turned into eleven months. Each week Claire and her uncle made the trek to the local clerk's office to file for a return pass to unoccupied France, but each week she was denied. She was growing numb to the word *no*. At first, she had been in denial—surely the officials would allow her to return to Lyon because she was a student—but denial had morphed into anger, which wore her down to weary acceptance.

"We showed him all of the papers," Claire said. "He claims it would be different if we lived in unoccupied territory, but citizens under German law are unable to leave their country once it is occupied."

"I have never heard of such ridiculous notions." Aunt Helene batted a green-stained hand as if the offensive words swarmed her head. "We are not at war with Germany. They have seen to that. They are nothing more than murdering, maniacal landlords to us now. Maybe tomorrow I should go in and speak to them."

"That way is closed to us now." Uncle Emile's brow furrowed, casting dark shadows across his weathered face. "I promised Claire's papa I would take care of her while she is here. I'll get her home."

Home. No place on earth sounded as close to heaven as her family's farm in America. In the first few months with her aunt and uncle, she had dreamed of returning to the university, but it was ridiculous to think of her classes when the country was in upheaval.

The thought of abandoning her studies crushed Claire. She'd worked so hard to get to the *conservatoire*. Her parents had beamed with pride the day she'd received her acceptance letter, her golden ticket to becoming a concert violinist, but to stay now would terrify them, not to mention herself. So far, her French family's farm had been cushioned from attacks, unlike the major cities, but how long could they remain safe from the roving Nazi war machines? When would they awaken to the screaming of bombs? Her aunt and uncle had been so kind, treated her as one of their own daughters, but they had enough to worry about. They didn't need Claire as an added burden. "Maybe I can go to the embassy."

"Mmm, which one?" Her aunt neatly snapped a peapod and scooped out its contents. "The bombed one in Paris or the one in Spain, which we're not allowed to travel to?"

"But I'm an American. Surely, they can't—"

"I was a young girl during the Great War and have not forgotten their ways. I will never expose my family, and that includes you, to the wickedness they are capable of."

Claire knelt in front of her aunt and touched her knee. "I would never let harm come to you."

A soft smile spread across her aunt's face. She reached forward and brushed her worn fingertips across Claire's cheek in the same way Claire's mother had. A deep longing for home swelled in her chest until she could hardly breathe.

Taking the papers from Claire's hand, Aunt Helene stood. "We are family, no? There are ways, but patience is key. Emile. Inside, *s'il vous plaît*."

Her aunt and uncle went inside, and Claire took up the vacated seat between her cousins. Wait. For how much longer? Hitler had marched into Paris not ten months ago and obliterated the country's morale. The great City of Lights now flew the hated Hakenkruez flag.

Casting off her straw hat, she took up the bowl her aunt had left behind and slid her nail down a pod, splitting it open to reveal its emerald gems. The repetition soothed her jingling nerves. With the smell of sun-drenched grass and cows surrounding her, she could imagine sitting on her own front porch shucking corn with Mama.

But the French chatter from the kitchen radio pulled her out of such thoughts. She was thousands of miles from home and not likely to return any time soon. "This sitting and waiting is almost worse than walking past that German guard post in the village. I can't stay here, but they won't let me go home either."

"You should join the Resistance!" Maurelle's elfin face lit with excitement. "Patriots doing what they can to stop the war. Think, *Cousine* Claire. You could aid downed pilots, smuggle goods across the border, and paper the towns with propaganda to resist the Germans at all costs."

"Smuggling. What an undignified thing for a lady." Odette looked to the open window of the house and dropped her voice. "I heard from *Monsieur* Andres, the baker, that a few local groups have turned to more murderous actions. Blowing up trains without regard to the innocent when there's only one German soldier on board."

"Or a group of German land surveyors?" The familiar knot of panic crept into Claire's stomach. It had taken weeks, but the authorities had finally discovered why her train had been destroyed. The handiwork of zealots. So many months later and she still awoke in the middle of the night covered in sweat with her heart pounding, the nightmare ever fresh. "No, I don't believe the Resistance is for me. Sight-reading a solo is all the danger I need."

Maurelle flipped her long brown braid over her shoulder. "If you say so. Perhaps, you could show us the jitterbug tonight, then Odette would finally have something interesting to tell Dillon when he comes back from the war. Where do you think he is?"

"Yugoslavia, possibly." Odette bit her lower lip as worry flitted across her pretty face. "He likes to be where the action is."

"I can't imagine why he likes spending his time with you then. You're so boring."

"At least I'm not a snot-nosed child."

Sensing the brewing storm between the sisters, Claire seized an opportune topic. "Who's Dillon?"

"Her secret fiancé," Maurelle whispered. "Mama and Papa don't know, not even I'm supposed to, but—"

"But you read a letter that was not yours to read." Odette's eyes blazed.

"You left it on the dresser next to my hairbrush. I merely glanced at it." Maurelle huffed and wiggled in her chair. "I would never snoop. Besides, I was tired of reading all those depressing newspapers Papa tries to hide from us. The Germans have started rounding up volunteers along the eastern borders to help in the workshops and munitions factories."

Odette snorted. "Volunteers, bah. Forcing the French to make bombs and bullets that will be used on their own people."

"You are lucky to be American, *Cousine*," said Maurelle. "They

cannot force you to go along with their horrible plans. Soon you shall be home, and we shall miss you terribly."

"Don't count me gone just yet. This morning the clerk told Uncle Emile that if we return again with my 'phony documents,' they'll arrest me." Gathering her frustration, she threw a handful of peas into the basket with more force than necessary. "Neutrality is no longer considered safe. Remember the radio news two nights ago? They arrested an American ex-patriot under suspicion of spying when he spilled his coffee on a German officer's boot."

Maurelle's eyes popped wide. "You are no spy!"

"I don't think the Germans are picky when it comes to rounding up suspects. They don't trust anyone, not even their own citizens."

"If you were a spy, you could smuggle yourself across the demarcation line to Vichy France." Odette leaned forward and dropped her voice. "I have heard of people doing this. Dillon mentioned it in one of his letters."

"I thought smuggling was undignified for a lady." Maurelle raised an eyebrow at her sister.

"As a smuggler, certainly, but it's an entirely different matter as the one being smuggled."

Smuggling. A ray of hope. She had no desire to join the Resistance, but if Uncle Emile couldn't get her out of the country legally, perhaps those people could help. They might be her ticket home to America.

"Are you sure the letter wasn't too full of kisses and tear stains to be readable?" Maurelle puckered her lips and blew kisses at her sister.

Odette threw a fistful of pods at Maurelle, who nimbly ducked the flying assault of legumes. "I told you to stop reading my things!"

As much as Claire had grown to love her cousins, she could only take so much of their bickering. Especially when she had a burgeoning idea. She jumped to her feet. "Excuse me, will you?"

A stray peapod hit the back of her head as she dashed into the kitchen. Aunt Helene stood at the stove stirring a pot of broth.

"Where is Uncle Emile?"

Aunt Helene glanced over her shoulder, frowned, then looked back at her soup. "You've peas in your hair."

Claire raked a hand over the top of her head. Peas pinged on the floor. "Do you know where I can find him?"

"Out in the barn. Was there something you need—"

Claire pushed through the back door and sprinted across the yard to the barn.

"Claire!"

She didn't stop to explain. She had to talk to her uncle.

"I want to find the smugglers." Claire swatted the backside of a goat as it refused to go into its pen. "If it's money they require, I have a little saved up. I was going to treat the family to a nice dinner in Paris when we went, but that's not happening any time soon."

Uncle Emile forked fresh hay into the trough for the mule. "It won't be necessary. They don't require money."

"You already know?"

"I've been making inquiries." His eye almost closed in a wink. "You did not think I needed to take so many trips to the baker, did you? Grab that fork."

Claire smiled, the steel bands around her ribs loosening after so many months of praying for a way out. Soon she could be breathing in the air of free France again. No Germans chasing her through the street, no threats of being thrown in jail, and—she swallowed hard—no family. They would have to stay while she slipped away. Love for these brave people filled her heart. She grabbed the spare pitchfork from the wall. "Thank you."

"Thursday after supper a man is coming by to sell me his pig. I'll refuse, we'll haggle, I'll refuse again, and he will leave with you and his pig in the back." Uncle Emile tossed hay to the cows. "Pack a small bag."

"Why didn't you tell me sooner?"

"I am telling you now."

She dug her fork into the mound and pitched the hay to the plow horse. "What will happen to you? What if someone finds out?"

"No one will find out. You will arrive at the contact's house, and from there he'll take you to Spain. You must do as you're told." He stopped, his fork frozen in the air with straw dangling off the end. "If something should happen along the way—"

"Nothing will happen," she said with more certainty than she felt. She had to believe in the best. If not, she'd crack. "I'll be cautious and do exactly as I'm told. I won't jeopardize the risks you are taking for me."

"Never tell anyone you are American," Uncle Emile said. "And trust no one outside your contact. People are struggling with the Germans' occupation, but some find their struggles eased by turning in escapees."

Claire strangled the handle to keep her hands from shaking. She could be captured. How would she escape then, or, more worryingly, how would she survive? She wasn't a trained soldier. Her best defense would be to curl into a ball and cry.

She sneaked a peek at Uncle Emile. Harsh lines etched his face like cracks in a granite mountain. He was tired and angry, but he was still fighting to find her a way home. Shaking herself, she vowed to never curl into a ball and cry. If her family was willing to risk their lives to get her to safety, she would make sure their efforts were worth it.

Straightening, Uncle Emile glanced through the open doors and frowned. The rumble of a motor drew near. Walking to the entrance, he shielded his eyes against the setting sun before spinning back around. "Get in the loft."

"What is it?"

"Germans. Don't make a sound, do you hear? No matter what,

not a sound. And remember what I told you." Taking the pitchfork from her fingers, he hung it back on its nail. *"Tout de suite!"*

Climbing the rickety ladder, Claire buried herself between two large mounds of hay. The motor drew closer until squeaky brakes pierced the air. Claire peeked through a slit in the splintered rails as a large truck with a canvas-covered bed pulled up the driveway. Three German soldiers with guns clambered from the back.

The passenger door creaked open. Out stepped an officer, the shiny metal pieces on his collar giving him away. "Emile Baudin?"

Her uncle nodded. *"Oui."*

"Ah, I am Colonel Schneider of the SS. A pleasure to meet you." His lips pulled back into a wolf's smile. "What a beautiful piece of property you have here."

"Merci. What can I do for you?"

"Your quaint village and many of the surrounding ones have fallen under my jurisdiction. I like to know and understand everything that happens within my command, including the people. Over the past few weeks, I have heard the name Baudin more than once and decided to come and meet the man myself."

"Many of the villagers know me for my goats. They produce the best milk and cheese in the region," Uncle Emile said.

Schneider grasped his hands together behind his back and pursed his lips. "No, that was not it."

Claire's heart tripped. They had come because of Uncle Emile's fuss at the government offices. Her fingers dug into the straw, crushing the slender stalks.

"I've heard rumors of a most unpleasant sort. You are unhappy with the current condition of your homeland," Schneider said. "I do not blame you, what with the upheaval of things and a new government taking control. Quite disconcerting to one's peace of mind, but when the change is for the better, then we must learn to adapt, to discover our new place in this new world. The Führer is helping us build that dream together. Do you understand what I mean?"

Uncle Emile pulled out his handkerchief and mopped his brow. "I'm afraid I don't, *monsieur*."

"It is all right, *Herr* Baudin. That is why I am here to help you. To give the French people a chance to work side by side with their new comrade Germans. Come, let us go inside so I may explain further to you and your family. I hear you have two beautiful daughters, *ja?*"

Schneider placed a hand on Uncle Emile's shoulder, turning him toward the house. One guard followed them while the other two remained next to the truck. Claire's breath blew hot and fast. Minutes ticked by, filled with nothing but the occasional *baa* of a goat and the chickens scratching.

Finally, the front door swung open and several pairs of feet tromped across the front porch. Claire's entire family marched into view, each of them carrying a small bag. One by one, they climbed into the back of the truck. Hot tears blurred the scene as terror gnawed a pit in her stomach. Where were they going? One of those atrocious factories?

The guards jumped in the truck and the engine roared to life. Kicking into gear, it rumbled down the driveway and onto the main road, leaving a trail of billowing dirt in its wake.

Claire pressed her cheek to the wood boards and cried until she was sure her heart bled.

Darkness filled the barn before she dared move from her hiding spot lest the house was being watched. Straw stuck to her cheek as she descended the ladder. Four rungs from the bottom, her foot slipped, and she crashed to the floor.

She tried to stand, but pain throbbed in her left ankle. "Applesauce and crackers."

She had to get away. The Germans would come back for the animals. They always did. Sickness twisted her stomach. With rumors of spies running rampant, they would take her in for interrogation. She'd heard horrible tales of those dragged into Nazi headquarters never to be seen again.

Hobbling into the house, she expected things to be thrown around and turned upside down, but everything was in its place as if the family had stepped out for the evening. The room she shared with her cousins was neat and tidy except for some drawers pulled out with clothes hanging over their lips. A few items were missing from the dressing table.

Claire found one of Maurelle's school bags and stuffed a few pieces of clothing and her wallet into it. In the kitchen, she gathered food, including the chopped carrots Aunt Helene had been preparing for supper. Would it be enough? Without the name of her contact or the meeting location, her only hope was to make it to the border of Vichy France. From there ... well, she'd find a way. She hoped.

Outside, the only light came from the pinpoint stars above. She took a shuddering breath and turned south. The direction of freedom.

Claire wanted to scream. Or cry. Either option seemed a good release for her raw emotions.

Dropping her bag to the ground, she sank onto the soft grass and leaned against a leafy oak tree to stretch her tired legs as the sun curved away from the midday point. The new position gave her an ample view of her swollen ankle. Three days of limping on it had left it a sickly purple and green color.

She scrounged in her bag for a wilted apple, which would serve as the day's allotted meal, and rubbed it against her arm to scrape off the bits of lint and dirt. It was dry and sour and the most delicious thing to hit her stomach since yesterday afternoon's carrots. If she didn't reach free France soon, she would have to risk going into a village for a loaf of bread.

With the last bite of apple, she tossed the core aside and leaned her head against the rough tree trunk, closing her eyes to the green grass and colorful field flowers. She'd seen enough of the French countryside to last her a lifetime. The few times she dared to catch a few winks, dreams of Nazis and Colonel Schneider ruined all hope of a peaceful rest. Always, the faces of her family haunted her thoughts, waking and sleeping.

A flutter of wings rippled overhead, annoyed squawks filling the once peaceful afternoon sky. Claire opened her eyes as a covey of brown quail took off from the tall grass and soared into the sky. How strange that they should all take off like that. Usually sudden flight occurred when—

Crack!

Claire screamed and ducked her head between her knees, covering her ears with her hands.

Crack!

Her throat closed around another scream as the gunshots rattled in her ears. A long minute passed. She was still alive. Something heavy touched her shoulder, drawing out the scream. Her feet kicked into motion as she tried to scramble away. A pair of scuffed shoes and the butt of a rifle appeared in front of her. Claire shrank back in fear as she glanced up at brown trousers, a faded blue cotton shirt, and, finally, a haggard face.

The man squatted in front of her, the lines of his face drawing together. He appeared to be in his midforties with blotches of rosacea on his cheeks. Pulling off a slouchy hat, he pushed a thick hand through greasy black hair. "*Mademoiselle?* Are you all right? I'm sorry I frightened you. There is usually no one in this field."

Claire nodded as she waited for her heartbeat to return to normal. He wasn't trying to kill her after all. "I didn't realize this was a hunting area."

"There is no need to shout, *mademoiselle.*"

"Pardon? Oh." She pulled her hands from her ears.

He twirled the hat between his fingers, watching her with deep hazel eyes. "What are you doing out here all alone? Is your house near?"

"No, I—I was just looking for the—the, ah ..." Her mind blanked. What was she supposed to say?

"Your ankle needs to be looked at."

"Yes, I'm afraid I haven't been able to find a doctor or ice."

"And you couldn't stay at home to rest it?"

Claire licked her dry lips. "No."

The man sighed and shifted his weight. "Best we get out of here then before the patrols come."

"What patrols?"

"Germans."

Panic shot through her like a shotgun blast. The grass swayed across the field, but no gray helmets poked out from among it. She clutched her bag.

"I can see this possibility distresses you as well." He stood and offered her his hand. "I suggest you come with me."

She shrank back as her uncle's warning rang in her head. "I don't know you."

"My name is Giles Desbaux. I live in a village called Montbaune a mere two kilometers from here, just over that hill." He pointed south with his hat. "I can offer you a cool wrap for your foot and a place to stay for the night if you need it. If you stay here, that injury may not heal right. Likely to leave you crippled."

Claire touched a tentative hand to her swollen ankle and winced at the sharp pain. It couldn't be that bad, could it?

"And then there are the field rats."

Rats? Crippled? Dying alone in a field with nothing but the starving rodents to keep her corpse company was not how she wanted to go. She took his hand, wincing as she moved her stiff ankle. "Claire."

He nodded and grabbed her bag, tossing it over his shoulder. "My truck is just beyond that grove."

"I'm sorry I ruined your shot. I won't mind waiting for you to continue if you wish."

Giles waved a hand. "Tomorrow I'll come back. It's getting close to business time anyway."

They made slow progress back to his truck, but Giles didn't seem to mind the pace. Claire did catch him frowning when another covey took flight a mere twenty paces away. Once in the truck, he turned the key, and the motor sputtered to life.

"What sort of business do you have?" she asked.

"Family business."

They drove into a small village, much like the one near Claire's family's farm, with stone and brick shops lining the main road. Women in calico dresses, farmers carrying grain sacks, and children holding their schoolbooks ambled in the street. A few of the men raised their hands in greeting as the truck motored by.

Giles stopped in front of a two-story building at the end of the main street. A massive poplar with leafy branches stood next to the front door. Made of dark, aged wood and stone, there were two tiny windows on the bottom floor and a crooked sign hanging on the building. White letters declared it to be *Les Trois Godets*.

"The Three Buckets. Do you own a restaurant, *Monsieur* Desbaux?"

"Not exactly."

Two steps inside and she understood what he meant. The overwhelming smell of sawdust and beer hit her in the face, swirling in her nostrils with the stiff scent of yeast. Four dim wall lights buzzed. The two windows provided just enough sunlight to highlight the bar along the left wall. Mismatched tables and chairs scattered around the dust-strewn floor while an upright piano stood on a small stage.

"Pauline!" Giles laid his rifle on the bar and motioned Claire further into the den. "Would you care for a glass of something?"

Claire glanced at the shiny bottles behind the bar. She'd made the mistake of getting into her dad's whisky one time on a dare from her brother. It had looked innocent enough until the first and only drop hit the back of her throat. The burning took ten minutes to go away. "No, thank you."

"I have coffee, tea, and well water. No wine, as my shipment has been delayed." He made a disgusted face. "The soldiers get sticky fingers during their inspections. Pauline!"

"What are you shouting for? I'm not deaf." Giles' twin, or who could have passed for his twin if he had a topknot of black frizzy hair, pushed open a curtain and stood with her hands on her hips. "We're missing three more cases of Merlot and—" Her eyes narrowed into slits as she spotted Claire. "We're not open yet."

"She's not here for service."

"Then what's she doing here?"

Claire wobbled forward, eager to take the heat off her rescuer. "I was trespassing on his hunting ground. Me and the quail."

Pauline's dark eyebrows rose. "What's a young girl doing out in the field to be shot at?"

"I stopped for a rest." She plucked at the loose string on her bag to distract her shaking hands. "I didn't realize it was a hunting field."

"Her ankle's hurt." Giles leaned his thick forearm on top of the bar. "Might be sprained."

"A girl like you sitting out in some abandoned field with a sprained ankle? You sure that's all there is to it?"

"It's the truth. I fell off a ladder."

Pauline silently assessed her. Claire's foot ached from all the walking. She needed to sit again but, more than anything, she needed this woman not to ask any more questions.

"You're about to wilt." Pauline marched forward, dragging a chair in her wake. She spun it around and pointed. Claire dropped onto it with a solid *thud*. Without waiting for a by-your-leave, the older woman picked up Claire's foot and placed it gently on top of another chair. She bent over the discolored skin. "Don't know if it's hurt too bad, but you shouldn't be walking on it. Where's your family, girl?"

Claire pulled her leg off the chair and tucked it behind her right leg. She felt too vulnerable propping it up, and the last thing she desired was to fall apart under the woman's judging gaze. Her belly trembled with unease. She pressed a hand to stop the gathering momentum, but it was too late. The rumble filled the silent bar room.

Pulling around a chair, Pauline lowered her stocky body onto the creaking cane bottom. Leaning forward, the hard lines of her face softened. "Where's your family?"

Tears pricked Claire's eyes. "I don't know."

"Have they passed on?"

"I don't … that is …" Pain welled in Claire's chest. She pushed it down with a heavy swallow. "German soldiers came for them. They said something about working side by side with Germans for the Führer. I hid in the hayloft until they left."

Behind her, Giles grunted. Pauline's nostrils flared as she spewed a string of curses. "They will never stop, will they?"

Giles slammed his hat back on his head. "I'm going to get Dr. Farman."

Pauline plied Claire with tea as they waited. Claire could almost relax if not for the older woman's steely gaze. At last, Giles returned with the doctor.

"It's not a sprain, but it is severely bruised," Dr. Farman said as he prodded Claire's ankle. "Rest for a few days before attempting to put much pressure back on it. Cold compresses every other hour will help to ease the swelling and speed healing."

"Thank you, doctor," Claire said.

"You're lucky you stopped under that tree when you did." Dr. Farman placed his stethoscope back in his black bag and snapped it closed. "Any more walking and you'd have a limp the rest of your life. Pretty girls like you don't need a limp to slow them down."

Claire placed her cracked teacup back on the table and reached for her bag. She rummaged around until she found her wallet. "How much do I owe you?"

Farman waved her away and turned to Giles. "I'll be around

tomorrow evening to collect. The '89 should be very nice."

Giles nodded. "*Oui*, with a shot of bourbon, no?"

"No, no. Marie Nequam is soon to deliver and the bourbon won't do for my hands. Remember little Pierre Tournay?"

"The cross-eyed boy?"

"*Oui.* I had two shots the night before he was born." Farman shook his head at the memory. "Never again."

Claire bit her lip to keep from cracking a grin. A bourbon-swigging doctor. Only in the country.

Pauline rose. "I'll get you settled in the spare room. It's not much, but I don't think someone as small as you needs a giant place to sleep."

Claire shook her head. "I can't impose on you like that. I thank you for the doctor, but I can't stay."

"The doctor told you to rest, no?" Pauline's eyes narrowed. "And your family is gone. Where else do you have to hurry off to?" Marching back through the curtain beside the bar, she left Claire with no choice but to follow.

Putting as little weight as possible on her foot, Claire pushed through the curtain and stepped into a storage space. A long, narrow hallway piled high with crates of glass bottles led right. In front of her was a rickety pair of wooden steps leading to a landing with three doors. Pauline waited by the first.

"Come on, come on," she said. "Unless you need help."

"I can make it." Grabbing hold of the worn banister, Claire managed to hitch herself up the stairs with a minimal amount of panting. How had she made it three days on her own?

Pauline opened the door to a small room with a narrow wooden bed, a window framed with blackout curtains, a chest of drawers with a porcelain basin and pitcher sitting on top, and a single chair with faded patches on its arms. "Not much but, like I said, it should do for you." Pauline ran a finger through the thick dust on top of the chest of drawers. "Hasn't been used lately."

"Thank you, *Madame* Desbaux. I'm very grateful for your

hospitality."

The older woman whirled on her with the speed of someone half her age. "One thing I won't have is too many thank-yous and apologies. Can't abide them every other sentence." She shook her shoulders as if spiders wiggled across her back. "You'll need to stay here the rest of the night. I'll bring you something to eat later on. Lord knows you need something on your bones. Do *not* come back downstairs."

Pauline shut the door before Claire could utter another word, so she mouthed a silent thank-you and set her bag on the floor. Walking to the window, she pulled back the dark, heavy curtains and peered out. The side of another building blocked the view, but if she angled to the right, she could see down the alley to the main street.

Her foot throbbed, sending tiny splinters of pain through her leg, so she left the window and eased onto the straw-ticked mattress. It was lumpy and smelled funny, but it was also the softest thing her bottom had sat on in days. Heaven.

But the feeling didn't last. Claire knew nothing about these strangers. Would they report her as a runaway? Plenty of people were willing to profit from such snitching. However, there had been no mistaking the hatred in Pauline's and Giles' eyes at the mere mention of Germans.

Perhaps it was best that Claire take the doctor's advice and rest for a few days. A bum foot would never get her to free France, and she could use the extra time to poke around for another group of smugglers. Hadn't Uncle Emile mentioned the underground dealers using clues to signal their whereabouts to one another? If she could figure out their clues, perhaps she could signal someone.

Easing her leg onto the bed, she peeled back the cold compress and grimaced. What had made her think she could last out there alone? Her new hosts seemed nice enough, but trusting was nigh on impossible these days. She'd have to stay on guard.

She glanced around the tiny room and its sparse furnishings.

Heaven? Or had she limped herself straight into a living … what?

CHAPTER 3

"These just came in, sir."

Michael took the papers from his sergeant. "*Danke.*" He looked back to his work, eager to continue the translations, but the sergeant remained at attention in front of his desk. With a sigh, Michael pushed the papers away. "Is there something else, Sergeant Dietrich?"

"Yes, sir. That is, me and some of the men, well, all the men really ..." Dietrich swiped away a sweat bead rolling from his strawberry blond hair and cleared his throat. "We wondered, want to ask if—"

"Do you have something to ask, or are you trying to stay away from working as long as possible?" Michael leaned back in his chair and crossed his arms over his chest. "You may not be busy, Sergeant, but I am."

Two bright spots exploded on Dietrich's cheeks. "Our shift ends in two hours, sir, and there's been static on the line since noon. With your permission, Eichmann has volunteered to stay behind."

"Stay behind for what?"

"For the rest of the shift." Dietrich's face darkened to deep red. "Last week the card game started early, and those post guards cleaned us out because they'd already stacked the deck in their favor."

Michael raised an eyebrow. "You want your commanding officer to give you permission to leave work for a card game?"

Dietrich's face purpled.

"Do you think the *Führer* leaves work early?"

"No, sir."

"Then do you think you deserve that special privilege?"

"No, sir."

"Work hours are from seven to seven, so I suggest you schedule a little more wisely next time."

"Yes, sir."

Michael opened his top desk drawer and pulled out a metal box, then fished out a set of keys from his pocket. After unlocking the lid, he took out a leather pouch and poured a handful of francs onto the gleaming wood. "Has Giles gotten his new shipment of wine in yet?"

"I do not think so, sir. Bottles seem to fall off the truck once they pass the guards."

After stuffing a suitable amount of coins back into the pouch, Michael tossed it across the desk to Dietrich. "That should help lighten the men's mood should the evening start without them."

Dietrich took the bag and weighed it in his hand before placing it in his pocket. He smiled. "Thank you, sir. Might we save you a bottle?"

Michael raked the leftover coins back into the strongbox and locked it shut. "No, not tonight. I still have two more stacks to go through before I turn in."

Dietrich saluted and turned for the door.

"If that card game manages to start before you arrive, be sure to let me know. I've been meaning to call on Lieutenant Ostermann for some time now. Perhaps we can discuss the penalties for his men cheating. Dismissed."

Michael waited until the door shut before letting a grin stretch across his face. It was almost too easy taking information from the Germans. With these kinds of soldiers, the war should be over in a matter of months. A Brit would never shirk his wartime duties for the sake of a card game. Still, letting them play meant he could get on the transmitter and send out his latest reports before the crew changeover. He glanced at his wristwatch. His contact wouldn't be on the frequency for another hour.

Grabbing the stack of finished folders, he walked to the corner filing cabinet and added them to the growing accounts of information. His fingers glided over the green folders, silently thanking each paper that was going to be sent to the British office in an effort to end the blasted war.

Rolling the drawer shut, he grabbed his mug and swallowed his coffee as fast as he could. It was black and bitter without any rationed sugar. He might as well chug an entire pot of ink if he couldn't savor a nice cup of English tea. The first time he'd been handed a mug of lukewarm bitterroot coffee he'd almost spit it onto a corporal's headset. After scouring the kitchen for anything else to drink, he'd been informed there was nothing left by the previous owners.

Michael glanced around at the fine furnishings of his newly acquired office. A heavy mahogany desk, thick Persian rug, antique light fixtures, oil paintings, and dozens of books on all subjects. It had belonged to a retired Jewish banker and his family. The family now resided in a work camp near the Polish border, except for the eldest son, who had been shot in the front yard when he tried to stop the Germans from appropriating the house. His body now lay in the back field where new COMMS workers could view it. A tale of victory.

"Jews are not human, Captain," Dietrich had explained. "They steal, lie, and cheat. How else do you think they came by this house?"

It took everything within Michael to keep from planting his fist in the stupid man's smirking face. Someday soon he hoped he could.

How many more would die? How many times would Michael be forced to stand silently while the inhumanity spread across the continent? How many more nights could he lie safely in bed before they came to get *him*?

He squeezed the mug handle. He would be safe. They would never find him out because he would do nothing to jeopardize this mission or the lives it sought to protect. Like the lives of the family that once lived in this home.

Shaking off the ghosts, he sat at his desk and opened the new files Dietrich had brought in. "One thing I can say for these *Jungen*, they're efficient."

In the short time he'd been assigned to the post, Michael's teams had cracked more codes and transmitted more shipping information and troop directions than any other COMMS posting in France, but efficiency had its drawbacks. Two stacks each with ten folders worth of drawbacks.

Michael rubbed his eyes to calm the stinging. A mountain of paperwork and less than an hour before his contact came on the frequency. He poised his red pen above the first translation. "Ok, back to work then."

"Dr. Farman sees no reason why I can't walk again with small breaks. The swelling has disappeared."

Pauline continued shuffling the glasses behind the bar. "Dr. Farman doesn't know you want to start wandering through the fields again with no place to go."

Claire handed her the next tray of clean glasses. "Whether he knows or not, I must continue on. I've already imposed too long on your hospitality."

Pauline plunked her hands on her wide hips and glared. "What's so important that you need to get back to hiding in the bushes? Have you a destination in mind?"

"I do."

Pauline raised an eyebrow. The Desbauxes had been kind during Claire's few days with them, never asking too many questions and sharing their rationed meals with her, but that didn't mean trust was implicit.

"All right, keep your secrets," Pauline said. "Wherever you're going, whatever you're planning, it's not safe out there for a girl like you. These are troubled times and getting worse."

"I have to try."

"I'm not your mother. You may do as you please, but you should know the stories of young girls caught out alone—"

The front door banged open, and loud male voices poured in.

"Quick. Upstairs before they see you." Pauline shoved Claire toward the back curtain.

She didn't have time to pivot before five middle-aged men in patched trousers and linen shirts sauntered into the room. Grins split their tanned faces as they spotted her. Claire tensed like a rabbit ready to spring.

"What's all this now, Pauline? A new barmaid for us?"

"None of your business, Ansell Medon." Pauline set five clean glasses on the counter, then filled them one by one at the tap.

"Oh, now don't flare that temper at me, Pauline," Ansell cooed as he blew her a kiss. "We're interested in visitors to our town."

"And what would your wife say to you welcoming such a pretty visitor?"

Ansell waved his hand and pulled out a bar stool. "She'd say I should spend more time at the bar and leave her alone at the house. The kids are bad enough, she doesn't need me adding to her troubles."

His friends laughed and joined him for their mugs of warm, frothy beer.

"Have you got a drop of whisky to spare? Feel I deserve it after hauling that tree stump up," one of the men said. "That thing had more roots than an ant has holes to crawl in."

Pauline studied the liquor bottles before choosing one on the end. "This one is almost used up. I'll have to look in the back for a full one." She started to leave but whipped back around to Claire. "Can't leave you out here but can't trust them to behave and not steal a swig while I'm gone."

"If you tell me where to look, I'll fetch the extra bottle," Claire said.

Frowning, Pauline flipped her glare between Claire and the men as they tried to hide their grins behind their mugs. "You wouldn't know where to look. I've my own sorting system back there." Drawing a deep breath in through her nose, she leveled a serious stare at the men. "I'll be gone thirty seconds, and you are to leave her alone while I'm gone. Is that understood, you sorry lot?"

Each man gave a solemn oath that he would be on his best behavior. Pauline grabbed Claire's hand and dragged her behind the counter. "You stay back here, and if one of them decides to even lean over the bar, clap him upside the head with the nearest bottle."

As soon as Pauline's skirt disappeared behind the curtain, the questions came like rapid fire from a gun.

"What's your name?"

"New in town?"

"Why haven't we seen you before?"

"Are you married?"

"Are you working here now?"

Waffling on how much she should divulge, Claire waited for silence. "I'm Claire, and I'm merely passing through. *Monsieur* and *Madame* Desbaux have been good enough to accommodate me for a while."

"How long may we enjoy your delightful company?"

"Enough of that." Pauline whipped back through the curtain, a scowl darkening her brow. "You all gave me your oath."

"Pestering the poor girl is the last thing we want to do. Just trying to be friendly." Ansell tipped the remaining splashes of beer into his mouth and pushed the empty glass across the counter with a waggle of his graying eyebrows. "Another."

"You can wait. I've got my hands busy with Eloy's vice." She plunked a full bottle of whisky on the counter and set to getting the cork out.

"I'll get it while you do that." Claire took Ansell's mug and set it under the tap, pulling the lever just as she'd seen Pauline do. Amber liquid turned to froth, foaming over the top, slopping down the sides and onto her shoes. "Oh, I don't think that came out right."

"Angle the glass and slowly straighten as it nears the top." Eloy leaned over the counter for a better look.

She tried again, this time stopping before the foam spilled over. Setting it on the counter, she smiled with triumph. "Much better that time, yes?"

"Yes, and no." He pointed to the settling foam and the one inch of beer in the bottom. "Takes practice."

"And you've had lots of that, I'm sure."

"I think I should be the one behind the counter instead of Giles. Let him plow behind the horses." Taking the glass from Claire, Ansell gulped the foam then wiped his mouth with his sleeve. "Where is the old man?"

"Drove over to Lecord this morning to see if their alcohol shipments arrived as expected." Pauline pried the cork out with her teeth and poured half a shot into Eloy's glass.

"Lots of items have been missing lately," Ansell said, sipping his beer. He tipped his cap back from his dirt-smudged forehead and wrinkled his face. "I'm sure our *landlords* might know something. Why don't you ask them about it?"

Recorking the bottle, she set it on the shelf and turned to place her palms flat on the counter. "If you're so interested, why don't you ask them yourself? Maybe ask when they plan to pay their tabs as well."

"Past my curfew by the time they come in or else I would."

His friends snorted into their glasses, but it was a cold sound that sent uneasy tendrils curling in Claire's belly. Landlords and curfews meant the Germans lurked nearby. How sad that these grown men could not stay out at night in their own town to share a laugh and drink. All the more reason for her to get out as soon as possible.

"You say our lovely Pauline was kind enough to put you up,"

Ansell said, drawing Claire's attention back to the men across the counter. "Traveling someplace nice? To kinfolk maybe?"

"That's a first, to hear my sister called 'lovely.'" Giles pushed his way through the curtain carrying two crates labeled FRAGILE. "Not the word I'd use."

"I've got a few for you as well." Pauline snorted. "What took you so long?"

"Got tangled at the gate. There were a few new guards on duty who were more than a little interested to see what was in the crates. Took four bottles this time." He set the crates on the ground, took a crowbar from under the bar, and began to pry open the lids. "A flea can't move in and out of this town without their noticing."

Eloy snorted. "Isn't that how they think of us anyways? At least you have booze to fend them off with."

"Humph, what's left of it."

Ansell slid his empty mug across the counter to Claire and smiled. "Another, please. Might find myself a little tipsy today after having such a pretty girl serving me as much beer as I like."

"Doesn't differ from any other day, no?" Eloy ribbed him with a hearty laugh. "Except it's usually Giles serving us."

"As I was saying earlier." Ansell smiled at Claire, ignoring his friend. "Where are you traveling to?"

"Here." Giles pointed down. "She came to see me."

Five interested pairs of eyes locked onto Claire. Behind her, she could almost feel fire shooting from Pauline's nostrils.

Ansell nudged his glass closer to Claire's unmoving fingers. "You came here? I didn't realize the Desbaux hospitality ran so deep."

"I knew her father in the war. God rest him." Giles flipped a look at Claire as he pried off the second lid. "Refill him while I get the bottles out, yes?"

Whatever his reason for lying about her, Claire was grateful. The fewer people who knew the details, the easier it would be for her to slip away when the time came. Too many questions brought the Germans' attention.

She took Ansell's glass. Her third attempt at the tap yielded a few more inches of beer and less foam. She slid the glass back to Ansell. If he was disappointed in the lack of beer, he didn't show it. "You said there are Germans nearby? What are they doing here?"

"They have a communication base not two miles out of town, at the old Dreyfus estate. Our insignificant village is centrally located for their operations. Plus, we have one of the better taverns in the region, as Giles knows how to keep the shelves well stocked."

"But they keep a close eye on who and what goes on here?"

Ansell nodded and lowered his voice. "They've made it their mission to become our personal watchdogs just like the last war. Most soldiers like to feel like big men in whatever town they're in. They're sure to notice you."

Pauline brushed past Claire, snatched an arm full of bottles, and dumped them into Claire's arms with a silencing glare. "Help me bring these into the back." She pushed Claire into the storeroom before stepping back into the bar. Even from the back room, Claire could hear the men squabbling. Seconds passed before Pauline shoved through the curtain again with an armload of bottles. "You ask questions too openly."

"I don't mean to cause problems, but it's better if I know what risks are out there. Ignorance won't do me any favors when I go."

Pauline took a step closer, her short stature not lacking one inch in irascibility. "So you're still set on traveling to God knows where without any sense of what's waiting for you. Do you not know what happens to girls on their own, or even whole families, if they're thought suspicious? That's what's wrong with young people these days. You don't think clearly. You don't plan. it's left to the rest of us to clean up after your mistakes. We don't need any more trouble here."

"I'm sorry if I've offended you. My circumstances are a bit unusual, but I assure you I won't impose on your hospitality any longer than necessary."

"Why not?" Both women turned to see Giles standing in the doorway. He let the curtain fall behind him, sealing in their privacy from the curious ears at the bar.

Claire frowned. "What do you mean?"

"Yes, what do you mean?" Pauline's face hardened.

Giles stepped in front of his sister and began taking the bottles from her arms, placing them on the wall racks. "She could stay here with us."

Pauline's mouth dropped. "Stay here? Another mouth to feed? Are you out of your mind?"

The bottles in Claire's arms turned heavy. "I can't stay, Monsieur Desbaux."

"And why not? Because you have some place else to go? I think not." His voice lowered to a soft, bear-like gruffness as he took the bottles from her. "A young lady with a proper place to live does not hide in fields eating apple cores. You have nowhere and no one, just a direction where you think your freedom lies."

"My university is in Lyon."

"You will never cross that border. Not without help."

Claire's gaze fell to the floor. Giles was right. She had nowhere to go. How did she ever hope to escape when every day hundreds of people found themselves arrested and placed on trains bound for who knows where? Fear had carried her this far, but she couldn't go on that way forever. She'd been a fool to think otherwise. She needed to find those smugglers to help her. That required money. The few francs she had wouldn't get her far.

"And how am I supposed to feed another mouth? It's hard enough with the two of us on those rations." Pauline paced the hallway like an agitated tiger. "Not to mention the bills we have to pay."

Giles shrugged. "She'll earn her keep."

Pauline stopped, hands on her hips. "How?"

"We could use the extra help. You've said it yourself."

"Did you see the foam she spilled everywhere trying to fill a simple glass? Not to mention all the attention from the men."

"She's right. I made a complete mess," Claire said.

"You'll learn and do whatever else needs to be done in exchange for a place to stay. And as far as those bums out there on my stools, they know their place."

Working at the bar would allow Claire to save a bit of money. She didn't know the going rate for smuggling humans, but whatever Giles paid her would add to the few pathetic coins jingling in her purse. She twisted her fingers together as she waited for the other shoe to drop. "Why are you doing this?"

A flicker of emotion passed in Giles' eyes, but it disappeared before she could put her finger on it. Grabbing two bottles of wine, he headed for the curtain. "When you've decided, tell Pauline and she'll put you to work."

Dumbfounded, Claire watched the curtain swish back into place. "He offered me a job."

"So he did." Pauline's gaze zeroed in on Claire like a gunner to his target.

Heat flared under Claire's collar. "And you don't approve."

"I don't approve of a young and innocent girl working in a tavern, and one who's been to the university to boot."

Claire shrugged. "I'm afraid my musical education doesn't mean much during a war. Too bad I don't play a magical pipe. I could find a cliff and lead the Nazis off the edge."

Pauline *harrumphed* and turned to a tray full of dirty glasses. "Upstairs. It's growing dark outside, so I'll expect your answer in the morning." Taking the tray, she walked to the kitchen hidden behind a wall of cognac and brandy bottles.

Claire grabbed a second tray and followed. "I'll help you with these."

Pauline turned back with a glare. "No, you won't. Upstairs. And don't even think of going back into the bar. Those men won't be there much longer anyways, not with the new crew coming in."

"Who's the new crew?"

Shifting the tray to her hip, Pauline's face darkened. "Germans, of course."

CHAPTER 4

Claire dropped the scrub brush into the bucket of dirty water and rocked back on her heels to stretch her aching back. It had taken an hour to clean the sticky mess on the floor. A week into her new duties and she ached in places she hadn't felt since working summers on the farm.

Still, she was glad for the employment and the much-needed funds it would provide for her ticket to freedom.

As she rose from a hunched position, needles of pain shot through her legs. She stamped her feet to get the blood going again before bending over to retrieve her cleaning tools. Her bottom hit the corner of the piano sitting center on a slightly elevated stage. Off-key notes tinkled in the air.

She tapped the yellowing C key. *Ting*.

"Ugh." She tapped the octave below it. "When was the last time someone tuned you?"

Glancing over her shoulder to ensure Giles was still gone, she popped open the top and peered inside. Bits of dust coated the strings, but otherwise, the instrument appeared in good condition. Perhaps tightening the strings was all it needed. Finding the C string, she tested the pin for resistance. It turned right away. Odd. She tried another. Loose. They were supposed to be tight. She turned the pin while tapping the key with her other hand until the *ting* came into pitch.

Tuning up the scale took several minutes, then she hit F. No matter which way she turned the pin, it refused to come to pitch. She stuck her face in the case for a better look. "I wonder if Giles has pliers and a flashlight."

"I do, as a matter of fact."

Claire banged her head on the side of the piano at the sound of Giles' voice. He leaned against the wall, a faint smile twitching his lips.

"I had to look." She rubbed her head. "And then it was so out of tune my ears nearly bled."

"I'm not surprised. It hasn't been played in fifteen years. Be right back." He slipped behind the curtain, then returned with a set of screwdrivers, pliers, and a large flashlight.

"Thank you." Picking out the needle-nose pliers and flipping on the flashlight, she dove back into the piano's cavity for a few quick twists. "Fifteen years is a long time for an instrument to sit still."

"Housed a cat for a time."

Frowning, Claire swung the flashlight back and forth in search of a bed of fur. "I know they climb into car motor compartments for warmth, but never a piano."

"Eloy sneaked him in when his wife threw the cat out of the house. Job was to catch mice, but he preferred to sleep. We'd hear him clawing at the strings early in the morning."

That would explain the pins. "I'm surprised it doesn't have more serious problems."

"No problems because no one touches it. Our mother was the last one to use it."

Claire tapped the F key. Better, but not quite. A few more twists and it sounded fairly reasonable to her ear. It would be so much easier with a tuning fork, but she thought it unlikely that Giles kept those in the back. She moved on to G.

"How did you come to tune pianos?" he asked between her tapping.

"My mother is a music teacher. She made sure my brother and I learned every scale and note on our family piano and hoped I would play it to go to the *conservatoire,* but I chose the violin instead. Easier to haul around." She laughed and turned the A-flat string. "All music touches the heart, but I believe the piano and violin are the best conveyers of its story. There, that should be a million times better."

Moving her tools to a nearby table, Claire pulled a chair over and sat in front of the instrument, pressing her fingers to the keys. Something close to proper-sounding notes hit her ears, bringing a smile to her face. *Mom would be proud.* With effortless movements from memory, her fingers glided over the keys, occasionally hitting one that needed to be fixed, but the melody could not be denied.

"*La Petite Poule Grise*. I have not heard that since I was a boy."

Claire turned to see the lines around Giles' eyes and mouth smooth as he stared off into a memory. She smiled and eased into a new song. It had been too long since she'd drifted away to music, losing herself in its comforting familiarity. Far from family and far from home, the simple songs from a life long ago proved a healing balm to her bleeding heart.

"Do you take requests?"

Claire's fingers stilled as she turned to see the Rowdy Bunch, her name for the regulars, standing in the doorway, grinning from ear to ear. They jostled forward to crowd around the piano.

"Why didn't you tell us you could play this old thing?"

"Do you know any Charles Trenet? What about that Josephine Baker?"

"Can you sing them too?"

Claire tinkled the keys to calm the raucous voices. "I can play almost anything you'd like, but I'm not much of a singer."

Ansell scoffed and patted her on the shoulder. "Why don't you let us be the judges of that, *ma chérie*?"

"You must be starved for entertainment."

Eloy sighed and leaned his elbows on the top of the piano. "The only time we hear singing is when they allow us to church once a month, and then it's like someone died."

Claire shifted on her seat. "Do you not have a radio, or maybe records?"

"We've taken to hiding them, so they won't find out we've been listening to the news. Which is why we need you to sing for us," Eloy said.

They beamed at her like hopeful children. They wanted a taste of the old life as much as she did, and not even her ill-used vocal pipes could deny them such a small thing.

"All right, have it your way." Claire laced and flexed her fingers over the keys. "But no teasing if I hit the wrong note."

They scrambled to take seats at the nearest tables, each leaning forward with their elbows on the table. She thought for a moment about what to play before the perfect song popped into her mind. She pounced on the keys.

"*C'est le retour des saisons, la joie dans la maison. C'est la vie qui recommence.*"

Her audience exploded in applause, so she dove into a second selection. After three beers and two more songs, Eloy joined her, then waited a full minute for his applause to tire out. Enrico Caruso himself never stood so proud.

The men rushed the stage and demanded *La Marseillaise,* which Claire happily obliged despite their off-key warbling. Tears pricked her eyes. Grandmère used to sing that song to her all the time. Claire tried not to think about what her family was doing back in Virginia. She liked to think of their lives going on the same as when she'd left, frozen in time. But how could they when they'd not had word from her in over a year?

She jangled the keys to knock the torturous thoughts from her mind, and out came Cole Porter's *Let's Fall in Love.* When the chorus rolled around for the second time, the voices died out until she realized she was the only one singing. The clapping and whistling had stopped as well.

"*Sieht aus, als wir rechtzeitig gekommen sind eine Feier zu geniessen.*"

Claire's hands froze over the keys. She swiveled toward the door where six vultures in Third Reich uniforms leered. Avoiding their eyes, she looked to the village men, paralyzed and ashen faced.

"Come, come. Why did the party stop?" One of the soldiers said in heavily-accented French, spreading his hands wide. "Not because of us, I hope. We like music as much as anyone. Play for us, *bitte*."

Panic seized Claire like the talons of a demon. She'd managed to avoid the enemy thus far, but her luck had finally run out.

"You haven't run out of songs already have you, *Schatz*?" He turned to Giles at the bar. "Wherever did you find this charming creature? And where have you been hiding her? Very naughty on your part."

Cheeks flaming red, Giles filled glasses brimming with beer and foam—his gesture for the less-than-likable customers—and carried them to the table closest to the bar, and farthest from the piano. "Won't you gentlemen have a seat?"

One of the other soldiers, with fewer shiny pieces on his collar, waved Giles closer to Claire. "Not there. We'd like to sit closer to the music. We may not be as rousing as the Frenchmen, but we can try for a solid stanza, can we not, comrades?"

"*Ja!*" The others pumped their fists into the air. They took the tables next to the village men and waited for Giles to serve them. His face a blank mask, the bartender set the mugs in front of them.

"Giles," the first young officer drawled, lighting a cigarette between his teeth and blowing wisps into the air. "You did not answer my question."

Giles placed the tray beneath his arm. "What question was that, Lieutenant Ostermann?"

"About your charming *chanteuse* and why you've kept her from us. Though I should say, she is quite cordial with the locals."

"My friend's child. Her parents died some time ago, but I consider her family. She has come to visit."

"Family. *Wunderbar!*" The man slapped Giles on the arm, grinning so wide the cigarette almost fell from his lips. "Will you not join her in song?"

"No, lieutenant. Who would see to the drinks?"

"Quite right. There's a good bartender."

Giles returned to his post behind the counter and looked at Claire with a silent plea to play along. She gave a stiff nod. The customers were always right, especially when they had pistols strapped to their sides. Any form of protest would bring the German ire down on their heads. She couldn't do that to Giles.

"Not having a sudden turn of stage fright, are you?" One of the soldiers hooted. His friends laughed until the lieutenant hissed them into silence.

"We are not being encouraging like her French friends. We should sing along. You, here"—he clasped a polished hand on top of the mercantile owner sitting closest to him—"what's that song you last sang?"

The mercantile owner's face blanched as his Adam's apple bobbed in erratic intervals. "W-we … that is … s-sing Cole Port … er."

Ostermann drew his hand back and took the cigarette from his mouth, tapping the ashes against the table. "I don't know any Cole Porter. Who wants to listen to ghastly American music anyway? Let's try something else, something hot. Can you do that, *Fräulein?*"

The urge to hurl her chair into the lieutenant's smug face sent blood racing to Claire's fingers. Cole Porter was about as hot as they came. Or at least he had been before the war kicked off. Who knew what passed for music under the Nazis' control? Likely something with Alpine horns.

"I will try my best, *monsieur.*" Smiling as sweetly as she could without choking, she launched into the last song she'd heard by Edith Piaf on Uncle Emile's radio. Hot? Maybe not, but the Germans would never know the difference if they could barely speak French.

"Bravo!" They cheered when she finished, clanking their mugs on the table. Giles brought over a second round. The soldiers grabbed more, but the villagers shook their heads. Eloy scraped his chair back and pulled his worn hat from a pocket.

"Not leaving us so soon, are you?" Ostermann puffed on another cigarette. The smoke curled upward around his head.

Eloy squeezed his hat between his hands and looked at his shoes. "I need to be getting home. The wife worries."

The lieutenant flipped his wrist over to look at an expensive watch. "But it's not even your curfew yet. She'll not be worrying, I assure you. I believe a wife worries when her husband comes home too early from the tavern, *ja?*" His friends laughed at the age-old joke of wives and husbands, but no one else found it quite as funny. "Come. Sit. Sit."

Ansell looked at Eloy and gave him the barest shake of his head. Wiping his glistening forehead, Eloy sank back into his seat.

"*Wunderbar!* Sing for us, *chanteuse*," Ostermann said. "Sing. The night is young, and it has been much too long since we've heard such a lovely voice."

Claire tried to keep her tone cordial. "What should you like to hear, *monsieur?*"

"Do you know *Lili Marlene?*"

"No, *monsieur.*" A lie. She knew the song from music history class and remembered the warmth it ignited when she'd read the sweet words. The only recording had been in German and sounded so charming at the time. Staring at the uniform in front of her, however, Claire changed her mind about the German appeal.

The lieutenant's lips curled into a smile. "We'll remedy that now that the music of the Fatherland is spreading for the whole world to enjoy." He cleared his throat.

"*Vor der Kaserne,*
 Vor dem großen Tor,
 Stand eine Laterne …
 Wie einst, Lili Marlene."

Claire shrugged. "I'm sorry."

"No? You still don't know it?" Ostermann shook his head. "It is easy. Let me show you." Stubbing his cigarette out on the table, he stood, adjusted his immaculate uniform, and walked over to her. "If you don't mind, I'll sit at the piano this time, and we can try the French version together."

Flabbergasted by the man's audacity, Claire slid out of her chair and walked around to the back of the piano to hide her knocking knees. What would her dear mother say? Looking toward the bar, Giles had stopped mid wipe with a glass dangling from his frozen fingers. His mouth slacked open, the rosacea spots on his cheeks burned bright. This was probably a first for his hole-in-the-wall bar.

"*Mademoiselle*, are you ready?" The lieutenant caressed the keys, bringing the piano to life with his touch. "And one, two, three—"

CHAPTER 5

Michael switched the headset to his left ear, giving his right one a break. Garbled voices on the other end argued back and forth in German about the number of provisions, or lack thereof, coming in for their troops. He rolled his eyes at the fourth accusation of the depleting supply of drinkable coffee. *Get used to it, mate. War requires we all suffer for the blessed Führer*. Even in his head, the word—or any word relating to Hitler—made him want to swish petrol.

He put the headset down and switched off the box.

Corporal Kruger looked up from the notebook he'd scribbled in. "Is there something wrong, sir?"

"How about letting me know when there's something interesting on the line?"

Kruger jotted a few more notes and nodded. "I can do that, sir, although today is going slow."

"So I heard. You'd think with a war on that our commanding officers could discuss something more important than coffee."

"Yes, sir. We can't blame them though for the sludge we have in the kitchen."

Sludge, chicory, or ground beans, it all tasted like dirt. Of course, some of the men had taken to adding drops of wine they'd bartered from the guard posts whenever tavern shipments came through. Every little bit helped in their minds.

"Sir, if you're looking for a bit of excitement, why not join us tonight at *Godets*?" Dietrich swiveled around in his chair, tearing the headset from his head.

"That's right, sir. You have not seen the newest entertainment in town." Kruger scooted closer. Excitement danced in his blue eyes. "What a dish."

Michael perched a hip on the edge of the desk. "Has Giles managed to smuggle something sweet past those guards? I could use a gelato cone."

Dietrich grinned. "Something sweeter. A dame, and not his sister. She's a cousin or niece of some sort."

"Wrong." Kruger tipped his chair forward. "Daughter of an old friend from the war. I heard it from Klaus who was there the first night. Giles was keeping her hidden, or at least for the locals, but now the secret is out. Only good that's come from those guards getting there early every night."

Dietrich leaned back in his chair, his hands pillowed behind his head and his gaze going to a far-off place. "Heavenly blue eyes with a figure to make a saint look twice. Voice of an angel." He scowled. "At least until Lieutenant Ostermann tries a duet."

"He did teach her *Lili Marlene*. A fair way to close the evening, if you ask me." Kruger surged to his feet and placed a fist to his heart. "*Vor der Kaserne*—"

Michael winced. His ears already hurt from the coffee argument. "I think we'll leave the vocals to the *chanteuse*."

"Come with us tonight, Captain. See for yourself."

He wanted to say yes, not for the girl but to escape the sheer boredom of the day and the mounting stack of papers on his desk. Not every day brought reports of a planned siege or bombing, but it was still better than sitting in a windowless bunker hundreds of miles away translating what the very men in this room bantered about. Unfortunately, the conversations about dames never came across his desk. That would've brightened those dreary afternoons. These days, women ranked low on his list of priorities.

Standing, he smoothed the front of his uniform and adjusted a button. "We'll see."

Hours later in his office, Michael switched off the short-wave transceiver, tucked it back into its battered leather suitcase, wound the antenna, and secured them both in the hiding hole he'd constructed behind the bookcase. Tonight's transmission had been short, with a clipped "received" on the other end from his contact.

Walking to the window, he pushed back the curtain and stared across the rose garden. Silvery moonlight glinted across the village's rooftops a mile away. In the peaceful quiet of night, it looked to be the most charming town. In daylight, one could see the harsh marks of the world they lived in. Military vehicles—jeeps, as the Americans called them—barbed wire, patrols, sandbags, and roadblocks shattered any notions of a quaint countryside.

He snapped the curtains closed and double-checked the hidden notch of his hiding hole. Stepping from his office, he locked the door with a brass key that he kept in his pocket at all times. "Lieutenant Hirsch!"

Hirsch rounded the corner from the workroom. "Sir?"

"I'm going into town for a while. You have the floor. I don't expect much to happen but, should the world fall apart, you'll find me at Buckets."

The young officer's eyebrows perked. "You are going to town, sir?"

"Should I not?"

"No, sir. I mean, yes, of course, sir. I mean, you can do as you like. It's just that you've never gone at night." Hirsch snapped his thin shoulders back and clicked his heels together. "Pleasant evening, Captain."

Michael took the military vehicle and motored into town, coming to a halt in front of the tavern. Darkness and quiet enveloped the town as curfew was in full effect. As he stepped inside the pub, a woman's voice reached his ears. When was the last time he'd heard a woman sing a French love song? Not since Joseph Goebbels took control of the airwaves. That was a man he'd have the greatest pleasure beating to a bloody pulp for starting his lies in that Heidelberg classroom.

The scents of cigarette smoke and fermented yeast floated

among the aged wood floors and brick walls. Michael breathed deeply, letting the colorful mixture blend with the memories of his childhood and the pub in his seaside village where he imagined the same old men still sat swapping stories.

The piano jingled, drawing him back to the girl. The men hadn't exaggerated. She was lovely with dark-blonde hair just past her slim shoulders. Long, graceful fingers flitted above the keys like hummingbirds. But it was her voice that caught him unaware. She sang of a boy and girl meeting in a garden, but instead of romantic elation, her tone left a haunted feeling. Whether she meant the words or not seemed to be lost on his men. They crowded as close to the piano as possible without banging into Ostermann's men, who'd managed to snag the closest seats.

Michael took the nearest chair at the back table, placing his cap to the side.

Giles bustled over with a glass of amber beer and set it in front of him. "It's been a long time since you've been here, *Capitaine*." He wiped the corner of the table with his apron.

"Been rather busy lately." Something flickered in Giles' eyes. Michael could imagine what the man thought of his busy schedule. Sneaking behind enemy lines, stealing and transmitting illegal messages, and saluting Hitler cronies. Strangely enough, that came easily to Michael. It was dealing with the looks of pure hatred from ordinary people that hit him hardest. But those looks meant he was doing his job. "I see you've added live entertainment while I've been away."

"She plays too fine to keep locked away."

Or Michael's men caught her before she had time to bolt for the stairs. "Does she plan to stay long?"

Giles shifted his feet, his fingers curling the corner of his apron. "She is visiting."

Michael smiled at the evasive answer and grasped the handle of his mug. "Let us hope her visit is not too short."

"Anything else I can get for you, *Capitaine*?"

"No, thank you. I'll just enjoy this for a while."

The song ended, and the men clapped. The girl half turned in her seat. Her eyes remained on the keys. "Any requests?"

"A love song!" Kruger shouted. "About a French girl."

"Do you have anything in mind, *monsieur*?"

"Uh …" Placed on the spot, Kruger scratched his head as if to summon a thought through follicle agitation. "I might … maybe like …"

Ostermann scowled at the boy until he looked around and spotted Michael in the corner. His mouth curved into a gracious smile. "Carry on, Corporal." He pushed out of his chair and made his way to Michael's table. "Captain, what a surprise to see you here."

"Every man needs a break once in a while. Sit, *bitte*." Michael indicated the chair opposite his.

Ostermann took the seat, swiveling it for a better view of the stage. He had a youthful cockiness barbed with self-importance. "Your men tell me how busy you are with the incomings. I suspect they'll only grow more and more frequent as we advance northwest."

"Staying busy and keeping on the alert is more gratifying than sitting on one's hands all day."

"I couldn't agree more, sir." Ostermann signaled for Giles. "That's why I'm always training and drilling the men."

"And then sending them off to a night's drinking after such long days."

"As you said, sir. Men need a break once in a while to keep their spirits up. What better distraction than a beautiful girl?"

Giles came to the table with a fresh glass of beer.

"And we'll have shots. Whisky."

Michael shook his head. He wasn't giving in to the sniveling boy's brown-nosing that easily. "None for me. I'm on call."

"Never mind." Ostermann waved the bartender away and leaned forward. He whispered, "Did you see the disappointment in his eyes? Greedy, just like all the French. Sometimes I think they're as bad as the Jews." Pulling out a pack of cigarettes, he shook one out and clamped it between his lips as he lit the end with an engraved silver lighter.

Looking away, Michael's gaze slammed into the girl's. A second later she turned back to her piano, but it had been long enough.

The girl from the train.

Trepidation squeezed every muscle in Michael's body as he slid to the edge of his seat, ready to spring to action. Did she recognize him or had his German uniform distracted her? One inkling of doubt and she could ruin the entire mission. A tremor ran down his spine. She could cost him his life.

On the train, she'd been the picture of loveliness in her bright red outfit as she'd babbled on to the conductor about visiting her family. The eagerness was now lost from her eyes, the exuberance gone from her stiff shoulders.

"It'll be much easier to identify them with the yellow stars." Ostermann's nattering jolted Michael back to the table. "Some of them can blend in so easily, but they'll no longer be able to hide like rats. They can't help what's in their nature. Should put those chambers to use, *ja*? Of course, if the one in Auschwitz is successful, then more can be opened for faster purging."

Michael's fingers curled around the handle of his mug. His nails bit into his palm as he longed to reach for Ostermann's throat. The Final Solution, the extermination of a human race, talked about like yesterday's headlines.

"Is that another American song?" Ostermann snorted. "She needs to find something else to play. The lyrics don't translate well."

Michael twirled his glass on the table, watching her fingers hit the keys with precision. Like a teacher. "Let her alone. American music is very popular right now."

"It's illegal under Goebbels' command."

"So is French music. Do you want her to stop entirely?"

Smoke curled from Ostermann's lips. "*Nein*."

Michael took a long swallow of beer. This was why he didn't come to the pub often. As the only other officer, Ostermann was required to speak to him and not fraternize with the enlisted. Still, if Michael had to speak to the cur, why not make him squirm a bit? "Lieutenant, I hear your boys are cleaning out mine at the tables."

"A fair stroke of luck."

"And what luck to have winning hands available before my men even get off shift. Then again, after twelve-hour shifts transmitting high-urgency messages to our commanders on the frontline, they are at quite the disadvantage against better rested players." Michael leaned back in his chair. The girl now sang of a woman living in a gray world because her lover had left. Strange she kept picking American songs.

Ostermann smoothed the sides of his pomaded hair. "I wouldn't say better rested, sir. We've had quite a time lately with false papers and people trying to cross the occupied boundary. Yesterday my men caught a couple trying to escape under a pile of hay on a farm truck."

Michael lifted an eyebrow. "Is that so? Fine job, Lieutenant. Your men's competence is a shining extension of your capable hand."

"*Danke schöne, Kapitän.*"

The final notes of the song drew whistling and clapping from the men as they begged for more.

"*Merci beaucoup.* Perhaps a little later I will play for you again when my voice is not so hoarse." The girl stood and closed the lid of the piano to a disappointed murmur from her audience. She turned to face them, but her gaze stared over their heads as if she couldn't meet their eyes. "In the meantime, I believe you have a card game to start."

With breath caught in his throat, Michael waited for her to notice him, but she swept off the stage and disappeared behind the curtain next to the bar.

Her voice rolled on in his head. Not a man to be taken off

guard, something in her words pricked his ears. Something in the way she accented them. He couldn't put his finger on it. Whatever her secrets, she would keep them—and his—for the night. The breath in his chest eased.

Not wishing to tempt fate, Michael tipped back the rest of his beer and threw a few coins on the table. Rising from his seat, he took his cap and tucked it under his arm. "Might I offer you a lift back to your post, Lieutenant? We're of no more use here."

"Kind of you, sir."

Once outside, Michael still couldn't shake the fear kneading in his chest as they left the village in darkness. Nor could he shake the girl's voice. An accent he'd heard before, but so unexpected to find in the French countryside. *This is what happens when I'm up past my bedtime. I start hearing things.*

"I don't see how he can expect me not to play. My secret is out. The Germans know I'm here." Claire stabbed her trowel into the earth and scooped out a rock. Flinging it over the fence, she rocked back on her heels and wiped away a trickle of sweat escaping from the kerchief around her head. "Besides, with the songs distracting them, those soldiers don't know how much they're drinking and paying for, or that I'm not a real singer."

Pauline grunted as she cut a head of cabbage and set it into her basket. "They wouldn't care if you warbled like a one-legged cat, but I've noticed more coins in the till since you've come." She glared across the rows of cabbage and radishes. "But don't think I'll start paying you for it. Girls like you shouldn't be out carousing with soldiers into the still of the night, and German soldiers at that. You should be at home letting some nice boy court you and get you a house and babies."

"I don't like singing for them any more than you like having them in there every night. I have to stare at the wall or above their heads just to make it manageable."

"Then I guess you won't like my offer."

"What might that be?"

Pauline put another cabbage into the basket and shrugged. "Business has improved since you've started playing. Giles runs around like a chicken with his head cut off trying to manage since I'm stuck in the back cleaning the bottles and glasses. He could use the help."

"Like helping him behind the bar?"

"Maybe. Or waiting tables."

"He doesn't even want me on the stage. What makes you think he'll allow me on the floor?"

"This is my bar too. He wheedled me into letting you stay. As long as you're here, you can help where needed. That was part of the bargain in the beginning, no?" Wisps of wiry black hair fell across Pauline's forehead as she hunched over the vegetables in front of her. "You can keep the tips."

Claire bit the inside of her lip to keep from smiling. Money for her escape fund, and from the Germans' own pockets. "Should I tell him?"

"No. Just do it tonight between breaks. He might be angry, but he'll get over it."

Claire sighed and studied her grubby hands. Had these filthy things really plucked the strings of a violin in a concert hall to the applause of white-gloved ladies and gentlemen? How had Claire's life ever spiraled to this point? From a full scholarship at a French university to a singing barmaid for the Nazis. Never let it be said life didn't have its twists.

If there was one positive thing from all of this, it was helping Giles and Pauline. Despite their bickering and oddities, they treated her with kindness and kept a roof over her head and food in her belly while many were starving to death. Being the local tavern meant the authorities turned a blind eye to the small garden they kept behind the building.

"There. That should be plenty for this week." Pauline dusted off her hands and lumbered to her feet. "We'll just add a few radishes and a bottle of chardonnay from the new shipment, and it should be good for the exchange."

Claire stood and swatted the dirt and pebbles sticking to her knees. Her silk stockings had given out long ago, reducing her to the cotton ones the mercantile could barely keep in stock before they flew off the shelves.

Inside, Pauline divided the vegetables and packed a basket, covering the contents with a worn green cloth. "Now make sure the baker gives you two loaves this time. No pinching me like the last time. Hurry and get going while I start the soup."

Looping her arm through the basket handle, Claire slipped out the back door and down the small alley next to the block. The baker's shop sat in the middle of town where it received the most traffic, though its wares grew less substantial by the week. The bell jingled at Claire's entry. "*Bonjour.*"

"*Bonjour.*" The baker took a customer's ration card and stuffed three rather flat rolls into a brown paper bag, then handed it to the woman. "A pleasant afternoon, *madame.*"

Clutching her bag to her chest, the woman nodded at Claire and left the shop.

"*Mademoiselle* Claire, I was wondering when I would see you today."

"We've been rather busy this afternoon." She patted the basket.

"Ah. Let's see what you have." Coming around the counter, he glanced out the window before turning to face her. "As you can see, I'm out of most things. I'm afraid this week's provisions may not be adequate."

Same old game. She lifted the corner of the cloth for him to catch a quick peek of the dark bottle nestled inside. "Are you sure?"

Stroking the sparse beard on his rounded chin, he turned his eyes to the ceiling. "I can see what I have in the back." He rolled his gaze back to her and held out his hand. "If you'll allow me ..."

She pulled the basket closer to her side with a smile. "May I join you?"

Knowing his part, he heaved a sigh and waved her into the back. After a quick negotiation, Claire tucked two fresh baguettes into her basket and left the bakery with a wave and a promise to return next week.

Two doors down, she stepped into the butcher's shop. The tangy smell of sausage and blood hit her in the face. Flies buzzed across the ceiling, flitting on the cuts of meat behind the counter.

"*Bonjour, Monsieur* Firmin. How are you today?"

"*Bonjour.*" The butcher slung a casing of orange-red sausage across a hook and wiped his massive hands on his bloody apron. His gaze fell to the basket at her side. "Come to the back."

She hated going to his work area. Hooks of all shapes and sizes hung from the ceiling, counters covered in dried and unidentifiable animal parts lined the walls, and the nauseating stench of blood and guts hung heavy in the air. The open back door let in the fresh air, but it also allowed more flies to buzz in on the afternoon breeze.

In the center of the room stood a wide table with long troughs around the edge. A young man stood at the far end hefting a cleaver over some animal's neck.

"Savon, look who is here," Firmin said.

Pushing a shaggy patch of brown hair from his face, the young man looked at Claire. His deep-set eyes widened, and red flames burst onto his cheeks. The cleaver in his hand faltered as he gave her a slight nod.

Wasting no time, Claire set her basket on the cleanest section of counter she could find and pulled out one of the baguettes. Firmin took the bread and stuffed it in one of the high cabinets along the wall.

"Savon, bring that box here."

Laying his cleaver on the table, Savon wiped his hands on his apron and walked to a large storage container half buried in the cool ground. Selecting a box from the several stacked within, he ambled around the counter and dropped it in front of Claire. Reddish-brown fingerprints smudged the corners.

With a deep breath to steady her stomach, she opened the lid to find some of the finest chops of liver, heart, kidney, brain, hooves, and other unidentifiable goat parts. She closed the lid and nodded. "Pauline will love this. A fine meal."

Firmin stuck his chest out. "Savon cut them just this morning, so they would be fresh for you. Didn't you, Savon?"

Savon's lip curled. "Better than those German pigs taking them." His gaze cut to Claire. "Why don't you spit on them when they come into the bar?"

"Because they would arrest me. Or shoot me on the spot. They don't take kindly to insults." Claire shook her head. What was he thinking, suggesting something so vulgar right to the Germans' faces? He must have a death wish.

"I wouldn't let them arrest you. Not if you were my girl."

The front bell jingled. Savon grunted and left to attend the new customers.

"I apologize for his forwardness," Firmin said. "He hasn't had the opportunity to speak with many women."

Claire smiled to ease the awkwardness left in Savon's wake. Tucking the box into her basket, she headed toward the back door. "We should have a few more carrots to throw in next week. Shall we say a few rolls and one baguette for a tenderloin or chops?"

Firmin ran a hand over his bald head. "The soldiers come for the tenderloins first thing. The best I could do is chops or shank."

"Deal."

He stepped in front of her, blocking her way to the door. "Why not go out the front to say goodbye to Savon?"

She smiled and sidestepped him. "I shouldn't make a big deal going through the main entrance." She patted the basket containing her secret stash.

Firmin's lips flattened into a thin line. "Of course, you're right. The back is more suitable for our business. Until next week, or hopefully sooner."

Back outside, Claire gulped in fresh air and hurried behind the row of shops. Coming out of the alleyway, a uniformed soldier stepped across the sidewalk in front of her. She slammed straight into his side, her nose bumping into his shoulder and her basket falling to the ground.

"*Excusez-moi, monsieur*. I did not see you." Tears welled in her eyes from the throbbing in her nose. Looking to the ground, she couldn't see her basket. Panic crashed down her spine.

"Allow me." He retrieved her basket from where it had dropped. He tucked the loosened covering back and handed it to her. "You should be more careful next time, *mademoiselle*."

Coldness swept through her limbs. She took the basket with trembling fingers and forced her gaze up. Brilliant blue eyes stared back. The officer who sat in the back of the bar, secluded by darkness and smoke. He stood a good nine inches taller than her, with a slender athletic build and reddish-brown hair slicked to the side. Seriousness marked his square jaw. Her gaze fell to the silver diamonds on his collar. "*Oui, monsieur*."

"*Capitaine. Capitaine* Reichner." Silver buttons glinted on the front of his gray tunic, blinding her with each breath. "And you are the *chanteuse* who has captivated my men."

He spoke perfect French without a hint of an accent. Or emotion.

She averted her gaze lest he see the fear blazing there. "They must not be very picky about entertainment."

"If you think your ability less than adequate, why put yourself through the pressure of performing?"

She pushed back a snort of laughter. Did he expect her to turn away a group of Nazis? She'd never be heard from again. "I enjoy playing, and it helps to pass the time."

"Where did you learn such a skill?"

"I come from a musical family."

"And somehow that talent skipped Giles?"

Her head snapped up as warnings zinged through her brain like tiny fireworks. Lies were too complicated. "We aren't related, though we consider each other as family."

"Ah, so you are merely visiting." He tilted his head forward, so the bill of his cap shadowed his eyes. Such a bright blue. "I hope you do not leave too soon. My men would notice your absence much too keenly."

Of course, they would. Why had she ever touched that stupid piano in the first place? Her fingernails clawed into the basket handle. "If you'll excuse me, *Capitaine*. I still have a list of chores before this evening, and I don't want to disappoint the men by scrubbing floors in the kitchen."

Clicking the heels of his black boots together, he bowed stiffly and gestured his hand to the side for her to pass. She held her shoulders as straight as she could and prayed her legs wouldn't give out as she made a beeline across the street and into the Three Buckets. The door had barely closed before her knees turned to jelly. She grabbed the door frame for support, resting her cheek against the rough wood.

Had he noticed what was in her basket when he picked it up? Would he raid the bar later for their desirable stock of bartered brains and organs? Would he interrogate her? Would she reveal the truth about herself?

His crystalline eyes haunted her as if digging into her secrets. She moaned, pushing off the wall. "Had to be a German officer."

She walked through the empty bar to the back room. In the kitchen, Pauline, Giles, Ansell, and Eloy had gathered in a corner behind a rack of glasses.

"What's all this?" Claire set her basket on the counter.

All four of them jumped.

Pauline fanned her pale face with a dish towel. "Don't ever do that again."

Ansell cursed and reached for the cigarette that fell from his cracked lips. He wiped off the dirt and stuck it back between his teeth. "Anyone else out there?"

"No, just me." Walking forward, Claire joined the group crowded around Giles' radio. It was cracked and glued back together in several places, but voices still managed to hiss through the box. "What's going on?"

"England and the United States are putting together some kind of agreement for the Allies. They're talking about their goals and what needs to happen after this war is over," Ansell said. "Fritz won't like it much."

"The Americans are getting involved?"

"They want to protect their trade with Britain and the Soviet Union and, once upon a time, us. Right now, they're only making a formal statement against the evils threatening world rule."

A disturbing mixture of excitement and fear rippled through her. If America got involved, the war would be over in a flash. She could go home.

Giles turned the knob as the reporter's voice crackled to an end. He placed the small radio under the floor and slapped the board back into place before turning to the men. "Bar's open."

CHAPTER 6

Michael paused at the door to the Three Buckets. He squeezed the doorknob, wishing it would snap in two. Frustration gnawed at his peace of mind.

He'd received no word from his contact tonight. It was the first time since he'd been assigned to COMMS that the wire remained silent on a reporting day.

Then there was the singing barmaid who held the key to Michael's discovery. Pressure like a giant rock lodged between his shoulder blades. If he didn't control his worries, the agitation would draw attention and suspicions would rise. It could blow his entire operation. Smoothing the front of his uniform, he whipped off his cap and tucked it under one arm, then opened the door.

He took a table in the back with no Ostermann in sight. His men sat at the front tables gathered close to the piano and its accompanist. Her gaze skimmed over the top of her instrument, never once looking at the enthralled crowd at her side. He remembered those deep-blue eyes on him yesterday afternoon, wide with terror. His lungs had burned from holding his breath, but the flicker of recognition never came.

Giles stopped at his table. "*Capitaine*, what is your pleasure this evening?"

"Largest bottle of whisky you have back there."

Giles raised a dark eyebrow. "The whole bottle?"

"*Oui*." A bottle, ten bottles, it didn't matter. Whisky had no more effect on his Irish roots than lemonade on a schoolboy. Tonight he wished otherwise. He needed the feel of oblivion sliding down his throat and seeping deep into his veins, and not even the consumption limit of two liters a week would stop him.

Two tables in front of him, Dietrich turned to say something to Kruger and spotted Michael. "Captain Reichner, join us." Dietrich pointed to the seat next to him.

The girl's fingers—why had he not asked her name—stumbled over the keys at Dietrich's outburst. Her eyes snapped to Michael through the smoky haze. Her jaw clenched. She tried the keys again, slow at first but gaining speed to finish the last notes of the song.

He never should have come back to the lion's den, but it was unavoidable. Something about the girl didn't sit right with him, and it drove him mad not being able to put his finger on it. A spy? No, she'd been too easy to follow on her backroom exchange with the butcher. Yet she resembled nothing of the girl he'd seen smiling without a care on the train. Better to discover her secret before she had a chance to blow his.

As the final notes drifted from the piano, she shot from her seat and hurried off the stage. The men clapped and continued their conversations while Dietrich, Lehmann, and Kruger dodged through the tables with a pitcher of beer, stopping in front of Michael's table.

"Shouldn't drink alone, sir."

"Have a seat then." Michael pushed his cap aside to make room for the sweating pitcher.

The girl barreled into Giles as he came through the curtain with a dark bottle cradled in his arm. He held the bottle out and pointed over her shoulder to Michael's table, but she shook her head. Giles said something more, and she took the bottle, placing it on a tray with a tumbler. Balancing the tray with two hands, she shuffled to the table.

"Ah, the lovely *chanteuse*," Dietrich cooed across the table. "Come to us for a personal serenade? How lucky we are."

"Are you not tired of my voice yet, *monsieur*?"

"Never."

Setting the tray on the table, she grabbed the bottle and loosened the cap. The glass wobbled in her fingers as she filled it with amber liquid. She slid it across the table to Michael before turning away.

"You can leave the bottle," he said.

When she turned to replace it, the bottle hit the edge of the table and fell sideways, sending a wave of whisky sloshing across the table. The men jumped back as the liquid rolled closer.

"Oh, *monsieur*! I am so sorry." She cupped her hands to stop the liquid from spilling off the edges. "How clumsy. I'm so sorry."

Michael set the bottle upright and tossed his cap onto his chair as the whisky seeped closer. "Towels. Do you have some?"

She raced to the bar, amber drops falling from her fingertips, and flung herself over the counter. Wiggling back down, she ran to the table and threw her armload of dishtowels on top of the whisky. With a few quick swipes, she had the mess cleared. Dropping to her knees, she began wiping the floor as well.

"*Chanteuse*, the bar does not seem to agree with you as well as the piano." Kruger checked his tunic and boots for stains.

Michael frowned. "Don't you men have a game to join?"

Clicking their heels together, they left for the poker game that was starting at a much drier table. Michael squatted next to Claire and took a somewhat clean towel to dry off a chair leg. "They're teasing," he said.

"I'm afraid they're right."

"Then why are you here? You don't seem like a girl who belongs in a bar singing for unruly soldiers and farmers."

Her fingers stilled for a second, long enough for him to imagine her mind whirling for an answer. "The war has taken my family. Giles and Pauline have offered me a place to stay. They can use the extra help."

He filed the information away, along with the peculiar way she pronounced the *r* on certain words. With the war exploding around them, everyone had secrets—he most of all—and any moment in her presence could spark the recognition that would doom him. Yet something in her innocent expression held him captive far beyond his soldiering investigation.

"Claire. What has happened?" Giles stomped to a halt behind her, his cheeks burning red as he stared at the soaked towels on the table.

"I'm sorry, Giles." Claire pushed to her feet, cradling the towels in her worn apron. "I spilled the bottle."

"I'm so very sorry, *Capitaine*. Please forgive her, she is new at this."

"An accident," Michael said. "The most damage is to your floor."

Scuffing a toe, Giles shook his head. "Not the first time, nor the last."

"I think it adds character," Claire said.

Michael dipped his head before anyone could see the corner of his mouth pull up.

Giles cleared his throat and turned to Claire. "Pauline might need some character added to the dishes in the back."

Claire dropped the soaked towels onto the serving tray and left.

"Allow me to bring you another bottle, *Capitaine*." Giles wiped his apron across the edge of the table. "On the house."

Before Michael could stop him—and call an end to the evening before something *did* happen—a corporal from the night crew ran into the room. Doubling over, he clutched his knees and gasped.

"What's the meaning of this, Corporal?" Michael snapped.

"Sorry, sir." The boy straightened, coughing as he tried to salute.

Pursing his lips as he struggled for patience, Michael waited until the coughing stopped and a normal color returned to the soldier's face. "Want to try again?"

Snapping a salute, the corporal panted. "Sorry, sir. Ran all the way. Incoming news. German cadet killed in Paris by French resistance. Reprisal expected immediately."

The rock on Michael's back crunched along his spine. "What

sort of reprisal?"

"They're rounding up citizens. Anyone in the vicinity or with ties to the assassin is to be shot."

Michael grabbed his cap and set it on top of his head. "Back to base, then."

Trying to rub the onslaught of bleariness from his eyes, Michael tapped out his message again. Crackling static, then dots shot through his headset. *Iron Shepherd. Repeat numbers.*

"How about grabbing a pencil and paper next time, lads?" Michael grumbled, pushing the black button to relay the number of Panzer divisions moving into Leningrad. He followed with a short recounting of the increased patrols of U-boats off the Irish coast.

Excellent, IS. WH out. The line went dead.

Michael pulled off the headset, relieving the pressure on his ears. He leaned back in his chair and closed his eyes. Those U-boats patrolled too close to his home, and he'd had no word from Mum and Dad in over two months. Not a surprise. It was hard getting personal messages across the lines. But, with their cottage resting on a bluff overlooking the coast, he worried and hoped each day to hear from them.

For their safety and sanity, he hadn't told them about his assignment. What would his German father think if he ever found out?

Someone hammered on his door.

Michael's eyes snapped open. The transmitter stared back at him. Leaping from his chair, he threw the equipment into its case and tried to shut the top. The knock came again. The lid refused to lock. Panicked, he ran his hands around the edges of the case and found the headset wire poking out the side. Shoving it in, he slammed the locks and pushed it into its hiding spot behind the bookcase.

Another knock. "Captain?"

Michael's eyes flew to the door. And the unturned key. He'd forgotten to the lock the door.

"Captain?" The doorknob turned.

Shouldering the bookcase with all his might, he slid it into place as the door squeaked open. Dietrich's head popped in. "Captain, are you in—oh, there you are. I knocked but did not hear you."

Michael smoothed the front of his tunic to calm his pounding heart. "What is it, Sergeant?"

Dietrich's eyes flickered to the bookcase then back to his superior. "A call for you, sir. Rather urgent, from Major Kessel's office."

Following Dietrich to the phone located in what had once been the front parlor, Michael took the waiting receiver. "Captain Reichner speaking."

"*Heil* Hitler. I am Lieutenant Lahm speaking from Major Kessel's office in Paris. The major is set for a short tour around the countryside, stopping at various posts for briefings and inspections. Very informal. He is interested in seeing your communication post. He should arrive a week from Tuesday with a small entourage."

Michael bit back the curse on his lips. "How long does the major wish to stay?"

"Most stops are one or two days, depending on how much there is to report. He likes to see a full list of daily events, procedures, and, of course, the impact they have on fulfilling our mission."

"Should I prepare anything special for him?"

"As I said, very informal. The major appreciates the simplicity of day-to-day tasks when he tours."

"We look forward to the major's arrival."

"If you have any further questions, you can speak with me, and I'll be happy to answer them for you. *Heil* Hitler."

"*Heil* Hitler." Michael dropped the phone back into its cradle.

Dietrich waited a modest distance away, but the wolfish light in his eyes gave away his eagerness. "Are we to host Major Kessel, sir?"

"Tell Lieutenant Hirsch I need him in my office in five minutes. In fifteen minutes, I want the men assembled for a briefing."

"Was anything else said, sir?"

Michael raised an eyebrow. "Should I call him back and allow you to ask for yourself, *Sergeant*?"

Dietrich had the grace to blanch. "No, sir. Thank you, sir." Clicking his heels together, he left the room.

One hour later, after briefing his men of the major's visit and locking his office door, Michael left the house to wander through the back gardens. The heavy scents of lavender, rosemary, and thyme clung to the air as the plants struggled to survive in a bed overgrown with weeds. He knew the choking sensation himself.

First things first. The transmitter had to be moved. Too close a call with Dietrich. That hound would stop at nothing if he caught a whiff of scandal or treason, and with the major coming, the office might be commandeered. There was a loose board under Michael's bed that might make an agreeable hiding spot.

He passed under a wooden trellis and continued along the path to where it bisected another. If he continued forward, he'd find the back corner of the lot with the decomposing body he never wanted to see again.

Michael pivoted away and continued on the grass past the walls of the garden.

Second thing, the major's arrival. An interruption, like most official visits. They said they wanted to see normal routines, but Michael had been in the military long enough to understand the dog and pony show. Pathetic. He couldn't remember the last time he'd stood for open ranks, but the officials expected it nonetheless. Michael would ensure his men didn't disappoint. With or without the spectacle, his men's boots gleamed like polished glass, every button shined, and every face was shaved. Pride in one's uniform was one thing. Standing at attention with colors bared for the vanity of an officer was another.

He stopped. Woods surrounded him now. Dirt covered the tips of his boots. So much for polishing them last night. He pulled at the hook holding his collar together to allow fresh air onto his neck. If he angled his head just right, he could probably see the steam rising from the tunic-oven baking his chest.

He continued on. The major would be easy to handle. German, British, Yank, Soviet—it didn't matter. All officers wanted to see efficiency, and Michael's men were the best at what they did.

Unease rippled down his spine at the thought. His men were the enemy, yet they performed their duties as all good soldiers did. If they'd donned the blue-grey of the Royal Air Force, he might be proud of them.

He shook his head. He couldn't afford such thoughts about the foe. He'd much rather think about the lovely blonde with a dimple in her cheek that deepened when she was embarrassed.

Michael stumbled to a stop. A woman, even a pretty one with the husky voice of a blues singer, was nothing more than a distraction. Why, then, did he fancy himself not minding that she'd spilled whisky all over his lap the other night? Would she have another cracking comment for that, too?

Pulling the cap off his head, he swiped away the sweat along his hairline. Her expressions were much too colorful and blunt to be French, yet she said them without thinking. It wasn't the only odd thing about her speech. Those *r*'s were rather flat.

The trickling of water drew his attention to where a towering oak stood next to a stream. Walking into the inviting shade, Michael slid down the trunk and stretched his legs out in front of him. The bubbling water tantalized his eyes closed. Drowsiness curled at the edges of his mind.

Dirt shifted under approaching footsteps. His eyes snapped open. A woman struck his foot. She screamed. He lunged forward, catching her before she smacked onto the ground.

CHAPTER 7

Pushing the hair from her eyes, Claire shrank back in terror. Back into the arms of the German captain. His breath fluttered the loosened hair on her forehead. He was half crouched and half splayed on the grass, cradling her from hitting the ground. Heat sprawled across her cheeks in a burning inferno of shame.

Her mind whirled. Those bright blue eyes. They'd seen her.

She'd been here before, like this. But she'd never stumbled over a man next to a tree before, and she'd certainly never fallen into a German officer's arms. She pushed away and scrambled to her feet. Where was her book? "I'm so very sorry. I didn't see you."

He stood and tugged his uniform into place. One reddish eyebrow quirked. "Making a habit of running into me, aren't you?"

"Not really. You just happen to show up in unexpected places."

The other eyebrow raised. "This is my fault?"

"No, but no one ever comes here, and I didn't expect to find you. I thought soldiers remained close to their posts."

"Everyone needs a break."

The sincerity in his words cracked her shell. Until she reminded herself that he probably meant a break from terrorizing innocent people and obliterating entire towns.

"I had no idea this was here." He brushed grass bits from his elbows and swept his hand out to indicate the stream. "I was out for a walk and came across it. I apologize if the spot was spoken for."

He didn't move to leave. She'd better. She took a step back.

"I'm not frightening you away, am I?"

Could he not understand why she didn't want to be anywhere

near him? "You've already claimed this spot for the afternoon, fair and square. I'll find another."

"Yes, but I'll—what's this?" Brow furrowed, he bent and retrieved a book from near his foot. "*The Three Musketeers*." He smiled as he opened it. "I haven't read this book since I was a boy. I loved the sword fights amidst all the treachery."

I'll bet.

"Do you have a favorite part?" His face was open and curious.

"No. I'm more the witty-character and whodunit type. *The Three Musketeers* was part of my school reading, but I find books much more enjoyable when I'm not required to take a test on them."

"You read often?"

"I like to, though I don't often get the chance these days unless it's Sunday."

"Because of your work at Buckets?"

"Partly."

He turned the book over as he examined the covers and edges, brushing off specks of dirt. "Pauline must be quite the taskmaster to only allow you Sunday afternoons for reading. Does she make you practice pouring beer to get just the right amount of head? I've tried it before and give credit to anyone who can do it properly the first time. It's harder than it looks."

"I practice when she isn't around because every time I spill I can see the dollar signs spinning in her eyes like a bad Ferris wheel."

He tilted his head to the side, cocking his ear forward as a thin furrow grew between his eyebrows. Claire looked to her toes, ashamed that she spoke so openly. She'd forgotten the simple happiness of talking about books with another person. His deep tones and persistent questions almost made her forget he was the enemy.

"Surely you don't intend to stay in the service industry for the rest of your life. You're much more at ease at the piano than behind the bar. Fewer accidents."

A smile threatened but she couldn't—wouldn't—let this officer pull it from her. "There isn't much demand for a non-graduated music student at the moment, but the men don't seem to mind. As you said, everyone needs a break, and if that out-of-tune piano can give them an hour or two of pleasure, then I'm more than happy to oblige. Of course, they'll change their minds as soon as I plunge a pitcher of beer into their laps."

He leaned forward, drawing her gaze up. "I could give you a few people to aim for, beginning with anyone who suggests a duet."

She bit her lip, but the smile came anyway. Oh, the pleasure that would flood her soul should she ever summon the courage to spill a tray onto that Lieutenant Oyster-whatever his name was.

The captain watched her closely, as if taking in every detail at once. Though she should've been nervous under such study, his gaze held nothing subversive. She had never seen such crystal blueness in a man's eyes before. Posture straight with self-assurance and a commanding air, she didn't doubt the man could stand beneath an erupting mountain and not rile. The thought of such a confident man sharing a book with her sent warm tendrils curling around her head as if she'd sat out in the sun too long.

A Nazi. The man was the enemy. She had no business being near him, much less giving into warm tendrils. "Excuse me. I need to head back."

His brow crinkled. "No, please stay. This spot is yours. Maybe I can find another one."

Claire shook her head. "Stay if you like. Pauline needs help scrubbing the chairs, and today we can do it without customers dropping in."

He held out the book, a hopeful light in his eyes. "Perhaps if we should meet again next Sunday, we can discuss this, or a new one if you've finished it by then."

"Doubtful." She let him wonder if she meant the book or the meeting. Taking the book, she tucked it under her arm and turned away. "Good afternoon, Captain. Enjoy the shade."

His secret was safe. For the time being.

Michael leaned his hand against the tree as she walked away. Sunlight hit the hair that fell loosely from under the faded red handkerchief tied around her head, turning the blonde waves into bouncing gold. Would it be as soft to touch as it looked? How hard would she slap his face if he tried it? Not that he would. He had no possible future with a woman. Not even one with eyes the color of a churning Atlantic storm.

Sighing, he pushed away from the tree and tried to force his thoughts onto a more productive path, but they skipped back to her. He'd blathered on like a schoolboy, though he had managed to make her smile despite her best efforts not to. It'd been a long time since he'd made a girl smile, not that he tried often. Now that he'd met a girl he wanted to see smile, he had to be wearing a contemptible uniform. And she, an American in France.

Without realizing it, she'd slapped him between the eyes with the last piece of the puzzle. She hadn't remembered to say francs instead of dollars. Bad luck all around.

How had she gotten to France in the first place, and who else knew who she was? A music student studying abroad stuck behind enemy lines was plausible. But was she a spy? Part of the resistance? Not possible. Her face gave away every emotion like the best Shakespearean actor. She'd be the worst spy ever. Still, she needed to be monitored.

Grabbing his cap, he headed back to base. First things first. He'd move the transmitter, then send word to his contact about the visiting major and the village's American girl. She might not be a priority, but they'd want her watched. Fine by him. The closer an eye he kept on her, the sooner he would sense her ratting him out.

The sun burned the back of his neck as he gained the garden

path once more. The wheels of his mind turned with delight as he realized the best way to both entertain the major and keep an eye on Claire. Hopefully Kessel liked to drink.

CHAPTER 8

Claire hefted the last crate of cigarette cartons onto the stack by the back door. She wiped the sweat from her temple with the back of her hand and took a long drink of water from the decanter waiting for her.

"What about this bottle here?" Pauline stood in the hall with her brother and another man whom Claire had seen once before. He'd come to the bar long after the customers had left for the night.

The man yanked the cork from the bottle and handed it to her. "The best I have from the Rhine."

Pauline tipped the wine bottle to her lips, swished, and swallowed. Her eyes slanted to Giles then back to the stranger. "Maybe the best in six more years. Don't play with me, Remy."

"It's hard to get the good stuff out of there these days. Keep it in the cellar for six years and use the other crates."

"Our customers are thirsty now." Giles crossed his thick arms over his chest as he nudged a crate with his toe. "Ten francs for the case. No more until you bring the good supplies."

The man blew a long breath through his nose. "I told you things are getting more difficult to transport. It's hard enough slipping this past the guards, and now you're getting picky."

"I'm already paying double what these are worth."

"Times are tough. Haven't you heard? There's a war on."

"Where's the beer?"

"Glad you asked." Remy walked to a covered crate and pulled off the canvas to expose three small casks. He yanked the plug from the bunghole and poured a small amount into a glass, which he handed to Pauline.

She swirled the glass, creating a tiny tornado of golden liquid and then tossed it back. She looked at Giles with a shrug. "Not bad. A milder hop than the last batch."

"The barley and rye aren't given enough time to ripen anymore." Remy fit the plug back into the cask. "Demand for it on the front lines can barely be met, so the factories are doing everything they can to speed the process up, even if it means sacrificing taste. This war can't end soon enough if only to get liquor quality under control again. A man has to save two months of rations for a decent drink these days."

Claire took another drink of water, fascinated by the black-market transaction carrying on in front of her. She glanced to the door, half expecting to see Eliot Ness come busting through. Or better yet, the Nazi captain. Never too far from her thoughts, she often found herself watching for his arrival. Ugh, why was she thinking about him at all? She smacked her palm against the crate's corner.

Three pairs of eyes snapped to her.

"Sorry," she whispered.

"Almost forgot about the cigarettes." Giles walked toward her, stopping at the crates by the door. Taking out a carton, he shook the box until one long cigarette fell into his palm. He rolled it between his fingers and under his nose, then handed it to Pauline for a try.

Repeating the rolling and sniffing, she nodded. "Good. How many cartons?"

"At least forty," Remy said.

Giles pursed his lips. "How many others are you supplying to this month?"

"Just two."

"Cut their supplies, and I'll pay double. Can you manage that?"

"I'll have some explaining to do, but I can manage. Besides, they never run out the way you do here. Must be some pretty persuasions." Remy winked at Claire.

"Mind your tongue." Pauline slapped Remy upside the head. "We run a respectable place here."

Remy rubbed his head. "I was only paying a friendly compliment."

The bell on the front door jingled. Giles cursed. "Claire, go and see who the thickhead is and throw him out. We're not open before noon." He grabbed an armload of crates and headed toward the cellar. "Remy, get those other boxes and bring them here. Quick."

Pushing through the curtain, Claire stopped in her tracks. Captain Reichner, the thickhead, stood at the bar with hat in hand. She swallowed hard to move the dryness from her throat. "I'm sorry, *Capitaine*. The bar is closed."

"I'm not here for that. I'd like to discuss business with Giles if he's available."

"I'm afraid he's not and won't be for some time. Perhaps you could come back later, during normal hours."

The captain stepped to the end of the bar. "That's what I'm trying to avoid. I'd like some quiet while we talk, away from the men."

He took the same firm stance he had the other day by the tree. Only today no sun burnished his coppery hair. Not that she should have noticed. "He's busy, but I'll ask." She headed toward the back room.

"I have something for you."

Claire stopped with her hand on the curtain and turned, her curiosity outweighing common sense.

Reaching inside his tunic, he pulled out a book and held it out to her. "I thought after *The Three Musketeers* you might like this one."

Gold lettering glinted at her from the red leather binding. *The Count of Monte Cristo.*

"It won't bite." He inched it closer to her.

"I'm sorry, I can't."

His eyebrows raised. "Read it already?"

She laced her fingers together to keep them from reaching for the novel. "No. But as you saw, I've not finished the other one, and there's no telling when I would get around to this one."

"Then it'll encourage you to read faster."

"Speed isn't the problem." She couldn't accept anything from him, the enemy, no matter how much she longed to.

He leaned forward and dropped his voice. "The taskmaster again?"

Meeting his eyes—those eyes that pierced into her soul—she smiled. *Nope. Just you.*

"*Capitaine*, what are you doing here so early?" Giles pushed through the curtain and stood next to her.

"He'd like to discuss private business with you, though I told him you're busy." Claire ignored the book still in Reichner's outstretched fingers.

Giles' gaze dropped to the book, then to Reichner, a deep frown pulling his mouth. "Is that so? I am busy but can spare a few minutes. Have a seat, sir, if you like. Claire, Pauline needs help in the kitchen."

Reichner dropped his hand. "I'd like *Mademoiselle* Claire to stay, please, if she consents. Part of this may concern her."

Giles waved her back into the room. Suspicions raised, Claire walked toward their table and perched on the nearest chair.

"I'll make this short." The captain sat, placing the book on the table and folding his hands next to it. "Major Kessel is coming next week to tour our facilities. I should like to bring him here. I shall pay in advance to help increase your supplies and, of course, pay for any costs that should accrue. Is this agreeable?"

Claire rolled her gaze to her lap. Was anything *not* agreeable when it came to the German army? Next to her, Giles' hands clenched until his knuckles turned white. As a self-made man, owner and proprietor of his own business, he couldn't even decide who to allow and turn away from his door.

Giles nodded. "Of course, *Capitaine*."

"Excellent. And for the entertainment"—Reichner turned to Claire—"you would be well compensated for your musical talents."

"There's no need to ask, sir. I play every night." His men had seen to that.

"Yes, but this will require longer sets than you customarily play with any special requests the major may have." He shifted toward her, brushing his knee against her skirt. "Only if you wish to accept. Otherwise, one of my men will have to play, and I'd rather listen to metal scratching across bricks. Your voice would be a welcome relief."

Her gaze flicked to the book lying between them. How foolish she was to think he cared for her to read it. It was merely a thinly veiled attempt to butter her up. Not that it mattered. He offered payment. Money she could use to get home. With Giles' connections, she might find someone willing to smuggle her for the right price.

Hope renewed, she nodded. "Of course, *Capitaine*."

Reichner's face relaxed into a smile. "Excellent. Tomorrow I can come by with the advance and perhaps discuss a few of the arrangements, say around 1400—ah, two o'clock? I know you are busy, so I'll see myself out now." Standing, he offered his hand to Giles. Giles rose from his seat and shook it. "Thank you, Mr. Desbaux. I appreciate your generosity." He turned to Claire and gave a stiff bow. "*Mademoiselle* Claire. Your generosity as well."

As he walked away, Claire snatched the book off the table where he'd left it. "Captain Reichner." He stopped by the front door. She walked to him and held out the book. "I won't have time to read this."

"You may take as long as you like."

"No, I don't think so."

"Please, it will give me an excuse to discuss it with you later." Adjusting the cap on his slicked-back hair, he left the bar.

Agitated, she curled her fingers into the book's spine. She

wanted to throw it in his face and tell him exactly what he could do with it. She'd almost believed his quiet teasing and earnest eyes. Another convincing Nazi tactic he'd been taught at boot camp, no doubt.

Uncurling her nails from the innocent book's spine, she tucked it under her arm. *Just remember, you'll be taking his money soon enough*. With that satisfying thought, she returned to the counter where Giles waited.

"What is that?" He pointed to the book.

"He thought I should like to read it, though I think it was a bribe for the extravaganza."

His cheeks darkened. Pulling a clean cloth from his belt, he picked up a mug and wiped the lip. "He's dangerous."

"I know. But impossible to refuse."

CHAPTER 9

The uniform pulled snugly across Michael's chest as Dietrich brushed lint from his collar. Michael examined his image in the mirror. Boots polished to perfection, buttons aligned, rank diamonds glowing silver, every spare thread clipped, epaulets straight, and Iron Cross gleaming on his left pocket.

That was why Claire couldn't stand to be near him. He remembered the warmth of her skin when he'd caught her. And how she'd leaned away from him in fear. And then there was the way her eyes flashed as if she wanted to bash him upside the head with a book. A book he only brought as a ploy to talk to her.

He pushed the tormenting thoughts away. "Did you check the ribbon rack?"

"Yes, sir." Dietrich eyed the colorful ribbons on Michael's chest once more and nodded. "Impeccable as always, sir. By the way, the baking soda worked wonders on my silver last night. Thank you for suggesting it." He pointed to the special skill badge on his left pocket.

"You can also use it with a little water to take the sweat stains off your inner collar and hat rim. Helps with the smell too. Is the jacket straight in the back?" As Dietrich stepped around him to check the lines of his coat, a knock came on the door. "Enter."

The door opened, and Lieutenant Hirsch stepped in with a smart click of his heels. "The major's carpool was spotted over the next ridge, Captain."

"How many cars?"

"Three. Two sedans and one Kübelwagen."

"Are the men assembled?" Michael asked as they left the room and went down the stairs.

"Everything is in order, sir." Hirsch held the front door open.

The entire COMMS detail, minus the three required to stay on duty, stood at attention in the front yard. Two German flags and the *Hakenkreuz* fluttered in the late morning air. Michael strode between the columns of his men for a quick inspection, pointing at a few crooked ribbons, a smudged boot toe, and waving hair. Buttons, medals, and belt buckles glinted in the sun.

As the first black motor pulled into the driveway, flags rippled on its bonnet. He took his place in front of his men with Hirsch at his side. Michael's heart pounded against his ribs as sweat trickled into his palms. He flexed his fingers to allow air between them.

The cars pulled around, stirring up plumes of dust before halting in front of the men. The driver and front passenger of the first car jumped from their seats to open the back doors.

A man stepped out from the back, laughing. "Oh, Ilsa. What a thing to say in the country." Short with a pale face, small eyes behind round spectacles, and a bristling mustache over a weak mouth, Kessel looked more like a bank teller than a military officer.

Michael snapped to attention. "*Heil* Hitler."

Kessel turned his attention to the forces gathered for him. "*Heil* Hitler. You must be Captain Reichner. I've heard much of the excellent work you're doing here."

"An honor to have you here, sir." Michael gestured to Hirsch. "This is Lieutenant Hirsch, our night officer."

"*Heil* Hitler!" Hirsch's chin was too high in the air and sweat dotted his upper lip.

Kessel's dull eyes flickered behind his glasses. "Enthusiasm. *Wunderbar*. Let me introduce you to Captain Ilsa von Ziegler of the SS, who is touring with me."

Stepping out of the car, Captain von Ziegler flashed a dazzling smile as she walked toward Michael. "Good day, gentlemen."

She was like no other woman in uniform Michael had ever seen. Tall and thin with platinum-blonde hair pulled into a bun at the nape of her neck, large blue-green eyes, and a bright red mouth. Her uniform skirt accentuated her curves, and a black belt cinched in the waist. Not standard issue.

Michael bowed. Hirsch followed his lead, although bowing much too low, as if for royalty. Straightening, Michael swept his arm to the house. "Won't you come inside?"

"Is all this for us? How charming." Ilsa held onto the major's arm as her heeled footsteps faltered on the uneven drive. "Not as many workers as the last base we visited."

"Our communications division is small, but we have the best interpreters. Much of the north-to-south communications come through here." Michael stepped into the house behind them. "I apologize, Captain von Ziegler. We didn't realize you were coming or we could have prepared more pleasant accommodations for you."

Plucking the cap from her head, she tossed it onto a nearby table and turned to him with a smile. "It's quite all right, Captain. I hope I don't put you out."

"She can have whichever room you've prepared for me." Kessel handed his cap to one of his trailing aides. "I can take the lieutenant's. A good-sized house, though I wonder how you can fit all the men and equipment in here."

"The men are quartered in the barn and garage. Lieutenant Hirsch and I are in the upstairs bedrooms." Michael led them down the hall to what had once been a formal dining room. "The transmitting station is just through here."

Ilsa pulled a small notepad and pen from her pocket. "Must a man be certified to operate these headsets?"

"All must possess a certain number of qualifications and pass a rigorous transmitting test in the ninety-eighth percentile or higher."

Scribbling on her pad, she then took the notepad from Kruger and perused the numbers and letters. "If we are able to intercept the enemy's codes, can they not do the same with ours? How do we prevent such a calamity?"

"Stealing secrets and tapping wires are a part of war, and even a part of peacetime. By changing our tactics and double-encrypting our messages, we can throw the enemy off and make it nearly impossible to crack our codes."

"Aren't you afraid of the locals listening in?"

"Every home and business was searched for radios or any device that could be used for listening, not that our concern was great. In this remote area, they're mostly farmers and simple-minded villagers, after all." Michael frowned as she jotted things on her paper. "Captain, may I ask what you're writing? Much of our work is classified and anything written down—"

She waved her pen at him. "I have authorization."

Kessel grinned. "Don't mind Ilsa. She keeps notes on everything. The better to root out problems."

Brilliant. Just what Michael needed, a Nazi hound sniffing around.

Ilsa tapped both notepads against her palm. "Have these villagers been questioned? Do any of them give you reason to suspect?"

"So far, we have had no reason to suspect any illicit activity in Montbaune. If that changes, Lieutenant Ostermann will be in charge of questioning." Michael attempted a light tone as he spread his hands to indicate the rest of the room. "I'm afraid COMMS is better suited to headsets and complex codes than hands-on duties."

The light on Kruger's station blinked, indicating an incoming transmission. He reached for his notepad, scattering papers and wires around until he noticed Ilsa holding it. "Captain? My notebook?"

She tossed it on the table and peered over his shoulder to watch as he wrote. "How many transmissions do you receive each day?"

"Every day is different," said Michael. "Some days nothing, some days as many as twenty, though some transmissions are merely gripes about the coffee."

She laughed, a tinkling sound that made Kruger jump. "Max and I discussed that yesterday morning, did we not, Major?

Thankfully, our *Führer* is pushing into more lands and opening more manufacturers. That will help increase the quantity and quality of our supplies. The Soviet Union is said to have marvelous tea with black cherries, and I dare say Kiev will have many of their influences."

Kessel squinted at Michael like a mole coming to the daylight. "Any news on that front?"

Did this man never listen to a briefing? News of the march Northeast was like reading last week's paper. "Our troops hope to take Moscow soon, sir."

"Good, good. And while our troops advance, our stationary forces can eradicate the problems within our own borders. I've seen much promise in dealing with the unwanted."

Michael's gut clenched. "On your tour, sir?"

"Last month, Colonel Fauster requested I look at some of the work camps. Ilsa can tell you more about them, as I preferred to remain in the offices while she took the tour. The smell was unbearable. The worst two days of my life, was it not, Ilsa?"

"The experience was rather enlightening." Ilsa patted the side of her immaculate hair. "Finally, a way to herd the undesirables into one place, so they're no longer tainting society. And the furnaces are enormous. They can burn all day and night, which accounts for the smell, or part of it. A powder or mint-scented hankie helps."

Bile flooded the back of Michael's throat. He recognized the beast prowling in her Aegean eyes, its thrill for blood purring deep in her soul. He clenched his jaw. "I'm afraid you'll find our duties much tamer."

She sighed. "Yes."

The day crew filed to their posts. Michael walked around, introducing each one with a short explanation of their jobs, expert languages, and the important missives they'd translated. They grinned like schoolboys at Ilsa as she made notes.

"And finally, this is Sergeant Dietrich." Michael stopped at the last station. "Our ranking enlisted man and my aide for lack of a lieutenant, besides Hirsch."

Kessel frowned. "An enlisted man serves as your aide?"

"Yes, sir. Sergeant Dietrich is a fine soldier and has proven initiative and leadership capabilities."

"Is that so?" Kessel turned a studious eye to the sergeant. Dietrich's chest puffed out. "Good for you, Sergeant. I like efficiency in all ranks. But, Captain, we'll have to get you a proper aide."

"We could use someone with Italian skills. With our countries joining forces, Italy will become a target for invasion and spies."

Kessel nodded as he picked lint from his sleeve. "Ilsa, would you like to freshen up? I know it's been a long journey."

"I'm perfectly content at the moment, Major." Resting a rounded hip against the side of Kruger's desk, Ilsa turned a catlike smile to Michael. "I noticed a garden as we drove in. Perhaps the good captain could give me a tour, and, maybe later, one of the village?"

Michael forced a nod. Better he give her a guided tour of the late roses than let her morbid fascination draw her out to the back corner to what lay decomposing there. "An honor. We can leave after we finish the tour of the house and get a bite to eat."

Entering the kitchen, Kessel glanced at the sandwiches and fruit Michael's men had scrimped together for the day's lunch. "Captain Reichner, please tell me there's a place in this wretched French countryside where a man can indulge in a good schnapps and whisky."

"Of course, sir. I know just the place." With just the girl Michael would like to see.

From behind the bar, Claire glanced at the clock, then at the scattering of soldiers at the tables. She was always nervous before a performance, but tonight was different. If this major didn't like her playing, she might not get paid. "Maybe he changed his mind."

Giles shrugged. "Eloy saw two cars and a military vehicle heading toward the house earlier today. And then there was the business with Firmin yesterday."

"Pauline wasn't too happy about the Germans getting all the best cuts. Why she considers tongue a best cut I'll never understand."

Giles dried off a tray and slanted a glance in her direction. "And what do you consider the best cut?"

"Steak, ribs, tenderloin. Normal meats."

"Expensive meats. Your generation forgets the traditional ways of eating."

"Oh, but Giles. The world is changing."

Giles frowned as the door opened and the long-awaited party arrived. "It hasn't changed that much."

Reichner, an officer who must have been the major, and a woman, also in uniform, settled at the captain's usual table in the back. Dietrich and two younger soldiers joined the enlisted men near the piano.

Time to get the show on the road.

Picking up a tray of full beer mugs, Claire walked to the captain's table. "*Bonjour*." She set down the beers and offered a tight-lipped smile. "Can I get you anything else?"

"Three schnapps and one whisky, single malt." Reichner handed the beers to his companions. He didn't bother looking at her.

Tiny rocks of disappointment dropped into her stomach as she walked back to the bar. The captain hadn't said anything about a woman being part of the tour. And why should he? She was just another uniformed person in Hitler's killing machine. Probably secretary to the major.

Claire repeated the order to Giles as she eyed the silk stockings and fashionable black pumps on the woman's slender feet. No secretary she'd ever seen looked like that.

Giles placed the drinks on the tray, then nodded. Taking a deep breath, Claire headed back to the table. "Three schnapps and one whisky."

Kessel took a sip of the whisky. Swishing it around his mouth, he nodded. "Amazing to find quality in this place."

"Giles always has the best." Reichner flicked a glance in Claire's direction. "I've told Major Kessel you'll be singing tonight."

"*Oui.*"

The woman turned to look at Claire as only another woman could. Claire felt like a country bumpkin in her patched calico dress and simple braid.

The woman's full red lips curved into a smile as she spoke in heavily accented French. "Entertainment from the rustics. How charming. First the drinks, and now a singing barmaid. However did you find such treasures, Michael?" She placed a silver cigarette holder between her lips.

The captain took a lighter from his pocket and lit the cigarette. "They're hard to hide in a small town, Ilsa."

Their conversation switched to German, so Claire retreated. Settling on the piano seat, she picked a lively French tune, then another, then a slower one. Her treacherous eyes wandered to the table in the back. Ilsa talked loudly and blew delicate smoke curls into the air as she touched the arms of the men on either side of her. Soon Kessel was three schnapps and two whiskies in and laughing louder than the piano could jingle. And Reichner—or Michael, as Ilsa had called him—sipped his beer, laughing and offering a word or two between Ilsa's. Never once did he look to the stage.

All that talk of wanting to discuss books and complimenting her lovely voice had knotted Claire's stomach the entire day, but now the rope frayed. She hated the feeling, hated him ignoring her, and, more than anything, hated caring that he ignored her.

"Hey, *chanteuse.*" Dietrich called out from behind his cards. "Play the *Marlene.* I need something close to German this night."

"Do you wish to end the evening so soon, *monsieur*? That is the song you always prefer to hear last." Claire's fingers drifted over the keys. What song would annoy them the most? "Unless you're trying to escape your bad hand."

Laughter exploded around his table as they nodded in agreement. Dietrich shook his head. "I'm doing quite well this evening actually. In fact, well enough to order another round. Play it for us, sweet like, and then we'll have it again to say *adieu* as usual."

Launching into the crowd's favorite, Claire sang it as close to sweet as she could, not that the men cared. She could sound like a horse. They were too sodded to notice.

Halfway through the second stanza, she looked up to find Ilsa waving her silver cigarette holder in the air. Claire's fingers stumbled to a halt. Was she being flagged down in the middle of a chorus?

"Is that how you sing it?" Ilsa put the holder to her mouth and inhaled, allowing the smoke to curl from the corner of her mouth. "How quaint the French make it sound, but nothing like the robust passion in German."

Stubbing out her cigarette and uncrossing her long legs, Ilsa rose and swayed between the tables to take a place next to the piano. With one manicured hand resting on top of the piano and the other on her hip, she began the first line in German. A mezzo-soprano, she was pitchy but not bad. Claire ground her teeth in annoyance. Why couldn't the woman croak like a frog instead?

At the end of the first verse, Ilsa stopped. Applause exploded around the room. Curtseying, she turned to Claire. "I'm afraid I don't know this in French. Can you keep up?"

Dumbfounded at the woman's audacity, Claire sat motionless.

"On the piano?" Ilsa tapped her nails on the wooden top. "Can you keep up?"

Claire nodded. She'd rather eat worms than accompany the woman, but she didn't have a choice. It was either play nicely or have another take her seat. Insignificant as it was in the scheme of things, her position at the piano was a small victory and her pride wasn't giving it up that easily. Not to a German cow.

Uncertain of what Ilsa wanted, Claire started playing a slow pace. Ilsa glared and bobbed her head for Claire to play faster. Claire obliged as the woman sang through three verses. At long last, the song ended. Determined not to give Ilsa another shot at German, Claire dove into an upbeat tune by Maurice Chevalier. How could she not feel better at the playboy's words?

Ilsa rapped her nails on the piano top. "I don't suppose you know any other German songs? Wagner or Charlie and his Orchestra?"

"I know a few." Dietrich threw his cards on the table and ran to the piano, gesturing for Claire to move. "Sorry, *chanteuse*, but you're lacking in this repertoire."

Biting her tongue, Claire stood. It wasn't just the usurping of her chair. It was something much bigger, something beyond her musical skills. Something that reflected the very soul of this cursed invasion. Tears pricked her eyes. From the corner of her eye, she saw Reichner. His head tilted toward her while all other eyes remained on Ilsa. A lump formed in her throat. She needed to get out, away from that place. Away from the pity in his eyes.

Rounding the corner of the bar, Giles grabbed her elbow before she could make the safety of the curtain. "Don't let them see you cry. They cannot win."

Claire sniffed and nodded.

"Go collect yourself, then come back ready to serve," he whispered. "A few more minutes of this goat and they'll be begging for you."

Knowing he wouldn't appreciate her throwing her arms around his neck, she gave him a wobbly smile instead. "Thanks, Giles."

"Go. Ten minutes."

CHAPTER 10

Want to get me a new aide who speaks English or Italian. Michael tapped out on the transceiver key. *Lieutenant.*

Several seconds passed before the response clicked into his headset. *We'll see what we can do. Updates on American?*

NSTR. Nothing significant to report. Unless one counted how much Michael thought of her despite every bone in his body screaming not to. Despite the training drilled into him not to get involved with people on the job. And despite the immense danger it could put her in. *Will investigate further while keeping eye on visiting Nazi SS captain. She's looking for something.*

Copy. Keep tab on Op Typhoon. And keep ear open for Pacific grumblings. Japan on the offense for holdings.

Roger. Not surprising as Japan had been on the warpath with China for four years. It was a logical conclusion they'd want to dominate the waters too.

Doing good job, IS. Over and out.

Out.

The compliment caught him off guard. This job wasn't a one-man show. He relied on the next guy as much as they relied on him. The possibility of his small part helping in any way kept him going day after day.

The clock next to his bed chimed half past four in the morning. A single candle lit the master chamber while the world outside slumbered in the black dawn. Wrapping the headset cords, he placed it and the transceiver back in its case under the bed before sliding the floorboards over top of it.

His stomach growled—a reminder that he hadn't eaten since

yesterday afternoon. More than anything he wanted to go back to bed and catch up on the months of sleep he'd missed, but his brain couldn't rest with images of Claire floating around. She hadn't spoken to him since before his guests had arrived.

A groan escaped his lips before he could stop it. His guests had overstayed their welcome by a week and were turning into more than a nuisance. Kessel blamed their extended stay on the changing tour plans of his commander, but Michael was sure Ilsa had something to do with it. The woman interrupted his men's work, begged to listen in on the headsets and to be driven into town every day with at least two escorts. Hirsch had come to him to ask how to handle her when she started pestering the night crew.

Then there was that notebook. She wrote down everything and kept it on her at all times. He needed to find a way to read what was in it. If she was looking for dirt, he needed to throw her off before she sniffed too close to his true identity.

He rubbed a hand over his aching eyes, wishing the day was already over so he could listen to Claire sing without interruption from Ilsa's caterwauling. Each moment in Claire's presence he expected the flash of recognition in her eyes, but the shock from the train explosion must have wiped him from her memory. Or he wasn't that memorable. He frowned, unable to decide which reason he preferred.

Pulling the pillows away from the base of the door, he tossed them on the bed and ventured into the hallway. He slipped downstairs and paused in the doorway of the control room. The nightshift sat hunched over their desks, pens scratching away as the messages came in. Hirsch patrolled behind them, stopping to read what they wrote and making a few quick notes in his notebook. A deep line marred his forehead.

Michael stepped into the lieutenant's view. "What's the report?"

Hirsch jotted a few more words, then looked up. "The British have started bombing Berlin. They have been going at it for the last few hours."

"Why didn't you alert me?"

Hirsch's young face paled. "I apologize, sir. I should have, but I wanted to let you rest unless it was necessary to disturb you. Things are quieting now." He handed his notebook to Michael.

Michael scanned the stats. Nothing unusual, and not the first time the lads had gotten the drop on the Germans. *Please, please, don't let us have lost any planes.*

"Do you have updates on damage?" Michael asked.

"No, sir. I expect to start hearing those soon."

With excitement and trepidation warring inside, Michael grabbed a pair of headphones and dialed into the Berlin frequency. Shouting hit his ears, panicked and angry voices overlapped with explosions. He wanted to hear every last bomb destroy its target. *Get 'em, boys, and then get back home.*

An hour later, the day crew arrived, ready for their morning brief and changeover. Except Dietrich. After the brief and a small talk with his men, Michael pulled Lehmann aside. "Where is Sergeant Dietrich?"

"I don't know, sir. I haven't seen him this morning."

"Go back to the bunks and see if he decided to take an extra hour of sleep. If he's not there, try the gardens, the kitchen, wherever he takes a smoke break. I want him in my office in ten minutes."

Michael tamped down his frustration. His second-in-command was never tardy. And with the major there. The last thing Michael wanted was to give disciplinary action in front of the brass.

He pushed open his office door and stopped. Ilsa stood to the side of the propped-open bookcase with her back to him.

Panic squeezed his chest. "Captain von Ziegler." He stepped into the room and shut the door, noticing a second person in the room. "Sergeant Dietrich."

"Ah, Captain. Maybe you can help us solve a mystery." Ilsa smiled, lipstick glistening like blood on a wolf's lips. "Having given us the liberty of your office while we're here, I decided to have a look around, as men can keep such interesting workspaces. The sergeant informed me there was something behind the bookcase, but I've yet to figure out what it is."

"It's a hiding spot." Michael leveled his most intimidating stare at her. "At least that's what I assumed it was when I found it."

"You knew this was here?"

"As you said, one takes an interest in new spaces he acquires. I found silver candlesticks, religious pieces, coins, and a family photo. For a time, I kept the lockbox there, but it became too much trouble to move the bookcase back and forth just for petty cash." Anger burned in his chest at the intrusion of privacy. He leveled it at Dietrich. "Your shift has started, Sergeant. I suggest you ask one of your comrades for a briefing and get to work. Berlin has been bombed."

"Berlin has been bombed?" Ilsa screeched. "Why did no one tell me?"

"It has been over for some time. Cleanup is in effect."

Red splotched Dietrich's neck as he backed to the door. "Of course, sir."

"And Dietrich." Michael waited several seconds as the sergeant's hand strangled the doorknob. "Report to my office as soon as your shift is over. I expect by then you'll have a good reason for missing roll call this morning."

"Yes, sir." Dietrich slinked out and closed the door behind him.

Ilsa touched a shaky hand to the shining blond poof of her hair and sank to the armrest of the nearest chair. "Did we have warning?"

"I don't believe so," Michael said. "We should have a damage report soon."

"Those poor brave men. And the women and children. Our great capital, how could it happen?"

It happened just as it had to Paris and Kiev and London. Because German egos would stop at nothing until they destroyed everything in their path. The price of war.

Michael steadied himself, maintaining a tight rein on his tone.

"England's air forces are weak. Their attacks are nothing but pebbles thrown against a metal fortress."

Ilsa nodded. Color returned to her pale cheeks as she took out a silver cigarette case and chose a stick. The faint whiff of tobacco soon filled the air. "You should watch your man. He has an eye for promotion. He made a comment to Max last night. I must say the major does not like subordinates jumping the chain of command. If we don't keep the order, we have nothing." She took a long drag, allowing the smoke to curl from her nose and frame her catlike eyes. "Anyway, I decided to see what all the fuss was about for myself. Let Max have a few extra winks of sleep."

How dare this woman reprimand him about subordinates knowing their place? Michael outranked her by ten months—an eternity in military time—and she'd marched into his command and snooped about behind his back with one of his sergeants. Talk about jumping the chain. Seemed Dietrich had found a willing ear to rat to.

Michael stifled his frustration. "You're right." He walked across the office and shoved the bookcase back to the wall. "Without order we have nothing. I will personally assure the major that it won't happen again."

"I understand, *Monsieur* Firmin," Claire said for the third time as she tried to shuffle out of the butcher's back door. "The major's touring party is causing quite the havoc all around town. Let's hope they leave soon, and we can get back to our usual business."

"If they did not come in here every day demanding fresh meat, I might be able to provide for my own customers." Firmin spat. "The stock was taken to the front lines long ago. How do they expect that I will have a cow or pig for them? And now they're taking the organs, feet, tongue, brains. Everything."

"We appreciate the hocks and knuckles you've been able to hide for us. They go a long way in making broth."

"I wish I could provide more."

She patted his thick shoulder, wanting to assure him. "We'll manage, all of us, even if the Nazis are trying to starve us out. Here." She broke off part of her bread loaf and handed it to him. "For the widow Lamarc. It'll go nicely with the tail soup."

"I will make sure it's in her basket."

"*Merci.*" Claire took another step back. "Until next week."

"You should not walk out alone. The Germans now patrol the village like locusts. Savon."

Claire's heart dropped into her stomach. "No, really. That isn't necessary. You're busy, and the bar isn't far."

"A lot can happen in so short a walk. Savon!"

Savon came into the back room. He wiped his hands on his apron and pushed the shaggy hair from his eyes.

"Walk Claire home," his father said. "I'll watch the front until you return. Go."

Claire could do nothing but offer the young man a smile. Savon's face turned pink as he shrugged out of his apron.

Once outside, gray clouds skittered across the sky as Savon walked beside Claire down the back lane. She pulled her thin sweater closer to ward off the cool September air.

"I have wanted to come to Buckets." Savon shouted as if she stood in the next town over and not next to him. Wincing, he cleared his throat and tried again. "I've wanted to come, but there's always work to do."

"The shop closes at five. Why not come after that?"

Darkness passed over his face. "The *other* patrons come then."

"The other—oh, you mean the Germans." Claire sighed and looked at the toes of her dirt-covered shoes. Michael's face flashed in her mind. "Yes, I suppose they do."

"They go to see you."

She attempted a laugh, but it sounded hollow. "I think beer is more of an enticement."

"Maybe at first, but now you're all they talk about when they come into the shop. The 'Songbird of Montbaune.' Lousy Germans. They don't deserve to hear you sing." His massive fists curled into tight white balls.

She tried to keep her tone light. "*Songbird* is hardly the word I'd use. They've just been deprived of real music for too long. War can do funny things like that. Why just the other day I suggested to Pauline we boil pinecones to add variety to the cabbage stew and—"

He grabbed her arm, pinching her skin. "Stop entertaining them."

"Ow! Savon, you're hurting me."

"Keep doing this, and they'll think you're no better than some brothel girl."

"How dare you!"

Three German soldiers ambled around the corner. Panic hit Claire.

"Ah, the *chanteuse*. What a rare thing to meet you in daylight," said the tallest of the soldiers. "And you're are not alone. Why did you not tell us you had a fella?"

Claire unlatched Savon's fingers from her arm. Red fingerprints marred her skin. "I don't. This is Savon Firmin." She recognized the soldiers from the post guard detail. They didn't come in as often as the other men but, when they did, they always left drunk. Beside her, Savon ground his teeth.

"From the look on his face, I think we've interrupted a lover's confrontation." The tall soldier took a long drag of his cigarette and smiled at Savon. "Can't blame you. The whole unit is taken in by her charms."

"Her charms are for the stage only." Savon grabbed Claire's arm and yanked her around. "Come on, Claire."

The soldier stepped in front of them and fingered the strap of the Mauser slung over his shoulder. "Now just a minute. We haven't finished our talk. You go back to chopping brains, and we'll see the lady home."

Savon moved in front of Claire, twisting her arm. "Leave us alone. You think just because you have weapons you can terrorize our country and do what you like. You need a lesson." Tugging Claire along, he brushed past one of the soldiers, knocking his rifle.

"Are you trying to disarm me?" The soldier shoved Savon.

Releasing Claire, Savon swung his fist at the soldier's face. The soldier shifted at the last second and Savon's fist grazed his cheek. The other soldiers grabbed Savon's arms, pinning them to his side.

"Very foolish of you, frog." The soldier sneered, wiping at the spot Savon had touched. Balling his fist, he punched Savon in the jaw. "For that little stunt, you get to watch."

Fear stabbed Claire's heart as the tall soldier turned to her. His eyes burned with fury, his thin lips trembling. He lunged. Claire screamed as his fingers clamped onto her shoulders. He pushed her against the wall. His sour breath scorched her neck as he leaned into her.

"Get off of me!" She jerked her knee upward, but his thighs kept her from moving.

"*Was ist denn hier los? Sie sofort loslassen.*"

The soldier snapped to attention, releasing Claire as he spouted something in German.

The booming reply could have sent the thunderclouds into hiding. Claire knew that voice. Clutching her sweater at her neck, she dared to peek up. Captain Reichner stood behind the guards who held Savon. Hands on his hips and blue eyes blazing, the captain barked an order. The three soldiers snapped to attention in front of him. At that moment she was glad she didn't understand German.

Reichner snarled an order, and the soldiers scurried from the alley without a backward glance. He turned to Savon. "What happened here?"

Savon's eyes narrowed.

The muscles spasmed in the captain's neck. "What happened,

Monsieur Firmin?"

"We're just French peasants. Dirt beneath your shiny black boots. Why do you care?"

Reichner took a deep breath. "Because I like to know the facts or as close to them as both sides will admit. There in the muddle, I may discover the truth."

"I was walking Claire home, and they came upon us. They assaulted her."

"And you tried to defend her?" Reichner turned his steady gaze to Claire. "Is that how it happened?"

She nodded. "Yes. Savon was trying to protect me."

Reichner kept his eyes on her for what seemed like several long minutes. The lines around his mouth eased. Claire's heart hammered against her ribs as she stared back, waiting for him to speak. "Thank you for your assistance, *Monsieur* Firmin, but I will take it from here. Please return to your shop. I shall see that the lady gets home."

Savon's chin jutted forward. "*I* will see that she is taken home. You should return to your men and instruct them on manners. We may be under your thumb, but this is still our country."

"Savon!" Claire ran to put herself between him and the captain. "You mustn't say such things."

"I should keep my mouth shut at all times, according to my father. I'm tired of keeping quiet. Tired of being shoved around." Savon glared at the captain. "He knows what we're all thinking."

Cold fingers of dread wrapped around Claire's insides. Normally so quiet, the boy couldn't seem to keep his mouth shut when their lives depended on it. "Please, Savon. No more." She turned to Reichner, ready to plead on her knees. Savon had a nasty streak, but she didn't want to see him beaten to a pulp because of it. "*Capitaine*, his tongue slips in anger."

Reichner flicked his gaze over the top of her head. "Even so, he should be mindful of who he's speaking to. Go home at once, boy."

"He's right, Savon." Claire turned and took his arm with a light squeeze. "Please go home. We don't need any more trouble."

"I want to walk you home."

"No."

Savon's teeth ground together as he shot the captain a look that could curdle milk. Spinning on his heel, he stomped off.

"Your boyfriend has quite a temper."

Claire snatched her basket. "He's not my boyfriend."

"I've never seen a man get that contentious over a woman he didn't care for."

"Doesn't he have a right to be put off? Or is that outlawed too?"

Reichner's eyebrows shot up. "You're angry with me."

Tucking the basket under her arm, she hurried away from him. He followed her.

"Do I not get a reason why? I think I deserve that after—"

"After what?" She spun around to face him and nearly slammed into his chest. She took a step back. "After saving us from your men? How heroic you are to call them off and send Savon scurrying away like a child."

Crossing his arms over his chest, his mouth tilted at one side. "You're not afraid of me, are you?"

"I'm more terrified of you than you could possibly know." For more reasons than she could say. Treacherous heart of hers.

"Because of this?" He plucked at the front of his uniform.

"You're just a man, but that uniform makes you something more."

"And what if I were to cast if off? Don a pair of patched trousers and a slouch hat covered in dirt from years of farming. What then?"

"It wouldn't change who you are. A falcon may lose its feathers, but that doesn't mean I'd start calling it a wren. You are what you are, and I am what I am."

She gripped the handle of her basket until the pieces of wicker dug into her palm. How did he unnerve her so much? And why did she care? Every time he came around he cracked a chink into her abhorrence of his very existence. Humanity hid beyond the gleaming buttons and shining metals on his chest, but she didn't want to see him that way. She needed to remember he was nothing more than a hated uniform with boots. Anything beyond that and she'd be guilty of emotional treason.

"I am just a man." He took half a step forward. His eyelids lowered to hood the blue rings of his eyes. "And you are just a woman."

"A conquered citizen of France."

"Are you sure of that?"

Blood drained from her head, leaving her cheeks cold and her mind numb around. "Is there something else you'd like to ask me, *Capitaine*?"

"As a matter of fact, there is." He paused. A lifetime's worth of heartbeats pounded in Claire's chest. Here it came. He knew who she was. "I was wondering if you've started that book I loaned you."

If she looked in a mirror right now, she swore her hair would be white. She expelled an unsteady breath. Her secret was safe for now. To keep it that way, she needed to get away from him, and fast. Turning, she started down the lane again in hopes he would get the clue. "No, I haven't. Your visiting officials have left little time for reading anything other than music."

Ignoring the hint, he followed. "Does the Three Buckets have many scores to choose from?"

"Only the basic selections that came with the piano. I found them stuffed under the bottom feet not long after I started playing."

"What about playing from ear? From records?"

"Pauline has one record, and it's from at least fifteen years ago."

Turning into the alley, she crossed the street with Reichner at her side. From the corner of her eye, she saw three German soldiers lounging outside the mercantile. Spotting her, they grinned and ribbed one another until their gazes shifted to Reichner. Blanching, they spun away as if not seeing her. The captain's presence was many things, but she never expected to feel an appreciation for it. With him nearby, less chivalrous soldiers were guaranteed to keep their distance.

Chivalrous? Oh no. When had she started thinking that about Reichner? Heat flooded her face despite the crisp air. She hurried for the safety of the bar.

"I can help find new arrangements for you. Perhaps records from this decade," Reichner said as they came to the back of the building.

"That's kind, but no, thank you."

"You mean you don't want to feel indebted to me. You'd rather keep me and the annoyances I bring at arm's length."

"I think it's best."

Two steps from the building, he put an arm out to stop her, his fingers inches away from her shoulder. Her eyes locked onto the button nearest his collar as her heart jumped to double time. He smelled of soap and starched wool.

"Are you always this stubborn, or only with me?" he asked.

Her gaze moved to his. Calmness reigned in the steady blue depths of his eyes. They called to her, and as the world whirled around them, she wished she could answer. Her throat grew thick. "I—"

The bar door flew open and banged against the wall. Giles glared out from the shadows. "*Capitaine*, a surprise to see you."

Reichner's arm dropped to his side. He clicked his heels. "*Bonjour*, Giles. I offered to escort Claire home as the weather is taking a dubious turn this afternoon."

Giles stepped forward. His dark brow creased into lines more ominous than the darkening clouds. "She's home now. Is there something else *I* can help you with?"

"No." Michael tugged the bottom of his jacket. "Though I would like to apologize for any inconvenience Major Kessel's extended tour may be causing you. Should the tab begin to run over your stock, please notify me at once, and I shall forward a new advancement."

"I'm well stocked for the time. Claire, Pauline is waiting for that basket." Giles moved to the side and jerked his thumb over his shoulder while keeping his stare on Michael.

Claire hurried inside as shame engulfed her. She couldn't even pull herself away from that man. How many times did she need to remind herself that he was the enemy? Pauline waited in the hallway, hands balled on her hips. The back door slammed shut.

Seething, Giles rounded on her. "What are you thinking? He's a Nazi!"

"I told him no, but he followed anyway."

"Why was he following in the first place?"

She resisted the urge to stamp her foot. She wasn't in the wrong. "It was a chance meeting while Savon walked me back from the butcher's. Three soldiers saw us and tried to start a little trouble. Savon defended me, but they persisted until Captain Reichner came around the corner."

"And where is Savon now?"

"The captain sent him home to prevent further trouble. Savon doesn't know when to keep his mouth shut."

Giles' lips clamped into a white line. He paced the hall with quick jerky turns. "Did they hurt you?"

"No." She hated lying, but Giles would never let her leave the bar again if he knew the truth.

He grunted. "Stay away from that German." Without a backward glance, he stomped into the bar.

"But, I wasn't ..." Claire stared at the curtain still swishing in his wake. "He followed me." She turned to Pauline, who stood in the kitchen doorway, tight-lipped and unmoving. "He's blaming me as if I brought that captain here on purpose. The captain does not understand the meaning of the words 'leave me alone.'"

"He's a Nazi, what do you expect?" Pauline trudged back into the kitchen.

Claire followed and placed her basket on a clear space on the counter. She pulled out the bread and dropped it into the bread tin. "I've never seen Giles so angry before. He's usually so, so … even-keeled around them."

"When they're paying customers, he is." Pauline huffed as she plunged her hands into the sudsy wash basin. "But some things never change."

"What do you mean?"

Pauline shrugged. "His demons are coming back to haunt him. I knew they'd never left, even after all of these years. How could they after that war?"

"You mean the Great War?"

"He was one of the lucky ones to come home, or so I told him. He thought otherwise. Never the same again."

Claire had seen the effects of war firsthand. Her grandfather had sailed on the battleship fleets to England over twenty years ago. More than once she'd caught him staring off into the distance, a hard expression on his face, looking like a stranger she'd never seen before. He'd shout and curse, crumbling to his knees until her grandmother shook him by the shoulders and the darkness passed.

"Giles doesn't blame you," Pauline said, dunking the washed glasses into the rinsing basin. "Just doesn't want a repeat. I guess you could say he sees you as his penitence."

Claire walked to the rinse basin to clear the soap bubbles from the mugs, then set them on a towel to dry. "What sort of penitence?"

Pauline shook her head.

Claire touched the older woman's shoulder. "Please tell me. Maybe it'll help me understand. I want to help, anything I can do to make myself less of a nuisance."

"You're not a nuisance." Pauline's hands rested in the steaming water. "Her name was Amaline. She was plain, but she was kind and always laughed at Giles' jokes. The war came, and he was eager to enlist. Foolish boy. They became engaged, and he left the following day."

Pauline sighed. "The Germans came, much as they do now.

Men and boys marched through the town looking for food and warm fires. And willing companions. I was too ugly for them, but Amaline with her soft smile …" Pauline gripped the side of the tub until her chewed fingernails turned white. "They thought to make an example of her, but she was so frail. She bled to death in her father's barn."

"Oh, Pauline. How terrible." Claire blinked back the tears pooling in the corners of her eyes. "Poor Amaline. Poor Giles."

Pauline sniffed and dipped her hands back in the water. "He blamed himself for not being there to stop it, to protect her. He sees a repeat of the past with you. Thank the good Lord he's let go of the bottle. For years after he tried to drink himself to death. Hand me that other tray over there."

Claire's heart ached for Giles and his lost love. Torn apart forever by the callousness of the enemy. Michael's face flashed before her. At times he seemed so sincere, almost kind. Could he commit such horrors? "I can't imagine—"

"No, and keep your mouth shut about it. No use resurrecting the dead. Go and wipe the chairs in the bar and then get the old curtains and my sewing kit out of the trunk at the foot of my bed. You'll need a few more sweaters before the cold sets in."

CHAPTER 11

"Don't you have a nice chianti back there somewhere?" Eloy pushed his half-empty glass back and forth in front of him on the bar. "My taste buds grow weary of Merlot."

"Try a beer," Giles said.

Eloy made a face. "Let the Germans drink their beers. I have higher expectations as a Frenchman."

"The major and his entourage took most of the good wines and beer." Claire poured him a shot of whisky to soothe his complaints. He could get downright cranky when his routine took a detour. "It might be a few weeks before we can get a new shipment in."

Eloy took the shot and tipped it back in one gulp. Plunking the glass on the counter, he glared at Giles. "Is this how you plan to operate your bar?"

Giles shrugged as he continued polishing a glass. "In wartime, I guess so. If you ever feel the need to march into Germany, you could always bring back a few casks or barrels."

Claire poured Eloy another whisky, which he shot back. "If I ever march into Germany, it'll be to kill that infuriating *Führer*. Can't even get a good wine thanks to him. Ansell will agree with me." He turned on his bar stool to eye his friend sitting at a table with two other men. "Ansell, would you not march into enemy territory for a good drink?"

Ansell flicked his hand in the air without turning from his companions.

Eloy frowned and turned back around. "Don't understand that." Leaning on his elbows, he motioned Claire forward, then whispered. "What's going on over there? Ansell always sits with me, but the past two weeks he's taken to sitting over there with them. Seen them in here much before?"

Claire shook her head. "They don't say much to anyone except Ansell. Maybe they're neighbors."

They'd entered the bar for the first time two weeks ago and taken a table in the back, away from the other patrons. They always ordered beers but rarely touched them and waved her away any time she approached. Their faces remained serious as they talked, never for longer than thirty minutes. Then, with a final sip from their beers, the two strangers would leave, and Ansell would take his place at the bar next to the locals. Despite constant cajoling, he never discussed them beyond calling them "old friends."

"Neighboring farmers, bah." Eloy snorted. "I've lived here my whole life and never seen them before. All I know is Ansell better keep his nose clean. People start doing things out of the ordinary, and those Germans get suspicious."

"Enough of that." Giles growled.

"You know it's true. Nothing's changed since the first time."

The rosacea spots on Giles' cheeks darkened. "Leave it alone, I say."

Claire lost interest in wiping the counter. "What do you mean by that?"

"As long as there are enemies, there will be those willing to fight against them."

"Soldiers, you mean."

Eloy shrugged. "Soldiers and ordinary people like you and me doing whatever it takes to send those Germans packing."

"That's enough," Giles hissed. "Do not get her involved in this."

"She's a right to know what's going on. Not like it's a secret what the Resistance is doing."

"The Resistance? Here in Montbaune?" Excitement shivered down Claire's spine. If there was one close by, they could help her get out of France. And then home. Maybe they could find information on her aunt and uncle. "They're adept at smuggling people out, yes? What about finding people?"

Eloy scratched his whiskered chin. "Maybe. It's a big system, sometimes organized and sometimes off the cuff. Always worth an ask. You got someone you want to find? Someone gone underground?"

"Don't we all have a loved one to find out there?" Claire bit her lip. As dear as the people of Montbaune had become to her, she couldn't risk her secrets getting out. The Germans could arrest her if they discovered the truth about her family's disappearance. It wouldn't take them too long after to identify her as American. She glanced at the secretive table where Ansell and the two strangers leaned their heads close together. "Do you think Ansell is a part of it?"

"Not saying yes and not saying no." Eloy peeked over his shoulder and frowned. "I've known that man all my life. Something's different."

"Why don't you ask him?"

"I've gotten chased off the few times I've tried. You'd think he'd tell me."

"Maybe he doesn't want to involve anyone for safety reasons."

"Exactly." Giles banged a glass on the counter. "We should not be discussing this. And you"—he turned to Claire with a scowl—"should not get so excited about the Resistance. They do dangerous work."

"Yes, but I thought maybe—"

"Maybe what?"

She squeezed the towel in her fist. Giles didn't have the right to treat her like a child, even if he was protecting her. She needed to talk to him without curious ears clinging to every word. "I'm excited to hear about freedom fighters," she said. "Gives us something to hope for."

"*Bonjour!*"

All heads swiveled as Ilsa von Ziegler stepped through the entrance, one hand propped on her hip and a generous smile on her lips. "*Bonjour.*"

Giles' scowl morphed into a bland expression. "*Bonjour, Capitaine.*"

Ilsa walked into the room, her pumps clicking against the floorboards. She stopped next to Eloy. "Might I have a seat next to you?"

Eloy nodded, tucking his elbows in close to his side.

Hopping onto the seat, she dropped her hat on the bar and scanned the bottles behind Giles. "Is it too soon for a gin and tonic?"

"Not if that is what you wish." Giles turned to gather the bottles.

"It is. I tire of beer. Women sometimes need something more delicate to sip. Cigarette?" She opened her cigarette holder and offered it to Eloy. He shook his head without looking at her. Ilsa's gaze drifted to Claire. "I don't suppose you would like one. You look much too young to be working in a place serving spirits."

Claire clenched the towel again. "I'm merely the entertainment, *Capitaine.*"

Smoke curled from Ilsa's lips. "So I've seen. Oh, thank you, this looks wonderful." She took a sip of her drink. "Delicious. I hope you don't mind me popping in like this. I know my crowd comes in later, but sometimes I get so bored with those men."

Claire blinked several times to keep her eyes from rolling. Ilsa bored? Then why hadn't she left with the rest of her party over two weeks ago? She came in every night with a new set of comrades as the others had switched to nightshifts. That kept Captain Reichner away from the bar and Claire's imagination preoccupied wondering what he was doing and when he'd come back.

Ilsa ran her finger around the rim of her glass. "I don't even know your name, my dear. I hear the men refer to you as *chanteuse*, which I take to mean nightclub singer. My French is not too bad except with the colloquial phrases. I get them so confused." She laughed and tapped the ashes from her cigarette.

"Claire."

"Ah, Claire. How pretty. I understand you're not from around here. The war has left you on the Desbauxes' generous doorstep."

The hair on Claire's arm prickled. "Giles is an old acquaintance of my father, and he's been gracious to provide me room and board."

"Ah. I assume your studies at the *conservatoire* have been put on hold because of the war?"

Claire's arm prickles turned into goosebumps. "You are well informed, *Capitaine*."

Ilsa's laughter spilled across the room like a thousand nails. "No, no. I just like listening to the gossip. Sometimes it's true and sometimes it isn't, but either way, it makes things more fun. Would you not agree?"

"I suppose it depends on what's being said."

"That is true. For instance, Giles"—Ilsa cocked her head in the bartender's direction—"I hear you have a way of obtaining the smoothest whisky and finest wine in the region."

Giles didn't bat an eye. "I pay my supplier well, and with the money from Captain Reichner, I've been able to afford some of the best stock for his guests."

"Yes, Michael—I mean Captain Reichner—is quite generous with his hospitality. He is also very gifted with languages. Can pick one out like that." She snapped her fingers. "Though with his unique abilities I can't imagine they'll want to keep him in the country long when Berlin could use his talent."

Claire did her best to tamp the ping of disappointment. Berlin. Headquarters and heart of the Nazis. Whether he stayed or went shouldn't matter to her. Or so she kept trying to tell herself.

"Is this the usual crowd?" Ilsa spun in her seat to look at Ansell's table, which had grown quiet since she'd entered. They sipped their beers and stared at the walls. "I thought there might be more people here."

"Sometimes there are and sometimes not." Giles left off the fact that many of the regulars had stopped coming by with the sudden increase of Nazis in town.

Ilsa swiveled back to face the bar. "You know everyone in town, don't you? I'm sure passers-through stand out like warts in so small a village." She pulled a notebook from her pocket and jotted a few lines.

Giles nodded as he wiped off the beer taps. "Anyone with a coin who doesn't cause trouble is welcome here."

"A businessman first and humanitarian second. I like that."

Ilsa liked it well enough to stick around another excruciating hour. Putting her two drinks on Captain Reichner's tab, she left with a promise to return in time for Claire's second show.

Ansell hopped onto the now unoccupied stool. "She asks a lot of questions. Wonder what she was writing."

"I thought she'd turn on me at any second. Like a lion on a zebra." Eloy shivered.

Claire took the empty glass from his shaking hands. "She didn't even talk to you."

"Sure was interested in you though. Probably jealous. You're much prettier. Don't need all that face paint she cakes on."

Ansell tipped back the remaining drops of his beer and belched. "Sings like a goat too."

Crisp autumn air breezed through the gaps in Claire's sweater, nipping at her skin despite her layered clothes. She scolded herself for not taking time to pull on stockings and Giles' castoff jacket, but after being in the same room with Captain Ilsa von Ziegler of the SS for over an hour, Claire had burst through the door as soon as she could. A few numb toes and fingers were well worth the price of ten minutes of peace and quiet.

Dead leaves crunched under her feet. The cold air and smell of dry bark heralded the changing season. "Why couldn't I have gone to school in Hawaii?" She shoved her hands deeper into her pockets. "A prisoner of the tropics, doomed to live among the palm trees and ocean breezes."

Nope. Instead, she was in cold France, serving beer, singing in a bar, being interrogated by a woman with the eyes of a viper, and forgoing all common sense with thoughts of a handsome enemy captain. Mom and Dad would be so proud.

Claire kicked a rock into the nearby bushes. Blackbirds screeched and took flight. "Sorry. Didn't mean to make you miserable as well."

"I thought I was the only one who made others miserable." Her enemy captain stepped from behind a tree.

Heat blazed across the back of her neck. Without realizing it, her feet had carried her to her reading spot by the stream. "I, uh … no, you're a little late today and lost the chance to someone else." She reached to tuck a wayward hair back into the braid curving over her shoulder.

"I doubt they had my irritating charm."

"Oh, I wouldn't say that." She looked at the dirt, over to a pile of dead leaves, the scattered stones by the brook, the broken twigs under the tree. Anywhere but at him.

"Will you tell me what drives you to assault innocent birds?"

"It's none of your concern."

"I apologize if I've offended you, Claire," he said. "I didn't mean to pry."

Applesauce and crackers. There he went again being kind. How was she supposed to hate him when he did that? She dared to look at him. "Why do you always do that?"

His brow furrowed. "Do what?"

"Act like you care? Show up right when I'm thinking of you— er … your presence makes it difficult for me to live as normal of a life as this war allows."

He stood tall, hands clasped behind him with the wind chafing the long hem of his overcoat. The corners of his mouth tilted down as he sighed. "Despite what you might think, or believe, I'd like to carve out a slice of normalcy too. I feel this war as acutely as you." He stepped forward, closing the gap between them until the edges of his coat swayed against her. "I can tell you're holding back something."

"I thought mass domination was what your country wanted, to start the reign of the thousand-year Reich. Not settle down to hearth and pipe."

"That is the goal of the Nazi party, among other things." Darkness passed behind his eyes as quick as lightning and then it was gone. "Many citizens, including myself, desire a peaceful life."

"But you're a soldier. You knew putting on that uniform was saying goodbye to a peaceful life."

"That does not mean I don't long for it."

Claire plucked the patched collar of her dress. "Not according to your comrade, Captain von Ziegler."

"Ilsa? When did you talk to—oh. Now I see why you are kicking rocks. Has she been at the Three Buckets all this time?"

"This past hour she enjoyed a drink or two with some of the village men."

"Was she talkative or asking questions?"

"Both."

"To you?"

"To me and the others."

"Was she interested in any one thing?"

"*Capitaine*," Claire said in the same exasperated tone she'd heard her mother use a thousand times, "if there's something you wish to know, perhaps you should ask outright. I find that speeds the process along."

"Very well." His eyes narrowed. "Did she seem like she was on the hunt for someone?"

"On the hunt? As in searching for a criminal?" Claire shook her head, trying to understand what he was driving at. "I don't think so. She was just interested in all of us."

Turning on his heel, he marched to the tree where she'd tripped over him. His back ramrod-straight, he stared over the bubbling water. "I come here every day," he said without turning around. "It's beautiful and quiet."

She nodded, unable to speak lest her teeth start chattering.

"Working nights keeps me away from Buckets, but at least I have a little time to enjoy this place before my shift starts. You haven't been here in a while. Since that day you fell on me."

"I did n—it was an accident."

He turned to look over his shoulder at her. A smile played on his lips. "So you keep saying."

Unruly butterflies swooped in her stomach. He came here every day and noticed she didn't, just as she noted his absence from the bar. Each figure that darkened the doorway sent her heart racing, then twinging with disappointment when it wasn't him. Later, as she drifted off to sleep, he was there on the curling edges of her dreams. Smiling at her.

He turned to her with eyebrows drawn together. "I assumed you were avoiding me after our last meeting."

"More like locked up." Horror crossed his face and her laugh fell flat. "Sorry. My attempt at a joke."

"From the way Giles glared at me, I see little to joke about. Was that man ever a boxer?"

"I don't think so, but he does lift a lot of heavy crates." A twig snapped in the bushes a few feet away. Claire jumped. A rabbit shot out of the undergrowth and bounced across the dirt into a new hiding spot behind a clump of oak saplings.

As it disappeared, Claire turned and snagged her sweater on a dried bush. "Perfect. More holes for the cold to sneak in through." Picking at the threads caught on the branch, her knuckles rubbed against the sharp nubs left by the fallen leaves. "Ouch."

Michael rushed to her side. "Allow me." Without flinching, he plucked her sweater free of its pointy captors. "Always getting stuck, aren't you?"

Claire circled her little finger around the hole and looked at him, confused. "Pardon?"

His smile fell. Bracing his hands behind his back, he looked away. "Nothing."

Scraping her fingernail around the edges in an effort to close the hole, Claire sighed and resigned herself to another late night of mending. "Giles is a good man," she said.

"I know he is. He only wishes to protect you."

The immediacy of his agreement caught her off guard. Michael saw the good and evil in men and was able to judge their true character without prejudice. Just one more tangle of confusion for her to unravel about this mysterious man. For him to be pure evil would be so much easier. At least then she wouldn't lay awake at night wondering why she couldn't sever the cord that pulled her to him. Her lungs squeezed tight.

"Claire, are you all right?" His forehead creased. "You're pale as a ghost."

"Just a little cold, I guess." She tugged the edges of her collar closer together.

His fingers flew to the buttons on his coat and slipped the first two from their hole. He paused for a split second before buttoning them back up. "I should not keep you out in weather like this. Please allow me to escort you home."

"You're not afraid of wine barrels being thrown at your head?"

The brilliant blue of his eyes warmed to sapphire as he smiled at her. "Not today."

Michael pressed his ear to Ilsa's bedroom door. The sound of splashing and an off-key *Biergarten* tune drifted under the crack. He fitted the skeleton key into the lock and slipped into the room, shutting the door quietly behind him.

The station's third bedroom had been transformed into a hazily—

lit boudoir. Hosiery hung from the curtain rod. Unmentionables had been draped over the foot of the bed and chairs. Shoes spilled across the floor and an assortment of feminine beauty supplies littered the dresser.

Why did women need so much stuff?

Steam spilled out of the bathroom, the door slightly ajar. Water sloshed as Ilsa sang in the tub.

He didn't have much time. He needed to find that notepad.

Scanning the room, he tried to imagine where she would place it for safekeeping. Start with the obvious. He searched the bed, under the rumpled covers, mattress, and pillow. Then the chair, dresser, and her suitcase. Digging his fingers around the inside edge of her suitcase, the bottom sprang up to reveal a false bottom. Papers filled the space. He grabbed them with anticipation. National Socialist Women's League. Lebensborn Program Application. Law for the Encouragement of Aryan Marriage.

Disgusted, he stuffed them back in the suitcase and scanned the room again. Where would she feel safe enough to put that notebook when indisposed? His gaze drifted to the bathroom. The last thing he ever wanted was to see her, much less in a state of undress, but maybe ... He moved to the door and squatted just out of sight. There, through the space she'd left open, was her discarded uniform. Michael pressed his lips flat, dreading what he had to do.

Something splashed in the tub. *"Drecksau!"* Ilsa cursed.

Michael peered through the crack. She clutched at her eyes, pressing the heels of her hands into them.

Seizing the opportunity, Michael snaked his hand past the door and grabbed the notepad from her uniform pocket. He rocked back against the wall, holding his breath. Too close for comfort. Flipping it open, he scanned the pages. Recounts of the camps she'd toured of the political prisoners, society degenerates, and Jews. Her pride in the efficiency of working them to death. Her thrill of the dogs attacking their bones.

Revulsion sickened Michael.

He flipped further. Notes about his command. Meeting him and his team. Word-for-word classified information. A curse leaped to his lips. He'd told her that was forbidden. The more he read, the more his name popped up. Dietrich was liberally sprinkled in, as well with a smattering of Claire. Mostly day-to-day observations with snide remarks in the margins.

He came to the latest entry dated that same day.

Michael thinks he's smarter than everyone. Looking down his nose with superior airs. It can only mean he's hiding more than the rest.

A note in the margins. *Get Dietrich to search behind the bookcase again.*

The entry continued. *Hiding things in his office, chewing out soldiers for attacking civilians, and now meeting with a peasant barmaid in the woods. Captain Reichner is indeed a man of mystery. One that I must unravel.*

Michael fought the urge to rip the paper to shreds. She'd taken to following him. Vile woman. He'd need to watch himself more carefully with Claire. He didn't need her dragged into this any further than she already was.

Possible Resistance fighters meeting at bar. Confirm with Gestapo Muller if suspects should be brought in for questioning. If suspects prove valuable—despite ineptitude—could be ticket out of disgusting country and on to Berlin.

The songbird could prove fallible to Reichner. Easy enough to find his secrets with her as bait or if Dietrich is just trying to get him out of the way. Then again, if Dietrich is right …

Ilsa pulled the plug in the tub with a *pop*. Water gurgled down the drain. Michael closed the notebook as his pulse kicked into high gear. Praying she was facing the other way, he stashed the book back in her uniform pocket and crept from the room. He locked it as quietly as he could and turned down the hallway, keeping his pace as normal as possible.

Ilsa's door opened behind him. "Michael?"

He stopped and turned. A slip of a robe barely concealed her body as a towel covered her head. "Yes?"

"Did you come to my room?"

"I knocked to tell you that dinner will be served shortly."

Her calculating eyes narrowed for the briefest of seconds. "Oh. Thank you." She closed the door.

Michael hurried into his room and leaned against the wall. Blood roared through his veins. She was on the hunt—and he was her prey. Little did she realize he was better at this game.

Claire's face flashed through his mind, pricking his heart. He pressed a hand to the spot to cover the recently vulnerable area and glanced at the floor where his transceiver was hidden. How could he keep her safe and complete the mission? Time was ticking. He had to move before Ilsa did.

CHAPTER 12

"I don't know how much we'll find out. So many have been taken and scattered." Giles braced his hands on the bar. Warm lantern light pooled on the worn surface.

Claire tried to control her voice as the din of the customers hummed behind her. "Please. I have to try."

"They could be anywhere. That is if they're still …"

Claire swallowed past the tightness gripping her throat. "If they're still alive."

"It is a possibility and one you must be willing to accept if you're determined to go through with this. It may be a dead end."

"I understand." Her words contradicted the doubt and fear roiling inside. One look at Giles' drawn face, and she knew he didn't believe her.

"Next week Remy comes with supplies. I'll put out a feeler then." He took a wet tray and buffed small circles on it with a cloth. "Time for you to get back to that piano."

Hope restored, Claire stretched on her toes and kissed him on the cheek. "Thank you for understanding."

His cheeks exploded red. "Go on now."

Heart lighter, Claire plucked the keys with gusto. It had taken many nights of arguing, but she'd worn him down. Someday soon she might have news of her family. Again and again, Giles had told her not to get her hopes up, but she refused to think of anything other than a blessed reunion. She'd go crazy if she gave in to the darker thoughts lurking in the corners of her mind.

And then there was Michael, his words seared into her memory. *I hope you do not leave too soon. My men would notice your absence much too keenly.* Would he miss her? The man could charm any *Fräulein* he wanted, but the thought of him sharing books with any other girl stirred her with irrational jealousy.

Heavy boots marched into the bar. She glanced at the door, but it wasn't the man she wanted to see. Ilsa, Ostermann, and two junior soldiers fanned across the back wall and surveyed the room. Ilsa's search stopped on Ansell and his two companions. With a smile, she gave the briefest of nods in their direction.

Ostermann and his guards surrounded the table with rifles pointed. "You are under arrest. Get up."

Ansell's companion with a heavy brow glared at Ostermann. "What are the charges?"

"Conspiracy and illegal actions against the Reich." Ostermann slapped the man in the back of the head. "Up."

Paralyzed with fear, Claire watched as the three men pushed to their feet and had their hands tied behind their backs. The strangers' faces purpled with rage while Ansell paled. He ducked his head and retched. Cursing, the guards jumped back.

"*Drecksau! Schau was du getan hast!*" Ostermann smacked Ansell across the face. "Do it again, and I'll flog you right here."

"That's enough." Ilsa buffed her nails on the sleeve of her jacket and held them out for inspection. "We didn't come here for shouting."

Ostermann leaned closer to Ansell. "You're cleaning my boots tonight with your own spit. A lesson in disgracing yourself on a German officer."

The heavy-browed man hunched his shoulders and dropped his chin. He bowled headfirst into Ostermann's chest, knocking him backward over a table. Plowing through the tables and chairs, he closed in on the curtained doorway leading to the back.

BAM!

The man hit the floor in front of the piano. A horrified scream rattled up Claire's throat. She slapped her hand to her mouth. Relief replaced fear as the man's back shuddered. Dark red blood poured from his left arm. Whipping off her apron, Claire fell to her knees beside him and wrapped the cloth around his wound.

"It's all right," she whispered. "Just stay still."

He moaned. "Have to get out."

"Get away from him." Ostermann flung chairs aside as he stomped toward them. "Get up, Dulcoate. And you." He grabbed Claire's shoulder. "Get back behind that bar. No more interference."

Claire squeezed Dulcoate's arm to ease the bleeding. "Please, Lieutenant. Let me bind his wound. He's bleeding badly."

"And what do I care about that?" Ostermann released her and gripped the pistol at his side. "Now, get away from him."

High heels clicked across the floor. Ilsa's nose wrinkled. "I don't think there's need for all this shouting, Lieutenant. This is a simple arrest."

"She's trying to help the prisoner."

Ilsa arched her finely shaped eyebrow at Claire. "Aiding and abetting a conspirator, are we?"

Claire's heart thumped into her throat. "No, I just want to—"

"Bring her along."

Ostermann's eyes widened. "But, Captain, she's not being charged with anything."

"Did I not just say aiding and abetting?" Ilsa's eyes narrowed. "She comes with us."

"No, please! Do not take her, *Capitaine*." Giles ran around the bar and stood over Claire, his voice cracking like wood under an ax. "She was just trying to help. She didn't know. Please, let her stay."

Ilsa rolled her eyes and walked away. Giles turned to Ostermann. "Please, sir. I beg you."

"You heard what the captain said." Ostermann looked down his long, thin nose. "You're lucky I don't run you in for housing the illegals, not to mention the overabundance of wine and whisky when there's a ration. Keep your nose out of it Giles, or you'll be next." He yanked Dulcoate by the back of his shirt and motioned for Claire to stand.

Giles grabbed her arm.

"Please don't say anything more. I'll be all right." She tried to smile as she squeezed his hand and moved his fingers away. Tears welled in his eyes as she kissed his cheek. "Thank you, for everything."

Ostermann grabbed her arm and pulled her outside along with Dulcoate, Ansell, and the third conspirator. She climbed into the back of a canvas-covered truck and sat against the side wall. No one spoke as the junior soldiers climbed in after them and posted themselves by the entrance.

The truck rumbled to life, shaking her every nerve loose. She crushed her cold fingers together to keep them from trembling as the truck sped down the road.

Don't give in to the fear. It'll paralyze your ability to think clearly and react. Her father's words replayed in her mind from when a boar had charged them while hunting. Easy enough for him to say—he always carried a gun. Her desire to survive would have to serve as her weapon.

Across the way, the third man stared straight ahead with his lips clamped in a white line. Next to him, Ansell's shoulders fell forward, his chin quivering. He searched Claire's face. *Forgive me*, he mouthed to her.

She nodded. It wasn't his fault. It wasn't anyone's fault except hers.

Dulcoate slumped against her. She looked down at the growing warmth against her arm. Her entire right sleeve was soaked with his blood.

Where was that irritating woman? Michael knocked three more times on Ilsa's door, but there was no response. He marched to his office where Hirsch was completing his end-of-day log. "Are you sure you didn't see her come back?"

"No, sir. Trommler dropped her off at the post guards' headquarters at 1600 hours. She assured him Lieutenant Ostermann would drive her back here after she did whatever she went there to do."

Michael checked his watch. 2000 hours. Four hours she'd been gone. "And she didn't give him any indication why she went there or how long she'd be gone?"

"No, sir."

Michael snatched the phone receiver and dialed the guard house's number. It rang with no answer. He slammed it back in the cradle with a silent curse.

Disrespectful, selfish, manipulative creature. She was a guest under his command and couldn't be bothered to let him know what was going on. For being an SS field agent, she wasn't very good at greasing the wheels. Or concealing messages from her commanding officer. Did she think her jewelry box was the best hiding spot? Had they not taught her anything at the secret police boot camp? Or maybe she was too busy making her own path to pay attention during Undercover Tactics 101.

"I don't want to do this to you, Hirsch, but I need you to cover my post while I retrieve Captain von Ziegler." Michael checked his watch. "Two hours at most."

Hirsch nodded and tapped a stack of papers on the desk. "Certainly, sir. I wasn't expecting to retire for a time with these."

"Good man. I hope one day they'll see fit to send us a new officer to help alleviate the burden."

"I nearly forgot." Hirsch pulled a piece of paper from his pocket and smoothed out the wrinkles. "Headquarters wired. They are screening several candidates and plan to send a new arrival in the next few weeks."

"*Wunderbar*. We could use the help, though I must say you do a fine job, Lieutenant."

"Thank you, sir."

Flinging on his overcoat and cap, Michael jumped into the military vehicle and sped down the driveway, turning in the direction of the guard post. Upon arriving, he hopped out of the vehicle but didn't wait for the scrambling corporal to open the door for him. Michael wrenched it open. Every man in the guard house jumped.

"Where is Captain von Ziegler?" No one answered. He glared at the sergeant sitting closest to the door. "On your feet, soldier. Do you not see a ranking officer in front of you? Where is Lieutenant Ostermann?"

The sergeant shot to his feet. "They're not here, sir."

"Where are they?"

"The Three Buckets, but that was over four hours ago, sir."

Trepidation exploded in Michael's head. In her hidden missives, Ilsa's commander had indicated rounding up conspirators, but Michael suspected she would have no qualms about blurring the line between the guilty and innocent. And Claire was in the line of fire. "Did they have plans to go anywhere else?"

"I don't know, sir. They took sergeants Thurman and Klein with them. And the supply truck."

"When they return, have Captain von Ziegler or Lieutenant Ostermann call me immediately. I don't care what time it is."

"Yes, sir."

Michael jumped back into the vehicle and pressed the gas as far as it would go. He should have seen this coming. Should have acted sooner to remove Ilsa as far away from Montbaune as he could. Since the day she'd requested to stay behind, he'd taken to searching her room, watching her incoming and outgoing mail, and, above all, keeping tabs on her. It didn't concern him that she wanted to arrest conspirators—it was happening all over Europe, and to the least suspicious people. But a Gestapo agent poking around under his own roof was too close for comfort. And to have her questioning Claire … the hackles on the back of his neck spiked.

He whipped the wheel around to dodge a pothole. Where was

that blasted moonlight tonight? Racing along the main street, he came to a screeching halt in front of the bar. Inside, German soldiers sat drinking and playing cards. Laughter and voices filled the room. His gaze leaped to the empty piano. And the blood stains next to it. His chest constricted.

Giles stood behind the counter, placing full bottles of liquor on the shelf. Michael marched over to him and pressed his sweaty palms against the counter. "What happened here?"

Without turning, Giles shook his head.

"Giles." Michael leaned closer, straining to keep his voice low. "I need to know what happened here."

Setting the bottles on the counter, Giles walked to the curtained doorway and motioned for Michael to follow. He stepped in behind him and let the curtain fall back into place.

Giles' pale face stood out against the darkness. "They took her."

"Claire?"

"She's why you came here, isn't she? Three French farmers mean nothing to you, but she—" Giles gripped the edge of a crate. "She's a good girl."

Michael took a deep breath before he forced out his next words. "Where did the blood come from?"

"She was trying to stop a man from bleeding to death. That's why the captain ordered her to be taken like a common thug. Tied up and thrown in the back of a truck with those other lawbreakers."

"Who shot the man?"

"The woman captain, when he tried to run."

Ilsa. And now she had Claire. "Where did they go?"

Silence.

"I know you don't trust me, but I need to know where they've gone. If you have any hope of ever seeing Claire again, then it's going to be me."

Silence stretched on. At last, Giles loosened his crushing grip on the crate. "Someone said they saw the truck turn on Dupont Lane near the old flour mill. East of town."

"Thank you." Michael turned for the curtain.

"What is your plan, *Capitaine*? It is four against one."

"Don't worry about that. I never fail to reach my objectives."

Back in the vehicle, he sped over the bumpy lane. His fingers hurt from the cold, but he didn't want to waste time fishing for his leather gloves. Not when he had to get to Claire.

He should have kept a better eye on her, should have kept tighter control of Ilsa. Should have … should have what? Forgotten his true purpose for being there? Jeopardized his whole mission? All for some American girl caught behind the lines at the wrong time?

He beat his fist against the steering wheel. Blasted if he did and blasted if he didn't. All his military training had taught him to keep it impersonal, form no attachments, and, above all, reach the objective.

He careened onto Dupont Lane. Pinpoints of light grew brighter against the bleak darkness of harvested fields. An old farmhouse loomed at the end of the road. As he drew closer, he could make out a sagging chicken coop to the side and smoke curling from the farmhouse's chimney. A supply truck sat in the driveway.

He pulled in and parked behind it. Pushing his coat back, he unstrapped his Luger from its holster and checked the magazine before sliding it back home.

Nerves ricocheted around his belly like the time flak hit the bomber he'd flown in as a serviceman. Things were easier then. No second-guessing who to shoot.

The front door swung open to a blinding shaft of light. A man stood in the doorway pointing a rifle at his chest. "Captain Reichner. What are you doing here?"

"I'd like to ask your lieutenant the same question," Michael said. "Where are he and Captain von Ziegler?"

The rifle lowered an inch, but the man didn't move. "They are here, sir, but I was told—"

"I don't care what you were told." Michael brushed past him. Stacks of broken furniture filled the corner, covering the warped floorboards. A single lamp burned on the mantel of the living room. Staleness and mold clung to the air.

The balding sergeant closed the door and slung the rifle over his shoulder. "I'll tell them you're here, sir."

Michael whipped off his cap and tucked it under his arm. "Take me to them."

The man licked his cracked lips. "Sir, I'm not supposed to let anyone in, at least not without informing Captain von Ziegler first."

Michael stepped forward until the tips of his boots hit the tips of the sergeant's. "I suggest that—if you wish to retain your rank until morning—you take me immediately. I'll even accept your pointing me in the correct direction."

The man pointed to the back of the house.

Michael swerved around him and started for the dark hallway.

"Wait. I'll show you." The sergeant scurried ahead of him and marched down the hall. He stopped at a door at the end of the hallway and knocked three times before pushing it open.

A round table blocked the back door, and two paint-chipped chairs stood in the middle of the crumbling kitchen. A black pot gurgled over the fireplace as the fire cast light into the room.

Three men sat against the wall to his right with their hands tied behind their backs. Claire sat between two of them. Fear squeezed Michael's lungs.

Ilsa stepped away from the kitchen counter. Smoke curled from the cigarette between her fingers. Her eyes widened. "Why, Captain Reichner, whatever are you doing here?"

"When you disappeared this afternoon, I began to worry. I sent out a few inquiries and"—Michael swept his hand around the room—"here I find you."

"Did I not leave a message with Dietrich? How stupid of me to worry you."

Michael clamped his teeth. Stupid didn't begin to cover it.

"As you can see, I'm perfectly all right." She waved her cigarette around. "And just a tad busy."

"So I see." He glanced at the prisoners with as much boredom as he could muster. Bruises covered the men. Ansell sported a split lip with dried vomit coating the front of his torn shirt. One man slumped over with a blood-soaked apron tied around his arm. Claire's shoulder kept him from falling forward. Her wide eyes turned to Michael.

He struggled to ignore their painful plea and turned back to Ilsa. "What's going on here?"

"Just a bit of cleaning up, if you will. Riffraff stirring the pot against our glorious *Führer*."

The man next to Ansell spat at Ilsa. "Your blessed *Führer*, you, and your whole forsaken country can go to the abyss. She-devil. Your reputation precedes you, but for all the claims of your beauty, I see nothing but your evil soul and an ugly mark. Ugly!"

"I warned you about your outbursts, Malet." Ilsa tapped her ashes into the puddle of spit.

Ostermann strode across the room and cocked his Luger in Malet's face. "One more word."

Malet didn't blink. "You're going to kill me anyway. Why wait?"

"Because we need you alive for the time being." Ilsa blew out an exaggerated breath. "Put the gun away, Ostermann."

The pistol's hammer released with a loud *click*. Ostermann shoved it back in his holster with a curse.

Ilsa stepped closer to Michael, her perfume wafting over him. The smell of death and torture. "Simple guardsmen are not ideal for this job," she whispered. "But what choice did I have when transportation to Gestapo headquarters in Paris couldn't be arranged until tomorrow? At least there I can ditch these buffoons and work with the professionals."

"Professional what?"

She smiled at him. "Interrogators, of course."

"Because you believe these men are conspirators?"

"I know they are."

"By what proof?"

"I didn't request to stay behind after Max's tour because I like the location." She laughed and drew from her cigarette. "The truth is I hate this country, but this is where they sent me. Now that I've flushed out the threat I can leave this blighted spot of a town. Between you and me, I'm hoping for a promotion. You'd think the frogs would have sense enough not to meet in bars where Germans are patrolling."

"Good work. I commend you, and your command will too." Michael flipped a disinterested gaze over his shoulder to the prisoners, then back to her. "Their information can prove invaluable. Names of Resistance members, lists, places, and routes. What happens once you're done with the miscreants?"

"Prison, work camp, or shot, I should say."

"And the girl?"

Ilsa glanced in Claire's direction then, to him. "She'll come too."

Blood strained in Michael's neck. "What are the charges against her?"

"Aiding and abetting."

He raised an eyebrow at Claire's apron tied around the nearly unconscious man's arm. She stared at Michael. Hardening himself to her fright, he rounded on Ilsa. "Aiding and abetting by tying her apron around a bleeding man's arm, which you shot, I believe, thereby preventing him from dying before you could question him? Is that what you meant?"

Ilsa's smugness slipped. "Well, she—"

"May I speak with you in private, Captain?" Without waiting for a reply, he marched to the door and held it open for her.

"Lieutenant Ostermann, keep an eye on the prisoners while I speak to Captain Reichner." Ice spiked in her eyes as she slinked to the open door.

Michael shut it behind them before gesturing toward the front room. Ilsa stalked to the empty fireplace. She reached a hand to pat her smooth hair, then trailed her fingers over the mantel. "How long have you known I was a Gestapo agent?"

"A while." He crossed his arms, his cap dangling from his fingers. "I was curious why you stayed so long after Major Kessel left, and I make it a priority to know everything about every person under my command."

"You spied on me?"

"Hardly. I'm in COMMS. It's my job to know what's going on and what's being said. When someone under my command starts questioning the locals, I start to put two and two together."

"Shows how good of an agent I am." She stubbed out her cigarette and popped a new one into the holder. The lighter shot a brief spark of orange against her profile.

"You're very good. Until you came, I didn't realize conspirators plotted right under my nose."

She smiled. "We all have our blind spots, Michael."

The hairs on the back of his neck stood at attention. "Indeed we do. And sometimes pride leads us to trample over our orders."

"I was ordered to bring these men in."

"And so you will. But the girl wasn't part of those orders, was she?"

"She involved herself."

"By tying her apron around a bullet wound? If you arrive with a prisoner who is, in fact, some innocent barmaid from the country, I guarantee your commander will run you up the wall and back again. Striking out on your own is not the military way."

Her shoulders sagged as her self-made ivory tower crumbled. Time to strike while the iron was hot.

"Speaking of the military way"—he braced his feet shoulder width apart—"I don't appreciate being undermined within my own ranks. You've used my men repeatedly without asking permission."

"But I couldn't ask you. I wasn't allowed to tell anyone."

"They are my men. When you employ them, everything you do becomes my business. And as far as not telling anyone, what are

Lieutenant Ostermann and two of his guards doing here? I assume they didn't drop by on a whim."

"I needed help taking the prisoners. I was told Ostermann doesn't fall under your jurisdiction."

"Why didn't you wait until tomorrow when the officials arrive?"

"Because I'm to meet them in Troyes. They are not coming here."

"You were expected to herd these conspirators by yourself?"

She flicked cigarette ash on the floor. "No, I—"

"With enlisted men you had no right to command? Without coming to me first?"

"As I said, I was told he isn't under your authority."

Michael stepped closer, looming over her. "I am the ranking officer in this area. One thing I cannot abide is disrespect for rules and courtesies."

"Courtesies?" she scoffed. "We're the same rank."

"*You* are a field agent with less than four years of experience."

Her eyes snapped. "You've made your point."

Not yet. "Stick to your orders from now on or I'll have a reprimand on Gestapo Muller's desk within twenty-four hours to inform him of how well you follow instructions."

"Since you put it that way"—she took a long drag of her cigarette, blew the smoke out through her nose, and stubbed the stick on the mantel—"I believe there's been a mistake."

Back in the kitchen, she hoisted herself atop the counter and crossed her legs. Reaching into her pocket, she pulled out fur-lined gloves and slipped her fingers into them, tapping the space between each finger with deliberate slowness, Ilsa flicked her gaze up. "Untie the girl's hands."

Ostermann's eyebrows shot up. "Untie her?"

"Are you hard of hearing?"

His mouth hung open. Michael reached into the top of his boot, yanked out his knife and handed it to Ostermann. Jerking Claire to her feet, he sliced the ropes in half, then shoved her forward.

Eyes wild, Claire looked at Michael. "What is going on? What have I done?" Tears streaked her face.

Ilsa rolled her eyes. "Pathetic."

Ansell struggled to his knees. "Where are you taking her? Please, I beg you, do not hurt her. She knows nothing."

"She's no longer your concern." Michael snatched his knife from Ostermann and grabbed Claire's elbow.

With all his might Michael wished he could assure Ansell that he was taking her to safety, to tell all three men to stay strong and face their futures with courage. But his admiration could never be expressed. They knew the risks and consequences. As brothers in arms, they would understand his silence.

Pushing Claire out the front door, Michael steered her toward the vehicle. She dug her heels in, jerking away from him as she tried to pry his fingers from her elbow.

"Do you think you're going to win against me?" He jerked open the door. "You won't get far in this darkness."

She braced her hands on either side of the door, refusing to get in. "How do I know this isn't some trick? Why should I go anywhere with you?"

"Because you want to live, and I'd rather not give contradicting news to Giles and Pauline. Now get inside."

She climbed in without looking at him. Michael jumped into the driver's seat and sped away. He waited until the house was out of view before decelerating to a more reasonable speed and glancing at the woman next to him. Hunching her shoulders, she sniffed back her tears and shivered.

Pulling to the side of the road, he put the vehicle in park and reached over the seat, fumbling around the back floorboard in search of the emergency blanket.

"Here." He flung the blanket around her and tucked it under her chin.

She froze as if he'd thrown a sheet of ice over her.

"I didn't go through all of that for you to freeze to death on the way back to town."

Her fingers curled around the blanket's edges. She sniffed. "Why did you?"

"Because you didn't do anything wrong."

"You sound so certain. Why do you care if I'm innocent or not? None of the other soldiers worry about what happens to one insignificant villager."

He seized the steering wheel. "Rules were broken here today. I will not tolerate such rogue actions against orders."

"You came all the way out here in the middle of the night to demand my release on behalf of regulations, yet you've turned a blind eye to the Bucket's well-stocked shelves for months." She turned to face him. Despite the darkness between them, he felt the questioning heat of her gaze. "Why do you suddenly care so much about rules?"

Feeling too much like a turtle overturned with its soft underbelly exposed, he vaulted out of the vehicle and paced the road in agitation. Of course she'd ask that. No Nazi soldier would've done what he just did. He could bluff all he wanted about rules, but if he dared to tell her the truth she'd think it a trick. But what if she didn't? He stopped pacing. What if, despite all this madness, she believed him? Perhaps he had found a soul in which to confide. For the first time in a long time, she gave him a reason to want to risk it all.

It would be the best risk or biggest mistake of his life.

Marching to the passenger side, he planted himself next to her door should she try to bolt. "Because I am not just some German officer and you, my dear, are not just some insignificant villager." He took a deep breath and squared his shoulders. He said in English, "The jig's up, Claire from America."

CHAPTER 13

He knew. He with his mastery of languages. How long had he known?

"I cannot understand you, Captain." Claire's French words warbled past the panic tightening her chest. "Why are you speaking English? I don't understand."

"Yes, you do," he said in a soft British tone. "My name is Captain Michael Reiner of His Majesty's Royal Air Force. I'm an agent in a special department sent to destroy the Nazis from within. I'm telling you the truth. Will you please trust me?"

Doubt and fear assailed her. What did he want? And why was he blocking her door? "I—I don't understand you. French. I am French, *monsieur*."

"You may be French, but you weren't born here. No French person says dollar when they should say franc."

That day by the river came rushing back. She had said that. A mistake he had caught. She touched her shaky hand to her head as dizziness encircled her.

"Ah, so you do remember. As I've said before, you have a horrible poker face." He shoved his hands into his coat pockets. His breath puffed out like smoke. "I know you're afraid to trust me, perhaps more so now than before. I hate this uniform more than you can possibly know."

Questions raced through her mind but voicing them was of no use. He would say whatever he needed to make her believe him, as she had done to make everyone believe she was French. The truth was too incriminating. If what he said was true, his confession was more than incriminating. It was a death sentence.

Taking a hand out of his pocket, he tugged on the front of the coat. "You've seen me out of this before."

Indignation flared at his matter-of-fact statement. She ripped off his filthy blanket and dropped it to the ground. "I beg your pardon. I may sing in a bar, but I'm a good girl."

"I wasn't suggesting otherwise." He took his hat off and tossed it on the back seat. "On the train to Montoire, there was an explosion. An ordinary man in ordinary clothes helped you off the train. Your foot was stuck, and he pulled it free. *I* pulled it free."

"Impossible. I was never on a train." But the memories of that day came flooding back in one mighty rush. The blue eyes. Those bright blue eyes pierced her through the chaos. She shook her head despite the vivid truth flashing in her memory.

"You wore red." Bending, he gathered the blanket and draped it around her shoulders once more. "And you said I smelled like fresh cotton and soap."

Her defense buckled. She hadn't told a soul about that man. About *him*. She sagged in the seat as the burden of terror lifted. He wasn't a Nazi after all. "What is it that you want, Captain Reiner? Not very clever, by the way." Her English sounded foreign to her ears after speaking French for so long. Rust tinged her words and pronunciation, but it felt good to speak openly again. Even if it was a trick, at least she didn't have to lie anymore.

He hinted at a smile. "I agree the name change isn't the most brilliant, but it's easier to manage the lies when they're close to the truth."

The strain and precision she so often attributed to his voice had disappeared into a soft lilt. Her fear began to dissipate.

"Is your story true? Are you a student? Your family was taken?"

She nodded. The blanket scratched her cheek, reminding her of the itching straw she'd hidden under in Uncle Emile's barn. "The officer said it was a work camp." Tears clogged her throat. The memory of her family cracked the dam. "I was trying to get to unoccupied France. I thought if I could just get there, then I could go home. Giles found me in a field with a twisted ankle and brought me to the Buckets. They offered me a job and a place to stay, no questions asked."

"They don't know who you are?"

She wiped her streaming nose on the edge of the blanket and shook her head. "No one does. Giles thought I was safe enough here, but when I found out Ansell was part of the Resistance … it's too late for that help now."

"I am sorry." He passed his hand over his face as he leaned against the jeep, or what passed as one in the German army. "There was no way I could get him out without drawing suspicion."

Claire's heart twisted at the thought of what lay in store for her friend. "Don't you know someone who can help? Have connections somewhere?"

"It's too dangerous, and the problem is beyond my limited control within Montbaune. Besides, Ansell and his friends knew the consequences. The greater the fight, the greater the ramifications."

"Like spying?"

"Exactly like spying."

Claire brushed her wet cheek with the back of her hand. "What if Ilsa finds out who you are? You stepped on her patent-leather toes tonight."

He pushed off the vehicle and straightened his coat. The military shield dropped back into place. "Let me worry about that. I'll take you home now. It's near midnight."

She still had questions but, as Michael walked around the jeep and climbed in, exhaustion overtook her. She'd ask him later when her brain wasn't bogged with secret identities, conspirators, and interrogations. They drove back to town in silence.

Michael stopped in front of the bar. It stood like a tomb, dark and silent.

"Are Giles and Pauline all right?"

"A little shaken, I imagine, but otherwise unharmed."

She turned to Michael, and her tongue went dry. What could

she say to the man who'd just saved her life? "Thank you," she said at last.

"It's nothing."

As if he did such things every day. Her heart jumped to her throat. He probably *did* do such things every day. Maybe not busting in on kidnappers like some cowboy, but with his spying. How many lives had he saved? Plots thwarted? This man who had come for *her*. Despite the cold, her insides warmed.

"Go inside, rest, but say nothing to Giles or Pauline about, well … you understand." He scanned the road. The lines around his mouth were not quite so harsh, and a lightness that had been well-hidden all these months softened his eyes.

With his façade dropped, she recognized the man from the train. So confident amid the hysteria. Heat crept up her neck at the memory of staring at him like a fool. And the way he'd stared back. "Were you a Nazi on the train?"

"Not yet."

"But you were—are—a British soldier?"

The corners of his mouth lifted. "Yes."

"Then why were you in France? Was it for reconnaissance?"

"My unique skills take me different places for different reasons. All for a good cause, but none I can explain."

"Or you'd have to kill me?"

"How would I explain the body to my commanding officer?" He winked.

"Nice to know you have a sense of humor beneath that uniform."

"I'm glad you finally see it." Stepping out of the car, he walked around and opened the door for her. "We'll speak again soon."

She climbed out, folded the blanket, and placed it on the seat. "Good evening, Captain Reiner."

"*Bonsoir*, Claire."

He gave a short bow and waited as she entered the building. Shutting the door behind her, she leaned against it and listened until the motor faded into the distance. Captain Michael Reiner of

His Majesty's Royal Air Force. And he had come for her.
Claire pushed off the door and raced to the stairs.
"Giles. Pauline. I'm home!"

CHAPTER 14

December 1941

Claire tripped twice as she raced through the woods, her vision blurring with tears. Michael stood waiting for her under the barren tree. "Is it true?" she asked.

"I'm afraid it is." Quiet sadness pooled in his eyes. "America is at war."

Claire grasped the tree trunk as she caught her breath. "But not with Europe."

Michael ran a hand along the back of his neck. "It's only a matter of days."

"How can you be so sure?"

"It's my job to know before anyone else does."

"Did you know this was going to happen?"

He shook his head. "My focus is here in France."

Claire sagged against the tree, hugging her arms around her waist. "All those poor people. On their way to church or cooking breakfast or scrubbing the ship decks."

Michael leaned his shoulder against hers. The smell of wool and aftershave mingled with the frosty December air in a comforting scent. Claire resisted the urge to inch closer.

"Did you have family on the islands? Neighbors or friends?"

She nodded. "Our neighbor's son, Dave, was stationed at Pearl Harbor for some time, but I'm not sure if he still is. My brother Rob is too young, but he turns eighteen soon. He'll want to enlist now."

"Is your family safe?"

"Yes, they live on a small farm in Virginia. I wish there was some way I could let them know I'm all right." Realization ripped through her. She whipped her head around to meet his eyes. "Can you get in contact with them? Let them know I'm alive? They have no idea what's happened to me." Hope burned in her veins like wildfire. "I'm sorry to ask. You've done so much for me already, and I understand the risk all of this puts you in, but if there's any way to get word to them I will forever be in your debt."

His lips pressed into a straight line.

Claire steeled herself for rejection.

"I make no promises, but I'll see what I can do. And I'll see about your French family as well."

She grabbed his hand and squeezed. "Thank you."

Surprise flashed in his eyes, but his fingers wrapped around hers. His warm touch sent heat waves crashing through her.

She let go before she made a fool of herself, sitting on the ground. The dead grass crunched beneath her and poked through her long cotton socks. First thing tomorrow, she'd fish in the old trunks for a pair of trousers or make some out of the heavy kitchen drapes as Pauline suggested. "If things continue as they are, I'll owe you more than I can repay in two lifetimes."

Michael hunkered next to her. "I'll think of it as an investment."

"No offense, but I think you'd make a lousy businessman."

"I'm willing to take the risk."

"Fair enough, but you've been warned. I don't have much money. I couldn't afford my studies at the *conservatoire* without a scholarship."

"Do you plan on going back?"

"Of course, but maybe someplace safer. There are plenty of terrific schools in the States, like the New England Conservatory of Music. Music is all I've ever wanted to do, to tour Europe and play the most famous halls in the world."

He chuckled. "Sounds easy enough."

"Sure. All I need is to finish my degree and then beat out every musician applying for the same once-in-a-lifetime slot. Piece of cake."

"You've managed to fool the German army about who you are. You'll cinch any musical challenge after this."

"I appreciate your confidence, but you've obviously never tried out for first chair violin in an orchestra. It's nerve-wracking, and the auditions are ruthless."

"Then I'm glad musicality doesn't run in my veins. I'd rather enjoy listening to it than know about the cutthroats backstage."

Claire laughed, reveling in the small joy of finding something humorous again. "What does run in your veins then, other than the ability to fool people?"

"Rather good at that, aren't I?" The corner of his mouth tipped as he rested a hand atop his bent knee. "Other than that, teaching runs in my veins."

No teacher of hers had ever looked like him or had the ability to turn her insides to jelly. His sharp intuition and penchant for courting danger belonged to a man of action, not one banging erasers. "I can't see you as a teacher."

"Because I'm not." He laughed. "My mum is a schoolteacher, and my da a professor of history. Or he was some years ago."

"How did they meet?"

"Mum took a summer course at Heidelberg University in Baden-Württemberg, which was unheard of for a woman, and Da was her professor. They got married a few months later, when she wasn't his student anymore, and shortly after"—he pointed at his chest—"I came along."

"Were you raised in Germany? Your accent … it's English."

He leaned his head close to hers. "Irish, actually. Confused yet?"

"Yes."

He laughed again. The sound was generous and cheerful. A month ago, she never would have pegged him as capable of such lightheartedness.

"My father is German, and mother is Irish. They wanted to

give me a quieter life after the Great War, so we moved to Ireland a month after the Armistice was signed."

"Seems you couldn't escape the war forever. Are they aware of what you do?"

"It's safer to keep some things in the dark, to protect your loved ones." His gaze rose to meet hers. The deep-blue orbs searched her soul. He crunched the grass between his fingers and looked away. "My da was a bit twisted when he found out I was coming back. We left Germany to get away from all of this, and then I put my foot back in the viper's pit."

"You're very brave."

"Or very stupid. The brave lads stare at the barrel of a gun every day on the field, dig in the trenches, and bomb from the air. I do what I can to make their missions easier."

"While also protecting the innocent. Every day I think about what might have happened if you hadn't come for me that night." She shivered and pulled her sweater closer at the thought of that hateful woman's eyes. "I worry she'll come back."

"That prospect isn't far from my mind either." His mouth compressed into a line. "But I'd rather face my enemy head-on than wait for her to skulk in the shadow. Until that day comes, I'll stick to the mission at hand."

Frustration washed over Claire. His purpose was brave and noble. What was she sacrificing by serving beer and singing silly love songs to strangers? "I wish I could do something more, roll bandages maybe, but how can you support the troops in a town occupied by the enemy?"

"Getting a might fidgety, are you? I know the feeling. But you're keeping the town's men in high spirits. Aye, that's a pun. I know my own men enjoy listening to you play."

"How can you speak so well of them?" She smashed a clump of dead stalks beneath her palm. "The worker bees thwarting air strikes and convoys."

"An argument I have with myself almost daily." A frown creased his brow. "They're good men. They work hard. They're trying to do their jobs. Just on the wrong side."

"Aren't you worried they'll find out?"

"Every waking minute. We all have our parts to play in the cogs of war, and this is mine. I would give the duty to no one else."

She shook her head in amazement. "You always sound so … resolved. How can you be so calm and sure about things?"

He tucked his chin to his chest. With a deep sigh, he lifted his eyes to search her face. "I'm not."

Something sparked within Claire. She didn't have much experience with men unless she counted her first kiss from Jimmy Dugan on the county fair's Ferris wheel, and she tried not to. Michael stirred emotions she didn't know existed. And now, knowing who he was, she didn't have to push them away.

But what good would come of falling for a man like him? His world was foreign, dangerous, and she was a music student who needed to get home. An ocean of reason divided them.

"Do you have a plan to leave?" he asked.

"Yes and no. I need to get home, but it's difficult without knowing who to trust outside of Giles and Pauline. And you." She smiled. It was such a relief being able to talk to him so openly. "Giles said he would ask his more discreet contacts about getting me into free France. But, he and Pauline don't like it when I talk about leaving. They don't think I'll last out there, but I can fit in an empty wine barrel in a pinch."

Michael looked at her as if she'd suggested flying to the moon. "You're going to stuff yourself into a barrel just to get to unoccupied territory? I suppose you'll use the same barrel to drift across the ocean. You might need to fashion a paddle first. A shovel could work."

"Ha, very funny. I'm not as good at this sort of thing as you are."

"And how many barrels do you think I've been in?"

She giggled and flicked a handful of grass in his direction.

"None. Your legs are too long."

A frigid wind picked up, scattering dead leaves across the ground. The smell of hearth fires punctuated the air. Claire shivered and tugged at her collar as she watched the sun drown in a blanket of gray clouds. "What time is it?"

Michael squinted at his wristwatch. "1400. Two o'clock."

"I'd better get back before Giles sends out a search party. He wants to do an inventory of usable chairs."

"How lucky for you. Let me help you up."

Michael stood and offered his hand. His hands enveloped hers, sealing them with a warmth that radiated all the way to her toes. How good it felt not to shrink away from him anymore. Her fingers curled around his, wishing she could savor his nearness all afternoon.

His gaze fluttered over her face, lingering on her lips. The once warm tingling burned to a heated rush. Too nervous to encourage it, she pulled her hands from his and tucked them in her pockets. "I'm glad you were here today."

"I hoped you would come."

Crunching rocks drew Claire's attention to the path leading to the village.

Savon, wearing no coat or gloves, stood glaring at her. "What are you doing here?"

"Are you following me?"

"Seems like you need a chaperone to protect you against your own foolishness."

Michael stiffened beside her. Why had she not taken more caution in meeting him? What if Savon had been listening the whole time? Horror slithered over her. "I don't appreciate your thinking you're my father, Savon. You have no right to follow me."

His chin jutted out. "You don't know what's best for yourself anymore. Not when you've hired yourself out as a *fille de joie* to the Germans."

A loose woman? Her mouth fell open on a gasp.

Michael swooped in front of her. "How dare you say such a thing to a lady? I demand you apologize at once."

"Or what? Pistols at dawn?" Savon sneered. "I hate to inform you, *Capitaine*, but that was outlawed years ago." He spat at Michael's boots.

"Do you think anyone would stop me from taking a shot?"

Savon's smug veneer slipped and, for the briefest and most unstoppable second, Claire wished Michael would forget the pistols and sock him in the face.

"Threaten me all you want. It's the only thing you Germans are good at, besides murder and seduction."

Michael stepped forward with hands clenched. "You need to learn some manners."

"And you think you're the one to teach me?" Savon nudged his chin in Claire's direction. "Or do you let your bawd take care of the action for you?"

Michael grabbed Savon by the neck and pinned him against the tree. "It's ten months in a labor camp for insulting an officer of the Reich. I can add another ten simply because I don't like you." Savon's face began to purple. "Maybe I'll save the guards the extra work and break your legs myself. Prisoners don't last long with broken bones."

A noise gurgled in Savon's throat. He beat against Michael's unrelenting hands.

"Stop it! Stop it this instant."

At Claire's command, Michael relinquished his grip and stepped back. Savon doubled over in a coughing spasm as normal color returned to his face. Claire clamped her arms to her side to keep from shaking. "You are nothing but a foul-mouthed bully, Savon. Get out of here before I box your ears myself."

"You're blinded by his lying tongue. I should've known it that day they attacked us in the alley. He came along like some grand knight to the rescue. He's not your kind."

"My kind doesn't strut around like they know what's best for everyone." Her voice shook with anger. "Leave. Now."

"I'm warning you, Claire, open your eyes. Or one day it'll be too late."

Michael grabbed Savon by the front of his shirt and jerked him forward until their noses almost touched. "Leave now, or I'll finish what I started a minute ago."

Savon's face turned purple as he struggled against Michael's hold.

"If not for yourself, then think of your father having to run the shop by himself. Business will suffer." Michael let go and took a step back.

Savon straightened his wrinkled shirt and cursed. He shot Claire a curdling look. "Don't say that you weren't warned." Spinning on his heel, he stormed away.

Claire's knees buckled.

She reached for the tree as Michael grabbed her by the waist. "Are you all right?"

"Never have I been called a … a …" She couldn't finish. "He thinks I'm a two-bit hussy."

"He's just angry because he feels he's been slighted."

"He can feel slighted all he wants because it's true after today."

"An affection slighted can be a dangerous thing."

Affection. The strength of Michael's encircling arms loosened the bands squeezing her heart. But with Savon's taunts still fresh in the air, she pulled away. "Savon deserves a wallop, but you wouldn't really shoot anyone would you? Sometimes it's difficult to tell if you're acting or not."

"If I don't appear in control, people will think I'm not, and I can't have that. Especially people with big mouths and loose tongues. I will only use force if there is no other option. I'm very good at what I do, but wanting to be with you isn't an act."

Claire released a heavy breath. No matter the circumstances, she didn't want Michael turning into a murderer. "Don't ever do that again. You could have killed him."

"Only if I'd wanted to. At the most, he would've lost consciousness for a few seconds."

"Must you be so blasé about it?"

"Do not for one minute think I take any action without account. The fear must be maintained or control is lost, though I do wish you hadn't been witness to it."

That was the most frightening part. She'd seen angry men before, but nothing like the cold collectedness Michael had exhibited. How many morals must he break to keep up the charade? He'd already broken so many rules to keep her safe, but he couldn't go on forever. At some point, the risk would become too great. For both of them. "I hate all of this."

"As do I." Michael took her arm and turned her down the path to town. "Take extra precaution when you come here again. It's too easy to be followed, and I'd rather Savon not be given an opportunity to corner you."

His words chilled her more than the wind. "Do you think he heard what we were talking about?"

Michael's mouth pressed into a firm line. His eyes flickered. "We'll find out soon enough."

CHAPTER 15

"Les étoiles brillent au dessus de toi ..."

Michael leaned back in his chair. For the first time in months, he was enjoying himself. The men's boisterous voices spilled across the room as they anticipated ringing in the New Year in less than one hour. Some of the men had even made party hats for the occasion. Not part of uniform regulations, of course, but for tonight Michael decided to look the other way unless they turned their celebration to kissing the piano player at midnight. *That* he would have to say something about.

How beautiful she looked with the ends of her hair curled and wearing a faded red dress reminiscent of the one she'd worn on the train. She smiled in his direction but quickly looked away. Michael bit the inside of his cheek to keep from smiling back.

"Dream a little dream of me." Her singing touched every part of his well-controlled spirit, swelling it out beyond its guarded perimeters to dangerous territory. He caught himself tapping along to the words. If he wasn't careful, she'd carry him away with her lyrical spell.

A gust of frigid air breached the door behind him. Heavy footsteps stopped beside him. "Lieutenant Klaus Hoffenberg reporting for duty, sir."

Michael stifled a groan as he turned in his chair. Couldn't they leave him alone for one night? Snow covered the lieutenant's thin shoulders and cap while mud stuck to the sides of his boots. Snowflakes glistened in his fair eyebrows. He shook from head to toe.

Michael frowned. "I didn't order any lieutenant."

"To serve as your aide, sir. I'm fluent in French with a smattering in Spanish."

Great. One more to worry about, and a personal assistant at that. Michael filed the annoyance away with all the others and gestured to the chair next to his. "Welcome aboard. Have a seat. A glass of beer will warm you in no time."

Hoffenberg shrugged out of his coat, spraying slush all over the floor and Michael, and placed it on the back of an empty chair. Giles hurried over with a tall glass of beer and set it on the table. Two long gulps and it was gone.

Michael waited until Hoffenberg stopped shaking before starting with the questions. "Lieutenant. Where were you stationed before?"

"Eastern forces for a while with a short stint in Brittany." Hoffenberg pulled a pack of smokes from his pocket and offered one to Michael, who waved him off. "Recently, I've come back from holiday. Spent some time enjoying the fresh air of the Highlands near the town of Arisaig."

Michael's annoyance dropped. He leaned forward in his chair, making sure to keep the code response exact. "Scotland, you say?"

Hoffenberg puffed on his cigarette and nodded. "Yes, sir. Have you been?"

"Some time ago. The weather and conditions left something to be desired."

"They remain the same, sir."

Running his finger around the edge of his glass, Michael smiled before checking the next tier of validation. "Tell me, is that white rabbit still there?"

Hoffenberg returned his grin at the reference to their knife-wielding instructor. "Indeed. And just as cuddly."

Hoffenberg checked out. The agency had sent Michael reinforcements.

Angling his chair to the stage, Hoffenberg settled back with his smoke and beer. It wasn't until Claire was halfway through a new song that he glanced at Michael. "Heard you had a little run-in with some Gestapo *Fräulein*."

"Word spreads fast."

Hoffenberg nodded. "Command isn't too happy about you butting in on that arrest, or so says their official response." He leaned over and whispered, "But I heard old man Nelson say it was good you got her to quake in her boots because not many men can withstand her charms. O' course I also heard it started over a woman." He turned back to the stage and lit a new cigarette after stubbing out the old one. "She's pretty, I'll give you that."

"She's American."

Hoffenberg's blond eyebrows lifted slightly. "Is that so? Bad for her because she's no longer neutral after that Pearl Harbor stunt, but good for us to get them in on this fight. Them Yanks don't know how to quit. When do we get to the dirty work? I mean, that's part of our job, right?"

Turning to take a good look at Hoffenberg, Michael noticed stubble on his pointy chin and hair curling over his ear. His uniform was crumpled, and one button on his tunic hung by a black thread. Out of regulations. As was his manner of speaking.

"You're not a military man, are you *Herr* Hoffenberg?" Michael asked.

The man shrugged. "Not really. My father told me to follow in his brick-laying shoes or join the army. I figured with guns involved the army would be more fun."

"Has it lived up to your expectations?"

"No. They didn't agree with my whisky-smuggling operations, so I was dishonorably discharged. Not much work a man can get with that hanging over him. Then one day I'm meeting with a potential client only to find out he's there to recruit me. I'm the kind they're looking for to do the dirtiest jobs. My reputation may not be squeaky clean, but I'm proud to defend my Belgium from these lousy Germans."

Michael resisted the urge to slap him upside the head. Did he not see the enemy surrounding them on every side? "Just remember that you're supposed to be one of them. Fighting for the *Führer*. We'll have to work on your military bearing."

"Not to your standards? I heard you mean business."

"However did you pass training?"

"By the skin of my teeth, but things are desperate. The SOE is scraping under the barrel now."

Michael shook his head as he took a sip of beer.

Hoffenberg's eyes turned serious. "I'll do whatever you ask, boss. Just let me kill a few of them every once in a while."

Beer snorted up Michael's nose at the man's blunt enthusiasm. He set his mug down and leaned forward. "Rule number one, *Lieutenant* Hoffenberg. No more talking about killing them. Patience and professionalism are the keys."

"Yes, sir."

"Second. Sit straight. You're my personal assistant and must remember bearing, even off duty."

Hoffenberg popped up in his chair like a weasel from his hole. Michael thumped him on the back with a laugh. "Not quite so rigid. We are in a bar, after all."

"In that case, I'll have another beer." Hoffenberg signaled for another drink.

Claire, who had stepped away from the piano for her break, brought two empty glasses and a brimming pitcher. "Good evening, gentlemen." She slid the tray onto the table, flashing Michael a triumphant look when it didn't topple over.

Michael's pulse raced at her being so near. And yet, still so far away. He straightened in his chair, clearing his throat. "This is Lieutenant Hoffenberg, my new personal aide."

Her smile tightened as she looked to Hoffenberg. "Welcome to our town, *monsieur*."

Hoffenberg stood and snatched Claire's hand to his lips. "*Enchanté. Mademoiselle* …?"

She pulled her hand back and rubbed it against her apron.

"Claire."

Michael kicked Hoffenberg in the back of the knee. He dropped onto his chair.

"New songs tonight," Michael said, drawing her attention. "They're a nice addition to the repertoire."

"New year, new songs, new chances." Her gaze softened at him. His chest swelled with warmth.

Hoffenberg grinned. "That sounds promising."

Michael shot him a look meant to blast him into a million pieces.

Hoffenberg waggled his eyebrows and lit a new cigarette.

"*Es ist fast Zeit!*" Someone shouted and motioned for everyone to raise their glasses.

Angling his wristwatch into the light, Michael saw it was seconds away from midnight. He pushed to his feet and raised his glass with the others.

"*Zehn, neun, acht … drei, zwei, eins. Prosit Neujahr!*"

Across the table, Claire watched him with a sad smile. *Happy New Year*, she mouthed silently.

His raised his glass to her. *Happy New Year, my chany.* She nodded and turned to make her way through the singing crowd to join Giles and Pauline behind the counter, giving them each a hug and kiss on the cheek. He wanted to join them, to slip his arm around Claire and assure them that things would not continue on like this forever. But he wasn't one for making promises he couldn't keep. He'd remain vigilant and wait while keeping Hoffenberg out of trouble.

Jumping on his chair and raising his glass high, the newly minted lieutenant grinned like a fool. "*Bleigiessen!* Who has the molten lead?"

He was nothing more than a stalker standing in the shadowy alley behind the bar. It was a gamble, but one worth taking should she come out to throw away the evening's bucket of wastewater and food spoils.

Michael checked his watch for the umpteenth time. The bar had closed an hour ago. It had taken quite a bit of rousing to get the men back to the command post. He ensured they were all accounted for then drove back to town, ducking in dark corners and sneaking around to the back of the pub like some thief.

He pulled his collar higher though his poor ears remained exposed. Numbness bit his feet despite the woolen socks, and even burying his hands in gloves couldn't stave off the cold from stiffening his fingers into icicles.

And all for some girl who may or may not stick her head out the back door.

Snowflakes danced in the sky like tiny cotton puffs. They landed on his nose, but he couldn't feel them. Five minutes more and he'd be a snowman. He'd give her four more minutes and then he was leaving.

His ear cocked, listening for a doorknob turning. Three minutes, two, one. Hunching his shoulders in disappointment, he turned down the alley.

Click. The back door unlocked.

Spinning around with heart racing, he peered around the corner. A slender figure with a long shawl draped over her head and shoulders carried a bucket to the back corner, where she emptied its contents. Michael stepped out of the shadow.

"Claire."

She gasped, swinging her bucket in the air like a cricket bat. "Who—who's there? What do you want?"

"It's me." Michael pushed his cap back so she could see his face.

"Michael? What are you doing here?"

"I wanted to see you. Just for a minute."

She lowered the bucket and took a step toward him. "Have you been out here the whole time? Are you crazy? It's freezing."

"I'm well aware of that." As if on cue, his teeth chattered together. He *was* crazy. "That song you sang tonight, *Dream a Little Dream* ... I found the words to be rather agreeable. Especially the lingering until dawn part." He was rambling like an imbecile. He took a deep breath and tried again. "What I mean is, it gave me—gives me—great hope."

She tipped her chin down, but not before he caught the smile on her lips. "Then I chose right."

"Aye, you did," he said in English. He stepped toward her until she was within arm's reach. Their puffs of breath curled together between them. Grasping her hand, he pressed a kiss to her palm. "Happy New Year, my darling *chany.*"

"Happy New Year, Michael," she whispered, curling her fingers over her palm. "I should be getting back before they come looking—"

"Of course. I shouldn't keep you out here like this." He backed away, not wanting to turn around lest he miss one second of her face.

"Why *chany*?" She asked as he neared the corner.

"The men call you *chanteuse*, but I figure I'm owed the privilege of a shortened version of your nickname. Do you object?"

"No." She pressed her fist to her heart and skipped back inside.

Though he was left in the snow once more, it didn't feel nearly as cold as before. In fact, he felt downright warm.

CHAPTER 16

K nock, knock.
"Enter." Michael didn't look up from his papers.

The office door opened. "This came for you, sir," Hoffenberg said.

Michael glanced up and took the note. It looked like a chicken had scratched all over it. "Who took this?"

"Kruger. I think he was a little nervous as it came from a major's office in Paris."

"You saw him write this?" Michael waved the paper in the air.

"He signaled me over when it mentioned your name."

"Can you translate then? The boy has an excellent ear for words, but his handwriting is atrocious."

Hoffenberg didn't bother looking at the paper. "You are being summoned to Major Kieffer's office in Paris and are ordered to report to 84 Avenue Foch at oh nine hundred tomorrow morning."

A ton of rocks hit Michael in the gut. Major Josef Kieffer was head of the Gestapo, and 84 Avenue Foch specialized in the interrogation of foreign special agents. Like the Special Operations Executive.

He folded the note and creased it with his thumb. "They didn't say why?"

"No, sir. I told Kruger to keep his mouth shut about it."

Rising from his chair, Michael walked to the window. Rain drizzled, turning everything to icy gray slush. Tiny steel bands wrapped around his brain and squeezed hard. *They know.*

But if they knew, then why not arrest him? Maybe they wanted to ease him in and make him feel safe before pouncing.

Michael tugged the hem of his tunic and turned around. "Tell Gestel to bring the auto around front in thirty minutes. He'll drive me to the train station. I'll speak to Hirsch before I leave but inform everyone that I've been called in for a quarterly report." He took a deep breath, dreading the next order. "If you do not hear from me by tomorrow evening, then we have been compromised. Get word back to HQ that there has been a breach. They will give you further instructions."

Hoffenberg's mouth dropped. "But, sir—"

"Second, if I don't return, take the transceiver and destroy it. Immediately. They will be listening for more messages coming out of here. Do you understand?"

Hoffenberg nodded.

"Good. No renegade stunts."

"Yes, sir."

Thirty minutes later, after informing a sleepy Hirsch and throwing an overnight bag together, Michael pulled Hoffenberg aside before stepping out the door.

"If it goes south from here"—his throat tightened—"tell Claire … tell her I'm sorry."

"I'll take care of everything, sir. You just take care of yourself." Hoffenberg stepped back as the arriving auto roared around the corner. "Pleasant journey, sir."

Number 84 Avenue Foch's white façade towered starkly against the gray morning drizzle. Black iron railings spanned each floor's windows, resembling teeth bared in warning to any who passed by. A promise to any who dared enter.

Michael tried to control his breathing. The words of de Vigny played through his head. *Wailing, pleading, crying—these are the coward's call. Assume your heavy and onerous burden, the one that fate has cast your way.*

Fighting the urge to flee, Michael took a deep breath and entered. The sterile foyer with black-and-white parquet floors included a bench next to the front desk. "Captain Michael Reichner here to see Major Kieffer," he said to the desk clerk.

"Papers, please."

Michael pulled the required identification out of his breast pocket and handed it to the sergeant for approval.

"Very good, sir." The sergeant handed his papers back. The black diamond *Sicherheitsdienst* insignia flashed ominously on his sleeve. "Fourth floor to the right. The stairs are over there."

Walking up the stairs, Michael looked neither left nor right as he ignored the lower ranking officials who stood aside for him. He acknowledged his superiors with brief nods. The unmistakable sound of transceiver beeps and button tapping came from an open door at the end of the hallway. Great. They had them here too.

At the fourth floor, an armed guard blocked the next flight of stairs. Michael kept his gaze straight as he entered the one open door ahead of him, knowing the horrors that went on one floor up. He stepped into an assistant's office full of bookcases, filing cabinets, and a desk with three phones on it. A gilded-framed picture of Hitler hung on the wall.

A captain with slicked-back hair looked up from a filing cabinet. Suspicion wrinkled his face. "May I help you?"

"*Heil* Hitler." Michael saluted. "I'm Captain Reichner. I have an appointment with Major Kieffer."

"*Heil* Hitler. Yes, you do." The assistant pushed the drawer in, locked it, and indicated a seat near the window. "Have a seat, please."

Michael sat, balancing his cap on his knee. He took several deep breaths to keep his fingers from twitching.

The man announced Michael's arrival into an intercom. Several minutes passed before a reply crackled from the other end. The assistant stood and opened the door for Michael. "You may go in now."

"Thank you." Michael stood and marched through the door.

Fanciful art dotted the cream walls of the major's office. Plush Persian rugs covered the floor. Airy curtains framed tall windows. The office belonged to a businessman with expensive taste, not the head of the secret police.

A middle-aged man with thinning hair stood in the corner watering a small plant. He hummed but didn't turn around.

Michael stood at attention. "*Heil* Hitler."

Kieffer turned slowly, raised his right arm in response, then turned back to his plant.

The silence stretched Michael's nerves like a snagged fishing line. A grandfather clock's pendulum ticked the seconds. All part of the torture process.

Setting the empty watering can on the table, Kieffer tweaked the plant's leaves before settling in behind his massive oak desk. The leather chair squeaked in protest beneath him. "Sit, Captain Reichner."

Michael tried not to laugh at the spindly chairs placed in front of the desk. More suited to a lady's tearoom, but it held his weight with only a few creaks.

"Did you have a pleasant journey, Captain?"

"Yes, sir. I had hoped to see some of the city, but the weather is rather preventative of such an excursion today."

"Mmm, yes." Kieffer turned his head to the rain-splattered window.

Michael took the opportunity to rub his sweaty palms against his knees.

"I hear your post is doing very well, with daily interceptions of the enemy's transmissions," Kieffer said. "Countless German soldiers' lives have been saved because of your efforts."

"Thank you, sir. My men do their job quite well, and I'm proud to serve with them."

Kieffer nodded, folding his hands on the desk in front of him. "I like to see a man who is proud to serve, and especially one who does a commendable job of leading. Poor leadership and those who take the rules into their own hands do not belong in our ranks. Which is why it distressed me to have a particular report come across my desk."

Not knowing what in the world the man was referring to, Michael nodded and waited.

"Ilsa von Ziegler has been at your post for some time, has she not?"

Too long. Like a barnacle Michael couldn't scrape off. "Yes, sir. First, as part of Major Kessel's touring entourage, and now on orders to arrest known conspirators in the area."

"But you did not know she was undercover?"

"I put the clues together at the end."

Kieffer smiled. "She said you were clever. Too much so to be stuck in some pig town when your talents could be used in Berlin."

"I wouldn't say clever, sir. Merely observant. Captain von Ziegler had a way of interviewing the locals that was more like an interrogation than an afternoon chat at the watering hole."

"Yes, well, that was one of her first assignments alone."

"Ah." Making excuses for poor performance. How about training agents better before sending them out into the field? Then maybe they wouldn't need to make excuses.

"But Captain von Ziegler was able to complete her mission and bring in the three conspirators, though they remain mute." Kieffer's gaze drifted to the ceiling. "We hope to have them talking soon."

Bile burned Michael's throat. If he closed his eyes and listened hard enough, he was sure he could hear the prisoner's screams.

"It's not unusual for the prisoners to refuse to speak," Kieffer said. "Trying to keep their supposed honor. But every once in a while, one of them will crack. Did you know the man named Ansell?" Kieffer inched forward in his chair, his gaze pinned on Michael.

"He is a farmer from the Montbaune area."

"Did you ever speak to him?"

"Not more than an occasional greeting."

"I see." Kieffer's shoulders relaxed. "This man, Ansell, was blubbering like a baby. Crying the name Claire over and over again."

Kieffer paused for a reaction, but Michael didn't give it to him. At least not outwardly. Inside, his heart was ready to leap out of his chest. *One, two, three, breathe in. One, two, three, breathe out.*

"Claire is a local girl who works at the bar," Michael said. "She plays the piano and sings for the customers."

"I see. Whoever she is, he was quite adamant about her innocence. I asked Captain von Ziegler about it. Her report never mentioned such a girl. Do you know why she left out the detail?"

Thunder rumbled as ominous clouds threw the room into darkness. Kieffer switched on a lamp. Its yellowish glow seeped across his desk, highlighting nothing outside of the small ring of light.

"She may have left it out because it was not part of the assignment. You'd have to ask Captain von Ziegler." Surrounded by shadow, Michael swallowed several times to clear the dryness from his throat. Asking for a drink of water was a sure sign of duplicity.

"And what happened to this girl who was arrested?"

"She was taken back home and told to mind her own business."

"Why not let her be taken? One more potential threat eliminated. Surely, after entertaining our soldiers every night, she would have overheard news to carry back to the resistors."

Michael sat straighter in his chair. "Because my men do not have loose tongues in public, sir. Like you, I cannot abide rule breaking. Captain von Ziegler had no call to take that villager, and I will not tolerate insubordination under my command."

"Von Ziegler was not under your command. She was under mine."

"Yes sir, but as ranking officer, I take full responsibility for anything that happens within the radius of my post. If we don't keep order, then we have nothing."

Kieffer's chair squeaked as he leaned back. "That is precisely what I tell my agents before they're sent into the field."

"Captain von Ziegler was kind enough to share it with me."

"I see. And what did you think of her? Ilsa." Kieffer propped his feet on the desk.

Chills broke out on the nape of Michael's neck at the sudden change in tone. "I think she is a fine agent. Ambitious, intelligent, and willing to do what it takes to accomplish her goals."

"And beautiful?"

"She is very attractive. Everything a German lady should be."

"More than some French country peasant?"

The chills turned to ice. "I beg your pardon, sir?"

"Come, come, Captain. We are both men who belong to a powerful nation. A nation that will someday rule the world. In this conquered land we will meet all manner of temptations. A dalliance is one thing, but when it comes to procreating, we must make sure it is with pure blood."

Michael dug his fingernails into his knee to keep from flying across the desk to knock the man's lights out. "I can assure you, sir, there has been no dalliance of any kind. My mission comes first, but when I do decide to expand our great empire, it will be with the right kind of woman."

Pushing out of his chair, Kieffer walked around his desk to perch on the edge. He crossed his arms over his chest and stared at Michael. "I can see why Ilsa was reluctant to bring you to my attention. Next to you, she looks weak and careless. One piece of advice for you, Captain." He leaned forward. "The next time you decide to act on your honorable intentions, don't interfere with my missions. Ever. Understood?"

"Yes, sir."

"Dismissed."

Michael's legs wobbled as he left the office. At the stairs, he gripped the brass handrail, hoping its coolness would calm the burning of his palms. Rain pelted the windows and lightning zinged across the black sky. The lights flickered as he marched down the stairs and toward the exit.

"Captain Reichner, sir." The front desk assistant called as Michael marched past. "The storm is bad, sir. Might I suggest you wait until it lightens and I can call a taxi for you?"

Michael shook his head and kept walking. Yanking up the collar of his overcoat, he stepped into the rain.

He had escaped the Gestapo. He would not stay in that building one second longer than he had to. Not when Hoffenberg was expecting his phone call.

CHAPTER 17

"Fish heads? What do you expect me to do with those?" Remy dropped the heads back onto the parchment with disgust.

Claire pushed it toward him. "The same as you would with pig tails and cow knuckles."

"Lady, don't you know how to make a deal? You offer me something I might actually want. And fish heads aren't it."

"I don't have anything else to offer." Except her stash of tips hidden under her bed, but she needed that for the journey home. Then again, if Remy refused to give her the names of those willing to smuggle people out, there would be no journey home.

Remy screwed his mouth to spit, then shot a glance at her before he swallowed. "No jewelry, fine clothes, old coins, vegetable seeds?" He snapped his fingers. "I traded two rabbits with the butcher. They should've bred a whole passel by now. Get me a few of those, and we'll talk."

"Firmin is protective of those rabbits. He gives them to the families with the most mouths to feed."

"That's sweet. Find me some better deals and then you'll have room to bargain." Remy started for the back door.

Claire grabbed his arm, then dropped it. "I'm sorry. I just … I have to get out of here."

His eyebrows pinched together. "You think you're the only person who wants to get out of this country? Last month I had a man try to sell me his front teeth for a ticket."

"In a few months, my garden will start to bloom. I can pay you in vegetables then."

Remy shook his head. "I don't do favors or give loans. Don't you have anything else now? Extra ration stamps, sacks of flour, coffee? The real stuff, not that chicory mess. Ah, what's that glint I see in your eye? You've got coffee?"

"Well, Pauline has a small can of it," said Claire. "But it's not mine to give away."

"They know you're trying to get out, right? Just ask her for it."

"No, I can't. She's saving it to celebrate the day that France is free again."

"She might be waiting a while." Remy started for the door again. "Look, if you're afraid of asking for a can of coffee, then you might want to reconsider trying to get out of here. Escaping takes backbone. Grit. Determination. Sorry, *mignonne*, but you don't seem the type to muck it."

He might as well have dashed her face with cold water. "I'll prove you wrong, *monsieur*."

"I'll be back next week for the lesson then." A grin broke across his pock-marked face. "*Bonne chance*."

As the door closed, Claire sagged against a stack of empty crates. What a complete failure. What payment could she come up with that was valuable enough to tempt him? Wrapping the fish heads back in their parchment, she marched into the kitchen.

Pauline glanced over her shoulder. "Didn't want the heads, I see. Worth a try, but when's a smuggler going to find time to add them to a boiling stew?"

Claire set the heads on a cutting board and pulled out a long knife to saw through the skulls. "He'll be back next week, so I have a little time to think of a better offer."

"Or none at all. Maybe it's a sign you should stay here. Where it's safe."

"Nazi-occupied France, or any occupied country for that matter, is anything but safe."

"So is trying to sneak past the Nazis." Pauline banged her spoon on the boiling pot, then started chopping cabbage. "At least if you stay, you'll have a roof over your head with a hot meal most nights.

Oh yes, and you won't be living in fear of getting caught and sent to a work camp."

Claire's heart squeezed. Was her family still alive wherever they were? If only Michael had news. She tossed the cleaned heads into the pot. "I have to try."

With her butcher knife Pauline hacked into a head of cabbage. "You'll leave us in the lurch. How many other girls do you think we can find that play, sing, and wait tables? We finally got you to the point where you don't spill anything."

Wiping her scale-covered hands on her apron, Claire wrapped her arms around Pauline's thick shoulders. "I've been practicing."

"What's all this?"

Claire looked up to find Giles glowering in the doorway.

"The girl still wants to leave us, but that old boot won't take fish heads for payment." Pauline shrugged Claire off.

Giles rubbed his shoulder against the doorframe and looked at Claire. "What's he want then?"

"Jewelry, vegetables, rabbits." Her gaze slid to Pauline's stiff back. "Coffee."

Pauline spun around cleaver in hand. "Coffee? My coffee? Why'd you tell him about that?"

"I didn't. He guessed, but I told him no because you're saving it to celebrate the day the Germans march out."

"Hmph." Pauline snorted. Something sparked in her eye before she turned back to her cutting board. "Should give it to him anyway, the old swindler. It's over a year old with hardly any smell left to it, but we can seal it tight and he'll never know."

Claire frowned. "I don't think giving him expired coffee will help my cause any."

Pauline waved a hand in the air and turned back to her cabbage. "Bah. He deserves it after selling me soggy cigarettes for New Year's."

"Firmin has rabbits. They get a high payout on the black market and Remy won't be able to turn it down." Giles fingered his faded suspenders, snapping them against his barrel chest. "I know he doesn't part easily with them, but maybe a few extra bottles of wine could change his mind."

"Maybe." Claire turned away and picked fish scales from her knife so as not to let Giles see the dread creeping over her at the mention of Firmin. She had no desire to set foot in that butcher shop ever again. Not with Savon sneering at her. He could expose her at any minute. Giles and Pauline might never trust her again if they knew. As terrible as that would be, it was nothing compared to what awaited Michael if his secret got out. She could never live with herself if his downfall came because of her.

And Michael. She had to be careful there too. After his sudden disappearance a few weeks ago, she'd flown into a panic fearing he'd been caught … or worse. When he came into the bar a few nights later as if nothing had happened, she nearly cried for joy right in the middle of a song. Under Giles' watchful eye, she barely had a moment alone with him, no more than enough time with Michael to assure her everything was all right.

It had been a wakeup call as to how quickly everything could change. One day he could be gone, or they could come for her, or for Giles and Pauline. Claire trusted Michael, but it wasn't wise to put all her eggs in one basket if she wanted to get out of France. If she wanted out, *she* would be the one to make it happen. Even if it meant leaving those she'd come to care for.

"Go over to Firmin's and ask if he'll make the deal." Giles pulled her basket from the shelf and put in two bottles of wine. "Take these and tell him he can have his choice of two more for the rabbits."

"But these are your best bottles. I have a little money stashed away that I can offer instead." Claire tried taking the bottles out, but Giles stopped her.

"Keep it for the journey."

"*If* there's a journey," Pauline muttered. "She should just stay here."

"Go on now." Giles looped Claire's arm through the basket handle and pushed her out the door. "The patrons will be here soon."

Claire's stomach knotted. Her once-simple plan to head south was turning into a strange saga of fish heads, soggy cigarettes, bargains with the butcher, and a complication of the heart dressed in a Nazi uniform.

"Claire."

Great. Now she was hearing him too. What she wouldn't give to hear her name in that Irish lilt—

"Claire!"

She looked up. Michael strode across the road, tall and confident. Her heart skipped a beat and she struggled to keep from running to him.

A smile lit his face as he drew near. "What are you doing out here? I thought you'd be getting ready for the day's performance."

"I'm—I have to run a quick errand."

His smile widened as his gaze drifted over her face. "I'm so glad to see you."

The knots in her stomach gave way to butterflies. If the time came, how was she going to tell him goodbye? "You're supposed to be on duty. Or does that consist of instilling fear into the hearts of the locals?"

"Not exactly." He glanced over his shoulder. The once-humming shop fronts stood silently behind his military Kübelwagen. "I ran out of black polish and was hoping to find some. I think the owner hides it from me in the back."

Claire glanced over Michael's shoulder to see Eloy peeking out the corner of his window. He gave her a short wave and scowled at Michael's back. "I think you may be right."

"Since my shopping trip has been cancelled, may I escort you somewhere?"

She ached to take hold of his offered arm. To brush her fingers over his exposed wrist. Instead, she gripped her basket tighter to keep from reaching out and stepped back. "It's not necessary."

"Because the entire town is watching us from behind their drawn curtains?"

"That's one reason." And because if he asked her to right now, she'd run away with him. "My destination is only a few steps away."

He eyed the covered outlines of bottles in her basket, then looked over her shoulder. A frown creased his brow. "I thought you were trying to stay away from the butcher shop."

She fluffed the linen around her cargo, not wanting to meet his eye lest his human lie detector sniff out what she was really doing. "Sacrifices must be made to get the best chops."

Eloy stepped through his door with a broom in one hand and the other balled on his hip, a scowl on his face. He started toward her.

"The town constable is coming. I'm glad you ran out of shoe polish," she whispered. Taking another step away from Michael, she announced in a louder and more annoyed voice, "Good day to you, *Capitaine*."

Even as she entered the butcher shop, she could feel Michael's eyes on her. For a split second, she thought of running back to him to throw her arms around him. She'd only been in his arms once, but she often dreamed of returning.

"Ah, Claire. What a delight to see you." Firmin grinned and wiped his hands on his apron. He eyed the basket in her hand. "Come, come to the back where we may talk."

The sound of a knife hitting bone drifted in from the back room. Savon. "No need, this will be quick." She put the basket on the counter and lifted the linen to reveal two green bottles. "Giles' best wine for two of your rabbits. And, you may choose two more from his stock."

Firmin's brow wrinkled. "You know I don't part with my rabbits easily."

"I understand, but you have a handful of them. You would hardly miss two from the newest litter." She pushed the basket closer to him so he could see the coveted labels. "What do you say?"

Firmin touched a thick finger to the 1921 Merlot, a wistful gleam in his eye. "You've never offered something this special before."

"I've never wanted live animals before."

He dropped his hand and flicked his gaze to her. "Savon. Come in here and bring our guest."

Savon stomped in, took one look at her, and glowered. Remy sauntered in behind him.

"Quick work getting over here." Remy grinned. "No wasting time. I like that. Comes in handy with this kind of work."

Claire ignored Savon and eyed Remy with suspicion. If he was here, he'd have no reason to deal with her for the rabbits and she'd have nothing left to bargain for the smugglers' names. "What are you doing here?"

"Giles isn't my sole customer. But you should be thrilled. Things can go much faster this way."

Firmin turned to Remy with a frown. "What kind of trade are you doing with Claire that she wants my rabbits?"

Remy rolled his eyes. "Get off the rabbits. You can breed a hundred more in a week with the two I left."

"You took the rabbits?" Firmin would never sell the two left. Not when he could make his own profits from them. With no rabbits to barter, Claire's plan was out the window. Hopelessness tugged at her. She'd have to think of something else.

Remy shrugged, but his eyes held no apology. "Sorry. Got to be quick if you want to deal with me."

"She wants to give them to the German." Savon spat.

All eyes turned to him.

Firmin spoke first. "My son, what do you mean by that?"

Claire clenched her teeth and stared at Savon, daring him to go on so she could hurl that 1921 Merlot at his fat head. "He thinks that because I have to sing and wait tables for the Germans, I've become soft toward them. And then he has the gall to call me … to say … unspeakable names."

Red singed Savon's ears. "You're sneaking around in the woods with that captain. You've been dirtied just by talking to him."

She slammed her hand on the counter. "How dare you?"

"Savon, shut your mouth!" Firmin's neck turned the same mottled red as his son's. "I will not have you talk that way to ladies and customers in my shop."

"Lady?" Savon snorted. "I'm sure she lost that some time ago."

"Shut up." Claire hissed. "You filthy little worm."

Remy leaned against the counter and grinned. "Guess this means any kind of engagement between the two of you is off. Not to mention the rabbits."

"As if I would ever consider marrying someone like *him*." Glaring, Claire grabbed her basket and marched out the door. It was enough to worry about finding another bargaining chip as good as the rabbits. Now she would also have to worry about Savon's accusations flying around town. They would kill Giles and Pauline. Even if Claire convinced them there was no affair, they might not ever look at her the same. And that would break Claire's heart.

What of Michael? Seeing him would encourage the accusations. But not seeing him … that would break her heart too.

Gathering a tray full of empty bottles and dirty mugs, Claire trudged into the back hall. Another hour and the soldiers would start to leave. It seemed an eternity before she would be able to disappear into the solitude of her room and forget the whole forsaken day.

"I hear your engagement is called off."

The tray quivered in her hands at the familiar voice. A hand shot from the dark and grabbed it before it spilled over.

"Hope you're not too disappointed," Michael said.

"Don't be absurd. He—were you listening outside the shop?"

Balancing the tray on the palm of his hand, Michael shook his head. "I've got ears everywhere. Remember?"

"Great. I'm sure the entire town now believes I had some kind of understanding with that swine. Despicable rumors."

"That's a relief. I'm terrible at picking out wedding gifts."

She glared at him. "Your flippancy doesn't help the matter. Who knows what else Savon has been spouting."

"Firmin put the fear of God into Savon after you left, but even so. That boy doesn't know when to keep his mouth shut. Neither does Remy. What business did you have with him?"

Nerves jittered down her backbone. This was not what she wanted to talk about. His nearness wreaked enough havoc on its own. "You know the trades we do with him."

"You didn't discuss illegal cigarettes and imported whisky though, did you?"

"It's none of your business."

Pots and pans crashed to the floor. A string of lively curses flew out the kitchen door. "Where is that mop?" Pauline screeched.

The mop and bucket leaned against the wall a mere two feet away. Another second and Pauline would stomp out the door and spot a very unwelcome German officer lounging in the hallway. Grabbing the tray from him, Claire shoved him behind a stack of crates. "Stay here," she whispered before snatching the mop.

She raced into the kitchen. Shoving the mop into Pauline's hands, Claire ran back out and ducked into the shadows where Michael hid. "You can't keep showing up like this or running across the street shouting my name or stalking me through the woods like some deer. People will get suspicious."

"And what suspicions might those be?" His husky voice buzzed in her ears.

"That I do more than sing to keep the Germans entertained. That I've become mistress to their captain. Why would they not think so when you rescue me from being arrested, loan me books, and stand in the alley for secret meetings after hours? Do you know the trouble, the hurt, this could cause? Which is all the more reason—" She licked her lips to steady her jumping nerves. "You should stay away."

He edged closer, setting her heart pounding. "That's why you've been avoiding me all night. I'm afraid you're not going to push me away that easily."

"Watch me." She jabbed him in the chest, but he didn't budge. "You've got a job to do here. An important one that needs no distractions. I've got a job to do too. To survive and get back home."

Candlelight flickered on his drawn face. "That's what you were speaking to Remy about, isn't it? Smuggling you out?"

"And what if it was? The fighting is getting worse every day. What if the Germans find out who I am? You won't be able to rush in like the last time. Ilsa may have been fooled, but others will not. I can't risk endangering Giles and Pauline like that."

"So you'd trust your life to someone like Remy? A swindler? That cheat would sell his own mother for the right price."

"I don't have the time or luxury to scruple over character flaws. If I wait too much longer, Ilsa could waltz in and march me to her torture chambers."

"Why can't you trust me to help? Given time, I can find a way to get you home."

"Trust is rather unreliable in your line of work."

He cursed under his breath. Good. If he got mad enough, he might leave. Then she wouldn't have to tear herself away from him.

"Claire, I can assure you—"

"No! You can't. You can't assure me of safety, of getting out of here, of you not getting caught."

"I am not going to get caught."

"You were just hauled away to Gestapo headquarters with no warning." She hissed, struggling to keep her voice quiet. "I was crazy with worry."

"But I came back, didn't I?"

"What if one day, God forbid, you don't?"

"I will not leave you here. I swear to it."

His determination to see her to safety cracked the fear around her heart. A ray of hope slipped inside, sparking a courage that she had kept buried beneath her self-preservation. Her gaze dropped to his mouth.

She must have been out of her mind thinking she could keep him at arm's length. Cupping his face, she stood on tiptoe and pressed her lips to his. He stood still for a second, then wrapped his arms around her.

Gliding her hand to the back of his neck, her fingers brushed the cold, studded insignia and stiff collar, so different from the warmth and gentleness of his kiss. He pulled her closer, circling his arms tighter until she could almost feel his heart beating through his chest. Life and all its problems faded away. She was alone with the one man who made her heart spin. Brave and true, he filled her world with possibilities she never knew existed. She could never let him go.

Pots crashed. Claire jumped back, heat burning her face and panic shooting through her. She peeked around crates. The hallway was empty.

She turned back to Michael, her pulse quickening. "You need to leave. Now."

"I can come back later. After everyone leaves."

"No. Get out of here before someone sees you."

She shoved him away, but even in a hurry he never lost his composure. He opened the back door and reached for her hand. "Claire?"

Despite the warning sirens in her head, she accepted the comfort he offered and took his hand. "Michael—"

Michael's gaze snapped to something over her shoulder. His fingers tightened around hers. "Allow me to explain."

Horrified, Claire dropped Michael's hand and turned around. Giles stood in the hall, hands on hips, mouth wide. He snapped it shut. "*Capitaine*. Have you lost your way?" Anger seethed in Giles' voice.

Michael lifted his chin and threw his shoulders back. "No, sir. I was merely—"

"I'll ask you to leave now." Giles' shoes smacked against the floor as he marched forward. "You may have all the business you like in the front, but not back here. Everything back here is off limits. This is still my bar."

"Forgive me, sir. I did not mean to overstep my bounds." Michael tilted his head in acknowledgment. "And I did not mean to impose myself upon Claire. It was my fault."

"Leave. Please."

"Good night, sir. Claire." Settling his cap on his head, Michael gave her one last look before closing the door behind him.

Claire clasped her hands to hold on to Michael's last touch of comfort. Turning, she faced the wrath bearing down on her.

CHAPTER 18

Claire swallowed hard against the panic flaring inside her. "Let me explain."

Giles' eyes snapped with fury. Air blasted from his nose. "There's nothing to explain unless you dare to tell me my eyes aren't to be believed."

"He's not who you think he is."

"No? Then tell me who he really is. As if you know."

Claire bit her tongue. She could never tell the truth about Michael. It could cost him his life, but the accusations against him were more than she could stomach. "He's good. He's kind and considerate. He's not like the other Germans at all. He hates this war as much as we do."

Giles slammed his fist on top of a barrel. "He's a Nazi! A cold-blooded murderer. Nothing else. They're all the same no matter how many lies they beguile you with to slip into your bed."

His words slapped her across the face, stinging her cheeks with anger. "That's not fair! Michael has never done anything to compromise me like that. He values honor too much. And how dare you accuse me of allowing a man such liberties?"

"*Michael*? You call him by his name? If you give him a name, he becomes a person, a man. He is anything but!"

"He is a person with a beating heart that's saddened and revolted by this ugliness. If you would only talk to him, you'd see—"

"I don't need to talk to him. I heard the lies before when I was a much younger man and tried to believe in the good in everyone. Their deception was a brutal lesson that I don't need to learn again." His chest heaved as he moved closer, pointing a finger in her face. "You are never to see him again."

Claire jerked away before his hand smacked her nose. "That's impossible if he comes to the bar."

"Then I'll lock you in your room."

"Like a child? You are not my father, Giles."

"No, but you are under my roof, and I make the final decisions." His lips clamped together as he spun away. Running a hand through his hair, he kicked the wall until his shoulders sagged. When he turned back to her, sadness lined his face. "You are not a child, and you're free to leave at any time if you wish, but while you are here, you'll not speak to him or see him alone again." He stalked to the curtain and whipped around, his jaw working back and forth. "Bah." He yanked aside the curtain and disappeared into the bar.

Claire bit back a scream. She glanced at the door and wished she could tear into the night and find Michael. They could steal away and leave this place behind forever. And go where? Ireland with his parents? What about her own home in America? There was also Michael's mission. His commander would be none too happy if he failed to complete it. And what about all the lives that depended on him? To ask him to give up his duty would be the most selfish thing she could do.

Before she could make such a foolish mistake, she raced up the stairs and shut herself in her room, sagging against the door. She could never do that to Michael. It would blow his cover and get them both arrested. Or killed. She squeezed her eyes shut as tears of frustration welled.

Pushing away from the door, she sat on the bed as the rage slowed, letting her sizzling mind cool. She was to blame for the impossible situation she now found herself in. Not Giles. He only meant to protect her, and she'd betrayed his trust.

If only she could tell him the truth. About Michael. About herself. But that could never be. Not until the war was over and the danger passed. The truth carried too many responsibilities. She wouldn't foist those on her friends. The less they knew, the safer they would be.

KNOCK! KNOCK!

Only one person battered the door like that. "Come in, Pauline."

Pauline came in and shut the door behind her. She hooked her hands in front of her and stared at Claire. "What was that all about?"

Claire looked away. How did she even begin to explain? No matter what she said, there was no right answer.

Sighing, Pauline crossed the room and eased onto the bed next to her. "A relationship with such a man is impossible."

The gentleness in her words drew Claire's attention. "He's not the monster Giles makes him out to be."

The customary sharpness in Pauline's gaze softened. "I see the way he looks at you, the way his eyes never leave you in the bar. And how you smile every time he comes in."

"Then you can see the goodness in him."

"I see how the heart follows without sense. If you continue with this man, where does it lead? What happens when the war is over? Think again if you have dreams of joining him in Germany. You'll be left here, where you've been labeled a Nazi mistress." Pauline leaned close as seriousness burned in her eyes. "Do you know what the villagers did to those women after the last war? They dragged them into the streets, tore their clothing off, and shaved their heads. No good man wanted them. Can you live with that shame?"

Claire jumped off the bed and paced the tiny room as the walls closed in like a cage. The truth of their identities wrestled on her tongue, desperate to burst out. She swallowed it back.

At least there was one part she could tell. Pauline wouldn't like it, but there was no point in denying it. "You're right. Captain Reichner flatters me with his attention. He's easy to talk to, and more than once he's come to my rescue when he didn't have to lift a finger. It feels good to attract a man like him, and if this war had never drawn us as enemies, I think we could have made a real go of it." She stopped moving to face Pauline. "But we are at war, and I don't want to end up like Amaline."

Pauline sucked in a breath.

"I also don't want to bring trouble to the bar by betraying the trust you and Giles have given me. I'm so grateful for everything you've done. You two mean the world to me."

The older woman sat quietly for a moment, then nodded. She rose from the bed and walked to the door. "Swear to me you'll never see him again."

"I promise." Claire's gut twisted over the falsehood. She never went back on her word, but the situation was so tangled that she could no longer determine if lies or truth were the better option.

After Pauline left, Claire moved to the window. She pressed her forehead to the cool glass as pain throbbed around her temples. Being on the wrong foot with Giles and Pauline was one of the worst things she had ever done. She depended on them far beyond the room and board. She needed their generosity and friendship. As unlikely as it had seemed, they'd become her family, and she'd hurt them by falling for the wrong man.

She gazed down at the alley and imagined Michael standing below as he'd done before. Tears welled in her eyes. "Please take me away from here soon."

CHAPTER 19

The transceiver beeped. *Do not jeopardize mission for one woman.* Michael pushed away his frustration and tapped back. *Mission is safe. Woman may not be.*

Mission not as safe as you think. Be on lookout. Name has crossed Gestapo papers more than once.

The Gestapo? Brilliant. One more reason to get Claire out of here. *Too close for comfort?*

Not yet. Keep nose clean as long as possible. Will alert if compromised like Berlin killings.

Dread prickled Michael's fingertips. *What killings?*

Guther and Schulze. Two weeks ago. Michael's gut twisted at the news. *Keep alert, IS. Over and out.*

Static crackled in the headset. Guther and Schulze. Dead. The words tapped over and over in Michael's brain. He'd dodged explosions beside those men for almost two months during SOE training. The Nazis would leave their corpses to rot and be eaten by crows as a warning to other spies. Like him.

With shaking hands, Michael put the transceiver back into its hiding spot. Clenching his fists several times, he willed himself to calm down. The war had taken so much and would continue to take until there was nothing left. Or until the Nazis were beaten once and for all.

He opened the door. "Hoffenberg!" His lookout hurried up the stairs into Michael's room. "I have a job for you." Michael closed the door. "I need you to take a message to the bar. Tell Claire I'll be waiting outside after the last customer leaves."

"It's a shame you got kicked out of there, boss. Don't know if

I'd be able to stomach getting banned from having a drink at the end of the day."

"I'm not banned. Just unwelcome."

Hoffenberg shuffled his feet. "She's pretty upset about what happened the other night. You can cut the tension in that place with a knife. Old man won't even look at her. What if she don't want to see you?"

Michael cursed himself. He'd caused the rift between Giles and Claire and, though he may never be able to completely heal it, he *could* take her away to safety. That was all Giles wanted for her. It was a twisted way to make up for the mess Michael had caused, but he would never feel ashamed of that kiss. Even if he never saw her again, he would always remember her touch and warmth. "Tell her I have no qualms about banging on the front door."

"Any word on when that blonde vampire is coming back? Been nice not having her breathing down my neck."

"I'll say." Michael rubbed the back of his own neck as if Ilsa stood behind him. "No, I haven't heard anything since she left for Paris. With any luck, the lights of the big city will be too much of a big a draw for her to return to the country." He could hope all he wanted, but something in his gut told him otherwise.

After Hoffenberg left, Michael attempted to complete paperwork until the bar's closing time. Finally, the hour came. He drove to town and parked at the end of the street, then walked to the alley behind the pub. Above, a window cracked open. Claire's head popped out as she searched the darkness below. Michael waved. She waved back and closed the window. A few minutes later, the back door opened, and she hurried toward him.

"Michael, if we're caught—"

He pulled her into his arms and pressed a kiss to her warm lips. She sighed against him, sending his blood racing. She was sweeter than anything he'd ever tasted. An entire lifetime spent holding this woman would never be enough. But first, he needed to get her out of there. Tearing his mouth away, he pushed her to arm's length.

Her eyes fluttered open. "You're crazy to come here. Every afternoon before the regulars come in, Giles takes to shining the shotgun he keeps under the counter. He never did that before finding you in the back hallway."

Michael rubbed his thumb over her chin and smiled. "He won't shoot me. There's no way he could get my body out the door without someone noticing."

"Want to bet?"

Clamping his teeth together, Michael tried not to let his frustration get the better of him. Giles wanted him for target practice. The Gestapo kept notes on him. Ilsa and Dietrich were thick as thieves, surely plotting against him. It was only a matter of time before he got caught. He dropped his hands from her arms. "You're leaving here. I'm not sure when, but soon. You need to be ready the moment I send word."

Her slender eyebrows shot up. "You … you've worked something out? But how?"

"Don't worry about the details. I'm still working on them." She didn't need to know that he hadn't started yet. He'd go off the cuff if it came to it. "Don't stop the charade just yet. You're doing beautifully, my *chany*."

She sighed and shuffled her feet over the dirt. "I want to tell them. Giles and Pauline. They deserve to know the truth after everything they've done for me."

"No." His voice was more forceful than he intended. He cleared his throat and tried again. "You cannot tell anyone anything. Not until this war is over. The fewer people who know, the less they have to hide if they're asked. Do not burden them with the truth."

Her eyes searched his. "Is this how you live every day? Keeping things locked away until you feel like an island, isolated from the world?"

"It's how I survive. And how you will continue to survive. After we beat those Jerries back, then you can tell them. Not before."

"You'll tell them with me, won't you?" She brushed her featherlight fingers over his cheek, branding his skin with her touch. "I won't have them hating you."

Yes. But he couldn't say it aloud. He would not promise her something that might never come to pass. She may be able to escape the war, but he was stuck until the bitter end. He prayed the war's end would not be his own.

He reached for her again. "I will do everything in my power. I swear to it."

CHAPTER 20

"You sure you want to do it this way, boss?"

"Can you think of a better way?"

Hoffenberg snapped a twig off a bush as they rounded the back corner of the house. "You lovebirds could sneak away in the middle of the night."

Michael shook his head. "The whole town needs to see her arrested, that way they'll keep their mouths shut. Instill a little fear."

"Aren't you afraid of what your girl's going to think when you label her a spy?"

"The angrier she is, the more believable it will be. After we get far enough away, I'll deal with her anger." Not to mention dealing with his commander. Michael would have a lot of explaining to do if he wasn't court-martialed first.

Pale moonlight illuminated a slush puddle on the garden path. Michael stepped high over it to spare his polished boots. "Have you spoken to your men already?"

"Got the confirmation yesterday. They'll be waiting to take her as far as the Spanish border where a contact should meet her with further directions. How far do you think she'll need to go before finding Allied troops?"

"Seeing as how Spain is divided on the issue, it might take some time to find friendlies. If she gets to Portugal, then she can find a supply ship or plane bound for England. From there the American embassy or the Red Cross can assist her in getting stateside."

Hoffenberg snorted. "Simple as that, eh? Glad you're in charge and not me."

"It's a lot of turning wheels, but the hardest part will be getting out of France with all the borders on lockdown and road patrols everywhere."

"Don't worry about that. My boys know how to handle them should the Jerries come along. They'll have enough ammo to light up the whole countryside." Hoffenberg kicked a snow-encrusted rock into the bushes and slowed his pace. "You sure you want to come back, boss?"

"My mission's not done here," Michael said. "I stay until headquarters calls me back. Or until there's a target painted on my head."

"Hate to point this out, but there's been a big fat target on you since the day you took the oath. You just keep making it bigger."

Michael's lips twisted. "This stunt will add the perfect bull's-eye."

"That it will. They'll wonder why you arrested this country girl only to have her disappear." Hoffenberg stopped and faced him. "Take her and run, boss. Go back to the island, get a farm, and raise a passel of fat babies. Forget all this."

Michael shoved his hands deeper into his coat pockets. It would be easy to slip away with Claire. To carve out a peaceful life somewhere, just the two of them. No more lying or living with the same men he was supposed to hate. Never again wear the uniform of a murderer. It would be so easy to give up, but ... "I'm not shirking my duty while our boys face the beast every day."

Hoffenberg groaned. "Guess I'll have to face them with you. Especially that Dietrich. I swear his eyes glow red."

"You haven't caught him snooping around again, have you?"

"No, sir. Just mumbles a lot when he's had a few too many at the bar. Seems to think he's going to be the big man around here someday."

"Guess he hasn't figured out that ticking off his CO is the wrong way to go about it."

Rounding the front of the house, Michael swept his gaze past the fence and barren trees. Just over the hill, nestled in the edge of darkness of Mountbaune, Claire would be starting her song. It had been over two weeks since he'd last seen her, and the separation was driving him crazy.

If he did nothing else, he would get her out before things fell around their heads. She'd be gone forever, but she would be safe. That was enough to give him hope. Hope that she could continue her music dreams and hope that he might have something to live for after the war.

A chill swept from the inky sky, ruffling the edges of his coat. On its tail came a chaser of burning logs and blackened chicory coffee. Kruger must be in the kitchen again. If only the next few months would zip by, so the sweet smell of roses filled the air. Ah, roses and … tobacco? His nose scrunched. "Did you light a cigarette?"

"No, sir."

Michael scanned the yard for movement. Nothing. Except a stylish black auto parked in the drive. No one around here owned an auto like that. What thickheaded bum was out driving after curfew? He grabbed his Luger as they approached the vehicle. He stepped to the driver's side window and peered in. Empty.

Hoffenberg pulled his Luger at the passenger side. "Empty, sir."

Michael touched a hand to the bonnet. Still warm. Cigarette smoke wafted toward him again. Flieger cigarettes. And only one person he knew smoked those. Dread shivered down his spine. "Ilsa?"

A warm, cherry glow smoldered near the front stoop. A lean figure with blonde hair silvered by the moonlight stepped away from the door. "Hello, Michael." Ilsa tapped her ashes onto the wilted rose bush. "Miss me?"

A curse, vile and bitter, clawed in his throat. "What are you doing here?"

Her thick overcoat did little to hide the swish of her hips as she sashayed forward. "Isn't she a beauty? Cream leather seats with hand stitching and she purrs like a kitten, though I couldn't begin to tell you what kind of engine she has. Whittler, my driver, could tell you the specifics if you—why, Michael. Is a gun necessary?"

He still had it aimed straight at her. He shoved it back into the holster. "Apologies, but we weren't expecting visitors."

"Yes, about that." She perched a hip against the hood. "I would have called, but we couldn't find a decent place to stop for the night. Have you seen some of the rat holes they call hotels around here? *Brutto*."

Her coy attitude raked across his nerves like a thousand nails. "Why are you here, Ilsa?"

"Always business first with you, isn't it Michael? Just like that night at the farmhouse. You were so adamant about following the rules." She threw her spent cigarette on the ground and crushed it with her shoe. "I've almost forgiven you for throwing me over for a peasant girl."

It hit him like lightning. She'd come for blood. His. "I must apologize for causing you such angst. It's an unworthy comparison, you and a simple barmaid. Like champagne to soda water."

She laughed and trailed a gloved finger across his coat, circling one of the silver buttons. "Flattery will get you far, Captain."

He forced a smile and shifted so her finger fell off his coat. "But following orders will get *you* even further, Captain."

"There you go again. Oh, all right." She huffed as she adjusted her fur collar. "Kieffer has sent me back to tidy a few loose strings. He feels we may have more spies in the area, and your post is the perfect place to catch them. It seems some of their operations use the radios to convey messages."

Of course, spies used the radio. Deciphering their codes was part of COMMS operations, and she well knew it. "A shame your last roundup didn't catch them all."

"Isn't it though? I think they're using our equipment and personnel."

"A plausible theory."

"A hunch really. The townsfolk have direct access to our soldiers.

It's so easy for them to eavesdrop or get a few of our men drunk enough to spill some secrets. Good beer, lively music, and a pretty face can do wonders on a Friday night."

Blood pumped through his head. Ilsa wanted Claire swinging right alongside him. "I wish you the best of luck as you track the culprits."

"That means a lot coming from you, Michael. I think we'll have fun doing this assignment."

Michael's ears buzzed. "We?"

"Well, yes." She blinked several times as if his misunderstanding surprised her. "I believe the traitors are using our radios, so I'll need to monitor them. Or rather your men will monitor them for me."

Frustration blazed in his chest. This broad was out of her Nazi-loving mind. "My men already scan the frequencies for such things, amongst a long list of other actions. I'm sorry, but we can't stop our fulltime operations just for you."

Ilsa's mouth flattened into a tight line. Reaching into her pocket, she yanked out a cigarette and lighter. "As disrupting as they are, these are Major Kieffer's orders."

With some major persuasion from her, no doubt. He pinched the bridge of his nose to ease the building tension in his head. And that blasted buzzing that grew louder with each second. "Bloody irritating."

Ilsa gasped. "I beg your pardon?"

"My headache. Might we go inside where it's warmer? It feels about ready to snow again."

Once inside, Michael shrugged out of his coat and hung it next to the front door. "Lieutenant, have a room arranged for Captain von Ziegler. I'm sure she's rather tired after her journey. Then take over for Hirsch while I speak with him in my office."

"Yes, sir." Hoffenberg clicked his heels and stomped up the stairs to make room for their unwanted visitor.

"Michael?" Ilsa followed him to his office. "I was hoping we might have a moment together before Hirsch comes in."

Michael squeezed the brass doorknob with all his might. Taking a deep breath, he pushed open the door. "Of course." Ilsa sidled into the room with Michael right behind her, but the room was already occupied.

Michael slammed the door behind him. "What are you doing in my office?" He glared at Dietrich, who stood with his hip cocked against the massive mahogany desk. The smirk disappeared from his face as he snapped to attention. Michael turned to Savon, who sat in a chair in front of the desk. "I didn't order any meat."

"I brought him." Ilsa sank into one of the overstuffed chairs by the bookcase and studied him through a veil of half-closed lashes. "I thought you might like to hear what he has to say. After all, it's part of what's brought me here."

Michael approached his desk and leaned across the gleaming wood top, searing Savon with a cold stare. "What are you doing here?"

Savon rolled a grimy cap between his thick hands. "She brought me." He jerked a thumb over his shoulder at Ilsa.

A muscle ticked in Michael's jaw. "I assume that's because you have something to say."

Hatred burned in Savon's eyes. "You won't like it."

"I'll like it even less if you keep dragging this on."

Savon's hatred burned brighter. "I might have the name of someone trying to flee the country. Someone who interests you."

"Is that right? Who is this person of interest, and why is this so important that you'd break curfew to come to a German outpost to rat him out?"

"Not him. Her."

Michael's heart sank like a mortar. *My darling Claire. I'm so sorry.* He pressed his lips together. "The singer. That's who you're talking about, isn't it?"

Savon's lips twisted. "You know it is. You're with her often enough."

"Play nice, Savon." Ilsa picked at her red nails, the sound grating

Michael's nerves. "You promised."

Michael allowed the corner of his mouth to tilt despite the curse curling his tongue. "You'd throw that girl to the wolves just because she rejected you. How chivalrous."

Red spilled across Savon's cheeks. "She's a traitor. Probably a Jew."

"What is it you want out of this?"

The boy peeked at Ilsa. She remained absorbed with her nails. "There's rewards for anyone caught trying to escape."

Michael dropped into his chair and laced his fingers over his stomach. "And you assume she's trying to escape because she has contact with Remy Legrand. Oh, yes. I know all about Remy and his supplies. There's not much in this town, or whole area for that matter, that I don't know about. I also happen to know that there are no rewards for turning people in because it's considered your civic duty to do so. Do you realize it's punishable to blackmail an officer of the Reich?"

"I offered the reward, Michael." Satisfaction glinted in Ilsa's eyes. "I thought it would make things go … smoother. For all of us."

"Clever deal and smart of you to take it, Savon." Michael steepled his fingertips. "But unfortunately, it's something I'm already aware of and have been for some time. Thanks for coming in. Sergeant Dietrich, see our courageous boy out."

"Now wait just a minute." Savon jumped to his feet with fists clenched at his sides. "You can't push me out like this. I want what's due me." He spun around to Ilsa. "You promised me things. You promised protection for my father's store."

"And you shall have it." Ilsa stared at Michael. "You already knew?"

"Why does everyone act so surprised when I uncover more dirt than a farmer at planting time?"

Pulling a cigarette from her pocket, she didn't bother with the holder as she lit the end and puffed. "I'm not surprised that you know, but that you would keep it to yourself."

"Of course, he's keeping it to himself." Savon twisted his hat until a seam popped. "Why should he leave his willing bedmate? It's true. I've seen them in the woods together. They're lovers."

Heat flashed across the back of Michael's neck. "Savon," he said, lacing his voice with annoyance, "did you ever stop to consider that interrogations go smoother with honey?"

"I'm sure you've got more tricks than honey." Savon's lip curled into an ugly sneer. "I know what's going on—"

"Sergeant Dietrich, remove this man from my office and these premises. I've had enough of his venom."

Dietrich grabbed Savon's arm and twisted it behind his back. "We told you to mind your manners. Out with you."

"You're a liar." Savon snarled. "*Vous et votre putain!*"

The door slammed shut on his curse.

Michael leaned back in his chair and scrubbed his face with his hands. "Please don't tell me you have more surprises tonight. I can't handle any more."

"Surprises? Ha, that's good coming from the omniscient one." Ilsa curled one leg underneath her. "If Hades froze over tomorrow, I'm sure you'd know about it before old Mephistopheles."

Michael snorted. "You give me too much credit, likening me to such a myth."

"Apparently not, if you already knew about the girl."

"Not all along. Your arrest that day got me to thinking, so really it was you who tipped me off."

"You could have told me instead of letting Kieffer grill me for two days straight."

He'd forgotten all about Kieffer and his orders. Michael's brain raced for a new option. "I have a plan that might make it up to you. In fact, if it's as promising as I hope it is, I'll let you have full credit."

"Oh?" A feline smile spread across her face. "I'm dying to hear this."

He leaned forward and braced his elbows on the desk. "Your arrival is rather fortuitous in that I've arranged to have the traitor apprehended in a matter of days. She'll be handed off to a small escort for interrogation."

Her smile disappeared. "No. I'll be the one to take her in."

Michael spread his hands in a helpless gesture. "My hands are tied as the arrangements have already been made, but I'm sure you can speak to their commanding officer about a trade."

"Do you have his number?"

"They're not the kind of unit you just call up. I'm afraid you'll have to wait until we join them after the arrest."

"I didn't come all this way to go back empty-handed, Michael." She took a long drag. "This is the kind of roundup I need to get headquarters off my back. To prove I don't belong in anyone's shadow." Her voice ended on a quiver. For the briefest of seconds, Michael almost felt sorry for her. Until he remembered the torture she intended for Claire.

He pressed the heel of his hand to his eye. The pain in his head pounded heavier than a Panzer division. With Ilsa at the lead. "All right. This is your show, but only *after* we have the prisoner in custody. We'll explain to the commander that you have priority from Major Kieffer."

"It's difficult for you to hand over control, isn't it?"

"You have no idea."

"Oh, I think I do." She crushed her cigarette into the ashtray and stood. "Don't worry, Michael. It'll all be over before you realize it. *Gute Nacht*."

Chills swept his spine as she left his office. Things were much worse than he'd thought. He'd have to let Ilsa arrest Claire.

CHAPTER 21

Claire added three more empty mugs to her tray and wiped off the unoccupied table. She'd stopped playing a half hour ago, but a few robust souls remained to tip back their last few drops. Two of them were from Michael's command, but they said not a word about him. None of them did. It was as if he'd vanished.

"Bring the mop around," Giles said as she passed him on her way to the kitchen. "Maybe it'll inspire the leeches to leave."

"We can hope." She sighed. "But if they haven't figured out by now that they've worn out their welcome, then we might be in for a long night."

Giles smiled, the first time all day. He opened his mouth as if he wanted to say more before looking away and brushing past her. Her heart cracked a little more.

Depositing her dirty dishes, she grabbed the mop and trudged into the front room. The men didn't even notice as she swabbed around their table.

What if Michael never came back? What if she was able to escape Montbaune before telling him goodbye? Did such a dilemma ever cross his mind? Would he look for her if she disappeared? For months now, she'd told him it was too dangerous to be together. Had he finally listened? Disappointment gnawed in her stomach. It was for the best, but it certainly didn't make it easier to accept.

She kicked the edge of the bucket, splashing dirty water over her toes. The men at the table glanced in her direction, then turned back to their beer. She dropped the mop in its bucket, rung it out, and started around a new table. A cloth strand hooked itself around a chair leg. Crouching, she set to unwrapping the string.

The front door banged open, followed by the thump of heavy boots.

"We're closed," she said.

The steps continued until they stopped right behind her.

"I said we're closed for the night, gentlemen." She turned to address them directly.

Lieutenant Hoffenberg stood with his hand on his pistol.

Fear sliced her chest, paralyzing her brain and legs.

"Get up, *Fräulein*." He grabbed her arm and jerked her to her feet.

"What's going on?" Claire twisted in his grasp, but his fingers dug into her skin.

"Still playing games, are you?" Her captor sneered. "Stop now and all of this will go much easier for you."

"I have no idea what you are talking about, *monsieur*. Please. Why are you doing this?"

"Because this is what becomes of spies and traitors."

The room went eerily quiet, like the center of a tornado. "No. It's not true." Her breath rattled. "I am no spy. You cannot do this."

"I'm afraid he can." Michael strolled in, hands behind his back. His face was a mask of granite. "And you're not French, are you?"

Her knees buckled, but the lieutenant's bone-cracking grip held her up.

"Two-faced, seducing pig!" Giles ran around the counter with a knife in his hand. "I'll cut your innards out and feed them to the vultures!"

Hoffenberg pointed his gun at Giles' stomach. "Put it down, old man."

Claire shoved the muzzle up. "No! Don't!"

Hoffenberg yanked it out of her hand and aimed for Giles' head. Twisting out of his grip, she threw herself in front of the gun. "Don't! Please, *monsieur*. Do not blame him."

Hoffenberg didn't move. "Put the knife down."

"*Brûlez en enfer.*" Giles spat and dropped the knife. Pauline rushed out from the backroom and ran to her brother's side.

Michael sighed. "Lieutenant Hoffenberg, why is this taking so long? Can you not arrest a simple girl?"

Claire turned to Michael, desperate to see the familiar comfort shining in his eyes, but she could not see past the coldness. His life was built on secrets, and she'd been able to trust him with hers. Or so she had thought. She searched his face for a sign that he had his reasons for giving her away. "Why are you doing this?"

"Because you are a spy. Is it not convenient that you should be found and taken into a village hosting a German communications post? Is it not also convenient you entertain soldiers after hours, when your free-flowing beer loosens their tongues? And, of all the men available, you chose me, the post commander, to flatter with your charms." The corner of his mouth twitched. "Did you really think it was working?"

Betrayal stabbed her like a knife. She once thought she could give that man her heart. How stupid she was! "You rat! All this time, you led me on. You let me believe—"

"I led you on? Hardly, though I did not discourage your attentions when you so blindly told me who you are. Next time you should be more careful about whom you trust." He shrugged. "If there is a next time."

"You lying pig!" Propelled by rage, Claire lunged at him, but Hoffenberg snaked an arm around her. She twisted in his grip, but he held fast. "You're supposed to be—"

The cold barrel of a gun pressed into her temple. "One more word and I'll blow your brains all over this floor. Your friends will spend days cleaning it up," Hoffenberg breathed in her ear.

"Gentlemen, is there not a more peaceful way of doing this?" The click of high heels terrified Claire more than the deadly steel pressed against her skin. Ilsa strolled around Hoffenberg and touched the pistol with one blood red nail, angling it away. "There. That's better isn't it? Men can be so unnecessarily rough, can't they?"

"Captain, I told you to wait at the car," Michael said.

"Why should I when we're here about a woman?" Ilsa shooed Hoffenberg's hands away from Claire's arms, then tied Claire's hands behind her back. "I'll take her from here."

"Don't hurt her." Pauline sobbed, clinging to Giles' arm.

Michael turned to them. "And what do you care what happens to a spy? She has been hiding under your roof the whole time."

Pauline cried harder. "We didn't know. I swear it, *Capitaine*."

Claire's heart crumbled as tears streamed down her friend's face. "Pauline, Giles. Don't believe him. I may not be who you think I am, but I am not a spy. If you want to know who the real traitor is, then—"

"Gag her." Michael's nostrils flared like a raging bull. "I'll not hear her poison any longer. Let the interrogators deal with her."

Ilsa slapped a perfumed handkerchief over Claire's mouth as she writhed about. Pulling the gun from her hip, Ilsa aimed between Claire's feet and fired. "Do you want to guess where I'll aim next?"

Claire stopped moving. Michael had not even flinched when Ilsa pulled her gun. Hot tears scalded Claire's eyes, but she was too angry to let them fall. She wouldn't give those soulless brutes the pleasure.

"Get her into the car before she starts wailing." Michael brushed off the sleeve of his coat. "Ilsa, your friends at headquarters are going to have their hands full with her antics."

"Don't worry." Ilsa smiled. "They'll know what to do." She shoved Claire forward, knocking the mop bucket over.

Water sloshed over the tips of Michael's boots. He kicked the bucket across the room. "Watch where you are going, clumsy girl."

Outside, Claire stumbled. As she steadied herself, her gaze jolted up to where Dietrich leaned against a black car.

Michael brushed past them and planted himself in front of the man. "Sergeant Dietrich. What you are doing here?"

Dietrich raised his chin. "I have orders, Captain."

"Not mine."

"Mine." Ilsa tucked her hands into fur-lined gloves, fluffing out the dainty cuffs. "You said this was my show after the prisoner was taken into custody."

"Sergeant Dietrich has nothing to do with the acquisition or transport of prisoners. He is a radio operator."

"I'm well aware of that, but he has provided numerous tips regarding spy traffic in the area. His services have been invaluable to me and will continue to be so."

Michael's back straightened until it looked ready to crack. "As his commanding officer, I will not allow it. Get back to base, Dietrich, before I write you up for insubordination."

"I am under orders from Major Kieffer, and I'm overriding you, Captain Reichner." Ilsa's eyes glittered with ice.

Claire's gaze darted down the street. If she ran for the alley, she could make for the woods and hide. She took a step. Hoffenberg grabbed her arm as his gun dug into her side.

"Very well, Captain von Ziegler," Michael said. "I'll allow Sergeant Dietrich to accompany us, but only to the outskirts of town. His job as an operator cannot be shoved aside for one mere girl."

Ilsa waved a hand in the air. "May we get in the car now? I'd rather not freeze to death in this pigsty of a town if you don't mind. Dietrich, drive."

Hoffenberg stiffened. "Captain, if you don't mind, I'd like to drive." One quelling look from Ilsa and he ducked his head. "Yes, Captain."

Hoffenberg looked at Michael before shoving Claire into the back seat. A heaviness engulfed her heart. She squeezed her eyes shut to keep the tears back. *Dear God in heaven. Help me.*

CHAPTER 22

The car bumped along the road, flinging Claire between Michael and the trigger-happy Hoffenberg. In the darkness, Michael could not see Claire, but he certainly felt her. Her leg scorched his whenever a pothole sent her sliding his direction. He braced his hands on his knees to keep from reaching for her.

He did what he had to do, but she wasn't safe yet. Ilsa was problem enough without Dietrich adding himself to the mix. They had something up their sleeves, but what? Michael's plan to drive Claire to the contact point had been simple. Now his mind raced through his options.

Yellow light spilled from the headlights across the dirt road and skittered into the engulfing woods, a mere pinprick of guidance on a cloudy night. Ilsa turned in her seat, frowning at Michael. "Where are these contacts you spoke of? They're supposed to be waiting to take the girl."

He shook his head. "*Geduld*." Patience.

Dietrich hit a pothole, jostling all the occupants. The auto sagged to the left. He cursed and slammed on the brakes.

"Why are we stopping?" Ilsa asked.

Dietrich got out of the car, bending near the front tire. "Blown tire." He made a popping noise. "Out of the car."

Ilsa, Michael, and Hoffenberg climbed out as Dietrich moved to the trunk. Hoffenberg peered at Claire. "What about the girl?"

Pressing his lips into a tight line, Michael reached into the car. Claire pushed herself against the opposite side and kicked at him.

"A little angry at me, I see." Michael grabbed her ankles and pinned them to the seat before she had a chance to imprint her heel on his face. "Will you please stop kicking so I can help you out?" He slid her toward him, catching her by the waist and hauling her into the night air.

"Why are you taking her out of the car?" Ilsa came around to the driver's side.

"She'll add unnecessary weight when we change the tire." Michael grunted as Claire bucked against him.

"Are you sure you're not giving her a chance to escape?"

Michael's fingers clamped against Claire's arm. "Are you insane or has the cold taken over your senses?"

"She's rather a pet of yours." Ilsa dug her hands deep into her coat pockets. "I thought since you saved her once that you'd want to try again. Maybe even join her this time."

"That's either a misguided accusation or a feeble joke. Neither of which I care for at the moment."

"You're right. The time for games is over." Pulling a gun from her pocket, she aimed for his head. "On your knees."

"Holster your weapon immediately, Captain." Michael reached for his pistol. "I won't tell you again."

"Why do you make this so hard?" She aimed her gun at Claire and marched forward until the muzzle pressed into her forehead. "Toss your weapon and drop to your knees or I'll splatter your girlfriend's brains all over this road."

Anger hissed in Michael's blood. He should kill Ilsa right here and be done with it. Claire whimpered, cutting through his murderous haze. He shoved her away. Throwing his pistol at Ilsa's feet, he dropped to his knees. "You drive a hard bargain, Ilsa. For no good reason."

"I wouldn't say that." Ilsa smiled. "Sergeant, if you please."

Dietrich hefted something bulky from the trunk and tossed it on the ground in front of Michael. His transceiver.

Michael glared at Dietrich. "Sniffed it out like a dog to a bone."

"You didn't make it easy."

"Was I supposed to?"

With a smirk, Dietrich pulled a gun from the trunk. "Your luck had to run out at some point, *Captain*."

"And you're just the man to ensure it happened."

"You did enough on your own, Michael." Ilsa tapped the tip of the muzzle against Claire's forehead. "A pretty face will get you every time."

"Let the girl go. I'm the fish you want."

"Maybe so, but there must be something more to her otherwise you wouldn't be trying so hard to smuggle her out of here. A few days in a dark room under an interrogation lamp should bring out that little secret."

A few steps away from him, Claire's legs buckled. She hit her knees with a cry.

"Pathetic." Ilsa rolled her eyes. "Lieutenant Hoffenberg, where do your loyalties lie?"

Hoffenberg clicked his boots together and saluted. "With our glorious *Führer* and Fatherland."

Ilsa kicked Michael's gun to the side. "Keep an eye on the girl. If she moves, shoot her."

"What's your plan now?" Michael asked as Hoffenberg retrieved his pistol. "To shoot me? Or do you have more torturous ideas, like locking me in a room with Dietrich?"

"You'll be locked in a room, I'm sure, far from your lady love, and put through a rigorous interrogation during which you *will* tell us everything we need to know about your spy operations."

"You sound rather certain that I'll cooperate."

"Of all people, you should know how persuasive the SS can be."

"Unfortunately, I won't have time to chat with your SS department." Michael kept his gaze on Ilsa as Hoffenberg shifted behind her and Dietrich. Drawing another pistol from behind his back, Hoffenberg trained it on Ilsa. "A schedule to keep, I'm afraid."

"Always trying to maintain control, aren't you? Even with a gun pointed at your head." Ilsa sneered. "In case you haven't noticed, you are at my mercy now."

"Listening to you cackle at one in the freezing morning is hardly merciful."

Ilsa slapped her pistol against Michael's cheek. "I can't wait for the moment when your body is beaten, your mind tortured to within an inch of insanity, the only hope left to you the promise of death. Then you will beg for my mercy."

"No. I won't."

Ilsa stretched her hand back for another blow.

Click.

"*Tsk, tsk.*" Hoffenberg pressed the muzzle of one gun to the back of her ear. "Ladies should not lose their tempers so easily."

The gun slipped from her fingers and hit the ground with a solid *thud*. Michael reached for it.

Dietrich lunged for Claire. He grabbed her hair and yanked her head back. "Touch that gun, and she dies."

Claire stumbled and fell backward, crashing into Dietrich. Yelping, he let go of her and leaped back with a nasty curse.

Michael grabbed Ilsa's gun and shot him. Blood spread across his chest, and he dropped like a rock. Michael swung his aim to Ilsa. "Same goes for you if you even twitch."

Ilsa held up shaking hands. "You're a dead man. I'll never let you get away with this."

Michael looked to Hoffenberg. "Tie her up."

Holstering his pistol, Michael pulled a knife from his boot and moved to Claire. She hunkered on the ground with trembling arms wrapped around her knees as she stared at Dietrich's lifeless body. He sliced through her ropes and helped her to her feet. Swaying, she touched a hand to her head where the gun had touched her.

Michael grasped her shoulders. "Claire, I need you to listen to me. I'm getting you out of here. You're safe now." She flinched, not looking at him. "I'm going to take this handkerchief off your mouth. Don't scream."

She nodded.

He slipped the handkerchief from her mouth. "Claire. My darling, I'm so sorry that—"

She kicked his shin. He doubled over with a howl. She punched him in the nose. Tears sprang to his eyes as she spun out of his grasp and ran.

Michael blinked to clear his vision as his nose throbbed. He took off after her into the woods. Branches slapped his face as he followed the sound of her footsteps. He was gaining. "Claire!"

A few yards ahead, she stumbled. He snagged her around her waist and lifted her clean off her feet. She kicked and clawed, but he squeezed harder.

"Stop and listen to me." He hissed in her ear. "Listen. I am not the enemy. Everything I have told you is the truth. My name is Michael Reiner. I'm a captain in His Majesty's Royal Air Force working for the SOE."

She twisted against him. "You gave me up tonight. What sort of ally would do that?"

"The sort who's trying to save your life. Stop kicking me, or I'll be forced to sit on your legs."

She stiffened. "Saving my life, are you? You and your Nazi friends?"

"Do you think I would've shot Dietrich if he and I were on the same side? I didn't want to do it, but he gave me no choice. I'll be wanted for murder now, in addition to spying."

"And Hoffenberg? Whose side is he playing for?"

"*Our* side. He's Belgian and has been trying to stick the Nazis every chance he gets. He has a small transport meeting us to take you—well, now us—to the border. The rest of the way we'll hoof it. May I release you now?"

She was silent for several seconds, her body relaxing inch by inch though an undercurrent of tension ran through her. Finally, she nodded.

"Are you going to run or take a swing?"

"Depends." He set her on the ground but kept a grip on her arm. She was breathing hard, but she'd stopped shaking. "Why didn't you tell me?"

"Because it needed to be real to be believable. You could never have acted your way through tonight. Ilsa would have spotted the lie in a second. And Giles and Pauline needed a reason to never look for you again. I do nothing without precaution and safety."

"I've noticed." She pushed a strand of hair from her eyes and took a deep breath. The last bits of tension eased from her shoulders. "What's our plan now?"

"Meet the guides, get across the border, and find transport to get you to the States."

"Home? To America?"

The hope in her voice punched him in the gut. He'd known all along that this plan meant giving her up, but it didn't lessen the sting. "You don't belong here, Claire. And since there aren't any Yanks in the area to hand you over to, it falls to me. Not that it would matter. I only trust myself to see you home properly."

She shifted closer. Moonlight slivered through the trees. Her pale face tilted up as her eyes searched his. "Why are you risking this for me?"

His blood pulsed at her nearness. "I think you know."

He reached out and brushed the hair from her face, tucking it behind her ear as his fingers wrapped around the back of her neck. His lips fell to hers and claimed her without hesitation. All his worry and fear vanished as his mouth moved over hers again and again. The heat of her touch purled through his veins, scorching his lips with desire. He pressed her closer, desperate to match his throbbing heart with hers. The kiss deepened with a low moan.

A strange bird twittered, and Michael pulled back with a groan. "*Ich komme.*" He lowered his voice and stroked her cheek. "Sorry. I'll have to finish that later." Grabbing her hand, they retraced their steps through the woods to the car. Ilsa sat on the ground next to the boot with her hands tied behind her back. He squeezed Claire's hand. "Stay quiet, and don't go near her."

Claire pulled her hand from Michael's and crossed her arms, staring hard at Ilsa. If only she could scorch the woman on the spot. "Don't worry about me."

Frowning, Michael hurried over to Hoffenberg.

"I moved the body out that way." Hoffenberg pointed to the woods. "Covered it with branches as best I could."

Michael nodded and rubbed the aching muscles at the back of his neck. Their night was getting longer by the second. "We'll have to move the car off the road and hide it in the bushes too. Cover its tracks. Make sure to—"

Claire untied the handkerchief still around her neck and marched toward Ilsa. "I believe this belongs to you," she said in English as she stuffed it into Ilsa's belt.

Ilsa's eyes bulged, but a gag muffled her cries.

Michael grabbed Claire's arm and hauled her away. "You can't follow a single order, can you?"

"No. Not after what she's done to me, to us, and the terror she's caused Giles and Pauline. She deserves to know how close she came to succeeding only to have it snatched away. That good will triumph over her evilness." Claire shrugged him off. "Are you going to leave her here?"

"The good captain doesn't think it's right to kill in cold blood." Hoffenberg frowned and checked his gun's magazine. "I, on the other hand, have no such scruples."

Michael shook his head. "I will not become what they are. Put her in the boot."

Ilsa bucked and screamed as Michael and Hoffenberg grabbed her arms and legs and stuffed her into the car. Hoffenberg shoved a cigarette beneath her gag. "To keep you company."

Michael slammed the boot closed. They pushed the car off the road and into the trees as far as they could. As he and Hoffenberg covered it with branches, Claire ran back and swept away the tracks. It wasn't perfect, but they didn't have time to fix it. Hoffenberg's contacts were waiting.

Clouds still blotted much of the sky, and the moon had passed its zenith. Claire had no idea what time it was, but they had been walking for hours, and she was struggling to match the men's grueling pace. Playing piano hadn't prepared her for this type of exercise. Michael took her hand, urging her to keep going.

They spotted a crossroads sign a few yards ahead. Once bright white and tall, the post leaned sideways with its town names worn off. "They should be near here." Hoffenberg cupped his hands over his mouth and whistled. The same strange birdcall she'd heard in the woods with Michael.

Silence.

Hoffenberg tried again.

Trepidation curled in Claire's stomach. What if the contact didn't come? What if he'd been caught? Michael seemed unconcerned as he stood with feet apart and hands clasped behind his back. She inched closer in hopes of absorbing his calmness.

Something howled from the trees.

"That's them." Hoffenberg grabbed the light and flashed Morse code in the sound's direction.

A light flickered from the bushes a moment before a man popped through them. "*Venez, venez.*"

At Hoffenberg's grin, Claire sagged with relief.

The man darted back into the shadows. The trio scrambled after him to find a flatbed transport truck and three other men waiting in the woods.

The man jerked a thumb to the truck. "Clothes are in the back along with your papers. No more last-minute surprises, Hoff. You were supposed to be here two hours ago."

"Sorry about that, Louie. We had an unexpected guest, and she forced a change of plans."

Louie glared. "Do you know how difficult it is to find two men's identification papers? Especially without the assurance you're going to use them."

"We do apologize for the inconvenience, sir," Michael said, "but it seems Hoff and I will be using them after all."

"Inconvenient for me, yes." The glare slipped from Louie's face as he smiled at Claire. "But not for the *mademoiselle*. Your setback is her saving grace. *Belle dame*. She will need all the protection she can get, and my men can only go so far." He grabbed two bundles from the back of the truck and handed one to her and the other to Michael.

Ducking behind the truck, Claire changed into the patched skirt that smelled of sheep and pulled on a pair of too-large shoes. She kept her sweater to remind her of Giles and tucked her new identification papers into its inside pocket.

Covering her hair with a handkerchief, she came around the truck to where Michael was standing. His lips were pressed into a tight line. "Are you all right?"

He grunted as he watched Hoffenberg bury their old uniforms. A deep furrow plunged between his eyebrows as he watched his recently removed boots disappear under a clump of mud. "I just polished them yesterday."

Biting back a laugh, Claire patted his arm. It was the first time she'd ever seen him out of uniform—aside from that day on the train—and my, what a treat it was. Wearing a homespun cotton shirt, patched jacket and trousers, scuffed shoes, and a slouched hat, he looked every bit the common farmer.

"Let's get a move on." Louie tapped his wristwatch. "You remember what the story is?"

"We're siblings hitching a ride to our family's farm because our home was destroyed in an air raid," Michael said. "Though it doesn't account for us traveling while it's still curfew hours."

Louie scowled. "This isn't the first time I've done this, soldier boy. We'll stop and wait to cross the first checkpoint at dawn. Now up you go, or you can walk if you don't like my plan."

Michael narrowed his eyes. Claire touched his arm before smiling at Louie. "We shall trust you and your men, as you know this area. The captain just likes to be aware of all the details. You should see him ordering eggs."

Louie shook his head as he and his men climbed into the truck. Michael took Claire's hand and marched around to the back, handing her up.

"What are you talking about, me ordering eggs?" His hiss was like steam blasting into her ear. "As far as I know we've never taken a meal together."

Hoffenberg threw himself on a patch of straw in the corner. "Relax, boss. We're supposed to be farmers now. Eggs are a part of life."

"I can't relax." Michael grumbled. Claire sat in the corner, and he eased himself next to her, propping his elbows atop his bent knees. "I'm not resting until we're on friendly soil again and far away from these Nazis."

Claire felt him coiling like a spring. One wrong move and he'd buck out. She supposed years of military training did that to a man. Or maybe it was being on the run.

The engine sputtered to life. Two of Louie's men scrambled into the back. Rifles glinted in the hay next to them. The younger recruit fidgeted with his collar, twisting his neck this way and that. Something about him seemed familiar. The sandy-colored hair, the long nose. She'd seen them before. But where? He turned his head and caught her staring. She smiled, but he looked away.

She scooted closer to Michael. "Michael?"

"Hmm?"

"We're going to be okay, aren't we?"

He looked at her, his face inches away from hers. His warm breath fanned over her cold cheeks. "I won't let anything happen to you." He took one of her hands and pressed his lips into her palm. "I swear it."

She snuggled into his side, resting her head on his shoulder. This time there were no brass buttons or diamond studs poking her. Just the smell of hay and soap. Of him. She sighed in peace. "I'm sorry I kicked you."

"And clawed me, and I think you even bit me."

"All that too." She laced her fingers through his. "From now on, I won't let anything happen to you."

A chuckle rumbled in his chest. "Oh? How do you propose to do that?"

She glanced at the rifles. "Any way I have to."

CHAPTER 23

Michael forced his gaze to the ground. Any look of rebellion and the checkpoint guards would string him up faster than he could pull the hidden dagger from his belt. But one more leer at Claire and he'd have them on the ground pleading for mercy.

"What farm are you going to?" one of the guards asked in horrible French.

"Our family's. North of Moulins," Michael said.

"That's near the border, isn't it?"

"*Oui, monsieur*. It's a small dairy farm."

The guard, a sergeant, eyed him with a smirk. "How can it be a dairy farm when all the beasts have been taken for soldiers?"

"I believe they have been allowed to keep one cow to provide milk and cheese for the village."

The sergeant's buddy, a young corporal with severe acne, stopped in front of Claire and gave her what he probably considered a Casanova smile. "It's dangerous to be traveling with so many men, *mademoiselle*. A girl as pretty as you should take extra care."

Hoffenberg twitched next to her. "She does not travel alone."

"Shut up. I wasn't talking to you."

"My brothers keep me well protected, *monsieur*." Claire kept her eyes averted.

"Brothers." The corporal didn't look convinced as he stared at Michael and Hoffenberg before glancing at their identification papers. "Why the difference in last names then?"

Claire tucked her chin closer to her chest as her voice quavered. "My husband was killed last month by an air raid. My brothers are all I have left."

The soldiers sneered and made lewd suggestions. Michael forced his hands to relax as fury surged through him. How many more times would they have to do this, and how long before someone slipped?

The sergeant handed back their papers. "Get on your way." His eyes roved over Claire as she climbed back into the truck.

The rest of their crew piled in behind her without a word. Louie started the engine and drove at a snail's pace that grated Michael's sense of urgency. It wasn't until the sun drifted past an hour did the tension begin to leave his body. His muscles ached from sitting so rigidly.

"How many more checkpoints do we need to get through?" Claire asked.

Michael shifted to stretch out his legs. "At least two more on this road, but the security will get thicker as we near the border." If they got that far. A vehicle piled with six men was asking for trouble. Not to mention if the hidden rifles and pistols were found. If it got too risky, they'd have to abandon the transport and make it to the demarcation line on foot.

"This was one of the easier ones." Lamarc, the youngest recruit, shifted on his patch of hay. "Some of them want to strip the whole truck for inspection, but this early in the morning they don't because their shift is almost up."

"How many times have you done this?" Michael asked.

"This'll be my fifth smuggle. I'm hoping to join the boys in Paris one day for more hands-on stuff."

"Like blowing up buildings and trains?"

Lamarc tugged at his collar and shrugged. "Only if there are Germans in them and only if it'll end this war so we can all go home."

"Where do you call home?"

"A small town near Montoire." Looking at Claire, Lamarc's eyebrows slanted together. "Forgive me, *mademoiselle*, but why do you keep staring at me?"

"I'm not sure." Claire shifted forward. "You look familiar. From a picture maybe. Or ... no, that's silly."

"You've seen a picture of me?" His face blanched as his eyes widened. "Where?"

"Calm yourself, Lamarc," his friend said. "She's probably mistaken."

"She's seen me before. Do you know what that means? It means others will have seen me. My cover's been blown." Lamarc hissed in the still morning air. "Where did you see it?"

Claire shrank back. "My cousin had—has a picture of her fiancé on her dresser. I'm sure it's just a coincidence. You look like him."

Lamarc's eyes narrowed. "Your cousin's name?"

"Odette Baudin."

"You're ... you're Odette's cousin?" Lamarc sucked in a deep breath. The hard lines of his face softened. With lightning speed, the softness vanished behind a narrowed stare. He swung back to Claire. "I don't believe you."

"Believe me or not, but my cousin is Odette. And her sister is Maurelle, and my aunt and uncle are Helene and Emile. You are her fiancé, aren't you?"

"You're trying to trick me. I don't believe you."

"Why on earth would I lie to you? If I was lying, how would I know that Odette wears a star pendant around her neck that you gave her?"

"You're tricking me to make me say something I shouldn't." He lurched toward Claire. "You're probably the one who gave them up to the Nazis! The neighbors told me when I went to find her."

"Enough." Michael shifted to put himself between Claire and Lamarc. "Sit, soldier, or I'll put you down."

The young man punched the back of the cab. "It was her!"

The truck swerved to the side of the road, brakes squealing. The engine cut off. Louie threw open his door and marched around to the back. "What's going on back here?" He glared at each person in turn. "Who's punching my truck?"

"We're all a little tired." Michael kept his attention on Lamarc. "Might be a good time for a break to stretch our legs."

"Fine, fine. Ten minutes and we're back on the road."

Michael made sure Lamarc was around the front of the truck before he allowed Claire down. "Why can't you ever make things easy for me?"

"I didn't mean to start anything, really I didn't." She picked straw from her sleeve. "You'd think he'd be glad to see the family of the girl he loves."

"You caught him off guard."

"Apparently I called the Nazis on my family too." She snorted and plucked a straw stalk from his collar. "I'm going to take a little walk."

Michael eyed the surrounding trees with interest. A few minutes behind a screen of pines would give him the chance to finish that kiss. "I'll come with you." He tucked her hand into the crook of his arm and started for the tree line just a few yards from the road.

"Oh, no. I don't think so." She grinned and stretched on her toes to kiss his cheek. "A little privacy, please."

"Fine, but when you come back, I have a few questions about this mysterious cousin of yours. Three minutes and I'm coming after you."

"You're awfully cute when you're bossy." Another kiss to the cheek, this one with a loud smacking sound, and she disappeared into the trees.

He couldn't stop himself from grinning.

Hoffenberg pounded him on the back. "Nice to have a woman to travel with. Keeps things from getting dull."

Michael scowled and smoothed the front of his rumpled jacket. "Where's Lamarc?"

Hoffenberg jerked a thumb at the truck. "Over there getting yelled at by his fearless leader. I'm sure I'll get blamed for all of this somehow."

Standing on the passenger side of the truck, Louie shook his finger at Lamarc, then pointed to the woods where Claire had disappeared. The boy's shoulders slumped as he shuffled his feet.

Michael nudged Hoffenberg. "Do you trust him?"

"I've known Louie some years. I'd trust my own mother with him, providing I stuffed her ears with cotton first. Whoever he picks for his team is on the up and up."

A low rumble rocketed tension into every muscle in Michael's body. His ears strained as he listened for the noise again. "What is that?"

"What's wrong, boss?"

Michael tried to zero in on the sound. There. Coming from the north, growing nearer. "Do you hear it?" He pointed to the hill.

"Yeah." Hoffenberg frowned. "But I wish I didn't."

A chugging motor grew louder, plucking every one of Michael's nerves like a stretched trip wire. A vehicle hurtled over the hilltop. Two Nazi flags flew from its hood. Rifle muzzles appeared over the sides.

Blood pounded in Michael's veins. He brushed his hand against the dagger hidden under his jacket. If only he'd kept that Luger instead of burying it along with the uniform. "Get ready."

Hoffenberg's hand moved to his pocket and the knife hidden there. "Already there, boss."

The vehicle stopped in front of the truck. Four Germans jumped out, but only the two corporals in the rear held rifles.

The highest ranked, a sergeant major, marched forward. His ferret eyes swept over the truck and Louie's men. "What are you doing here?"

Michael kept his head down but remained aware of the new arrivals' every move. He didn't recognize any of them, but that didn't mean they wouldn't notice him.

"Did you not hear me?" The sergeant major stomped his foot. "Or are all of you frogs conveniently deaf?"

"We are traveling to our family's village, sir," Louie said, walking forward. "We've stopped for a rest."

"A rest? It is still morning. Do you lack the stamina for a long journey, or have you been breaking curfew? Where are your papers?"

Fishing into their pockets, the travelers produced their identification papers. The sergeant major quickly examined them. Except Michael's and Hoffenberg's. He took his time studying those, frowning over each one. Blood rushed to Michael's head.

"Look at me," the sergeant major barked, holding the photo next to Michael's face.

Michael lifted his head, catching the man's gaze for a second before he dropped it to his shoes. It burned him to behave as a terrified civilian, but that's what the Germans expected, and they held the guns. For now.

An ugly frown crossed the sergeant's face. "This photograph does not look much like you."

"I'm sorry, sir, but it's the only photograph I have."

The corporals snickered. The sergeant major motioned for his fellow sergeant to join him. "Does this man resemble this photo?" he said in German.

The sergeant squinted. "Maybe. A little fatter in the face."

"It's not him. He and his friend match the description of the spies who stole that car and left the beautiful captain in the trunk."

"Then who are the rest of these men?"

"Fellow conspirators." He turned back to Michael. "Isn't that right, Captain Reichner?"

Michael mounted a blank but somewhat confused look on his face despite panic turning his bones to jelly. "*Pardon?*"

"Come now, Captain Reichner, or whatever your name truly is," the sergeant major said in German. "We're not stupid, and neither are you by all reports. Except for one thing. You left your hostage alive. Captain von Ziegler was found this morning with a marvelous story of how she was left to die. She gave excellent descriptions of you and your man here. Lieutenant Hoffenberg? And some girl."

"Monsieur, je ne comprends pas ce que vous dites." Michael spread his hands in a pleading gesture. Where was Claire?

"You know exactly what I'm saying. It degrades us all for you to act otherwise."

Hoffenberg snorted and crossed his arms. "Should've shot 'em when we had the chance, boss."

Michael took his military stance with feet wide apart, and arms crossed over his chest, every muscle in his body straining for action. "Too late for that now."

The sergeant major's mouth cracked into a malicious grin. "There. Isn't it better to speak in the father tongue?"

"Watch your tongue, Sergeant." Michael took a step forward. "You're addressing an officer."

"And you're addressing a man with rifles aimed at your head. Dunst. Fleischer. Keep the bead on Captain Reichner and his friends while I radio in. This catch should be worth a promotion. Maybe even a medal. Keep an eye out for the girl. She's around here somewhere."

Spinning on his heel, the sergeant major marched back to his vehicle and picked up the radio. Dunst and Fleischer motioned Michael and Hoffenberg to the ground.

With the Germans holding all the cards, Michael had no choice but to comply. Rocks pressed into his knees as he knelt in the road next to Hoffenberg. Michael held his breath as he listened to the static voice on the other end of the radio. They wanted him and Hoffenberg to be brought in alive for interrogation. Once he was ordered to stand, he'd have only a split second to wrestle the rifle from the guard. Any longer and he'd be dead.

Louie and his men stood with hands raised a few feet away. They needed a distraction. Anything to draw attention away from the truck. Then Louie could get one of the rifles hidden under the carriage. Michael turned his head a fraction of an inch to catch Louie's eye.

"Looking for your girlfriend?" Dunst pressed the tip of his rifle to Michael's head. "Face front!"

Michael faced forward again, waiting for his moment to strike. *Dear God. Keep Claire away. Far, far away.*

CHAPTER 24

Raking her fingers through her hair, Claire hit a snag. More than one, actually, since her hair had blown into knots during the windy ride. She sighed. A rat's nest it would remain until she had a proper brush in hand.

She tied the kerchief back over her head and inhaled the woodsy air. Cold and piney, it brought relief from the burning truck exhaust. Her legs and backside enjoyed the reprieve too.

Michael had done his best to keep her comfortable, insisting she sit on extra hay and wear his mittens to keep her fingers from falling off. He'd promised that one day soon she would have a warm bed and nothing to fear, but he'd never mentioned himself. She knew he intended to continue his mission. But not if she could help it.

She picked her way back through the woods. Her three minutes must have passed, but Michael had yet to come stomping after her. Either he'd relaxed his stance on order and discipline or … her heart tripped.

Rushing to the tree line, she ducked behind a wide trunk, peeking around it. She smothered a cry. Michael and the others knelt in the road. Hands behind their heads. Guns pointed at them.

If she could catch Michael's eye, he'd know she was there, but he stared straight ahead. How could she help them? If only she could get into the truck and … and … what? Run over the Germans? The soldier by the jeep would shoot her as soon as she turned the key. Applesauce and crackers. Couldn't the Germans give them a break?

For the first time in weeks, a ray of sun peeked from the clouds, glinting off the gun barrels and truck grill. Claire shielded her eyes from the sudden brightness. Maybe if she could get their guns—the guns! Hidden under the truck. *Thank you, Louie.*

The truck sat a few feet away. If the Germans kept their backs to her, she could duck behind a wheel without being seen.

Sucking in breaths to calm her jackhammering heart, she darted toward the large front wheel and hunkered down behind it. She stuck her hand behind the tire and groped for a handle. A muzzle. Anything that felt like a weapon. Nothing but greasy nuts and bolts.

She fumbled under the runner until her fingers brushed against a handle. She pulled, but it didn't budge. Wiping her slick palms against her hip, she tried again. Nothing. She peered around the side of the wheel to make sure she was still safe, then ducked her head under the running board. Two hooks held the gun in place. It felt like a ton as she lifted it into her shaking hands. It wobbled, hitting the rocky road with a *plunk*.

The soldier stopped talking to his radio. Claire snatched the gun and crouched behind the wheel. Gravel crunched. She tried to calm her mind the way her father had taught her on hunting outings, but it didn't work.

The radio crackled. The soldier continued his conversation. Claire sent a flurry of thank-yous heavenward.

It was now or never.

Crawling out from behind the wheel, she walked toward the jeep, holding the gun in front of her. Numbness dulled her senses, but her brain whirled. Stopping behind the soldier at the radio, she raised the gun and pushed it into the back of his neck. *Click.*

He froze. *"Was willst du?"*

"Déposez la radio."

He dropped the radio on the seat and raised his hands above his head. *"Et maintenant, mademoiselle?"*

"You're going to release my friends over there."

"No, I'm not. One word from me and they're dead."

"And you along with them." She pressed the gun harder against his neck until the skin around it turned white. "You're a sensible man, yes?"

"With a gun at my neck, I most certainly am."

"Excellent. Now walk. And no funny business."

With shoulders erect, he stalked around the back of the truck, stopping behind his men. *"Sie gehen lassen."*

One of the riflemen looked at him. *"Was ist das?"* And then he saw Claire. He swung his rifle around and yelled.

Claire's prisoner shook his head. She peeked over his shoulder. Louie and his men stared with their mouths hanging open. Hoffenberg crowed, and Michael … it was the first time he'd ever looked surprised.

The Germans continued arguing. Claire pressed the gun farther into her prisoner's neck.

"Genug. Freigeben." His voice quivered.

The gunmen lowered their rifles.

"Tell them to drop their guns. Step back with their hands on their heads." Claire ignored the tremble in her hand.

Her prisoner repeated her message. The gunmen opened their mouths, but the leader held up his hand. They placed the rifles on the ground and took a step back, lacing their fingers atop their heads.

Claire caught Michael's eye. "Would you mind taking it from here, please? I believe you're better at this type of thing."

Michael shot up, his eyes never leaving the soldiers. He flicked a hand toward Hoffenberg. "Get the guns."

Leaping to his feet, Hoffenberg grabbed the weapons and cradled one to his chest while handing the other to Louie.

Michael took the pistol from her captive's belt and aimed it at him. *"Zum Boden."*

His commanding tone broke through the dizziness of Claire's brain. Spots danced before her eyes. What had she done? "Michael, I—" The strength in her legs vanished.

Michael pulled her against him, stroking her hair. *"Shh*, it's all right now, my brave girl."

She shoved the gun into his hands and collapsed against his chest.

"My darlin' lass." He crooned in his soft lilt. "Whatever put such a mad idea into your head?"

"I know you had the situation under control." She shuddered, clutching his shirt. "But you were taking too long."

Squeezing her tight, he pressed a kiss to her forehead. "You're right about that, but next time—"

Pop! A gunshot ripped through the air.

"He's running!"

Claire turned to see a soldier sprinting away. Hoffenberg took aim. His shot hit the dirt at the fleeing man's heels.

Michael stepped away from her. He brought the pistol up and fired. The runaway dropped to the ground. *"Slán agus beannacht leat,"* he whispered.

Claire stared at the prostrate body. Two more shots exploded. She jumped, horror seizing her. The remaining German soldiers crumpled on the ground, blood oozing from their heads.

Michael blazed with fury as he turned on Hoffenberg and Louie. "What is going on?" His fingers clamped around his gun as his shoulders shook with barely bottled rage. Never had he been so terrifying.

Hoffenberg shrugged. "They would have talked, Captain. We had to."

"They could have been sent in as prisoners with Louie. The enemy is of more use alive."

"Yes, sir."

"If you decide to get trigger-happy again, consult me first, understood?"

"Yes, sir."

Michael pinched the bridge of his nose as he sucked in several loud, deep breaths. His shoulders sagged. Claire wanted to put her arms around him, but she knew comfort was the furthest thing from his agenda. There was a mess to clean first.

He dropped his hand and pulled his shoulders back. "What's done is done." Marching to the jeep, he grabbed the radio. A voice crackled over the line. Taking a deep breath, he launched into a frantic tirade of German. His arms flailed about, pointing to the bodies as if the radio operator could see him. Back and forth they went for several minutes before he switched the radio off again.

Michael was right. What's done was done. Claire turned her back to the gruesome scene on the road. "What did you tell them?"

"That my patrol came across a bloody scene before we were attacked by traitors from the woods. Gunfire ensued, but they escaped heading north. A new patrol should arrive soon to help us look for them. Roadblocks are being set within a ten-mile radius. We need to leave. Now." Rummaging in the jeep's glovebox, he pulled out a map and slipped it in his pocket. "This should come in handy."

"These too." Louie tossed Michael and Hoffenberg rifles from the truck. To Claire, he handed a sack. "Food. You'll need it."

Claire hefted the bag to her hip. "Are you sure you won't come with us?"

Louie shook his head. "It's better if we part ways here. You should arrive in San Tolosa in two or three days. My brother, Hernando, will be waiting for you."

Hoffenberg's brow scrunched. "You've got a brother named Hernando?"

Louie smiled grimly. "We are all brothers in this fight."

Claire slipped around to Lamarc, or Dillon, as she now knew, and took his hand in both of hers. "I'm sorry we had a rough start, but I'm glad we got to meet. Odette spoke well of you."

Sadness lurked in the corners of his eyes as they searched hers. "I only wish I knew where she was."

"Me too." Tears clouded her vision. She gave him a quick hug. "Take care of yourself, Dillon."

She waved goodbye to the fighting Frenchmen, then tramped

behind Michael into the woods, matching his soldier's pace. He kept ahead, always scanning the trees for possible threats and only turned back once to help her down a steep decline. He never said a word. She managed to keep up, but by nightfall, she felt like the frayed strands of a fiddle bow.

"We'll rest here for the night." Michael pointed to a clump of pines.

Pushing aside the lower branches, they stepped into a small enclosure with bushes providing a decent barrier around the tree trunks. Quite cozy given the circumstances. Claire brushed together a pile of pine needles and plopped down as fast as her aching muscles would allow. She opened the sack Louie had given them and scrounged out a hunk of cheese and a few strips of jerky.

Hoffenberg grabbed his share and ducked back outside. "Perimeter check," he said around a mouthful of food.

The thick grove allowed wisps of moonlight in—just enough to see outlines—but at least it blocked the wind. Claire hugged her knees to her chest to preserve as much body heat as possible. If only they could light a fire. Oh, what she would give to warm her fingers and nose. To roast a hot meal. To ... see. Something brushed against her leg. She swatted at it and prayed it was an errant leaf and not a spider. "I wish I had a flashlight."

"Too dangerous. Patrols could see it," Michael said as he stalked by. The man was oblivious to physical discomfort.

"Is that why you didn't bring one from that jeep?"

"Partially. If we're caught with a German torch, then we'd be in double trouble." Twigs snapped as he pivoted and paced. "Same reason we didn't bring their guns. They don't take kindly to having their things filched."

"Come and sit. You're making me dizzy." She patted the leafy seat next to her. "Just for a little while."

He stopped moving. Finally, he sighed, easing next to her with a grunt. "These shoes pinch a bit."

"I'm sure Louie was only thinking of practicality when he gave us these old tattered things. Sturdy over well fitting." She thought of the red leather pumps she'd purchased for her trip to France. They were the most fashionable thing she'd ever bought, and they pinched like the dickens, but she was too proud of them to care. After days like today, she couldn't believe all the effort and saved money she'd put into a silly old pair of shoes.

"I think they've had close to thirty years of breaking in." He stretched his long legs out and rotated his ankles until they popped. "I know Louie did the best he could, but these are a wee tight."

She poked him in the shoulder. "Maybe your feet are too big."

"Men are supposed to have big feet. We'd look strange with dainty ones like you."

"Ha. You should tell my mom that. She always says I have my dad's feet, which are anything but pretty."

They laughed, but it was a strange sound. Like Mozart playing in the lull of battle. How could anything sound so jovial amid such ruin? They could do with a little Mozart today.

Claire laid her cheek on top of her knees to study what she could see of Michael's face. "What did you say to that man when you … after you … after he fell?"

Michael rolled a twig in his palm for several long seconds. "It's an old Irish saying. Goodbye and blessings with you. My grandmother used to say it when she left someone's house."

"It's an odd thing to say to a man you just … an enemy, I mean."

"I don't relish killing any man." The twig rolled off his fingers to the ground. "I regret you seeing it. I don't ever want you to see something like that again or see *me* like that. The look in your eyes…" He dropped his head and stared into his hands. "I don't think I'll ever forget it."

"Michael." She took both his hands. "If he had gotten away, he might have come back to hurt us, or Louie or Lamarc."

A rough laugh tumbled from his lips. "You and Hoff should have a chat."

"No, thanks. He's a bit more rogue than I prefer." She shuddered, remembering the bodies in the middle of the road. "You said it yourself. This is war and what's done is done. Let's just get out of here in one piece, okay?"

"That's something else we need to talk about." Michael took his hands from her grasp. "Since Portugal is claiming neutrality, no Allied bases have been established within its borders, though there are troops on the ground. It should not be difficult to find you a place on one of their convoys back to England. I'll write specific instructions to the commander that when you arrive, he will need to—"

"Absolutely not."

His eyebrows slanted. "Beg your pardon?"

"No. I refuse."

"Refuse to take my instructions?"

She crossed her arms over her chest. "I'm not going anywhere without you. Convoy, tank, plane, or whatever."

"You can't stay here."

"Fine, then you come with me."

"I haven't finished my assignment."

"In case you've forgotten, you and your henchman killed a man and locked an SS officer in a car trunk before running off with an American. I'd say your cover is blown."

"As long as there are troops in harm's way, I have a job to do." He took a deep breath. "I don't want to leave you, Claire. Do you believe that?"

"Of course I do, but that doesn't mean you can ship me off wherever you please."

"You're going back to America, and that's it."

Her throat tightened. Home. For so long it was the one place she'd wanted to be yet couldn't get to. Now, the opportunity to leave was in sight, but the thought of leaving Michael left her heartsick. How could she tell him goodbye? Was she expected to pick up the pieces of her life on that western shore without him?

The bushes rattled as Hoffenberg stepped into camp. "Might get a little snow tonight." He stopped, glanced at the two of them, then started to back out. "Sorry. I'll come back."

"Stay. We don't need footprints giving away our location." Michael sounded as pleasant as a prickled grizzly bear. "We could all use a little rest. I'll take first watch." He leaned in close to Claire's ear, his breath tickling her neck. "We'll talk about it later."

He could talk all he wanted. She needed to start rethinking her plans. Plans that included him.

Hoffenberg fluffed a handful of leaves, then fell onto them. He was snoring by the time he hit the ground. Tired as she was, Claire knew trying to sleep was going to be as easy as cornering a ghost. Michael tapped his fingers against his leg, drumming tension. Capturing his twitching hand, she flung it over her shoulder and cuddled into his side. Instantly, warmth seeped into her chilled bones. A few minutes later, the tension ebbed from his shoulders.

She smiled and closed her eyes. They may not have many more nights together. She would gladly take whatever she could get.

The rock digging into his right hip was the only thing keeping Michael awake. Exhaustion did not begin to describe the weight pulling at his eyelids. The warm, soft body pressing against him called him toward a silvery dreamland.

Thirty more minutes. He could last that long before waking Hoffenberg for the second watch. Surprisingly, the man's snoring hadn't woken Claire or notified the Jerries.

Claire sighed in her sleep, sending a puff of breath into the air. What he wouldn't give to start a blazing fire for her, but all he could offer her now was body heat. If they got out of France alive, the first thing he would do was order a hot bath and soak until his fingers and toes wrinkled beyond recognition. Then he would wrap himself and Claire in wool blankets and sit next to an enormous fireplace while drinking real coffee.

He shifted his legs, sending pins and tingles up them.

Who was he kidding? A hot bath? Warm blanket? Real coffee? It would never happen, at least not for him. He'd be lucky if he got a fresh change of clothes before being sent out to the field again. That is if he wasn't arrested for abandoning his post.

He tucked Claire's hand farther into the crook of his arm, making sure to cover every inch of her exposed skin. Even if he couldn't enjoy a few comforts, he would make sure she did. And he'd make sure she enjoyed them far away from here, no matter how much she argued. And no matter how hard it was to say goodbye.

CHAPTER 25

R ain pelted Michael's back as he peered out from behind a low stone wall. The mission church of San Tolosa squatted at the edge of town. Its bell raised high on the roof clanged wildly in the wind. A yellow light glowed through the stained glass while a red flag waved over the door.

The rest of the street was deserted. Each house's windows had been shuttered against the storm. Two German vehicles sat in front of the cantina.

Michael ducked back to where Claire and Hoffenberg waited next to the wall. "This is the place. We'll have to run."

Hoffenberg squinted against the raindrops. "Any patrols?"

"None visible, but the police station is two doors down from the church. Bound to be German soldiers in there." Michael glanced at Claire. She hunkered in the mud, trying to shield her face from the rain. "When I say go, run."

She nodded.

Michael took one last look at the street. "Go!"

They shot out from behind the wall and streaked across the muddy road. Claire slipped behind him. He turned around, grabbed her hand, and yanked her along. Racing to the church, Michael grabbed the door handle and turned. Locked. Cursing, he knocked. Nothing. He pounded. Lights flickered in the sheriff's office window. He pounded again. Handing Claire his rifle, he rammed his shoulder into the door. It groaned against the force.

"Hoffenberg! On the count of three. One. Two. Three."

They threw themselves at the door. It crashed open. They scrambled inside, slamming the door behind them. Michael held it closed as the wind tried to open it again. "Get me that board to bar it in place."

Hoffenberg held up the splintered board. "Can't, boss. You broke it."

Click.

Claire screamed.

Metal pressed against the back of Michael's head. "You disturb the peace of God's house, *señor*," a man said in poor English.

Every muscle in Michael's body tensed. He held up his hands and slowly turned around. Cold black eyes and the barrel of a pistol waited for him. Either this was the wrong place or his information was outdated. He needed to think, quickly. "We seek sanctuary."

"This is a sanctuary for all, but I must ask what trouble follows you to break down my door at this hour."

"We've traveled a long way. From a place near Louis, in France."

The coldness in the priest's eyes evaporated. He secured the pistol to his leg and clapped Michael on the shoulder. "Welcome, *mi hijo*. I am Father Hernando. Come. You need warmth and food."

The tension eased from Michael's body, though his senses remained on alert. Claire stood close to him but not touching as her gaze locked on Hernando. The tiniest flicker of a smile curled her lips, easing away the weary travels of the day.

"You are not who I expected, but then Louie likes to send me surprises." Hernando picked up a slender rod leaning against the wall and slapped it over the door handles to hold them in place. Wrapping burly arms around Claire and Hoffenberg, the priest ushered them down the aisle of his small church. Candles burned on the altar, flickering shadows on the wooden pews and saint statues.

"Thank you, Father." Claire shivered as she trudged alongside the round priest. She glanced over her shoulder at Michael. "You don't know how long we've—"

German voices shouted outside.

Michael grabbed his rifle from Claire and spun toward the

door. Hernando shoved him back. "You'll destroy everything. Get behind the Blessed Virgin!" He pointed to a statue of a woman behind the altar.

Racing for cover, Michael, Claire, and Hoffenberg dove behind the statue as the church doors banged open.

"What are you doing in here, priest?" a man asked in German.

Hernando replied in Spanish. The German cursed the priest's inability to speak a more cultured tongue before switching to a crude Spanish.

Claire's fingers clawed into Michael's back as he pushed her against the statue. Her breaths raced along with his heart. Next to him, Hoffenberg clutched his rifle. Two sets of boots marched down the aisle as Hernando babbled. Cloth tore and metal pinged as if a curtain had been ripped from a rod. The feet came closer. Michael's finger hovered over the trigger. Wood scraped and clattered against the floor.

"*No, por favor!*"

The Germans laughed as their footsteps retreated. They barked something else before the doors banged shut. Hernando huffed what sounded close to a curse as his sandals slapped against the floor.

"They'll be back." He skirted around the statue and motioned them out. "This way. Quickly!"

Claire's hand shook in Michael's as they followed the priest. The Germans had shoved the pews and tipped over the altar. The once-lit candles splayed across the floor in sticky globs of wax. Hernando pushed aside the torn curtain to the confessional and pressed against the back panel. It clicked open to reveal a hidden space.

Hernando pulled a stubby candle and lighter from beneath his brown robe and handed it to Michael. "Down you go. Watch the steps."

Handing his rifle to Hoffenberg, Michael lit the candle and ducked into the darkness. The feeble light bounced off rough walls and steps leading down. He took Claire's hand as she stepped in behind him and started down the stairs. Coolness rushed up to greet him as the musty smell of stone grew stronger. At the bottom of the stairs, the space opened up into a room.

"This place was built during the Inquisition." Hernando followed them down holding his own candle. He walked to the far wall and lit a sconce. "While we all wish for people to come to the true faith, my brothers and I do not believe in torturing others for different beliefs. A creed that led me to join a new brotherhood of resistance."

He lit several more sconces until light flooded the room. The basement was roughly twenty by twenty meters with a partitioned-off corner and a tall bookcase that sagged with books and jars. A small table with four chairs clustered in a corner. Across the space was a second flight of stairs.

"I h-hope we didn't c-cause you any t-trouble with the soldiers." Claire's teeth chattered as she hugged her arms around herself.

"They like nothing more than to create trouble." Hernando's eyes widened as he looked at her. "*Señorita*, you are shivering. Come at once and put on something warm. Here, there are things for you." He motioned her to the screened-off space.

Claire moved behind the screen and gasped. "Oh, a bed. How lovely. And clothes!"

"I hope they will do."

"Perfectly. Thank you. I mean, *gracias*."

"*De nada*." Hernando came back around the screen carrying blankets. He tossed them to Michael and Hoffenberg. "This is all I have to offer you right now. Tomorrow I will check the mission barrel. If I had known you were coming, I would have made sure to have a change of clothes for you. Wait a moment, and I'll bring you something to eat."

He disappeared up the second flight of stairs. Michael and Hoffenberg stripped out of their wet clothes, leaving on their knickers for modesty's sake, and wrapped up in the thick blankets.

Footsteps clattered on the stairs. They reached for their rifles.

"Do not shoot. It is me." Hernando popped his head around the corner.

Michael sighed with relief and leaned his gun against the wall, but within easy reach.

Hernando carried a platter of cheese, bread, grapes, and a jug of wine with three glasses. "I'm sorry I can't offer you more. Most of my food I have to hide from the Germans." He set the platter on the table and poured a liberal amount of wine into each glass. "*Por favor.*"

"It's a feast. Thank you." Michael took one of the cups and drained it dry to relieve his parched throat. The wine calmed his galloping pulse. "I apologize for not warning you that we were coming with the lady. It was a last-minute change of plans."

"It usually is with Nazis involved." Hernando massaged his tonsured head. "We'll talk more in the morning. Rest well tonight. You're safe here, but do not, for any reason, leave."

"Thank you, Father Hernando."

"*Buenas noches.*"

The priest trudged up the stairs. A single click resonated between the stone walls. Locked. No one was coming in, and, most certainly, no one was going out.

Michael rubbed his tired eyes. All he wanted was one good night's sleep out of the elements. Not even the cold floor could deter him. "Claire? Are you coming out? Hernando brought food."

She didn't answer.

"Claire?" Michael moved to the partition and rapped on it. "Are you all right?"

Silence.

He peeked around the divider. She lay curled up on the bed under a mountain of blankets sound asleep. Smiling, he stepped in and brushed a wet strand of hair from her cheek. Poor darling. How he wished he could spare her from this hardship. It was a dangerous enough trek for a trained soldier. The miles of walking over unfamiliar and uneven terrain wore him to the bone, but she hadn't uttered one word of complaint. He saw it in her eyes, though, and it grieved him more than his own exhaustion. She was the most important mission he'd ever undertaken. He would die before failing her.

Leaning down, he kissed her cheek. "Sleep well, my *chany*. We're close to freedom."

Claire jerked awake. A scream stuck in her throat as tears coursed down her face. A candle flickered nearby, highlighting her surroundings. She recognized nothing. Panic scuttled up her chest until memories flashed back. Running through the rain. Nazis. A priest.

She groped at the blanket covering her neck. She needed to breathe. The panic started again as the Nazi voices rang in her head.

Footsteps came. The bed sagged under additional weight and strong arms wrapped around her, pulling her close.

"*Shh.* It's all right." Michael pressed a kiss to her forehead. "You're safe here, Claire."

She melted into him and the fear ebbed away on a tide of relief.

"You were having a nightmare."

She nodded, scratching her cheek against the rough blanket wrapped around his shoulders. "It was raining and the Nazis were coming. They reached out for me. I couldn't find you." More tears pricked her eyes.

"Just a dream. It's over."

"But it's not, is it? We're still not free."

"We will be soon. I promise." He stroked her hair, easing the tension from her shaking limbs. "Try to think of something pleasant."

"Like Paris in the springtime."

"Paris is hardly pleasant at the moment."

"Before the war." She sighed and wriggled closer to him. "When it was full of possibilities and beauty. One day, I'll see it when it has those things again." Closing her eyes, her mind drifted on a sea of calm black. Michael's arms anchored her, giving her a haven against the storm raging outside. "Michael?"

"Hmm?"

"Stay with me. Please."

His breath hitched. Swinging his legs up on the small bed, he sat against the headboard and pulled her head down to rest on his chest. His heart beat strong and true under her ear. Claire curled her arms around him as, one by one, her dreams glided on the ebb and flow of his steady breathing, lulling her into a peaceful sleep.

CHAPTER 26

"You will know the safe places to stop by the red tablecloths hanging from clotheslines." Hernando unrolled a map of Spain across the table. "It's a sign among the Resistance fighters."

Claire leaned forward in her chair to find their place on the map. They'd come so far, yet Portugal's border was still such a long way away. "Your red flag wasn't on a clothesline. It hung above the door the night we arrived."

"It's unseemly for a priest to hang his clothes for all the congregants to see, so I don't have a line. Most churches hang their signs above the door."

"The Germans aren't suspicious?"

"Not when I go into a long sermon about the sacrificial blood of Christ and all who enter my doors being offered the free gift of atonement. The Nazis don't like hearing that they have to ask for forgiveness." Hernando frowned as he looked beyond her shoulder and jumped off his seat. "*Señor* Hoffenberg. I have asked you, again and again, to stay out of the sacramental wine. You have already drunk this month's allotment, and I've had to add water to next month's."

Across the room, Hoffenberg froze with the jug in his hand. "Sorry, *Padre*, but you wouldn't begrudge a man a few extra drops."

"What will I tell my congregation this Sunday when my shelves are empty?"

"Listen, if they drink this every week, they'll understand why it's all gone. It's delicious."

Michael swiveled in his chair and glared at his second-in-command. "Give back the wine and stop offending our host."

A flicker of humor sparked in the priest's eye. "I take no offense. I'm accustomed to seeing many drunks stumble through my doors."

"I'm not a drunk!" Hoffenberg glanced at the jug cradled in his arm. With a huff, he crossed the room and popped the cork back in it before setting it on the table. "Aftertaste is a bit sour."

Hernando pulled the jug closer to himself and sat. "As I was saying, watch for the signs. There aren't allies in every town, but they're close enough to give you food and shelter every few days. *Señora* Teresa will be the next contact if you follow the path I've laid out."

Claire's stomach rejoiced at the prospect of having food ready for them. Better than having to forage, as they'd done through France. "How will they know they can trust us?"

"*Dios aplastará la cabeza de la serpiente.* God will crush the serpent's head. You must remember that and repeat it only when asked for the code phrase."

Claire tried it, but her tongue struggled against the musicality of the words. Michael, however, said everything precisely but without the delicate roll. Hoffenberg was nearly perfect.

"It's the wine. Gets me in the spirit of things." He nudged Michael. "Spirits. Get it, boss?"

Michael ignored him and turned back to the map, muttering over distances divided by daylight and other practical things he worried himself over.

Claire settled back in her chair and continued her stitching. Hernando had found a sizable piece of flannel which she had cut into three. It may not be as practical as calculating the miles to Portugal's border, but on the cold nights to come she and the men would appreciate an extra pair of warm knickers.

Hernando pointed to something on the map. "When you leave tonight, this is where—"

The bell in the corner jingled, indicating someone had entered Hernando's home. His heavy eyebrows drew together. "Washerwoman's early. Excuse me a moment."

He trudged up the stairs that led away from the church. Hoffenberg waited for the lock to slide shut, then scurried behind the partition. A second later he came out chugging from a new bottle of wine.

Claire clicked her tongue. "Father Hernando won't be happy with you."

Hoffenberg shrugged. "What he don't know won't kill him. Unless you tell him."

"You're perfectly capable of getting into your own trouble without my help."

He toasted her with his bottle and brought it to his lips again for another long swig. He held it out to Michael. "Want some, boss?"

Michael batted it away without taking his eyes from the map. "I prefer not to indulge in stolen goods."

"Didn't see you complaining when we took those stolen rifles from Louie."

"Yes, well ... that's different."

"There! All done." Beaming, Claire held up the first pair of finished underpants. One leg was slightly longer but overall not bad. "What do you think?"

Michael and Hoffenberg looked between her and her red-and-black masterpiece, then at each other. Michael cleared his throat. "Um, what are they?"

Claire flushed. She remembered her dad and brother had such things drying on the clothesline back home. Perhaps European men were different. Heat crept up her neck. "You know ... to go under ... to keep you warm."

A grin broke across his face. "Very thoughtful of you. Do we need to try them on for alterations?"

Heat flashed across her cheeks. She threw them at him across the table. "Smarty-pants."

The lock above clicked. Footsteps hurried down the stairs, and Hernando burst into the room, panting. "You have to leave. Now."

Michael snapped to attention. "What happened?"

The priest's brown robes flapped about him like chicken wings as he folded up the map and shoved it at Michael. "The soldiers are ransacking the town. If they find the extra provisions in my home, they'll know I'm hiding people. *Vámonos!*"

Panic hit Claire. She leaped from her chair. "Have they followed us here?"

"News of fugitives travels fast, but this wouldn't be the first time they've caused trouble for the sake of scaring the locals."

"But we've put you in grave danger."

"Nonsense, my child. God has placed you in my keeping, and I will do His bidding for as long as He calls me to it." Hernando braved a smile and patted her cheek. "Now, come."

Gathering their few items, Claire tucked them into a sack. She shook her trembling fingers and tied a knot to secure the sack. "Wouldn't it be safer to stay here rather than expose ourselves?"

Michael shook his head and grabbed a rifle. "If the Germans find something suspicious in Hernando's house, they won't leave him alone. We'll never be able to leave, and no one else will be able to hide out here."

Claire nodded as she slipped her hand into his, the touch immediately steadying her nerves. They followed Hernando up the stairs. At the top, he peeled back a flap of canvas and peered through a peephole. He pushed against the wall, and it creaked open. Stepping through the opening, he motioned them out. They scrambled into a small living space. Hernando pushed back a bookcase.

"Take these." He grabbed two small bags from a kitchen table and tossed them to Claire. "It's not much, but it'll last for a few days."

She quickly stuffed them into the sack of clothes and hugged it to her chest as if her life depended on it. Perhaps it did.

Michael crossed the room and flattened himself next to the door. "Where are we to meet the cart?"

"In the western woods. Near the stream and the old mine. Half a mile from here." Hernando peeked out the window. The gray of afternoon light speckled his face.

Michael stuck his hand out. "Thank you for everything—"

"I'm taking you to the woods."

"Not necessary. I can find it. I won't allow you to be caught with us."

Hernando laid his hand on Michael's arm. "This is my mission, *mi hijo*. I will see you to the end." Bending down, he unstrapped the pistol from his ankle. "Time to go."

The ground was slick with mud as they crept out of the back of Hernando's house. Twilight's muted grays and blues melded everything into shadow. Claire forced her gaze to stay on Michael's back lest she imagined a Nazi instead of a tree as they raced into the woods. That must have been how Dorothy felt in Oz when all those horrid trees terrorized her.

On they ran, dodging limbs and tripping over rocks. Claire's lungs burned as her ears pricked for any sound of footsteps following. The thin trickle of a stream sounded through the bushes. The cart had to be close.

Hernando slowed and swerved behind a large oak. He motioned for them to get down. Claire flattened herself behind a tree. Michael moved in front of her like a shield while Hoffenberg hid on their other side. Muted voices drifted between the trees. Michael stiffened. Claire forced her breathing to quieten so she could hear.

German voices.

She gripped her sack tight. She could use it as a distraction if need be. Hopefully that would give her enough time to run. Or hide. Hernando motioned to Michael who nodded in return. Adrenaline zinged through Claire's body, readying her for action.

Stowing his pistol in his voluminous sleeves, Hernando stepped out from behind the trees. *"Buenas noches."*

Claire peeked around the tree. Two soldiers held a village man

Songbird and the Spy

between them. The man's nose bled as he begged. A cart and donkey stood behind them next to the stream. Their ride.

One of the soldiers released the man and shouted at Hernando. The priest smiled and kept walking toward them. The soldier pulled out a gun and aimed at Hernando. Michael whipped around the tree and fired. The German crumpled to the ground. Aiming at the other soldier, Michael walked forward giving commands in German. The soldier released the man, who ran around behind his cart.

Michael motioned the soldier to the ground. *"Nieder."*

The soldier dropped to the ground with his hands raised. He glared despite his shaking arms. Michael said something else. The prisoner shook his head.

Crack!

The prisoner slumped to the ground as blood oozed from his chest. Hernando shoved his pistol into his belt. "Never leave a survivor."

A sweaty hand clamped over Claire's mouth and dragged her behind the tree. "Squeak and I'll cut you, *kleine Maus.*" The German voice breathed in her ear.

Claire stiffened as he pressed a knife to her throat and hauled her against his body. Michael called for her. Her mind scrambled for escape, but the man's arms held her like steel bands.

"Claire?" Michael came around the tree. "We need to go—" He stopped dead in his tracks. Fury darkened his face. *"Lässt sie los."*

The knife pressed into Claire's neck. She whimpered as warm drops spilled down her throat. The German shouted at Michael. Knuckles white, Michael slowly lowered his gun to the ground while keeping his gaze on the man. He shouted again, and Michael held his hands up, his face deathly calm. Claire scanned the trees. Where were Hoffenberg and the priest?

The man's arm tightened around Claire as he dragged her backward. She dug her heels into the dirt, the sack bouncing across her knees. The sack! She swung it and smacked the side of the man's head. His grip loosened, and she flung herself sideways, grazing the knife against her throat. Michael sprang forward and tackled the man to the ground.

They writhed like snakes on the grass, the blade a dull gleam of metal between them. Elbows jabbed, and knees hammered amid their grunts. They flipped, and Michael landed on his back. The German heaved down on top of him, the knife grasped between them as the point lowered toward Michael's heart.

Claire scrambled for Michael's gun. Throwing it to her shoulder, she took aim and squeezed the trigger.

The German arched up, blood welling from the hole in his chest. He slumped forward, then moved no more. Claire clutched the gun as disbelief washed over her. A horrible drowning sensation numbed her.

Hoffenberg and Hernando raced through the trees. Hoffenberg pushed the dead man off Michael and knelt beside him. He spoke, but Claire couldn't make out the words. A hand closed over hers. She looked up. Hernando. His mouth moved, but she couldn't focus. Only one thing stuck in her mind.

"I killed him." The confession broke her submerged spell. She shoved the gun into Hernando's hands. "Take it!"

She raced to Michael's side. A dark red line sliced from his pectoral to his stomach. No! Dear God, no. Her fingers fluttered to his wrist for a pulse. It was weak.

"It's not deep, but he's losing blood." Hoffenberg pressed down on the wound. "He needs stitches."

Hernando stepped behind him. "You have no time for that. You must go. Now."

Michael's teeth grit together as he pushed away their hands. "Don't worry 'bout me. I-I'll make it."

"You'd better. For now, a binding will have to suffice. Once we're a safe distance away, we'll sew you. I've my sewing kit." Claire looked frantically about for something to use as a dressing. "Didn't we pack bandages?" She dug through the sack and yanked out the flannel underpants. With a quick jerk, the seams popped open. "Lift him."

Hoffenberg and Hernando eased Michael into a sitting position, and Claire wrapped the bloomers around his chest and stomach, tying off the crude dressing. Michael grunted, but didn't utter a word.

Not looking at the German's body, Claire grabbed her sack and climbed into the back of the hay-filled cart as Hoffenberg helped Michael crawl in behind her. He laid down, pain creasing his face.

"It'll be all right." She smoothed the hair from Michael's pale forehead. "Just don't die on me."

"I'll try not to." He attempted a smile, but it didn't push past the agony in his eyes. He moved a hand protectively over his chest as Hoffenberg settled on the other side of him.

Hernando spoke quietly with the driver. The man wiped the blood from his nose and climbed up to the bench to take the reins.

"I'll take care of the bodies and tracks." Lines creased Hernando's brow as he looked down at Michael. "Yarrow will help him heal. There's a patch of it I often collect from a mile north of here past the edge of the wood. See to it quickly, or I fear an infection might take him." He covered the three of them with hay. "God bless you on your journey."

Claire took his hand and squeezed. "Thank you for everything."

"Go in peace, *señorita*." He smiled and piled hay on top of her head.

The driver clicked his tongue, and the cart jerked into motion. Michael's hand reached for Claire's. She laced her fingers through his clammy ones to stop the trembling. Could the cart not go any faster? They hit a rut. Michael moaned.

Claire stroked his face. "It will be all right, darling. I promise." But her promise rang hollow against Hernando's words. *Quickly or infection might take him*.

Infection could take a flying leap. It wasn't taking Michael anywhere. Not on her watch.

CHAPTER 27

Claire held up her needle. Orange light from the campfire danced on its silver surface. "I've never sewn up a person before."

Hoffenberg jerked back as if she'd stuck him. "And you think I have?"

"I'm sure your seedy background has led you to more than one back-alley brawl. Certainly you've patched up a buddy or two."

"Doesn't make me qualified."

Michael grunted from his prone position between them on the ground. Sweat dotted his ashen brow. "Keep arguing and there won't be any use in patching me up."

"None of that talk now, boss. Your lady here is going to sew you up tight as a drum while I mash this yarrow to keep the fever at bay." Hoffenberg ripped the leaves off the stalky green plant and ground them with a rock.

Michael's eyelids fluttered closed. "Get it over with."

Claire pressed a hand to his forehead. He was burning up. Squelching her flaring panic, she turned to the fire and passed the needle several times over the flame. The one time she needed alcohol and not a drop to be had.

Taking a deep breath, she poised the needle over Michael's bare flesh. Hoffenberg had shaved the ruddy hairs from Michael's chest so they wouldn't interfere with the stitches. His uneven knife strokes left a pale path of Irish skin in its wake, the muscles well-defined below the surface.

Michael flinched with her first pass of the needle but quickly set to gritting his teeth as his hands clenched at his sides. Firelight bounced across his contorted features and over the planes of his body. The heat warmed Claire's face. Sweat trickled down her back, but she dared not move any further away from its guiding light. It was chancy, lighting a fire to begin with, but their driver had taken them to a cleft in a rocky hillside saying it would be safe enough for their emergency purposes. The Germans had never ventured that far on patrol. Hopefully they wouldn't make an exception that night.

By the time she tied off the final knot over Michael's stomach, Claire's hand had long since stopped shaking despite her pounding heart. A thin sheen of sweat covered his body, and his head twitched. She checked his pulse. Strong but fast. Too fast.

She looked to Hoffenberg. "Do you have the yarrow ready?"

He handed her a tin cup with yarrow-steeped water. "Get it into his gullet while I put the rest of this on the wound. Should help to stop infection. Dirty kraut must've had a filthy blade."

Claire held the cup to Michael's lips. "Open up." Michael twisted away. She pulled his head back and grasped his chin. "You need to drink so we can get that fever down."

Michael cracked his mouth open, and she poured the tepid brew between his lips. He coughed but swallowed. She tipped the cup again. Finally, he drained the contents and collapsed.

"Do you have any more?" she asked Hoffenberg.

He shook his head as he dusted the green flecks from his hand. Exhaustion smudged under his eyes. "Used the last bit of it. Does he need more?"

Claire stroked the matted hair from Michael's face as her heart clenched. "We'll know in a while."

A while came and sweat drenched Michael as spasms gripped the long lines of his body in feverish torment. Claire dipped a pair of the flannel underpants in the last drops of water and bathed it over his burning skin. The water evaporated as if washed across a skillet.

She passed the cup to Hoffenberg. "We need more water. And yarrow."

"There's a stream around the other side of the hill, but the yarrow is a good quarter mile away if I can even find it by moonlight. It was tricky enough identifying it without the flowers."

"Do the best you can."

Michael twisted and smacked her hand away from his face. She grabbed his arm and pinned it to his side. He continued to thrash beneath her hands.

Hoffenberg grabbed Michael's other arm. Concern pulled his mouth down as he glanced at Claire. "You all right?"

She waved him off. "Fine. Go, please."

Firelight delved into the creases of Hoffenberg's face, aging him years beyond his youth. "Maybe I should sit with you awhile. At least until he calms down."

"I'm afraid he won't calm down until we can break the fever."

Hoffenberg's lips pressed together. With a quick nod, he eased to his feet and slung one of the rifles over his shoulder before hooking the canteen to his belt. "Douse that fire. I'll be back as quick as I can."

He sidled through the entrance and slipped into the night. Claire tamped down the fire until only the embers glowed a dull red then sat next to Michael, the other rifle resting nearby. She stroked his brow and hummed softly as he shook against the heat demons pilfering his body. Never had she felt so helpless.

In the glow of the flickering embers, her hands flushed red as if covered in blood. Sickness roiled in her gut. Were they not bloodied? She'd killed a man.

She clenched them together, desperate to rid herself of the feel of the gun. She had killed and then hours later she'd used those same hands to preserve life, Michael's life. But now she might lose him too.

She grasped Michael's hand and brought it to her quivering lips. "Don't leave me. Please don't leave me here alone."

Claire woke to the early rays of sun slanting off the walls. A sharp pain jolted down her neck as she straightened her head from its odd angle. Rubbing the aching spot, she glanced down at Michael and gasped. His smooth, dry brow was pale, but his chest rose evenly in sleep. She placed two fingers to the pulse beneath his jaw. Strong and steady.

"Thank God!"

Hoffenberg shifted from his lookout position near the entrance. "Is he awake?"

"No, but sleeping soundly. I believe he's out of danger."

A tired smile crossed his face. "He should be after what you've done. I've never seen a nurse more dedicated to her patient."

"This nurse wouldn't have made it far without her aide. Thank you." He picked up his gun and checked it, but not before she noticed the pink staining his cheeks.

Claire pulled back the jacket she had draped over Michael and examined the wound. The black thread marred his pale skin like tiny railroad tracks. She smiled in relief. The yarrow had done its job.

Michael's eyes cracked open to a sliver of blue. "You certainly are pretty to wake up to." Sleep thickened his voice.

Claire stroked the side of his face. Her heart pattered with happiness. "Good morning. You gave us quite the scare."

"My apologies." He shifted and grimaced, then gingerly touched his chest. "This is going to make walking difficult."

She placed her hands on his shoulders to keep him from rising. "We'll take it easy."

"No, we need to move. The longer we stay in one place, the more danger we're in."

"Michael. You've been sliced open. You move around too much, and those stitches will bust. I'll run out of thread if I have to fix you again."

His gaze drifted to the packed-dirt walls of the crevice. Pale sunlight washed over the top and filtered down to them. "Nightfall then."

Claire looked to Hoffenberg for reinforcement, but he merely shrugged. She sighed. The mission stopped for no man. Not even a recently stabbed one.

CHAPTER 28

"How much longer until Lisbon?" Claire stifled a yawn. Dead on her feet, it took every ounce of willpower to put one foot in front of the other.

"Two or three more days if the weather stays fair," Michael said as he marched ahead of her.

Two weeks had passed since his run-in with that German knife. The wound was healing nicely, thanks to Hoffenberg's foraging for yarrow. Only after a steep climb or particularly long day would Michael hint at his discomfort. Stubborn man. He'd only admit to his pain if he fell down dead. Even then she had her doubts.

Claire ached to take off her shoes and rub her raw feet in the grass, but by now they were welded to the socks and leather after weeks of sloshing through rivers, mud, and every other unimaginable situation. She tried not to complain, but some nights it was impossible to keep the tears at bay. "Can we stop for a moment, please?"

Michael turned back. Concern creased his face. "Are you all right?"

She nodded as she put a hand to her aching back. "Just need to catch my breath, so neither of you has to carry me over the next hill." And so Michael didn't pop a seam.

"A rest sounds good to me." Hoffenberg plopped on top of a rock and opened the satchel slung over his shoulder. "I've been smelling this bread and apples all day. About time we dug into them." He divided the shares they had obtained from a resistance safe house two nights prior. Polishing an apple on his grimy sleeve, he took a large chomp of the fruit. "My favorite part of traveling.

You get to try all sorts of food from very nice ladies."

Michael examined his apple. "I'm waiting for the day someone throws in a big juicy steak with roasted potatoes."

Claire stared at her apple, its blood red color taunting her. The shock of the gunshot rippled in her hands. The lifeless stare of the German still sought her in the darkest parts of her nightmares. She dropped the apple and rubbed her hands together, desperate to wipe away the blood.

"Claire. What's wrong?" Michael's sharp voice jerked her back. He picked up the apple and held it out to her. "Eat."

She lurched to her feet. "I'm not hungry."

Grabbing the canteen, he took her elbow. "Come with me."

They walked the few yards away to a clear, tumbling stream. Claire knelt on the grass and stuck her hands in the icy water, trying to wash them clean.

Michael squatted next to her. "Tell me. And don't say nothing is wrong."

Claire scrubbed her numb fingers together. "I killed him." It was no more than a whisper, but the words clanged in her ears.

"You had no choice. He was going to kill me."

She squeezed her eyes shut. "Don't do that. Don't justify what I've done. I'm a murderer now, just like them."

"You did what you had to do, but not because you wanted to. Your remorse proves that you're not like them. You could never be like them."

She opened her eyes and pulled her hands from the water. "What of these? How can I ever play again with murdering hands?"

"The same way I can do this." He stroked her cheek with the backs of his fingers. "War forces us to do terrible things for the sake of survival. You must find the strength to forgive yourself. If you don't, the guilt will eat you alive."

"Looks like we're intruding on a private moment." A heavily accented voice cut through the haze.

Six men dressed in dark-green fatigues emerged from the trees behind Michael. One of them shoved Hoffenberg to the ground in front of them. Portuguese soldiers. With rifles.

"Captain, I believe you were called. That means you're in charge here." The man closest to Michael nudged him in the back with his toe. "Which means you should set a good example and not cause any problems."

"You have me at too much of a disadvantage to cause any problems," Michael said.

Claire's heart drummed in her ears. Not again.

"Stand up, all of you." The soldier grabbed Michael's arm and yanked him to his feet. "Put your hands behind your backs."

Claire and Hoffenberg did as they were told. When their hands were tied, the soldiers escorted them through the woods to a covered truck. The lead soldier swept his hand to the back of it. "All aboard."

"I thought Portugal was neutral," Claire whispered to Michael as they climbed in and sat with their backs against the cab. Three of the soldiers came in after them while the other two sat up front.

"That doesn't mean we tolerate troublemakers sneaking across our borders." One of the guards kicked her foot.

She glared at him. "We're not troublemakers."

Michael glared at her. Good thing his hands were tied, or they'd be clamped over her mouth like a steel trap.

The guards snickered. It sucked the fire out of Claire, leaving her with an empty, aching gut.

The truck rumbled on for hours, swerving around like James Cagney's getaway car. Then, without warning, the driver slammed on the brakes, and her head thumped against the back of the cab. She bit her lip to keep from crying out. The three guards jumped down and signaled for the prisoners to climb out.

Claire blinked against the bright sun. They stood in a large courtyard in front of a sprawling white stucco building. Purple bougainvillea climbed the walls, and numerous potted flowers sat beside a double set of open French doors. Gauzy white curtains billowed on the breeze. It looked so peaceful, apart from the armed guards walking along the roof and around the gated walls.

The first soldier motioned to his men. *"Trazer à menina."*

Two guards grabbed Claire by the arms and dragged her toward the open doors. "Michael!" She twisted and kicked, landing a blow to one of their shins, but they didn't release her.

"Let her go!" Michael yelled.

Terrified, Claire dug her heels into the ground, but the men yanked harder. "Where are you taking me? Michael!"

"Claire!" She twisted her head to see a guard point a rifle at Michael's chest. His shouts followed her inside, up a sweeping staircase, and along the arched corridors. She pulled frantically against her captors' grip, but they held tight, stopping in front of a thick wooden door with black iron hinges. One knock and the door opened.

An old woman with a wizened face and a long black braid looped over her shoulder smiled at Claire. *"Vêm em, meu filha,"*

The men dropped Claire's arms and cut her bonds. Then, they left without a word. Bewildered, Claire moved into the room, rubbing her sore arms. Thin white curtains fluttered in front of open windows. A four-poster bed and the scent of fresh flowers filled the airy space. A large copper tub stood in the middle of the brick floor.

"Where am I?"

The woman smiled a toothless grin. *"Casa do bode branco."* She reached for Claire's coat.

Claire took a step back. "No. I don't understand."

"It means house of the white goat." A young woman close to Claire's age with a long black braid swinging across her back walked in carrying two buckets of steaming water. "Of course, it's been changed to Fort White Goat now by the residing soldiers."

The old woman slipped Claire's coat and kerchief off, then tossed them in a basket before Claire had a chance to react.

"Forgive my grandmother." The young woman poured the

water into the tub. The faint scent of roses wafted from the steam. "She hates dirty things."

Claire pressed a hand to her head. "I must be dreaming. A very bizarre dream."

"No dream." The girl pulled a cake of soap from her apron pocket and placed it on a stand next to the tub. "Or we would be out of a job. It was exciting to hear a woman was coming."

"You heard I was coming? How? What is all this?"

"This?" The girl swept a hand around the room. "This is for you, Claire."

Claire grabbed hold of the bedpost before she slid to the ground. "I beg your pardon?"

"Michael Reiner. Captain of His Majesty's Royal Air Force. 23217208."

"That's it? You can tell us something more." The guard swung his leg as he perched on the edge of the desk.

"Michael Reiner. Captain of His Majesty's Royal Air Force. 23217208." Michael stared at a painting of the ocean on the wall behind the desk.

"We already know that." The guard sighed. "How about the girl. Where's she from and where are you taking her? Planning to get all the way back to jolly old England from here?"

Michael forced his fingers flat on his knees. "Michael Reiner. Captain of His Majesty's Royal Air Force. 23217208."

The guard groaned. "How many times are we supposed to hear that?"

The door banged open, and footsteps marched across the floor. "As many times as you ask him questions, Sergeant. Get off my desk."

The sergeant hopped off the desk and rendered a British-style salute before scurrying out the door.

"You're about to cost me a boatload of paperwork, Captain," the newcomer said in English and slammed a handful of folders on the desk as he rounded it. Short and squatty with a bald spot, he glowered at Michael.

Michael glanced at the British crown insignia on the man's collar. "Sir?"

"Major Thornbush." His bottlebrush mustache twitched as he planted both palms on the desk and leaned forward. "I've been waiting for you to show up ever since you informed command of your hairbrained idea to smuggle a girl out of the country. And not just some girl—a Yank. Now, because of some fiasco involving an SS officer, you're on the run too."

Michael jumped to attention. "Sir, I can explain."

"You'd better because I'm dying to know why you've abandoned your post and taken another man with you."

After two hours of explanations and drilling questions, Michael's mouth felt like it was full of cotton balls.

"They'll put you back in the field," Thornbush said. "Not in France of course. You're too much of a liability now."

"Yes, sir. I expected that."

"They want you back in England for a full debriefing, and, most likely, a good rear chewing. But, according to your file, you are too valuable to demote or slap in the brig."

Michael shifted in his chair. At least Thornbush wasn't talking treason. "I've been chewed out before, sir."

Thornbush's mustache twitched. Rising, he walked to a small table lined with bottles and glasses. He poured Michael a full glass of water. Michael drank it like a man in the desert.

"Now, about this girl," the major said. "Are you sure you want to send her back to the States?"

Michael nodded. "She belongs with her family where it's safe. They don't even know if she's alive or not."

"They do."

Michael jumped to the edge of his chair. "Sir?"

"According to your commander, you once requested they send word to her family in America. I understand they sent a telegram some time ago."

Relief poured through Michael like a sweet rain. Now he could tell them she was coming home. The bittersweet reality twisted his gut. She was leaving him, but she'd be safe. "Sir, where is Miss Baudin?"

"Being taken care of." Thornbush's lip twitched as he eyed Michael up and down. "You may see her later after you're scrubbed free of the pigsty you've been rolling in."

Michael resisted the urge to lift his arm and sniff. Had he been filthy for so long that he no longer noticed the stench? Poor Claire.

"I have a transport leaving on Friday." Thornbush sat in his chair and pulled a stack of files toward him. "You, your lady friend, and Lieutenant Hoffenberg will be on it. After that, you belong to the boys on Baker Street. Dismissed."

Michael stood, saluted, and marched from the room in a daze. The last few days began to take their toll. Of all the scenarios he'd imagined, he'd never anticipated being rescued by British forces. And now he had a ticket home. Though he was bound for possibly the worst dressing down in military history, it was still better than being shackled in the Glasshouse or Colchester Garrison.

A guard escorted him to a room where a tub filled with warm water awaited him. He soaked and scrubbed every inch of his body, taking special care around the thick pucker of healing skin slicing from just below his heart to his navel. When the water turned cool, he stepped out and slipped into a fresh set of fatigues. After tying his boots, he glanced in the mirror and immediately regretted it. A scarecrow stared back at him. His hair brushed against the tops of his ears. Thick red whiskers swept across his jaw and throat. Eyes shot with red.

He scratched his chin, rasping the thick hairs beneath his short nails. "I may not be able to take care of the sleep problem yet, but I can do something about this."

Rummaging under a pile of towels, he found a grooming kit. After lathering up, he swiped away the beard with the razor, then used a small pair of scissors to trim the hair above his ears. The rest needed a professional's touch, but at least he would be presentable for Claire again. He ran his hands over his British dress with pride. Now to go and find the lady.

After leaving his room, he descended a flight of stairs to the first floor and walked along a breezeway with a courtyard on one side and a garden on the other. Rounding the corner of what appeared to be a library, footstep thundered behind him behind him. He turned in time to catch Claire as she launched herself into his arms.

"Michael!" A shower of kisses fell on his cheeks, neck, and forehead, with the sweetest of all landing on his lips. He pulled her close, suffering the slight sting across his chest, and inhaled her rosewater scent. She dropped her arms from around his neck and slipped her hand into his. So soft and warm. "Where have you been?"

"Cleaning up for you." He squeezed her fingers, relishing how perfectly they fit between his. "Apparently my efforts have not been in vain."

She grinned. Her shining hair fell around the shoulders of a blue dress that turned her eyes to fire-glazed sapphires. And her shoes didn't have holes in them. "No, they haven't. What else? And don't lie to me because Hoffenberg saw you dragged into a room."

Michael sighed. No avoiding it. "I had more than a few questions to answer. It seems they've been expecting us."

"Yes, I know."

"How?"

"Carmo and her grandmother, Ines. They serve as maids upstairs. They also said we won't be staying long."

He nodded. "We leave Friday for England."

"England? I've never been there." Her eyes brightened with excitement. "I'm sure it's different now with the war on, but I would still like to see it. Will we have time for you to show me around a little bit or do you need to report straight away?"

His heart constricted. "I'm afraid there won't be time. I'm to report to the office in London, and"—he swallowed past the dryness in his throat—"you'll need to be on a boat or plane without delay."

Her fingers twitched in his hand. "Why do I need a boat or plane?"

"Because you're going back to America."

"No."

"Claire, we've talked about this."

She dropped his hand and balled her fists on her hips. "Don't use that I-know-better-than-you tone with me."

"In this case, I do."

Footsteps sounded in the distance. Taking her elbow, he guided her into the library and closed the door behind them. She stalked to the middle of the room and braced her feet apart. If she had a cape, she could have been a matador, and a lovelier opponent he'd never faced.

"I know you're trying to keep me from harm's way by sending me back to my family, who have probably been grieving over me for the past … however long I've been here. I can't even remember." She pressed a hand to her head.

"Counting your time at the *conservatoire,* almost three years, and they're not grieving. My command post was able to notify them. I was informed during my briefing session a little while ago."

She rocked back on her heels. Mist sheened her eyes. "Thank you. They must have been worried sick. What about my aunt and uncle?"

Michael shook his head. "No news yet."

Claire stood quietly for a moment staring at the wall. Then, with a loud sniff, she blinked back the moisture and squared her shoulders. "My family knows I'm not dead. There's no reason to travel across the Atlantic to tell them something they already know."

"You don't think they want to see you after all this time? To get you away from the war?"

"I'm sure they do, and someday I will, but not now."

Michael ground his teeth in frustration. "This isn't a discussion, Claire. I'm telling you—"

"And I'm not one of your soldiers to boss around. Last I checked I could make my own decisions."

"What is it you've decided to do? Where are you planning to live? What about money?"

"I'll find a job in England. According to the BBC on Giles' radio, the USO has set up camp in London. They're always looking for entertainers." She raised her chin. "I realize you have a duty to complete, but this way there won't be an ocean between us."

"Why are you being so stubborn about this? Can't you see I'm trying to do what's best for you?"

"What's best for me is to be with you. In France, Germany, England, or the Arctic Circle. I'm not leaving you, and if you force me, I'll find a way to come back. You know I will."

He wanted to ask her to wait for him, to be the one he came home to when the war was over. But common sense rallied against it. She needed to be safe where he didn't have to worry about her. Someplace where the ravages of war didn't explode around her day and night. A cottage on the coast perhaps.

It took everything in him to keep from closing the distance between them and claiming her lips, leaving no doubt of how much he cared for her. Instead, he crossed his arms, clamping his hands against his sides. "Most likely, I will not be reassigned in England, and you cannot follow me to the continent. Can't you at least see the reason in that? I may be gone a long time. This war could stretch on for years."

"I'll wait."

"And if I don't come back? Claire, you need to understand that there's a very real chance that I may not come back at all."

"I realize that." Her gaze flickered to the ground. "But I'm not going to sit halfway around the world wondering and waiting. I'm going to be as near to you as possible."

The corner of Michael's mouth pulled up. "You're a stubborn one, you are. Can't for the life of me figure out why you want to stick around."

Clasping her hands behind her back, she sashayed toward him. A saucy smile played across her lips. "I kinda like you. What can I say?"

"Another mystery."

She stopped in front of him. "Are you kidding? A trilingual Irishman in uniform. What a catch."

"I can also ask, 'Where's the pub?' in Italian." Grabbing her by the waist, he pulled her against him. Her lips moved sweetly under his, igniting a fire that burned him. He wound his fingers into the damp curls at the back of her neck. The scent of roses and the warmth of her arms tantalized his senses.

"Oops. Sorry, boss."

Michael pulled away to see Hoffenberg standing with the door wide open. "Are you here for a reason, or are you just taking in the views?"

"Major Thornbush wants to see you."

"He saw me not two hours ago."

Hoffenberg shrugged. "This time he wants us both in there. I figure if it's a lashing, they can kill two birds with one stone."

Michael grunted and turned back to Claire. He ran a hand over the front of his uniform. "One of these days I'm going to kiss you without interruption."

She brushed a few specks from his shoulder and patted his cheek. "I'll be waiting."

He started for the door.

"Does that mean I can start looking for apartments once we get to England?"

"It means I'll think about it. And they're called flats." Michael closed the door on her hopeful face and marched down the hallway with Hoffenberg. "Find out if you can get messages in and out of here. I need to send an immediate telegram to Ireland."

"Letting the folks know where you are?"

"Not exactly." They paused at Thornbush's aide's desk. "I thought I might prepare them for the sudden arrival of a houseguest."

With the telegram sent to his parents, Michael sat at the desk in the room he shared with Hoffenberg. Pulling out a fresh sheet of paper and pen, he took a deep breath.

Dear Mr. and Mrs. Baudin,

My name is Captain Michael Reiner. I have had the privilege of knowing your daughter for the past year while stationed in France. During our time together, I have come to know no finer or braver woman than Claire. I love her as dearly as the breath I take, and with your permission, I would like to ask for her hand in marriage. I promise to take care of her, treat her with the respect she deserves, and always be faithful. I apologize for the suddenness of my declaration, but times like these have a way of opening a man's eyes to what truly matters. I hope we all may meet someday, but until then I remain yours.

Respectfully,
Michael Reiner

CHAPTER 29

London, England

Claire twisted this way and that in front of the mirror, marveling at the feel of a real satin slip gliding over her skin once again. A thrill of anticipation pebbled her arms.

The velvet curtain rustled. "Are you decent, miss?"

"Yes, come in."

The curtain pushed aside, and the sales clerk of Bourne and Hollingsworth glided into the dressing room. Four more outfits draped across her arms. "Utility clothes. More functional and less expensive to produce now that materials are being rationed."

Claire selected the top garment and slipped into it. The dark blue dress fit her like a box. Its only adornment boasted of two pockets and three buttons down the front. She tugged at the scratchy collar. "No."

"Your gentleman has requested to see them all."

"He may never want to look at me again if he sees me in this."

The woman smiled with understanding as she hung the other garments on a hook. "They get used to it when the whole country is wearing them."

Taking a deep breath as her excitement sagged, Claire stepped out of the dressing room to the showcase area lined with gilded mirrors and floral wallpaper. Michael reclined on a pink velvet settee with one foot resting casually atop his opposite knee. His eyebrows rose as she moved forward for inspection.

Claire brushed her hand down the skirt as if that would make it better. "Maybe in another color."

"On the dais, please." He pointed to the platform in the center of the room.

She stepped on the raised area. Her reflection bounced across the dozens of mirrors, catching her from every angle. Not one of them did a whit of good.

Snapping on her pincushion wristband, the clerk marched to Claire and tugged at the excess material hanging around her waist. "We can take it in several inches for a better fit but remember it won't be as figure hugging as we may like. You must be able to move freely during a bombing raid."

Claire gulped and stood still as the woman measured and pinned her. Standing back to admire her work, the woman nodded. "Splendid."

"Is it?" Claire frowned at her reflection. The garment swallowed her.

"It will be once we add the finishing touch." then slipped it from a pink box, the clerk slipped the pocketbook over Claire's arm. "Standard black goes with everything and look." She pointed at a small compartment built into the bottom. "A perfect fit for your gas mask."

"*Très chic*." Claire spun on the dais and held the purse aloft in a model pose. "What do you think?"

Michael nodded. "Stylish indeed."

"A moment, if you will, while I pop into the stockroom to see if they've brought in the new shoes." The clerk disappeared with a swish of her measuring tape.

"If we're going for practicality, I hope the shoes have buckles that can double as shovels should we need to entrench ourselves." Michael took a sip of his tea from the dainty china the clerk had provided. "Or a cup and saucer for tea. Much more British."

"You're enjoying this too much."

"Yes, I am. As you should be."

Easy enough for him to say. His civilian trousers and jacket were tailored perfectly to show off his broad shoulders and trim waist.

Claire fingered one of the buttons on her bodice. "You shouldn't spend your clothing rations on all these new clothes for me. A few blouses and sensible skirts will do me fine."

"What happened to that fashionable girl I met on the train? Has she suddenly turned schoolmarm on me?" Setting down his cup, he walked to her and took her hands. "Claire, we left France with nothing but the clothes on our backs. I want to do this for you. Let me."

He'd spent a minimum amount of his clothing rations on himself, declaring the rest were for her. With no money of her own, she had no option but to let him. It had prickled her pride but allowing him to help had led them to a level of intimacy they had never shared before. He wasn't simply buying her a cup of coffee, but an entire wardrobe to rebuild her life. A life she wanted with him.

Slipping her hands from his, Claire laced them behind his head and drew him close as love swelled her heart. "It'll cost you for that privilege."

His blue eyes twinkled. "Oh? What's the price?"

"A club sandwich with a slice of chocolate cake."

"That would cost a lot of ration stamps. Bacon doesn't come cheap."

"A kiss then."

He kissed her softly, setting off tiny fireworks.

"Ahem." The clerk cleared her throat.

Michael pulled back without a hint of remorse. Claire's cheeks burned.

"You're in luck. This is the last pair in your size." Kneeling in front of Claire, the woman pulled a pair of brown low-heeled Oxfords from a shoebox and slipped them onto Claire's feet.

The stiff material encased her entire foot. She sighed with acceptance and glanced at Michael in the mirror. "No buckles."

"The metal was needed to make arms." The clerk squinted at Claire's legs. "Oh, dear. We'll need to do something about those right away."

She hustled Claire back into the dressing room and whipped a pair of rayon stockings from her smocked uniform. "Silk is needed for parachutes, I'm afraid. If you don't care for these, Max Factor makes a brilliant pan stick to paint on the color." She leaned in and whispered. "Tea works in a pinch. Have a girlfriend help draw the seams."

What was the world coming to when the German army forced ladies to dip-dye their legs like Easter eggs?

The curtain rustled, and a dress was thrust into the room. "Try this," said Michael from the other side.

All thoughts of eggs disappeared as Claire unpacked herself from the box dress and wriggled into the floral dream. Sprays of white flowers covered the red A-line dress. A dozen tiny buttons glided down the back and a smart collar set it off to perfection. She tapped her toes with excitement as the garment slid over her thighs.

"It's from three seasons ago, but it's a dream on you." The clerk clasped her hands with a wide smile. "I have just the thing to top it off. Back in a dash!"

She left, but Claire couldn't wait for her to return. Grinning from ear to ear, she glided out of the dressing room and slinked toward Michael. He sat up on the settee, nearly sloshing his tea, and whistled. "That's more like it."

She twirled and laughed as the hemline floated out around her knees. "Where am I supposed to wear this in Ireland?"

"You'll wear it here with me and again when I return. It's the closest thing to what you wore when I first met you." Rising from his seat, he grabbed her hand and twirled her. "Onstage with your violin would be perfect too."

Her laughter faded. She stared at her hands as thoughts of playing again surged from where she had kept them locked behind guilt-ridden bars. Her nightmares had eased, but the dead German was always there, crouching in the recess to spring forth when her guard fell.

"It will get easier. I promise."

She met Michael's sympathetic gaze and pushed aside the thoughts. Today was for rebuilding what had been lost. She kissed him soundly on the cheek. "I love the dress."

An hour later, Claire had a brand-new suitcase stuffed with outfits, underclothes, shoes, three hankies, and a brush and comb set. Michael forked over the clothing rations and instructed the purchases to be delivered to her hotel room later that afternoon.

They left the store and strolled down the sandbag-lined sidewalk. One block ahead, church bells rang, their solemnity echoing between the gray buildings. Men dressed in their finest uniforms marched out of the front doors and stood on the steps, saluting as a flag-draped casket was carried out. A young woman in black, holding onto a toddler, reached out a trembling hand as the box passed. The gold band on her left hand winked in the sunlight. Claire gripped Michael's arm as the woman's outstretched fingers fell short of the casket. A loud sob rustled the veil covering her face.

Michael removed his hat and Claire dipped her head as the casket and its mourners proceeded into the churchyard. The bells sounded their mournful toll as they continued down the sidewalk in silence.

A tightness lodged in Claire's chest. She dug her fingers into Michael's arm. So alive and strong, she could never think of him otherwise, but how quickly it could all change. Was the knife incident not proof enough? How easily she could become that woman in black. Claire peeked up at him. He looked straight ahead, expressionless. As if sensing her gaze, he covered her hand with his and squeezed. The tightness in her chest eased, fractional though it was, but she would take it for all it was worth.

They walked to the bustling hub of Trafalgar Square, and Claire breathed a tiny sigh of relief as the noise drowned out her morose thoughts. Buying ham sandwiches wrapped in wax paper and two apples from a cart, they sat on the steps of the National Gallery with other Londoners taking a late afternoon lunch.

Claire bit into her sandwich. "This is the most delicious thing I've eaten in a long time. You can't go wrong with bread, meat, and cheese."

Michael chewed thoughtfully and swallowed. "I'm not complaining, mind you, but I'd give a full rations book for a proper lamb stew."

As they ate, sunlight danced off the double fountain waters, the carefree splashing sounds filling the square. The statues of Lord Nelson and his four lions kept watch as people hurried along, their faces tired but not anxious or fearful. And no wonder. The war had touched them all certainly, but Nazis didn't march among them. Scars from the Blitz over a year ago still marred the city with its cratered buildings and piles of rubble, but today the sun shone brightly as men and women wrapped their arms about each either. A small slice of heaven.

"It's so strange to be out like this. Sitting where we like without fear of being arrested." Claire dusted the crumbs from her hands. "I still find myself looking over my shoulder, waiting for a German soldier to appear."

"Plenty of soldiers here, but they're the good guys."

"Yes, *you* are the good guys." She squeezed his arm. "Only a good man would sit for three hours in a women's dressing area without a single complaint."

He leaned back on his elbows as his gaze swept leisurely over her. A smile curved his lips. "Getting you all to myself, examining you from every possible angle without looking like a lecher, and, most importantly, no one shooting at us. Trust me, *chany*, I have no complaints." He touched the brim of her new white straw hat. "Not to mention the beautiful smile you've worn all day."

"It's exciting getting a new wardrobe, but I'm happier just to have you with me." She kissed his cheek. "Thank you for everything."

"I like spoiling you."

"I like that you like to."

"Is there any place else you'd like to go?" Closing his eyes, he tilted his face up to the warm sun. Having removed his hat, his hair gleamed copper, and the lines around his mouth eased. Claire had never seen him so relaxed. It made her heart skip.

"I need to find a beauty counter. My toilette of lately has consisted of cold water and a sliver of soap that dries my skin out. Clothes help make the woman, but a little rouge and mascara can go a long way."

"You're beautiful without all that paint."

"Thank you, but trust me. I think you'll appreciate the lipstick look too." She leaned close to his ear. "I promise to try and not get it on your collar."

Grinning, he opened his eyes. "Won't mind if you do." Standing, he offered her his hand. "Yesterday, when I asked at command for shopping recommendations, a captain mentioned his wife goes to Harrods for beauty supplies." He looked in the direction of the Admiralty Arch on the other side of the square. "We'll have to take the bus."

Claire took his hand and stood. "Oh, no. Let's not go to Harrods."

"You just said—"

"I know, but I'd much prefer to walk around and enjoy the weather with you today. I'll go tomorrow while you have that meeting with your commander. Having you watch me put on mascara is not something we need to experience together." Not with all the weird faces she made. She tossed their sandwich wrappers and apple cores in a trash can and took his arm. "Come on. You can show me Buckingham Palace. I want to wave to the king and queen."

CHAPTER 30

Claire jittered with nerves as she stood on the tarmac. No matter how fast she tapped her toes, the numbness would not leave her legs. What was taking him so long?

The clock below the traffic control tower clanged twelve thirty. Another ten minutes and her flight would depart. She glanced across the tarmac at the other brave souls boarding the plane to Ireland. More like one of the toy planes her brother played with as a child. Would it have enough power to get off the ground without crashing into the gate at the end of the runway?

The small plane started, black smoke billowing into the air, covering everything in its smelly path. Its propellers came to life, droning like a thousand bees. Claire whipped the handkerchief from her sleeve and held it over her mouth and nose. Thank goodness the sales lady had added a drop of rose water to it. Claire wanted to move to the waiting area, away from the fumes, but Michael had told her not to move while he ran inside to make a last-minute inquiry.

A boy in uniform approached her and raised his voice above the noise. "Boarding's begun now, miss! I'll take your luggage if you like!"

Claire nodded. "Yes, I suppose that would be best. Thank you."

He picked up her suitcase and carried it to the plane. Claire's heart dropped as she watched it go. It was the first purchase she'd made in over two years. No, she hadn't made it. Michael had. After three days together in England, their time was up. Tears pricked the corners of her eyes.

Finally, the side door to the hanger opened and Michael stepped out. Tucking his flight cap into his belt for the no-salute zone, he jogged over to her. "Sorry. That took longer than it was supposed to," he said. "Flight crews and paperwork don't always mix."

"I was getting worried you wouldn't be back in time."

"Nonsense. You think I'd let my girl go without seeing her off?" He grinned. Even over the roaring engines, she could hear the heartbreak in his words. "When you get to Aldergrove, Lieutenant Johnston will escort you to your next hop, and from there you'll take a taxi. You have the address? If you forget, just tell the driver Aldo Reiner's cottage. Everyone knows everyone in Wicklow."

Claire nodded and patted her pocketbook. "I wrote it all down."

"And the letter?"

"You mean the one explaining why a strange Yank is landing on your parents' doorstep? Right here." She patted her purse again.

Clasping her upper arms, Michael stroked his thumbs over her shoulders. He probably meant it to be reassuring, but it scattered what was left of her nerves. "They *are* expecting you. Just don't let them pull out the family albums. You'll be stuck for days. What's wrong?"

She tried to smile, but the tears blurred her vision. She bit the inside of her cheek to keep them at bay. "I wish you were coming with me."

He squeezed her arms as his jaw stiffened. "You know I can't, my *chany*."

She nodded, not trusting her voice. The last thing she wanted him to see before they parted was her breaking apart. He needed to know she could handle it, even if inside she was crumbling. "Do you have orders yet?" She asked past the lump in her throat.

"A few more weeks here and then off on assignment."

Fear grabbed her. "Not in German uniform again?"

"No. I'm sure my picture is pasted on every wanted poster in every Nazi office by now." He grimaced. "They're assigning me to a civilian post. Might even get to grow a beard."

"Just shave it off before you come see me." She ran her fingers along his jaw, committing to memory the stubbled skin and squared bones for the long lonely days ahead.

"Boarding all passengers!" A crewman's voice called over the droning engines. "All passengers on board!"

"Michael." Claire buried her face in his neck. He swallowed several times and tightened his arms around her. She clung to him, frantic to hold on to their last precious moments.

His lips brushed the side of her neck. "Claire, I'll come back for you. No matter what happens, I will do everything I can to get back to you. You do believe that, don't you?"

She nodded as the tears slipped down her cheeks.

"No matter how long it takes." His hands angled her face up. His lips traced her mouth, searing her all the way to her toes.

She crushed herself to him, the flames of desperation ready to devour them. She tried to memorize his taste, the scent of his shaving cream, the contour of his lips. A voice announced final boarding.

But they'd had so little time.

Michael pulled back. Reaching into his collar, he slipped a chain over his head and pressed it, with its two metal tags, into her hand. "Take these. So you can have a little piece of me with you."

"But won't you need them?"

"Identity tags are the last thing I need when I'm supposed to be blending in." He ran a thumb over her cheek and caught a tear. The muscles in his throat constricted.

Claire closed her fingers over the tags, still warm from his skin. Her heart shattered over the fragile reminder of mortality she held now in her hand, but it was nothing compared to the devastation in his eyes.

"I love you, Claire," he whispered, kissing her again. "I will until the day I die."

Tears clung to her eyelashes. She pressed her handkerchief into his hand then kissed his lips, claiming him. "I love you, Michael. Come back to me." One more kiss and she tore herself away. She kept her head high and eyes forward as she walked across the tarmac. If she dared a look back, she'd never get on that blasted plane.

Somehow she found her seat without her wobbly legs giving way. The plane rumbled down the runway and soared into the sky. Pressing her face to the glass, she searched for Michael. As the plane drifted higher and farther away, she could still make out a solitary figure standing far below.

She kissed the tips of her fingers and pressed them to the glass.

The tantalizing scent of foaming sea caps and tilled earth wafted through the truck window as it curved along the cliff-side road. Claire could almost feel the ocean spray from the white cresting Irish Sea fanning far below. Each turn along the bluff led to a more surprising and more beautiful view of sharp crags, scattered rocks, and gentle hills. And always a plush carpet of green. Never had she seen such a lush, wild land.

"A shame it is, tae keep young folk separated," said her driver, Seamus O'Finnigan. Neighbor to Michael's parents, he had offered to take her when she couldn't find the taxi driver. Seamus surmised he was in the pub for his afternoon libations. "The war causin' so much tragedy. 'Twould do the county good tae have a weddin'."

Claire whipped around. "A—a wedding?"

"Well, o' course. Why else would a lad ask a lass tae stay with his parents while he's off fightin' evil?"

Because I gave him no choice. She faced the window to hide the heat rushing to her cheeks. Marriage.

Of course, she'd thought about it—dreamed about it—but all those hopes had come second to survival for the past few years. How strange to be thinking of such normal things again. Strange and exciting. And to celebrate with the whole—she twisted back to Seamus. "Did you say the county?"

He nodded, popping the pipe from his mouth and tapping the ashes over the side of the door. "O' course. Everyone's been waitin' on ye tae get here. They all want tae be seein' the girl who finally captured the soldier's heart."

Her heart jumped to double time. An entire county of strangers waiting for her, a Yank fresh from war-torn France.

"There it is." Seamus pointed to a whitewashed cottage with a thatched roof overlooking the bluff. Roses arched over the front door. "Welcome to Rose Cottage."

The truck sputtered to a stop at the front gate. Claire's hand shook as she reached for the door latch and stepped out. She checked her straw hat and straightened her collar in the windshield's reflection. *Please like me.*

Seamus got out. "Ye go on tae the house while I bring yer bag."

Taking one last breath, Claire pulled her shoulders back and walked along the pebble-covered path. Before she made it halfway, the front door creaked open and out stepped an older, red-haired woman with Michael's striking blue eyes. A tall man with spectacles followed two steps behind.

Without a word, Michael's mother opened her arms wide. Claire fell into them without a second thought. Warm tears fell on Claire's neck as long, masculine arms circled her and Michael's mother. Relief washed over her like a balm reviving her tired soul. It had been too long since she'd felt a mother's embrace.

With a loud sniff, his mother pulled back and wiped her eyes with her apron. "Claire. I'm Irene, and this is Aldo. We're so happy to have you here. When Michael told us …" She blinked and held Claire's hand between hers. "You must tell me about my son. I want to know about my boy. We haven't heard from him in so long."

Claire nodded, squeezing Irene's fingers. "I left him in excellent health though a bit thinner than I would like. He's sent you both letters."

Irene's eyes widened with delight. "D'you have them now?"

"Yes, they're in my suitcase—"

"Irene, let the girl breathe. She's only just arrived, and we don't want to scare her. Forgive us, *mausi*. You're the only link we've had to Michael in some time."

Claire turned to look at Aldo and gasped in surprise. He spoke with a light German accent instead of Michael's soft lilt, but he looked exactly like Michael, plus a few gray hairs.

She smiled. "You must be so proud of him. I know I am, and I'm delighted to be here with you, though I'm sorry we didn't give you much notice. Everything happened so quickly."

"*Och*, enough of that." Irene waved a dismissive hand. "I won't have you feeling less than you belong here, not when Michael cares for you as he does. Aldo, get her bag. I'm sure she needs a wee rest after all her traveling. I hope you like lamb, Claire darlin'."

Ushering her into the house and up a flight of rickety stairs, Irene directed Claire into a bedroom. It was simple and clean with a bed, washstand, and a wardrobe against the wall. And a spectacular view of the beach below.

"Michael's room." Irene ran a hand over the small dresser. Not a speck of dust streaked in her wake. "Though he hasn't seen it in years. I hope it suits."

"It's more than I could ask for. Thank you, Mrs. Reiner. Oh, wait. Let me get your letters." Claire flipped open her suitcase and pulled out a bulging envelope. *Mum and Da* scrawled across the front in Michael's bold hand. "For you."

Irene took it with shaking fingers and pressed it to her heart. Another tear slipped down her cheek. Smiling, Claire hugged her. There had been too much crying.

"Thank you. I'll leave you to rest for now. Wash up. We'll have tea when you're ready." Irene patted Claire's shoulder and closed the door behind her.

Claire blew out a rush of air that lightened her spirit. She was at Michael's house. And his parents had welcomed her with eagerness and happiness. She twirled in the center of the room as the days, weeks, and months of uncertainty receded in the blossoming of hope.

Salty sea air beckoned her to the window. Blue stretched out as far as the eye could see. Her heart tripped. This was the same view Michael had seen growing up. And now he had given it to her. She touched the dog tags hanging beneath her cream blouse.

"Be safe, my darling. And don't worry about your parents. We'll take good care of each other."

CHAPTER 31

1944, France near the Belgian border

Michael ran his thumb over the miniature painting of Claire. One day he'd have a real photograph taken of her, but until then he'd treasure this keepsake from their short time in London when she'd sat for a street artist. It seemed a lifetime ago.

"Heard from her, boss?" Hoffenberg squatted next to him as they waited in the tree line.

Michael tucked the painting into his breast pocket, next to his heart. "No, but the post isn't reliable anymore. Not out here."

For two years he and Hoffenberg had been working with resistance fighters crossing the French and Belgian borders. The SOE had given them orders to seek out and destroy all enemies by blowing up trains, sabotaging weapon depots, and creating overall mayhem. It would be their death sentence, like so many agents before them, if caught.

Michael pushed the thought aside. Dwelling on morbid facts wouldn't get the mission done. "Where's our new radio operator?"

Hoffenberg rubbed a hand over his grimy face. "Should've been here forty minutes ago. Unless the Germans shot the plane down. That would be the third one they've taken this month."

"One hour and twenty minutes left in the drop window. If he's not here by then, we'll pack it up and head out." Michael scanned the overgrown field before them, then looked to the sky. Cloud wisps scuttled in front of the pale yellow sun. "Don't like these daytime drops. The Germans can see the parachutes for miles. Like a homing beacon to our location."

"Those decisions are made by the big boys back in Blighty. You should have a word with them."

"Wouldn't make a difference. I'm still on their unforgiven list. I told them being stuck out here with you was punishment enough."

Hoffenberg grinned and lit a cigarette. "A grand pair we make, eh?"

A distant droning broke the still country air. Michael's ears perked at the now-familiar sound of an approaching Lysander Mark III. A black dot flew into view. The engine cut, and the plane descended, skimming the field. A pack dropped from the plane, then a figure.

A cold sweat broke out across Michael's back as it always did when watching a drop. "Let's go." Hunching forward to keep a low profile, he and Hoffenberg ran across the field with pistols at the ready.

Reaching their target, they found him grappling with his pack. Hoffenberg knelt and kept a lookout.

"Hurry up," Michael hissed.

"Can't." Eyes wild, the operator yanked at his pack, the straps tangled. "I can't get it on!"

"Keep your voice down. Get your gear and follow me."

They raced back to the cover of the woods where Michael had left their rifles. He leaned against a tree as blood pounded in his ears. The hard part had only begun. "Untangle it. Quickly."

The man's wide eyes turned to him. Sweat dripped down his face. "Yes, sir."

"Reiner. That's Hoffenberg."

"Nate." The young man shook as he straightened out his gear. Finally, he slung the pack on his back.

Michael nodded. "Let's go. We have an hour before we're supposed to make contact, and we're nowhere close to our calling radius."

They kept to the woods and far from the road where German patrols were known to travel. Having trod this path more times than he cared to count, Michael recognized the tree marks identifying how close they were to the town. They crossed a small stream and climbed behind a moss-covered boulder. He checked his watch. Right on schedule.

"Lille is over the next rise." He looked at Nate. "Get the equipment set up. We'll need to make contact first."

"Right-o." Swiping the sweat from his face, Nate set up his gear and slipped on his headphones to make the call.

"I give him a week." Hoffenberg muttered around a cigarette.

"Better odds than most." Michael shook his head as Nate fumbled over the switches. "Calm yourself, man. We have time."

"Not that much." Hoffenberg muttered again. "We signal too long in one area and the Germans will pick it up. They'll be on us like spit on a glass."

They couldn't afford for that to happen. Again. The mortality rate for radio operators was catastrophically high with many of them not lasting the first month in the field. Michael had lost five under his watch. If Nate didn't get his nerves together, he'd add to the statistics.

After several minutes of signaling, Nate removed his headphones and switched off his equipment. "The operatives are set up and ready for contact as scheduled."

Pulling a map from his pocket, Michael spread it over the ground. "We're here. We need to go here." He pointed at the black dots for Nate's sake. He and Hoff could make the trip in the dark with their eyes closed. It was too easy to fall into complacency though, so Michael never took one step for granted. "The Germans patrol the streets, but there's a smaller contingent of them in this neighborhood. That's where we get in. We're to meet the operatives there at twenty hundred hours."

Nate nodded. "What do we do until then?"

Michael eased down to the ground. His legs ached with relief. "We wait."

Nate settled silently next to Michael and clasped his hands over his stomach. Hoffenberg, however, managed the time by yanking up every blade of grass around him.

Finally, under the cover of darkness, they crept from the woods and made their way to the outskirts of town, its inhabitants locked safely behind doors for curfew. The stifling summer air shifted through the empty streets and across Michael's brow as he slipped into the shadows of a café. He glanced up and down the street. Seeing no movement, he motioned Hoffenberg and Nate to make a run for the church twenty yards away. Michael dashed after them and into the churchyard, hunkering behind a row of headstones. A grisly meeting spot if there ever was one.

Michael checked his watch. Two minutes past the appointed time. He signaled to Hoffenberg, who whistled a low bird call. Nothing. A minute later he tried again. Silence. Michael frowned. The contacts were never late. Unless they had been compromised. It would then be up to Michael and his small team to set the bridge explosives without backup. Where would he obtain the extra Comp B for demolition on short notice?

Hoffenberg whistled again. A twittering reply came from the back corner of the church. Michael sighed with relief. Hoffenberg repeated the call which was answered immediately. Michael stood up.

"*Guten Abend*, Michael."

Ice filled his veins. He slowly turned. "Good evening, Ilsa."

"I thought you'd be dead by now." Ilsa pointed her Luger at Michael and came around from behind an ornate headstone.

"Funny, I had hoped the same for you."

"Yes, I'm sure you did." A cruel smile twisted her lips. "I spent several weeks recovering from hypothermia. Being locked in the trunk of a car in freezing conditions will do that to you."

"Perhaps you should have given in. I hear it's a rather painless way to go."

"Sorry to disappoint." She glanced over his shoulder and *tsked* as Hoffenberg aimed his pistol at her. "I wouldn't. You're outnumbered."

Three German soldiers rose from behind a crypt, rifles pointed at them. Michael kept his gaze on Ilsa, careful to maintain eye contact lest he give away his contacts. But he couldn't ignore the knot cinching in his stomach. How had Ilsa found him?

He smiled to cover his trepidation. "Taking no chances this time, I see."

"Not with the two of you. Throw your weapons over there."

Michael and Hoffenberg did as ordered and stood with their hands up. Nate trembled between them clutching his radio case.

"Is this your new operator? Hopefully he's more cautious than the last one." She pointed to the end of the churchyard. Four bodies dangled from a tree limb. Michael's contacts. "He led us straight to the whole team. You'd think they'd cover their tracks better."

Hatred spiraled through Michael as the urge to strangle her nearly turned his vision red. "You finally hunted me down. Shoot and get it over with. Listening to you talk is torture."

"You have no idea what sort of torture I have in mind for you." She shifted her aim and fired at Nate. Blood welled out of his chest. He dropped to the ground without a word.

Michael cursed. The black words ricocheted off the church wall.

Ilsa shrugged. "I only need the two of you. Less fuss."

Pop! Pop! Pop!

Bullets sprayed around them, pinging off headstones. Michael and Hoffenberg hit the ground.

"Who's shooting?" Hoffenberg scrambled for cover.

Michael dove next to him and raised up enough to see over the top of a freshly dug grave. The German soldiers were shooting across the street. Figures darted in the café. Resistance fighters! Michael looked behind him. Ilsa raced out of the churchyard and around the corner.

He knocked Hoffenberg in the shoulder. "Stay here!"

Leaping to his feet, Michael took off after Ilsa. Her footsteps echoed off the stone walls. He clipped right behind, gaining on her. She turned down an alley. A dead end. He had her.

Michael stopped at the entrance and pressed his back against the wall. "You're trapped."

Her feet pattered over the cobblestone like a rat looking for a hole. She pounded against the brick walls, her rasping breath loud in the darkness.

"Give up."

Pop! Pop!

Brick chipped off the opposite wall where her bullets hit. Five down. Three to go, unless she reloaded. He pulled the knife from his belt. He'd have to time it just right.

"Still there, Ilsa?"

"Waiting for you to make a move so I can put a bullet in your brain."

He laughed. "You were never a good long-distance shot." He darted across the alley, flattening himself against the opposite wall.

Two more shots rang out. One left. Taking a deep breath to calm his racing pulse, he threw himself behind a set of trash bins, rattling their lids as he slid to his knees.

Bang!

Michael gasped as pain seared his thigh. Warmth ran down his leg.

Click. Click. Click. Her gun was empty. Now or never.

Michael staggered to his feet and walked toward her, menace seething in his blood. Agony burned in his leg, but only death would stop him now. "Give up now, Ilsa. You've got nowhere to run."

"And make you look like a hero for capturing a German SS officer? You should know me better than that." She reached into her pocket and pulled out a magazine of bullets. "We could have been great together, Michael. We could have done wondrous things for the Fatherland, but the only thing left for me to do now is kill you. I'll enjoy hanging your carcass alongside the other traitors."

"Last warning. Put the gun down."

"Then I'll find the girl." She slid the magazine into the bottom of the pistol. Her red lips curled up. "Too bad you won't be around to see what I have in mind for her."

Michael rushed the last few steps and sank his blade to the hilt in her belly. "No, too bad for you."

Her eyes widened as her mouth formed a perfect O. She fell back, landing on the cobblestones with her legs curled gracefully beneath her. She touched the knife sticking out of her middle and smiled. Her gun flashed up.

Bang!

It hit Michael like a bolt of lightning. White flashed before his eyes. He fell backward as blackness swallowed him.

CHAPTER 32

July 1944, Ireland

With a flick of her wrist, the bandage unrolled from Claire's fingers, and she began the repetitive task again from her station under the first-aid tent. Across the airfield, the USO orchestra swung its way through "Yankee Doodle Dandy." Snare drum and cymbals collided in a bright clash at the end of the song and the audience of American servicemen and Wicklow residents erupted in applause.

"Ask your mom to buy you an ice cream and keep to the shade." Vera, the other aide who was straight off the nurses' boat from Philadelphia, patted a sunburned little boy on the head and shooed him out of the tent. She flopped in the chair next to Claire. "These Irish are going to use up my aloe vera stash. They should know to keep that pale skin out of the sun."

"The sun comes out so rarely, they get excited."

"They get burned is what happens. Guaranteed we'll see most of these people again tomorrow in the hospital."

But not the one person I want to see. Claire scanned the crowd in vain, hoping to spot the one man she longed for above all others. Two years of dreaming of Michael's return had yet to summon him. So she kept busy to ease the loneliness.

The orchestra launched into "You're a Grand Old Flag" with a flutter of violin strings. Claire's heart skipped at the familiar sound. No. No more violin. No more music. She had found something else to occupy her at the hospital, perhaps not as fulfilling as playing a new score, but at least she was helping the troops in some small way.

Vera jabbed her in the side with a tongue depressor. "Why don't you get up there on that stage and show them a thing or two? I hear they're leaving next week to tour Europe."

"What are you talking about?"

"Don't play dumb. I've heard the rumors about you and that fancy French conservatory you went to. Gave it up to go on the run with that man of yours."

Claire bit back a groan. The only thing the residents of Wicklow loved more than a good story was telling it to everyone who passed by. "That was a long time ago. Before the war, before … things happened." She stared at the lopsided bandage in her hands. How could she ever dare to play beautiful music again with murdering hands? Each pluck of the string would be a stab of guilt. Michael had said forgiveness was key, but it was a task easier said than done.

The first-aid doctor came around the tent's privacy screen squinting at his watch. "You girls can go on break. The next volunteers should be here any minute with the extra crate of burn cream. These Irish and their skin problems will be the death of me."

Claire tucked her rolled bandage in the box of supplies and bounced out of her chair, eager to be away from the taunting orchestra strains.

"You in a rush, honey?" Vera called after her.

"I need food."

Vera wrinkled her nose. "Don't know if I'd call it food what they eat round here. The locals eat nothing but potatoes, and the army has nothing but gruel."

"Not today. Can't you smell that?" Claire took a big whiff of the succulent air. "Good ol' barbeque in honor of America's birthday. I intend to celebrate until they have to roll me home."

Interest sprang in Vera's eyes. "Do you think they've got funnel cakes?"

"Let's go find out." Grabbing Vera's hand, Claire zig-zagged her way through the invited throngs of local civilians and military personnel. It seemed everyone within a fifty-mile radius had turned up for Glendalough Army Air Force Base's Fourth of July Spectacular.

Following her nose, she jumped into the hamburger line.

Vera's hand slipped from hers. "Sorry, doll, but I'll have to miss out on the funnel cake. I got a cute pilot winking at me. How's my lipstick?"

Claire peeked over her friend's shoulder at the smarmy flyboy then looked back to inspect Vera's thin red lips. "Right on the money. Hey! If he asks if you want to see the plane's underbelly, tell him no!"

Vera waved and dashed off to her afternoon romance while a knot of jealousy tightened Claire's stomach. She longed to hold Michael's hand and lean her head on his shoulder just like all the other girls did with their beaus. Soon. The storming of Normandy beach a month ago had blazed hope throughout the Allied world that the war wouldn't last for much longer. Michael could finally return home to her, and they could stroll hand in hand without looking over their shoulders. Just like she'd dreamed.

"What'll it be, sweetheart?" The hamburger cashier's nasal New York accent cut through Claire's daydreaming.

"One cheeseburger with all the fixings. Do you have funnel cake?"

He jerked a thumb to the next tent over before scribbling her order on a pad of paper. "Four bob."

"Four bob? That's outrageous."

"You wanted all the fixings." He shouted over his shoulder to a grizzly man flipping burgers on a flaming grill. "Cheeseburger! The works!"

Claire dug in her coin purse and handed over the inflated amount. The beef patty sizzled on the open flame, its thick aroma curling through the air to wave under her nose. The griller slapped it between buns and loaded it with slices and bits from heaven before sliding it across the table to her. Cradling her treasure, she wove through the crowds to where Aldo and Irene waited for her on a picnic blanket spread under a tree.

"This does not taste like bratwurst." Aldo held up a hot dog with one bite taken out of it. His bushy eyebrows drew together in accusation.

Sitting, Claire balanced her plate across her knees. "That's because it's a hot dog. I told you it wasn't sausage."

He took another tentative bite and chewed. "It should be. Who would want to eat something named after a *hund*?"

Claire shrugged and picked up her burger with both hands. Tomato and pickle juice streamed down her hands. She bit into it. Long-forgotten flavor exploded in her mouth, and she nearly died on the spot. Just like her dad used to make.

"I can't understand why the two of you enjoy so much beef and pig. Lamb is better for the digestion." Irene held up her bowl of lamb stew that she'd brought from home and dipped her spoon into the thick contents. She smiled at Claire. "I thought the orchestra played wonderfully. Don't you think so?"

Claire shrugged. She knew where this was going and, like the times before, Irene would not convince her to play again. "Well enough from what I heard at the first-aid tent. We were rather busy dealing with sunburns. It'll make for a lot of work at the hospital this week."

"Well worth it after today. For too long we've had nothing to celebrate," Aldo said.

Claire looked around at the airfield turned fairground. Children raced around with red, white, and blue balloons. Families sat at tables or on blankets eating while others bobbed for ducks, played ring toss, or joined in the baseball game behind the food tents. She could have plucked the warming scene straight out of America's heartland.

She took a drink of the apple cider Irene extracted from her picnic basket. "I suppose they felt it was safe enough to throw a big shindig now that the Allies are pushing into France."

Aldo nodded as he examined his dubious hotdog. "It's the foothold we need. Soon our boys will march to Germany, and we can finally end the fighting."

Irene reached over and squeezed his hand. "Michael can come home."

"*Ja, Schatz.*"

A mixture of sadness and fondness spiraled through Claire. She desperately wanted Michael home, but she was beyond grateful for the blessing he had given her in his parents. She'd come to know and love them as her own.

A lanky figure in uniform cut his way through the crowd, making a beeline for them. Major Farrow, the air base's British liaison. Stopping at the edge of their blanket, he removed his hat and tucked it under one arm before pulling a yellow telegram from his pocket. "Mr. and Mrs. Reiner."

Claire's stomach flipped. *Michael.*

Aldo grabbed the telegram and tore it open. "Michael's been shot. Missing in action."

Claire's ears buzzed as the blood rushed from her head. Shot. Missing. No, not her Michael. He was too careful, too clever. They couldn't have endured so much only for him to be lost to her somewhere across the Channel.

Aldo stood, the telegram quivering in his hand. "Shot where? Where is my son?"

"I'm afraid we don't know, sir," the major replied calmly. "The last word we received was that he was shot near the Belgian border while on a mission. We have been unable to reestablish contact with his unit to determine further information. My sincerest apologies."

Claire jumped to her feet as the need to know overruled fear. "We don't want apologies! We want answers! Are you sending in men to find him?"

"We have operatives all over the country with their own orders to complete. The army cannot override its mission to search for one agent. However, I can assure you that we are doing everything we can to—"

"Then send me! If the army can't spare personnel, then I'll find him. I blended in as a Frenchwoman once. I can do it again."

Major Farrow sighed. "Miss Baudin, as well as you were able to pass for a Frenchwoman, your face is well-known to the German army. British intelligence still intercepts reports from Nazi transmissions that you, Reiner, and Hoffenberg are to be arrested on the spot. Even if you weren't wanted by the Germans, there is no way the army will allow an untrained person to go on a suicide mission."

"So that's it? The army is going to sit back and cross their fingers that Michael's not … d-dead?" Tears clogged her throat. She turned away.

Aldo laid a hand on her arm. "Calm down, *Schatz*. We're not giving up hope." He spoke again to the major, but the words drifted past Claire.

Sitting around waiting for news was worse than knowing for sure if Michael was d—no, she couldn't even think that possibility. She wouldn't think it! Michael was alive, and she needed to get to him. The army's stance on her involvement was clear, but there had to be another way. Blast this war!

Frustration tearing at her, she paced, ignoring the people laughing and skipping all around her, acting as if her world hadn't just crumbled in on itself. The warmup notes of the orchestra danced across the field, teasing her with their joyfulness. They sought only to entertain the troops, but did they ever think their marching songs were a summons to the battlefields of death?

Still, she had once dwelled in the hopefulness that music brought. When all else had failed, music had shone a bright light through the darkness of Nazi occupation. She missed seeing Giles', Pauline's, and all the villagers' worried faces ease from their daily troubles each time she sat down at the piano. The simple act had buoyed her spirits as much as theirs. If only for a few hours, they could all forget about the war lurking at the front door. Claire'd had purpose then. Music had been her gift.

Until it had been snatched away the second she'd pulled that trigger.

The opening notes of "The Star-Spangled Banner" trumpeted over the crowd. Chills broke over Claire's skin. Music had brought her out of the darkness and led her to Michael. Perhaps it could do so again. Vera had said the USO was leaving for Europe in two weeks. If Claire could join them, she'd be that much closer to Michael—wherever he was.

Heart pounding, she walked toward the stage. The orchestra was bound to perform somewhere close to Belgium. Word would get out that she was looking for him. She'd make sure of that.

"Claire! Where are you going?" Irene's voice stopped her.

Claire turned around. "To join the USO. It's time I picked up the violin again."

CHAPTER 33

December 1944, Brussels, Belgium

The military headquarters' clerk blinked across the desk at Claire. "Like I told you yesterday, and the day before, and the day before that, there's no news on Captain Reiner."

"Then I'd like to speak with Major Worth. If you're incapable, then I'm certain—"

"Look, miss. I've passed the major your notes, but he can't meet with every person coming in here and demanding to see him. You're not the only one looking for some missing soldier."

Claire folded her hands tightly to keep from wringing his scrawny neck. "Captain Reiner is not just *some* soldier."

"I'm sure to you he's not, but we've got more caseloads here than we have time to deal with. If something comes in, we'll let you know. In the meantime, keep doing what you're doing." His squinty gaze swept over her in lewd suggestion. "The boys sure appreciate a pretty girl from home to look at."

"I'll be back tomorrow."

"I'll look forward to it as always."

Casting him a shriveling glare, Claire marched out of Allied Headquarters located in a once-elegant hotel on the Place Rogier. British and American soldiers catcalled as she walked by the packed cafés where Benny Goodman blared from a BBC radio station. She kept her chin high but didn't look at anyone, as any sort of acknowledgment was taken as fair game. She had no desire to be pulled onto some stranger's lap for a kiss. A mistake she'd learned the hard way.

A few blocks over, she slipped down a side alley and entered the back door to another hotel where the USO had booked its performances. Feathers, sequins, tap shoes, and brassy trumpet notes swallowed her up as the entertainers bustled about in preparation for the night's show.

"Five minutes to curtain!" The balding stage manager shuffled between the performers with a cigar clamped between his lips. He stopped in front of Claire, blowing dirty smoke rings. "You're late, sweetheart. Lots of boys out there waiting to hear you play, and it won't do them no good if you're tardy thanks to some GI Joe."

"I'm hurrying, Mr. Abram. Never been late before."

"Yeah, well. First time for everything." Chomping his cigar, he turned his scathing attention to a gaggle of star-spangled dancers leaning against the scenery.

Claire hurried to the dressing room and slipped out of her coat and dress. Two of her most precious possessions dangled over her heart on a long silver chain. Michael's identity tags. Five months of touring with the USO orchestra around Europe and she'd yet to find him. Her throat constricted. Soon. It had to be soon.

She slipped into her dark-blue performance dress and tucked the chain safely beneath the bodice, then hurried out to find her violin in the musicians' corner next to the stage.

"Any luck today?"

Claire pulled her case from behind a tuba and turned around. Dinah Shore, America's sweetheart, leaned against the wall sipping tea from a chipped cup. Stones glittered around the neck of her dark pink dress in sharp contrast to the bullet-ridden walls around them. Claire shook her head. "Nothing."

"Oh, honey. Want me to go with you tomorrow? I can charm that little clerk while you slip into the major's office."

"I highly doubt that will help my cause but thank you."

"Being famous excuses many faux pas." Dinah squeezed Claire's shoulder. "You and Michael will be together soon. This war can't go on forever, and you know what they say."

"No news is good news? That's what people say when they

don't know what to say."

"Don't you just hate that? Listen, I'm going to have the band play 'Dream a Little Dream' tonight just for you. That was your song, right?"

Claire nodded. "He always liked me to sing it for him."

"Sing?" Dinah's eyebrow shot up. "All these weeks and you never mentioned singing. Quite a multitalented girl."

Claire laughed. "Talented? Not really. Just a girl trying to find her love song."

"Aren't we all, honey?" A burst of drums and horns announced the start of the show. Dinah drained her cup and set it on a makeup table. She took Claire's hand and squeezed. "I'll see you out there."

Claire picked up her violin, the familiar weight soothing and comforting. Each night she played, the scars from France healed a bit more. She could find joy in the strings once more. Michael may not be in the audience tonight, but plenty of others were. They were someone's Michael, and she owed them a night of hope.

She glided onto the stage with the orchestra and took her seat in front of the conductor. They opened with "The Star-Spangled Banner" to thundering applause, then the drums rolled as Dinah swept onto the stage with a dazzling smile and wave. Adjusting the mic to her level, she shielded her eyes against the glaring stage lights. "Are you boys out there? I can't see a thing!" She turned to the musicians. "Let's lay that trumpet on them. Give me 'Blues in the Night.'"

Claire's fingers moved to the swanky notes as she scanned the crowd packed into the lobby of what was once a fine Brussels hotel. Plenty of smiling faces but not the one she hoped for. The song ended, and the audience whooped and hollered.

"I'm going to do something a little different tonight, hope you don't mind. Hope she doesn't mind." Dinah turned around and pointed at Claire. "Come on up here, honey."

Claire's eyes popped open. What a way to broadcast her presence. Handing her violin to the second chair, she walked to the microphone. Lights blinded her as the adrenaline pounded in her ears.

Dinah's arm slipped around her. "This is my friend, Claire, and she's got a fella fighting out there. Since he isn't here to listen to her sing, maybe you'd like to. What do you say?"

More cheers and clapping. Claire's heart leaped to her throat as her mind went blank. "I don't remember the words," she whispered to Dinah.

"Sure you do," Dinah whispered back. "Just sing to him."

Claire gazed out to the sea of blackness. She imagined one man sitting at the back table wearing a scuffed jacket and loose shirt opened at the throat, watching her with an easy smile. She sang only for him.

"Stars shining bright above you." Her voice wobbled. Michael. Think of Michael. "Dream a little dream of me."

The men murmured as the crowd rippled. Men in the back started clapping as a shadow slipped from their ranks and wove its way to the front on a swell of cheers. The dark figure jumped on the edge of the stage and moved toward her. Dark jacket. Shirt unbuttoned at the throat. Hair glinting copper in the light. A flash of bright blue before the figure swooped in and kissed her. Words stuck in her throat at the shock of contact. Hands, large and warm, clasped her face in a touch so possessive the illusions fell away.

Michael.

He dipped her back. Claire threw her arms around his neck, pressing herself into him with an urgency of colliding souls. Tears streamed down her cheeks and around their crushed lips. His mouth broke away as he swept her into his arms. Clapping, whistling, and hollering erupted all around, but Claire buried her face in Michael's neck, clinging to him like a life preserver in a vast ocean of nothingness. His strong fingers curled into her as he carried her from the stage. A door kicked open and cold air swirled around them. Claire didn't give her bare arms a care as his pulse beat frantically against her cheek.

"Claire." His soft brogue thickened with emotion. "Claire, my *chany*."

Their lips sought one another, finding and taking. Desperation forced by years of separation drove out gentleness.

Michael set her down and cradled her face. "Claire, please don't cry." His thumbs stroked at the tears slipping down her face as his own eyes glossed over. "What are you doing in Belgium?"

His voice caressed her soul like drops of rain to a desert. After two long years, there he stood. "Oh, Michael. We received a telegram saying you'd been shot and missing in action." She dashed a tear from her cheek. "I came to find you myself."

"You brave little fool. If I wasn't so happy to see you, I'd thrash you over my knee for such recklessness." A lump moved in his throat. "I've lain awake every night with you floating in my thoughts. I thought I was dreaming again, seeing you on that stage."

She pressed a kiss to his neck and tasted the salt of her tears. "Do I need to pinch you?"

He cupped her face in his warm hands. His brilliant blue eyes seared into her. "After all this time … I wasn't sure you'd still want me."

"I told you I would wait forever."

"You were supposed to wait in Ireland."

"It turned out to be too far from you. How could I wait when I didn't know if you were alive or dead?"

The brilliant blue of his eyes turned deep as a river. As he lowered his head, Claire raised her lips to meet his. So soft, so sweet. She curled her fingers into his hair, savoring his taste, his warmth. His touch ignited the passion within. He traced every curve of her mouth, pulling a soft moan from her lips. She pressed into him, not wanting to leave a breath of space between her and this man her heart beat for.

He grunted, cutting through her haze of desire. "I'm afraid you've got a cripple on your hands, my *chany*."

She took in the scratches and bruises on his face. "I don't care about any of that. You're alive, and that's all that matters to me."

"Wish I could say the same for the shrapnel buried in my leg." He bent over and hitched his pant leg. Claire gasped. Angry slashes of skin cut his muscular calf, the ragged edges pulled together with black catgut sutures. Lacerations cut like whip marks around his ankle and knee, and green and yellow bruises mottled the remaining skin. "The pain isn't so unbearable anymore." He dropped the pant leg. "The good news is I can feel a storm coming on much sooner than I use to."

His attempted joke did nothing to stop the sadness crushing her heart. "How did it happen?"

"Firestorm with the Jerries. Ilsa found me. She's dead." Michael cleared his throat and shifted his weight. "Would you mind if we took a seat? I forgot my cane in the vehicle, and my leg gets ornery when I stand too long. Or leap onto stages."

She spotted two apple crates heaped on top of a rubble pile. She grabbed them and turned them over. "Finest in the house."

"Quite possibly the only ones in the house."

Sitting, she took his hand and slowly rubbed the back of it. Cuts crisscrossed his knuckles. As the euphoria of their reunion settled, she gazed at him fully for the first time. A swath of red whiskers covered his jaw and curved into a mustache, highlighting his stark cheekbones. Purple smudged under his eyes, and his clothes hung on his usually erect frame. Her heart twisted. "Where have you been?"

He looked away. "Coordinating the liberation from deep underground. A different city or town every week. We never lingered, and once we had the Germans on the run, we had to stay on their tails. That night with Ilsa, I lost a lot of blood. The locals took me into hiding until I was well enough to travel again. I'm sorry I couldn't get word out."

"You scared the daylights out of us."

He brushed a finger under her chin. "If I'd known you were

tracking me down, I would've made my whereabouts known sooner. Then I would have at least known to look for you here. It's good to see you playing again."

"I wasn't sure I'd ever pick up an instrument, not after what happened, but you were right. I needed to forgive myself, and music is helping me do that. It's helping to heal those bitter wounds, and mine were turning poisonous."

"Music is a part of you, Claire. It's always been your dream. Don't let go of it."

"I won't. Not again." She smiled. "In fact, there's a fine music academy in Dublin that I can apply to once the war is over."

"You could've applied now instead of touring around a war-shackled country where you have no business being." The glint in his eye told her he was only half teasing.

"As if that's stopped me before. Besides, I couldn't wait one day longer. Being apart from you, not knowing where you were, or if … you gave me no choice. I searched every town we stopped in, hoping you'd come to one of the shows."

"I'm not even supposed to be here tonight, but the corporal who picked me up wanted to catch a glimpse of the American girls with the great gams before driving to headquarters. He'll have lost his stripes come morning for insubordination."

"You came to yell at him for ogling the women only to find yourself crashing on the stage to kiss one."

"I couldn't believe my ears. For a moment I thought I was back in France." Michael laced his fingers between hers. "Like you were calling to me."

"I was, for so long, and I would have kept doing it until I found you." More tears crowded her lashes. She blinked them back. "Do you have to go back?"

He grimaced. "Not much good in the field with this busted leg. So far, they've kept me dancing between Belgium and France, but it won't be for much longer. This Battle of the Bulge should determine things fairly soon."

"That's wonderful news!"

"Speaking of wonderful, Hoffenberg is with a unit taking the munitions factories along the German border. He's gotten wind of a Baudin family working near Bastogne and is headed there soon."

Claire's heart tripped with joy. Her family. They could be safe and sound on their farm in a matter of weeks. "I can't wait to see them again."

"As soon as Hoff sends word, I'll take you to Montoire myself, but we'll stop in Paris first. In the hands of the Allies, it's a celebration night and day. Perfect time for a honeymoon."

"Sounds like when Mardi Gras hits New Orleans every— honeymoon?" The air left her lungs in a *whoosh*. "D-did you just say what I think you said?"

"It's where you've always wanted to go, isn't it?"

"Well, yes." She swallowed against her dry throat. "But are you sure you want me as a wife? I mean, I *am* an American."

A mischievous grin spread across his handsome face. "After all the time and effort I put into you, do you think I'd let you slip the hook?"

"So I'm stuck with you?"

"Afraid so, my *chany*. But I've one more thing to ask." He leaned in close, his warm breath fanning across her cheeks. The entire world seemed to hang in suspense. "Did you ever read that book I lent you?"

"Michael." She poked him in the chest. He captured her hand and flattened it against his heart, pulling her forward. Laughter tumbled out as she wrapped her arms around him. "Just like you to stick to business even during a proposal."

"Business, eh? I believe I've got two years' worth of business to attend to, and somehow I don't think you'll object."

She brushed her fingers across his jaw, relishing the rough feel of him. His pulse surged beneath his warm skin. He'd come back to her, just like he promised. "When have you ever known me to object, my dear Captain?"

He raised an eyebrow. "How much time do we have?"

"Forget it. Just kiss me."

"Yes, ma'am."